HAUNTED BY MYTH

What Reviewers Say About Barbara Ann Wright's Work

The Mage and the Monster

"I have truly enjoyed reading the novels in 'The Sisters of Sarras' series by Barbara Ann Wright. …I've been delighted with all three books. The story of Gisele and Vale is a fitting conclusion to this series. It takes the characters and the narrative of the first two books and pulls us into a story that includes danger, adventure, and war. It's also a chance for some, including Gisele and Vale, to find love and acceptance. There are quite a few twists and turns in the plot. This tale will definitely keep you wondering as you read."—*Rainbow Reflections*

The Scout and the Scoundrel

"The second lesbian fantasy romance in Wright's The Sisters of Sarras trilogy takes to the military for a delightful character-centered story about trust and loyalty. Sarassian Commander Zara del Amanecer is socially awkward and ultra-rational. As punishment for a recent faux pas with a Colonel's daughter, her scouting squad is the first in an experiment in using prisoners as recruits, putting flirty, smart-mouthed thief Veronique 'Roni' Bisset under Zara's command and setting the stage for their opposites-attract romance. …Series fans will not be disappointed." —*Publishers Weekly*

"What made this novel so special were the characters, especially Roni and Zara. Zara grabbed my heartstrings from the beginning and never let go. She has this loveable, everything-is-black-and-white, no-filter personality that often gets her in trouble. …Roni is a perfect foil for Zara's character, and the chemistry between them grows steadily as the two are thrown together. …This is a thrilling fantasy/adventure novel with a lovely enemies-to-lovers romance that I thoroughly enjoyed." —*Rainbow Reflections*

The Noble and the Nightingale

"Wright sets up the Sisters of Sarras lesbian fantasy romance trilogy with solid worldbuilding, a delightfully awkward couple who bridge social realms, and an entertaining adventure that leaves plenty of room to grow. ...By the end, Wright has established strong personalities for Adella's two sisters and taken the suspense plotline to the brink of war between Sarras and the Firellians, setting up strongly for the next volumes. Readers will be pleased."—*Publishers Weekly*

"Only Barbara Ann Wright can weave a satisfying romance from nothing more than looks of longing, stolen kisses, and hand-holding. ...*The Noble and the Nightingale* is an entirely satisfying addition to the shelves of Barbara Ann Wright, who somehow finds fresh ways to blend fantasy and romance with characters worthy of their settings."—*Beauty in Ruins*

Lady of Stone

"Yet another stellar read from Barbara Ann Wright, *Lady of Stone* is a wonderful blend of magical fantasy and lesbian romance that had me eager to find out how it all ends, and yet reluctant to have it end." —*Beauty in Ruins*

Not Your Average Love Spell

"...a solid little fantasy tale with a lot of really cool elements. ...Wright plays to all the tropes...in a way that keeps the story fresh while preserving the surprises. ...As for the romance, that was surprisingly sweet and amusing, with four women at the heart of the story who are entirely likable...the spark of attraction and the emotional connections are undeniable."—*Fem Led Fantasy*

"...a great story filled with magic, wondrous creatures and adventure but what I really enjoyed about the book was the way that the characters grew. ...It is a great thing to read in these trying times and I took hope from it. The story pulls with enough magic to feel like a fully fleshed

out fantasy world while keeping our heroes relatable and engaging. ...I give it a full hearted thumbs up and you should definitely check it out."
—*Paper Phoenix Ink*

"[*Not Your Average Love Spell*] is an entertaining...romantic fantasy adventure comedy? (I'm not sure how to categorise its Venn diagram of subgenres, either.) Starring an agoraphobic witch; a bright, curious, talkative homunculus; an archivist/scholar with a revolutionary bent; a knight who—at least initially—believes wholeheartedly in her order's mission to stamp out magic; and an invasion of genocidal warriors, *Not Your Average Love Spell* takes its characters on an entertaining ride and delivers all of them a happy ending. (Except for the genocidal warriors. Their happy ending would be terrible for everyone else.)"—*Tor.com*

The Tattered Lands

"Wright's postapocalyptic romance is a fast-paced journey through devastation. ...Plenty of action, surprises, and magic will keep readers turning the pages."—*Publishers Weekly*

House of Fate

"...fast, fun...entertaining. ...*House of Fate* delivers on adventure." —*Tor.com*

***Lambda Literary Award Finalist*—Coils**

"...Greek myths, gods and monsters and a trip to the Underworld. Sign me up. ...This one springs straight into action...a good start, great Greek myth action and a late blooming romance that flowers in the end..." —*Dear Author*

"A unique take on the Greek gods and the afterlife make this a memorable book. The story is fun with just the right amount of camp. Medusa is a hot, if unexpected, love interest. ...A truly unexpected ending has us hoping for more stories from this world."—*RT Book Reviews*

Paladins of the Storm Lord

"This was a truly enjoyable read. …I would definitely pick up the next book…the mad dash at the end kept me riveted. I would definitely recommend this book for anyone who has a love of sci-fi. …An intricate novel…one that can be appreciated at many levels, adventurous sci fi or one that is politically motivated with a very astute look at present day human behavior. …There are many levels to this extraordinary and well written book…overall a fascinating and intriguing book."—*Inked Rainbow Reads*

Thrall: Beyond Gold and Glory

"Once more Barbara has outdone herself in her penmanship. I cannot sing enough praises. A little *Vikings*, a dash of *The Witcher*, peppered with *The Game of Thrones*, and a pinch of *Lord of The Rings*. Mesmerizing. …I was ecstatic to read this book. It did not disappoint. Barbara pours life into her characters with sarcasm, wit and surreal imagery, they leap from the page and stand before you in all their glory. I am left satisfied and starving for more, the clashing of swords, whistling of arrows still ringing in my ears."—*Lunar Rainbow Reviews*

The Pyramid Waltz

"…a healthy dose of a very creative, yet believable, world into which the reader will step to find enjoyment and heart-thumping action. It's a fiendishly delightful tale."—*Lambda Literary*

"Chock full of familiar elements that avid fantasy readers will adore… [*The Pyramid Waltz*] adds in a compelling and slowly evolving romance. …Set against a backdrop of political intrigue with the possibility of monsters and mystery at every turn, the two women slowly learn each other, sharing secrets and longing, until a fragile love blossoms between them…"—*USA Today Happily Ever After*

For Want of a Fiend

"This book will keep you turning the page to find out the answers. …Fans of the fantasy genre will really enjoy this installment of the story. We can't wait for the next book."—*Curve*

A Kingdom Lost

"There is only one other time in my life I have uncontrollably shouted out in cheer while reading a book. [*A Kingdom Lost*] made the second. ...Over the course of these three books all the characters have blossomed and developed so eloquently. ...I simply just thought this whole novel was brilliant."—*Lesbian Review*

The Fiend Queen

"After reading this series Barbara Ann Wright has made my favorite author list. Her writing always seems to sweep me away to another world. The pacing, characters, and language were all perfect. ...I am so addicted to Fantasy now. I knew fantasy was one of my favorite genres but it was always hard for me to come by a consistent source of fantasy books. After finishing the series A Pyradisté Adventure I knew that I had found a diamond. I can't wait to read the rest of Barbara Ann Wright's works. ...Read it! I am obsessed and I don't know how I will ever want to read a non-fantasy Lesfic ever again. I literally felt drunk off the series. Even after I was done with this book I thought about it constantly for at least two days."—*Lesbian Review*

Visit us at www.boldstrokesbooks.com

By the Author

The Pyradisté Adventures
The Pyramid Waltz
For Want of a Fiend
A Kingdom Lost
The Fiend Queen
Lady of Stone

Thrall: Beyond Gold and Glory

The Godfall Novels
Paladins of the Storm Lord
Widows of the Sun-Moon
Children of the Healer
Inheritors of Chaos

Coils
House of Fate
The Tattered Lands
Not Your Average Love Spell
Haunted by Myth

The Sisters of Sarras
The Noble and the Nightingale
The Scout and the Scoundrel
The Mage and the Monster

HAUNTED BY MYTH

by

Barbara Ann Wright

2023

HAUNTED BY MYTH

ISBN 13: 978-1-63679-461-7

THIS TRADE PAPERBACK ORIGINAL IS PUBLISHED BY
BOLD STROKES BOOKS, INC.
P.O. BOX 249
VALLEY FALLS, NY 12185

FIRST EDITION: DECEMBER 2023

CREDITS
EDITOR: CINDY CRESAP
PRODUCTION DESIGN: SUSAN RAMUNDO
COVER DESIGN BY INK SPIRAL DESIGN

Acknowledgments

Thanks again to everyone at BSB: Rad, Sandy, Cindy, Ruth, Stacia, Susan, and everyone else who works tirelessly behind the scenes. You're seen and loved.

Thanks to my fabulous writing groups and my awesome writer friends. You make the job worth it.

And thanks as always to my mom, Linda Dunn. I tried to think of the best way to say how grateful I am for the life you've given me, but there just aren't enough words. I love you.

Dedication

For Mom. There aren't enough words.

Chapter One

Chloe's side burned from running, and the muggy air of a Texas autumn leached the sweat from her every pore. Her job often took her down some strange paths, but she rolled with it, took pride in dependability. It was just a shame that it often included running through small-town parks at one a.m., chasing the ghosts of Confederate officers.

And this particular bastard was fast.

Chloe spotted his ghostly shimmer through a gap in the line of trees that separated this tiny park from the courthouse and businesses of Main Street. He'd switched directions yet again, but if Chloe stopped, her feet would refuse to restart. Who knew someone named Chester M. Goodspeed would live up to his name even after the son-of-a-bitch had died?

When Chloe had arrived at the park, Goodspeed had been hanging out near his statue, ranting about sacrilege and history and shame on everyone. He'd seemed to think people could hear him, a sign that he'd been summoned rather than hanging around for over a hundred years.

A crane and a flatbed truck had sat nearby, no doubt waiting to take the statue down, but the workmen had been gathered around their equipment, shaking their heads. For two days, the statue removal had been thwarted, plagued by mishaps like cables coming loose, random shocks from equipment, or the controls of the crane acting up, all things a ghost could manage. And there had been so many that local officials suspected sabotage.

And they were right. They just didn't know that all the petty problems had been caused by the unquiet dead. Of course, they couldn't see or hear him, bless their hearts. No, that was her privilege alone.

She'd loitered, watching the confounded crew as Goodspeed had used charges of ghostly energy to work cables free of their moorings or trip the foreman, all while yelling curses they couldn't hear. She'd almost admired his tenacity. And she'd watched too long. He'd gone still, staring at her, and she should have looked away, but she'd been seized by a fit of obstinacy and had met his eye.

When spirits knew she could see them, they knew she could end them, some awareness of the dead. He'd vanished. Lucky for him, the crew had already decided to try again tomorrow. One a.m. had forced him out of hiding, the witching hour calling forth all the unquiet spirits in the world.

Chloe glanced at her watch where a timer ticked down. She had just over forty minutes to send Goodspeed's spirit to the other side, or he could vanish, ready to rematerialize tomorrow and mess with the work crew again. She couldn't banish a ghost in front of an audience without answering a lot of questions people didn't want answered.

"Shit, shit," she said, wheezing but grateful for the cardio she got in when she wasn't tracking down monsters or chasing ghosts through parks or museums or graveyards. Most spirits weren't very powerful, thank God. Any power they had only came from how many statues or carvings or figurines they had in the world and how well they were remembered.

Chester M. Goodspeed was but a drop of history.

Thankfully, she'd brought a flood.

"Ready to tap out?" Chloe heard in her mind, the tone teasing but with enough affection that she didn't want to press further and say that she could handle it.

"Yeah," she said, slowing and putting her hands on her knees as her breath came so hard, her throat ached. Her satchel felt like a bag of lead across her right shoulder. "But only…because you…don't get tired."

Ramses the II, third pharaoh of the Nineteenth Dynasty of Egypt, Chosen of Ra, the greatest ruler of the New Kingdom appeared before her and held out a hand lined in the blue fire of the powerful dead. "Pay up, chump."

Chloe glared up at him. "After…you catch him."

He shrugged before looking around, cracking knuckles he didn't have to crack. Chloe counted herself lucky he wasn't pretending to stretch with one leg on a tree. She'd seen up that pleated kilt one too many times.

"He's there," Chloe said, pointing toward the farthest edge of the park. Goodspeed was trying to hide beneath a clump of bushes, but the soft white glow gave him away, especially with no moon and only the orange shine of old streetlights lining the road.

"Run right and cut him off," Ramses said. "I'll steer him toward you."

Easy for him to say. Chloe threatened her body into moving again. Goodspeed couldn't go far from his statue, and he wouldn't be able to outrun Ramses for long. She could still redeem herself. She dipped into her pocket and grabbed a plastic baggie full of salt and cayenne pepper. That should hold his ass long enough for her to banish him. She popped open the top, grabbed a small handful, and cocked her arm back, planning to nail him when Ramses chased him around the corner.

There, his glow rounded a tree. She launched her arm forward, the cloud of dust catching the light.

Someone screamed and coughed, a woman's voice, and a small dog started barking like a fiend. The light swung crazily, shining over a leash and a rabid-looking chihuahua and a person trying to wipe their face while light came from their phone.

"Shit," Chloe yelled. "Sorry…I…" She looked behind the dogwalker but couldn't see any glow.

"Are you fucking crazy?" The dogwalker backed into the dark street, towing the squirming dog that looked ready for some hearty disemboweling.

"Sorry…I'm…security," Chloe stammered, nerves swallowing the usual excuse she had ready. "Just…go home." Out of the corner of her eye, she saw the bright blue glow of Ramses on the other side of the park. Goodspeed had switched directions on him, too.

Ha.

Chloe turned her back on the dogwalker before she could do something like start filming and darted between two trees and through some shrubbery, hoping to catch Goodspeed on the other end of the park this time. She had to promise her body three full days free from workouts before it would run again. Stupid ghosts and their stupid stamina.

She was still a dependable gal, but right now, she would have been tempted to return to the days when ghosts and magical creatures hadn't recognized her, when her mother had still been the chosen monster hunter, her sister had been next-in-line for the job, and she could pretend the world was normal.

"Come on, come on," she muttered, hurrying for the right corner this time. She glanced at her watch again. Thirty minutes left to get him.

"Damn." They might have to pack it in tonight and come back tomorrow, especially now that the dogwalker was still shouting.

And another voice answered hers.

Chloe turned, stumbling, trying to run backward while she peered through the trees. The strobing amber lights of a security car bounced around the park.

Oh, that was all she fucking needed.

The security car passed by where the trees and shrubs hid her, but the dogwalker had no doubt pointed in the direction she'd gone.

The car stopped at the corner. The ghostly glows headed straight for it. The security guard wouldn't see them, but if Goodspeed was smart...

"No," Chloe yelled. "Ramses, stop him." She ran harder, breaking through the trees just as the security guard set foot on the sidewalk, and Goodspeed dove into him as if into a deep pool.

"Shit." Chloe lunged, but the security guard turned in a jerky dance, limbs flailing as if he was being attacked by ants. Goodspeed really didn't want to get banished. He wasn't that strong of a ghost, so possession would sap his strength and push him out of the man's body soon enough, but before that, he could use the man to hide, use him as a hostage, maybe.

Or use him to kill. There was more than pepper spray on that hip.

Chloe jumped into a hedge as Goodspeed drew the guard's gun. She rolled behind a tree and halted, trying to hear if Goodspeed was coming after her now. "Come out and face me, you swine," Goodspeed said with the guard's mouth. "The Confederacy shall not be defeated so easily."

"Oh shut up," she muttered.

Ramses walked through the tree and knelt by her side. Stuck in a human body, Goodspeed wouldn't be able to see him as well, if at all. "What are you thinking?" he asked quietly. "Wait him out?"

That sounded like a fine idea, except the dogwalker was yelling, "Did you get her? She threw something all over me and Tiger."

Chloe rubbed her forehead and groaned. "We've got to do something before he shoots her or someone else. I'm not taking Tiger home with us."

Ramses cocked his head expectantly, brows raised. "You know what we have to do."

"Being possessed won't make my body impervious to bullets."

He waited, and his look continued to speak volumes. They had to disarm the guard quickly, and though she was getting better at self-defense, she wasn't as good as the leader of an ancient army.

And combined, they were both stronger than they'd ever be alone.

But goddamn, she hated being possessed.

"Fine." Chloe shut her eyes. The double vision while merging still nauseated her. A series of tingles passed over her skin, but she didn't jerk around like the guard. She was used to being possessed, and it helped that Ramses wouldn't do it without her permission.

And it helped knowing that no other fucking ghost could.

When she felt herself stand, her eyes opened. The feeling of being a passenger in her own body had been the hardest to accept. She felt like she was staring at the world's largest TV as she bent low and crept through the darkness. She sounded less noisy now than when she'd been in control. If only she didn't still feel as tired, as if she should still be panting. But Ramses never felt her fatigue. He could push her farther than she could on her own.

And he never had to deal with the consequences, like that one time he'd broken her rib.

"Oh, quit complaining," he said in her mind, their mind.

"And as I was about to think, it's not fair that you can hear my thoughts like this."

"It's a feature. We're quieter this way. Now, shh, I have to listen."

Chloe fought down her irritation at being told to shush in her own mind.

The dogwalker said, "Hello? Sir?"

Goodspeed didn't bother to respond, and Chloe listened hard for footsteps. He was probably easing down the sidewalk, listening for her, too.

"What are you…oh my God," the dogwalker shouted. Tiger yipped, then squealed as footsteps hurried into the night. Good, she was running away, but she'd probably call the police, which meant Chloe had to wrap this up even quicker.

"I know, I know," Ramses said in their shared mind. Chloe was about to censure him for not paying attention when he leapt through a gap in the bushes, scaring the hell out of her. By the shriek of alarm from Goodspeed, she wasn't the only one.

They tackled the guard's body, and a stab of pain came from where her knee collided with the sidewalk. She would have winced or recoiled, but Ramses pushed through. With a move she could never re-create in a thousand self-defense classes, he flipped the guard over. The gun bounced from his fingers, and Ramses knelt on his back. The guard's body was larger than Chloe's, stronger, but Ramses had never let that stop him, even when it should have. When the guard struggled and heaved, Ramses bounced his head off the sidewalk.

Chloe winced. "For God's sake, don't kill him."

"I won't. I've just got to shake him…loose." He gave the guard another jolt to the head.

Chloe bit back her disapproval. All they had to do was knock the guard out. No one could manipulate a body that couldn't move on its own anymore. She just wished it wouldn't be so hard on the mortal body later.

The guard finally went limp. "Yes," Chloe and Ramses said at the same time, though they'd have to save the high five for later.

Goodspeed burst from the guard's body like candy from a pinata, and Ramses leapt from Chloe's body at the same time. He pounced on Goodspeed, their spectral forms passing through a few bushes, hovering slightly as they lost their focus to stay near the ground.

Chloe gasped, the pain in her knee a sharp knife. Figured. She shambled forward, following Ramses and Goodspeed. Physical strength didn't matter so much in a contest between spirits. Neither could hold the other for long. But Chloe didn't need long. She got another handful of salt and cayenne from her pocket. "Now!"

Ramses flung Goodspeed away, and Chloe got him full in the face.

Goodspeed froze, his form rippling, caught by the salt and weakened by the pepper.

She wanted to whoop in victory, but she had no doubt that she'd soon hear sirens in the distance. She swung her satchel to the front of her body and unzipped it hurriedly, not needing any light to find her carefully packed tools. With a small hammer, she drove two long iron nails through Goodspeed's spectral boots. He shrieked and sunk until the nails were embedded in the ground.

"Your time is come, spirit," Chloe said, her heaving breath somewhat spoiling the effect of the ancient words, but luckily, that didn't matter. "Your body covers you no more, and you are but dust." With a tingle of power running through her, she placed a loop made of rowan branches and red thread over his head and brought it down through his chest. It dragged a little as it passed, his will fighting hers, but it was no use. "The wind in the north calls you." A faint red line appeared inside him, rippling like a string in a creek. It followed as she took the rowan loop all the way to his feet. "The rain of the south invites you."

His lips worked as if he was trying to say something. Chloe shook her head. This always went easier if they just gave in, but she couldn't interrupt the ritual to tell him that. Not that he would have listened anyway.

Chloe brought the rowan loop back to his chest, the red line following, becoming darker, more tangible than the spirit who held it. She tilted the loop and followed his right arm where it was stuck straight out from his body. "The earth of the west summons you." She came back down the left. "The fire in the east compels you." When she moved to his chest again, the red spread through him like the blood that had once run through his veins. "Your kin await you, spirit. Move along unto eternity and pass easy."

He shivered once as if letting loose the biggest exhale of his life. Then, he was gone.

Chloe didn't know if Chester M. Goodspeed deserved to pass easily from this world to the next, but those were the words she had to say, and it eased her mind to think that spirits moved on to somewhere better, somewhere they could see their folks again.

"Chloe, move your ass."

She put her tools back in her satchel and rolled her eyes. "You have no poetry in your soul." And all her aches and pains were hollering for her attention. She always wished she could lie down and nap after a banishment, but she could hear sirens now, and she couldn't afford to be caught. Not like the time she'd been pulled over, and a highway patrolman had found what he'd called, "a bunch of woo-woo junk," in her back seat.

Hunting ghosts and monsters would have been hard anywhere, but damn, it seemed doubly hard in Texas.

Chapter Two

Illegal poker games weren't hard to find, especially for a demigoddess like Helen. One only had to look in the right places. And perfect the right look, of course, something that would attract the right target, someone who could introduce her to the right people.

Too bad she couldn't just walk into a game unannounced and alone. But no one knew to fall to their knees in worship anymore.

Sigh.

Helen glanced at the mirror in the bathroom of the lobby of the Majestic Hotel in Miami and thumbed through the dossier on Kirk Abados on her phone, making sure she could get everything right. He clearly preferred blondes in their mid-twenties. She looked at her reflection and focused, moving her dark hair through the color spectrum until it shone a honey blond. She fixed it back with a barrette, then softened the edges of her jaw with her glamour, making her look a bit younger than she usually did and infinitely younger than she was.

Check and check. He also seemed taken with green eyes and willowy figures. The eyes were easy; she'd always managed to change their hue whenever she liked. Check. And she'd lucked out by already having the right build.

She took a deep breath as she studied herself. Even though she'd retained the power to change her hair and eye color and use her glamour to shift her appearance in other ways, her confidence still stuttered.

Her magic had a tendency to slip nowadays.

She suppressed another sigh. At the height of her power, she could have appeared as something straight from Abados's dreams, using a glamour so powerful, she wouldn't have had to open her mouth to have him falling to his knees as she'd once had kings, goddesses, and the entire city of Troy. Hell, she wouldn't have needed any game at all to get what she needed.

But she'd outlived the thriving belief in the old gods. With only a handful of believers worldwide and fewer festivals and sacrifices every year, even the power of a demigoddess waned.

Helen straightened her neck, telling herself not to be so damned maudlin. She had purpose. And not even time could dull her natural charm.

She left the bathroom and loitered in the lobby, watching for her prey. Having inside knowledge about where criminals tended to gather never hurt, either. Her smuggling contacts never let her down there. If only they'd been able to get their hands on the ambrosia. Still, it was amusing to get her hands dirty now and again, and she was so close to success, she could almost scent it on the wind. All she had to do was convince one human to introduce her to one poker game and win the ambrosia off one other player. Simplicity itself.

"You ready?" she said, ducking her head as she spoke quietly.

"Born ready," Maurice said from near her left shoulder. She felt the air move as his tiny wings flapped. He was invisible to the eye, and only those with a connection to magic could sense him. Many fair folk were the same, one of the few reasons why more of them had survived to modern times than any of the other non-human races.

Helen dismissed Kurt's dossier from her phone and tucked it in her inner jacket pocket and straightened her skirt. The outfit had also been carefully chosen with Abados in mind. Red, his favorite color, a suit that hugged her body in all the right ways. Glasses and the barrette holding back her hair completed the look of a woman who was all-business... until the right man came along and let out her inner sex goddess.

What a crock.

And if that didn't work, there was always the short, thin kladenet strapped to her back underneath her jacket. Every woman needed a self-swinging sword on her side in case of trouble. She offered a prayer to Aphrodite that this would work. She wasn't about to let another ancient creature die while she could prevent it.

When Abados strolled into the hotel, two hundred and twenty pounds of spray-tanned sleaze in an expensive suit, Helen followed him to the reception counter. She paused behind him as he began checking in and pretended to be looking for someone.

When Abados turned, Helen moved as if to step past him, fighting the urge to tense as Maurice caught her foot and tripped her, sending her lurching into Abados's arms, right on target.

Helen caught herself on his arm, forcing him to grab hold of her. And right as their eyes met, she feigned a look of shock, making sure her pretty eyes were wide, her lips gently parted. He stared, clearly gobsmacked. He probably didn't need Maurice undoing her barrette and letting her golden tresses flow freely around her shoulders.

But what the hell.

A look of rapture passed over his features. By the time he figured out that he'd never have her, she'd secure everything her charges needed in order to survive. She waited until his back was turned to smirk and sent a prayer of thanks to Aphrodite, who might not even be able to hear her anymore. Despite that—and their tumultuous past—it never paid to be too cocky. She needed all available power in her corner.

They sat in the lobby, and Helen spun a sob story about needing money and let Abados gently pry out of her that she needed a certain trinket held by one of the people who'd be attending a local poker game. Not the ambrosia. She didn't want to risk admitting her true desires, though Abados looked too smitten to care. He barely waited for her to finish her chain of falsehoods before he snatched his phone from his pocket and told her he only needed to make a few calls to "set the wheels in motion."

Helen sat back and smiled and waited.

"You might want to look a little less like the cat that ate the canary," Maurice said from somewhere near her neck.

She shrugged, though she schooled her face into a more sad but hopeful expression.

Maurice sighed, stirring the hair on her nape. "Of course, by the look on that arsehole's face, you could have been saying a load of gibberish, and he'd be making calls and setting wheels. Or you could have just commanded him to lead you to an illegal underground poker game and not waste all this bloody time."

She rubbed her neck and hid her mouth behind her elbow. "I couldn't risk him shaking off the glamour. If anyone should understand that, it's you."

"No one's ever shaken off my glamour, sunshine."

Helen fought the urge to roll her eyes. "I'm sorry I suggested otherwise."

He huffed but seemed to accept the apology. Fair folk were touchy about their powers and their honor, no matter that many seemed as crooked as a dog's hind leg. Maybe they just didn't like having that pointed out.

When Abados returned, he was beaming. She pretended to listen as he told her about the game she already knew about, the players she'd already researched. He wanted to win the item for her, but a shot of magic and a pretty smile convinced him to let her play on her own. She probably didn't need to add, "And if I lose, you'll console me, won't you?" but she liked seeing his knees turn to jelly.

When they finally reached the small but clean room above a dry cleaner's where the game was to take place, Helen pushed her glamour, watching two of the men respond and one of the women, all of whom stood as she entered and seemed happy to let her join their game. The final two, who Abados introduced as Fatma and Ali, sister and brother, glared at her intrusion, even taking Abados aside to have a quiet word.

Helen shook hands with the others, watching their faces carefully so she could tailor her expression for each. Miniscule muscle movements and quick glances told her volumes, and though it had been ages since she'd had to change her expressions so quickly, going from flirty to shy to carefree, she rather nailed it.

Even if she did say so herself.

She felt the touch of Maurice's tiny hand on the back of her neck. "The ambrosia's in a bag by the third chair over," he whispered. "The others have got some pretty good stuff as well. When do you think they'll start betting it?"

Not until well after the money was gone, no doubt. Which was why she'd have to cheat to make sure they got the ambrosia as quickly as possible. And she didn't feel bad about any of her advantages. After all, these people would take advantage of her if she let them. And she'd already put three of them, plus Abados, off their stride. They'd have to fight to pay attention to the game rather than her. She wasn't even unduly worried that Fatma and Ali seemed to be the current owners of the ambrosia. They could be the world's greatest card sharps, but they didn't have an invisible fairy on their side.

She did lament the fact that the criminal underworld knew something of the actual underworlds, something the world at large remained ignorant about. These criminals would no doubt give their eyeteeth for the location of her sanctuary, but that was something she'd never reveal, just like she didn't plan for anyone to guess that she knew the value of true ambrosia.

The sight of the fat wad of cash she pulled from her suit pocket finally convinced Fatma and Ali that she was worth keeping around, though Fatma still stared, her dark eyes full of distrust if not outright disdain. She wouldn't be won by a pretty smile. At least her brother seemed to prefer to focus on the cards. Helen met Fatma's stare and lifted her brows as if daring her to make a move.

Bold. Probably stupid, but she'd never been able to back down from a challenge. Maybe she had more in common with the fair folk than she thought.

Fatma gave her nothing but a twitch around the lips that might have been the beginnings of a smile or probably indigestion. Helen put it out of her mind as the game began. The other woman at the table, Crystal, was the designated dealer, so Helen saved her charms for the actual players. She bid or called or raised, worrying her lip sometimes, trying to seem like she couldn't control her face. She didn't win every hand; she wouldn't risk these people knowing she was cheating. No doubt she could fight her way out, especially with the kladenet. But even a self-swinging sword couldn't win every combat, and her charges didn't need her laid up while she healed. Besides, the crooks at this table might bring her more unlooked-for gifts in the future.

"This big dude is trying to bluff a straight," Maurice whispered in Helen's ear. "And Ali's got a full house."

She'd already figured out the bluff. The "big dude" had a massive tell in his twitchy index finger, even though he tried to hide it with his other hand. But a full house beat her two pair, and she needed a win this round in order to stay in the game. She tapped the cards, silently asking Maurice to get a look in the deck and move the cards she needed.

He chuckled, his cold breath nearly making her shiver. "Such an expense of energy will require extra vittles, quality ones."

Helen held in a frown. She couldn't risk nodding or shaking her head. Demigoddess or not, she wasn't making a deal with a fairy without a ten-page contract. She picked up her water glass and whispered, "We'll see," just before she drank. That was the best answer he was getting.

"Aye," he said with another sigh and a dash more brogue than usual. "Give me a bit of a distraction."

Like what? She couldn't very well point and shout, "What's that?" Everyone would suspect her of tampering with the table. She'd have to lean on the winsome naivete she'd been hoping to instill. She only wished playing dumb didn't feel like setting feminism back fifty years.

When the bet got around to her, she said, "Check," something she could only do if everyone else had also checked. Which they hadn't.

"Sorry, sweetheart," Abados said, giving her a look with so much pity and condescension, she almost let the kladenet out to play. "The bet's already at one-fifty. It's either call or raise."

"Oh, sorry, I wasn't paying attention." She batted her lashes and could almost feel him trying to decide if he wanted her money more than her. Ugh. She fumbled with her chips, dropping some on the floor. Even if only two players helped her pick them up, the others wouldn't be closely watching the deck.

And Maurice could move objects faster than anyone could follow. It did expend a lot of his energy, and she would try to find him a reward later, but she'd never agree to anything vague where he was concerned. When she, Abados, and the big guy righted themselves, she called, and no one seemed to have noticed anything was awry. She got a better full house than Ali's on the next deal.

A quick look of surprise passed over Crystal's pale face when she dealt Helen's cards. Oh ho? Did one of the other players have the dealer working for them?

"I think the dealer's crooked," Maurice whispered in Helen's ear. "Trying to cheat us? The cheek of it. I ought to give her a walloping."

Helen caught a hint of real danger in his tone. Hating being cheated while already cheating was just another dichotomous part of his nature. She shook her head slightly, disguising it in a stretch. She'd rather figure out who Crystal was cheating for and beat them at their own game.

But as the rounds ticked by, she still had no proof, but her money was on Fatma and Ali. Or maybe just one, whichever didn't want to risk losing the very artifact they'd brought to the table, maybe.

The two other men were out of the game, banished to the corner before the real prizes came out, leaving just Helen, Abados, Fatma, and Ali.

"I've stopped that Crystal cheating twice more," Maurice whispered, though he sounded louder, his tone flatter, a bad sign. "I managed to thwart her, but—"

A soft buzz interrupted his words, and Helen's vision blurred. She had a moment to gasp before it cleared again. The others looked at her while she was still reeling, and she put a hand to her chest and sipped some water, forcing herself to smile but using the sudden nervousness she felt. "Sorry, just got a little lightheaded."

Abados gave her a sympathetic look. "After this, I'll take you to the best seafood restaurant in town. Anything you want, babe."

She fluttered her lashes again as if he was God's gift while she resisted the urge to throw up on his suit.

Maurice lightly pulling her hair was a nice distraction…at least until he spoke. "That was glamour," he practically growled. "She has fairy blood, and she's pulling a glamour on me?"

Oh shit.

Helen tried to control her breathing, wishing she could say some soothing words and calm him down. Crystal likely didn't even know Maurice was in the room, but that didn't matter. Fairies disliked having their honor besmirched, they hated when others tried to cheat them, but they positively loathed when anyone sought to out-glamour them. "Easy," she said around another cough and drink.

"No one outcons me."

"Maurice." She tried to smile disarmingly as Fatma looked her way. "Let it go," she said behind her teeth and her water.

"Fuck that. It's the principle of the thing."

"You don't have principles." Now everyone was looking at her, and she felt as if she was trying desperately to put a cork back in a bottle.

Or a tiger in a cage. Myths about fairies often mentioned their stature or speed or magic. But Helen knew from experience that they were very, very strong for their size.

Especially when they were pissed.

It was almost a relief when the table launched upward as if swatted by a giant hand. At least the room didn't feel as if it was holding its breath anymore. Helen dove away just as everyone else did, cursing Maurice and the fact that she understood why he felt he had to deliver this particular walloping. But how in Hades was she supposed to have known that one of the people she'd be spending the afternoon with could use glamour?

Everyone was talking over everyone else. Crystal screamed as she flew to the side, straight into Abados. They both toppled. Helen's mind raced for a plausible explanation but came up empty, especially after Crystal's ear was pulled straight up, making her cry out again as she stood rapidly, her arms flailing.

"Think you're smart, do you, low blood?" Maurice shouted, his voice filling the place for all its high pitch. "Queen of the goddamned fairy mound?"

A slight spark came from Crystal's fingers. Maurice grunted as he let her go, his small body outlined in white fire for no more than the beat of a heart.

Helen gawked. Crystal must have more fairy blood than she realized. She began to feel the same urge to protect her that she did her charges, but Maurice wouldn't kill her. Or rather, by the look of things, Crystal wouldn't let him.

Still, she couldn't just let them wreak havoc. She pulled a small flat jar of the Maurice Contingency Plan from a hidden pocket in the waistband of her skirt, uncapped it, and threw a line of superfine gold glitter into the air. Crystal's head snapped toward it as if on a string, and Helen knew Maurice would do the same. They'd both be drawn to the sparkles by their fairy blood. Helen grinned, never regretting the day she'd learned that those descended from the fair folk accounted for sixty percent of all glitter-based purchases.

It was just a bonus that the glittering cloud now hovered between her and the other poker players. The two who were already out of the game had fled down the stairs. Everyone else's eyes were on Crystal.

And Fatma's bag was on Helen's side of the glitter cloud.

She grabbed it and ran for the stairs. Hopefully, it also contained some money, but nothing was more important than the ambrosia. "The police are coming," she shouted as she reached the ground floor, sending the employees of the dry cleaner's running in all directions, adding to the chaos. Maurice could take care of himself after the glitter fascination wore off, and meanwhile, she could get—

"Hold it," Fatma yelled from the stairs.

Shit.

Helen ran down the hall toward the rear doors of the building, pushing out a heavy door into a sun-filled alley. She darted to the right and turned a corner, but a dumpster blocked her way. "Fuck." She turned, but Fatma slid around the corner, her shoulders heaving as she breathed hard.

She didn't seem in the mood to talk as she tied her long dark hair in a knot at her neck. "That's not yours," she said, nodding toward the bag.

Helen reached back and drew the kladenet. "Feels like mine." The short thin sword went into a guard position in her hand. It would do all the fighting for her.

"Oh, honey, that's so cute," Fatma said as she drew a small pistol from the pocket of her black leather jacket. "But now the bag feels like it's mine again."

Well, shit. But Helen wasn't afraid. In another time, she might have enjoyed this encounter. There was something about women who were armed. Could have been the take-no-shit attitude. Fatma's bronzed skin and tight jeans would have helped. But not anymore. Helen was too tired of lamenting all her yesterdays, and her past had permanently purged all desire from her life.

Luckily, her heart didn't need to be in this encounter in any way. A self-swinging sword didn't necessarily need a wielder.

Helen let it go, and it dropped nearly to the ground, enough for Fatma to begin a smile, a look that morphed to confusion as the sword rose again, hovering in the air between them. "Attack."

"What the fu—ah!" Fatma screamed as the sword lunged toward her, point-first. It slapped the pistol out of her hand as she brought it up, leaving a line of blood across her knuckles. She fell backward, hand to her chest, screaming again.

"Halt," Helen commanded, pausing the sword an inch from Fatma's throat. Helen kept the smirk off her face as she strode forward and picked up the pistol. "I hope you don't look on today only with regret," she said to Fatma's terrified expression. "Against any other opponent, I'm sure you would have done well." Then, she looked to the sword. "Subdue."

The kladenet flipped over in midair, and Fatma barely had time to gasp before the pommel rapped against her forehead, and she lay still.

Helen grabbed the kladenet and secured it to her back again. She tossed the pistol into a trash can and walked back by the rear of the dry cleaner's, wondering what the others were up to inside, but it wasn't worth the risk to find out. And Maurice would catch up soon enough. Someone who'd been alive for thousands of years wouldn't be defeated by some criminals, a human with fairy blood, and a jar of glitter.

Helen swung the bag over her shoulder and sighed. All part of a day's work in running a sanctuary for mythical creatures. And she hadn't had to launch a single ship.

CHAPTER THREE

When Chloe woke up in the shitty motel bed, fatigue still had a heavy hand upon her. After she'd gotten in the night before, she hadn't had the energy to shower, but now she wished she had. The smell of cayenne on her hands brought up too many memories of ghosts, real or otherwise, and her mouth tasted like a raccoon had been nesting in it.

Still, when she opened her eyes, she didn't move. Near the foot of the bed, Ramses hovered on a chair next to the flimsy desk, his hands laced over the toned abs sported by his statues, never mind that he'd probably never achieved that look in real life, but he'd always appeared as a mash-up between his various statues and what he'd really looked like. He'd once counted himself lucky that he wasn't stuck with the tied-on pharaoh beard and a heavy-looking pectoral every time he appeared.

His dark skin was slightly tinted from his own blue glow, and that was currently rivaled by the light from Chloe's laptop as he streamed a TV show, the closed captioning flashing across the bottom. She sometimes bemoaned the amount of money she spent on streaming services, but he was addicted to at least one show on every goddamned platform, and he only had to use a jolt of ghostly energy to switch between them after she got him set up each night.

She'd never say no to his hobby. The money was worth it to entertain him while she slept. Even if he promised to stick around and watch over her, she felt better knowing he had more reasons to stay, that she could see him every time her eyes flickered open.

After all, it only took a flash of time for people to disappear forever.

A depressing thought, one that often haunted her mornings, sending her down a depressed spiral that felt like a metal slide in summer. And it had been hot the day of the wreck; she could still feel sweat dribbling down her spine and the pain in her chest from the seat belt. Pain like that wasn't supposed to linger like a badly healed bone, but she could summon it like someone had surely summoned Chester M. Goodspeed's ghost.

Stop it. Think of something else. Any goddamned thing but the wreck.

Like the EMTs working to bring her mom back to life?

No.

Or the way they'd pulled Jamie out of the front seat and covered her with a sheet as if she was furniture being stored for winter?

Oh, fuck you, brain.

Her mind seemed to be saying, "Fuck you right back," as she recalled the floaty feeling when they'd loaded her on a gurney, a feeling made more intense by the golden glow detaching from her mom's body like steam off asphalt. The glow had hovered over Jamie briefly, then had ignored her, their mother's chosen successor, much as the EMTs had.

That gold glow had come for Chloe, invisible to everyone else, hers alone now, even after her mother's heart had restarted.

Chloe put a hand over her eyes and tried to get her asshole brain to shut up and leave her be, but once it started down a spiral, it had to take its flesh, just like the hot slide she'd imagined it to be. Jamie had been the chosen one. Jamie had gotten the training. Chloe had been twenty-two, studying to be a tech writer, for fuck's sake. Tech writers did not go out and hunt ghosts and goblins in their spare time.

And so she'd been overjoyed when they'd loaded her mom in the ambulance beside her. For so many reasons. The EMTs had brought her mom back to life, but the golden glow still hovered in Chloe's periphery; the family gift seemed disinclined to return to its former owner. She'd felt it, too, scratchy as a wool blanket, yet cold as the hand of death, and just before she'd finally surrendered to her concussion, she'd seen Ramses's spectral face for the first time.

Great. We're all caught up. Can we move on?

Chloe lowered her arm to watch Ramses now. They were distantly related, but after having over a hundred children in life, he had descendants all over the world, scattered by oceans and time. She didn't see any resemblance between them in his aquiline nose or patrician face—though they had the same bronzed skin tone—but it was comforting to wake up every morning to family who couldn't leave her.

Would Jamie have felt differently?

"Shut up," she muttered. She made herself move, welcoming the twinge in her swollen knee. She couldn't get too distracted by the past. She was the dependable one, never letting anybody down, and she'd be damned if she'd let a freaking grief spiral carry her away. She'd crammed a lifetime's worth of training into the year after Jamie's death while her parents had been wrecks, their marriage dissolving. She had absorbed her familial duty and the trappings that would keep her alive. Now she was an expert at twenty-five. How many people could say that about anything?

"How did you sleep?" Ramses asked, his striped nemes slipping over one shoulder as he turned.

"Good and terrible."

He clucked his tongue. "You always wake up early and brood after a late-night job."

Chloe rubbed her aching neck. "I'm fine."

"You're clenching your fists like you do when you think about Jamie."

She sighed, long and loud, hoping he'd just drop it. He'd never gotten to share this work with Jamie, share a mind with her, bonding as he did to only one member of the family at a time. How much of Jamie's memories would he have carried and shared?

When Chloe didn't reply, Ramses sighed and stood, one hand hovering over the laptop long enough for a flicker of ghostly energy to pause the show. "Move over," he said, waiting until she'd scooted to the middle of the bed before sitting beside her, hovering just over the covers. His nemes flickered and vanished, leaving his short, and surprisingly red, hair, the look he sported whenever he seemed to have a mind to comfort her.

She gripped the duvet and wanted to say that she didn't need comforting like some little kid, but she had moved over for him. Had he ever comforted his actual children like this? He never said much about his life, and the only secret he'd revealed about his death was that his heart had been judged heavier than a feather by Anubis. Instead of being devoured by Ammit, he'd been given the choice to return as a spirit and lighten his heart so he'd one day be able to join his family in the afterlife.

"You've always been brave," he said. "It wasn't enough for you to swing across the monkey bars. You had to get on top of them. You remind me of Zahra."

The person who'd bound him to Chloe's family over a millennia ago. She couldn't ask if he said the same thing about everyone he'd been bound to, scared that it might be true. She needed strength like Zahra's today.

But it could wait a bit. She leaned toward him. He didn't have a solid presence or the warmth of a living body, but she felt his great store of spiritual energy, a feeling that had grown more comforting than flesh and blood as time went on. "I had something to prove back then. I got tired of watching Jamie and Mom and feeling like I was outside looking in."

"And now you've proven yourself time and again."

"Tell that to my asshole brain."

"Very well. Hear me, O Brain of Asshole-ishness, and obey," he said close to her head, making her giggle. "Stop waking Chloe up and making her doubt herself."

With another chuckle, she sagged against the headboard. "Thanks, Pharoah."

"My pleasure." He smiled gently. "Now, about our wager from last night…"

She nodded and put her hand out. She hadn't been able to banish Goodspeed on her own, so she had to pay her debt. "I'll get Apple TV."

"Yes!" He grinned and put his hand near hers, making the hair on her arm stand on end as they went through the motions of shaking hands. "Now, are you going to shower or go back to sleep?"

"Shower." She shifted toward the other side of the bed.

"Good. By the look of you, I'm counting myself lucky that I have no sense of smell."

She chucked a pillow at him as she snorted a laugh and stood, taking her overnight bag and shuffling into the bathroom. "I really hope we don't have to investigate anything else for at least a week."

Ramses appeared in front of the laptop once more, crossing his sandaled feet on the foot of the bed. "I feel I do have to remind you that a few months ago, you complained that you didn't have enough to do."

She rolled her eyes. "Tell that to my knee."

"Hear me, O Knee—"

She barked a laugh and shut the bathroom door.

With a long sigh, she leaned against the shower wall and let the warm water wash over her, easing her tense muscles. Could she have been happy being a freelance tech writer and editor? Maybe. It was what she'd imagined after she'd put away adolescent dreams of being a monster hunter like so many of her ancestors. There was just so much about that life no one had mentioned: sore knees and self-doubt and the hard water of hotel showers, when she had to use damn near the whole tiny bottle of shampoo to feel clean.

But the work crew at the park would be able to take Goodspeed's statue down now, and no one else would get hurt.

She smiled at herself in the mirror as she dried off. *Take that, O Brain of Asshole-ishness.*

❖

Under cover of darkness, Helen made her way to the large beach hut she'd rented, the bag containing the ambrosia slung over one shoulder. She'd spent the rest of the afternoon under an umbrella on the sand, reading a book on her phone and sipping a frozen Jack and Coke, a thoroughly pleasant way to spend a few hours. Maurice had yet to put in an appearance, but she wasn't too worried. If he'd proven anything in their acquaintance, it was that he could take care of himself.

Though, without her transport, he would find the journey back to her island a little grueling.

Pegasus whinnied a greeting as soon as Helen opened the door to the hut. "Hello," she said, finally letting herself really relax as she stepped inside and turned on the small overhead light. The soft glow reflected off Pegasus's white coat and feathered wings. "I return triumphant. Sorry I took so long. I had to wait for dark."

He pawed the ground, a gesture of congratulations, and tossed his head in his equine version of a shrug.

"Thank you. One quick call and we're on our way." She dialed the satellite phone at her villa on the island.

The Sphinx picked up quickly. "Morningdale Orchids, how may I direct your call?"

"It's me." She made a mental note to ask how the Sphinx's latest business venture was going. Rare orchids couldn't be that easy to grow and sell, but the Sphinx liked to keep busy. "We're about to start back. Did the regular delivery come?"

"Not yet," the Sphinx said. "But I'll meander toward the dock and take a look. Maybe I'll meet the smugglers there, give them a fright."

Helen tried to quash the flutter of panic in her gut, telling herself that it was a joke, that the Sphinx knew the protocol, but, but... "Um, someone who can pass for human should—"

"And that's a fail," the Sphinx said, their tone implying that Helen was the epitome of uncool. "You must have had a hard day, babe. Relax. I'll find one of the naiads or someone to go check, don't worry."

Helen sighed and took a deep breath. Fighting the urge to repeat herself, to remind, to reiterate, to warn if necessary was a Sisyphean struggle, but the Sphinx was right. It had been a hard day, or at least, a busy one. Pretending to be a bonehead, then flirting with Abados had taken a lot out of her.

"You really need a fuck buddy," the Sphinx said.

"Oh sure. I'll make a dating profile, shall I? 'Undying demigoddess seeks adoring worshiper for casual fun in whichever random city she's forced to go to once a decade.' The requests will come flooding in."

"Is there any point in me saying that you have admirers aplenty in the sanctuary?"

"Do you really want to rehear my speech on how I can't fool around with those under my protection?"

"Nope."

"Same."

The Sphinx chuckled. "You didn't happen to, uh, score anything else while in town, did you?"

Helen rubbed the bridge of her nose. "Why can't you grow your own weed?"

"Maybe someday, I will. But I'd rather learn while already possessing some. My arthritic paws will thank me."

"I'm sorry," Helen said, her frustration dulled by shame. "Like you said, it's been a long day."

The Sphinx made a kissing noise. "I'm sorry for keeping you on the phone. Come home. I'll start the cocoa. You can have yours in the bath."

"Sounds like heaven. Hey," she added, "now that I think about it, I already arranged for a shipment of your 'medicine' to be delivered tomorrow from our smuggling contacts."

"Bless you, my dear. I'm sorry I ever doubted. Fly safe."

Helen hung up and checked outside again. Since the moon had already set, she saw nothing but the bright lights of the avenue that fronted the beach. If any lovers were entwined nearby, they'd have to draw their own conclusions about hoofbeats and flapping wings.

She switched off the lights of the hut, and Pegasus followed her outside. She lifted herself onto his back with ease, holding tight with her knees, though Pegasus would never throw her. Now, all she had to do was—

"Wait!" Maurice's voice.

Helen sighed and chuckled. Right on time. Maurice sounded out of breath when he reached them. Pegasus gave a soft whinny of hello.

"How did you get away from Crystal?" Helen asked.

"Didn't until just now." Pegasus's mane brushed over Helen's knuckles as Maurice tangled himself in the strands so he didn't fall off on the trip.

She frowned. "Was she that powerful?"

"In magic, no. In her other charms—"

"No, stop. I don't want to know." But her mind was already working. Logistically, how would they—she shook her head. *No, ugh.* Still, she had a duty to ask, "And she's all right? Staying out in the world?"

"She doesn't need your sanctuary," Maurice said, and she could hear an undercurrent of irritation, affront that any of the fair folk would need her help. That he needed her help.

"I just wondered if she wanted a place where she could relax, be herself."

He was silent for a few moments. She waited patiently, Pegasus shifting under her as they stood on the beach. In the dark, it was almost like they were both invisible. He only ever shared deep thoughts when he couldn't see her well. Or when he was drunk on mushroom wine.

"She likes it out in the world," he finally said. "In ways that I tired of long ago." That was the closest he'd come to not only thanking Helen but admitting the sanctuary was home.

Still, she hid her smile, even in the dark. The unpredictability of fairies had already been proven today. She did feel the need to add, "Me too," letting him know that the thing he didn't want to say, that she wasn't supposed to know, was known and understood and reciprocated. Though, no doubt they'd stay the kind of family who was uncomfortable with hugs and punched each other in the shoulder to show affection.

One quick word to Pegasus and they took off over the ocean, heading toward the small island that had managed to stay lost among many others in the Caribbean. Long ago, Helen had used her then-substantial savings to buy it, when she'd decided that relics of myth like herself needed a sanctuary. After living so long, there seemed little else in life to hope for.

Even those with a bad reputation deserved someplace they could thrive. Otherwise, they'd wind up captured by humans or in various underworlds, many falling under the care of the unscrupulous dead, or so her contacts had told her.

But even that sounded better than nothingness after death. Helen didn't see why any creature needed to risk death or what came after when they might live forever if left alone. If only humanity was less selfish about sharing their world with anyone who didn't fit their narrow view of the universe. Even science had an exception to every rule. She was personally a big fan of both science and mathematics, and both fields acknowledged the concept of endless possibilities.

If only humans could be as...bendable.

Helen leaned her head back as the wind combed chaotically through her hair. She closed her eyes to the starlight and let memory overtake her. She'd loved humans once, had loved among them. She'd even been able to contact the dead for the past few years, ever since the walls between the levels of the Greek Underworld had been brought down. The living who had the power of mediumship could now hear the voices of those in the Elysian Fields or the many realms of Tartarus.

Still, as happy as talking to those she'd loved made her, Helen hoped the mortal-turned-god who'd assumed the mantle of queen of the Greek Underworld wouldn't keep the throne. What if she decided to tear down the final wall, the one that would let the dead rise from the grave?

She couldn't even imagine the chaos that would cause. Even the elder gods hadn't done it, and those creatures were unhinged.

Or what if the new queen decided that the survivors of all the old myths should step into the light? Helen had vowed to never, ever mingle freely with humanity again, not without a disguise. Not if she'd have to hear those two little words. Every day. For the rest of existence:

Of Troy.

As if she'd never done anything in her life but be forced into the wrong place at the wrong time.

Pegasus's whinny brought her back to herself. She was clenching his mane too hard.

"Sorry," she tried to call above the wind. *Count to ten. Breathe. No need to dwell on ifs and maybes.* What mattered was that she'd had a successful trip and was returning home to a bastion of safety and the best friends a demigoddess could ask for. She was a survivor, not a whiner, and that meant she owed her help to those who weren't so great at surviving.

As if summoned, Maurice began to glow, his tiny body outlined in fairy fire where he was tangled in Pegasus's mane. He was staring at her with luminous green eyes, his wings folded behind him like a moth's and his head thrust forward, feathery antennae tilted toward her. His handsome face peered at her from the dandelion-like fluff of his hair and beard. He mouthed, "Are you okay?" slowly, as if he knew he'd never be heard over the wind.

She nodded, choking up, touched at the words and floored at the fact that he'd risked visibility to utter them. She forgave him for everything about that day. He might even have factored that into his decision about whether to appear. Still, she loved the little bastard. Someone with as short a temper as his would have been discovered long ago if they didn't have her sanctuary. And so, she had an obligation to keep up her sanctuary. Simple logic.

If only all her problem children would realize the fact that running loose in the world and causing trouble would only get them attacked by missiles or torpedoes or something, even if they tried to keep low profiles. Any murders or kidnappings they might commit were going to be noticed, either by law enforcement or monster hunters, especially those who possessed some psychic ability. For them, anything out of the ordinary equaled evil, never mind the fact that they owed their gifts to some very extraordinary ancestors, some of whom she'd met.

Some of whom she'd trusted.

Two of whom had betrayed her.

But we're not going to think about that.

With Pegasus's speed, it only took four hours before Helen caught the flash of one of her warning buoys. They kept anyone from innocently straying too close to the island, a registered site of previous nuclear tests. She or one of her charges had a long history with local pirates, smugglers, and the rulers and politicians of the various countries nearby. They remade those connections with every generation so local residents and visitors were routinely warned away. And if someone did reach land, the creatures there were more than capable of magically rattling their brains a bit before releasing them back into the world. A thick canopy of trees kept them a secret from the air, and the island itself wasn't large enough to be considered the newest tourist spot.

Isolated. Perfect. Just a tad lonely, but she had to expect that just from living so long.

CHAPTER FOUR

Helen passed the dock and aimed for a particular patch of trees. It was only a glamour designed to fool airborne eyes, but she couldn't see through it. Pegasus seemed to, or more likely, he knew his food was down there somewhere. He was an immortal, intelligent horse, but he was still a horse at heart.

They passed through a dark blur, and Pegasus alighted gently on the lawn. Beneath the glamour, the clearing was lit by a single floodlight and a string of bulbs that led from the landing area to her house. Helen slipped down just as Maurice fluttered away with barely a good-bye. Helen thanked Pegasus with a kiss on his soft nose, then sent him on his way to the paddock.

With a yawn, the Sphinx rose from where she lay beneath the wooden lattice of a huge gazebo. "Good flight?" Though nowhere near as large as her namesake statue at Giza, she was still impressive at eight feet tall, with her muscular lioness body and a dark, feminine head. She wore her black hair in a multitude of braids that were currently pulled into a twist behind her.

Helen put a hand to her back and stretched. "About the only thing that went as planned." She sighed before the Sphinx could point out that some of the island's denizens would love to get out once in a while, no matter how the plan went. "I'm sorry. I know all I do is whine lately."

The Sphinx shrugged one tawny shoulder. "Understandable." She looked back as Helen followed her to the huge solarium attached to the house. "It's still no fun to listen to, don't get me wrong." She winked.

Helen breathed a laugh. The solarium was lit by a few softly glowing lamps rigged with large footpads so the Sphinx could turn them off and on. As Helen sat on a small chaise lounge next to a much larger one, the Sphinx gently pulled the huge glass door closed. Cool air began trickling in from the main house, and Helen slipped her shoes off, luxuriating.

"You might not want to get too comfortable," the Sphinx said, a hint of apology in her golden eyes.

Helen held in the epic sigh she really wanted to let out. "Why? I thought there was a bath and cocoa in my future."

"We could wait until you have a drink in hand. Maybe one of my special cookies?"

Tempting, but Helen shook her head. If she drank or took anything, a sigh could quickly become a tirade, rant, or another episode like the one that had destroyed the building that had stood here before the solarium.

When the nereid Psamathe had first showed her face at the sanctuary after betraying Helen centuries ago.

I thought we'd decided that we aren't going to think about that.

Right. "Just tell me that nothing's gone wrong with our, um, rehabilitating brethren," Helen said.

"No, all the prisoners are accounted for."

"Sphinx, we've been over this. Beings like the Lamia—"

"I know, I know. Everyone is capable of redemption, and all our 'rehabilitating brethren' need is more time to see the error of their evil ways." She waved a paw. "But we don't need to get into any old debates because they're all still here."

Helen was too tired to make a true retort. "So why am I not getting comfortable?"

"I think there might be a griffin near a place called Waxahachie in Texas."

Gods. She knew where Texas was, at least, and it wasn't too far, even if it was huge. And a griffin wouldn't be that much trouble to corral. And if it had been imprisoned and shipped to the area, at least she'd have someone to take her bad mood out on. "And how do we know this?"

"Well, one of the nereids heard it from a whale who got it from a naiad who still lives near Galveston, and she—"

Helen nodded. "I get the picture." The water creature gossip network was vast, but luckily, it was also surprisingly accurate. "Any signs it's in grave danger or being horribly mistreated?"

"Oh, I wasn't suggesting you go right this minute."

Helen fought the urge to glare. "Then what did 'don't get too comfortable' mean?"

"It's a figure of speech, touchy. A way to break news that might not be completely welcome. Go drink your cocoa in the bath that has been lovingly prepared for you, then get some sleep. You're far too grouchy for company."

"I take back every mean thought I've ever had about you." And she did, too, now that a bath and a hot drink and bed were all in her future again. But she did feel the need to add, "And I'm not grouchy," over her shoulder. "Overworked? Yes. Stressed? Most definitely. Do those add up to understandably vexed? Absolutely. But grouchy is a whole other world, one where only cranky children live."

She decided to ignore the muttered, "Sounds about right."

❖

After a long day spent doing nothing but recovering, Chloe felt much better, even if she had to do that recovering in a shitty motel room. "I'm glad we decided to start staying an extra night after ghost cases," she said as she gnawed on a breadstick. "Even if it strains the budget."

Ramses didn't take his eyes off the laptop that sat between them on the bed. "I always found a day of rest essential after a battle."

"But you had lots of wives to help you unwind after a hard day." Not that she was jealous, no sir.

He snorted. "It's cute that you think multiple wives didn't come with their own problems."

"But lots of benefits."

He rolled his eyes. "If it's companionship you seek, finish your pizza, don your finest come-hither outfit, and we will take this town by storm."

Chloe barked a laugh. She'd never taken anywhere by storm, and even if she owned a come-hither outfit—whatever the hell he imagined that to be—she hadn't packed it. And this town didn't look like the friendliest place for "young woman seeks same."

But he knew all that, and after a moment, he dropped his arm and gestured to where her phone sat on the nightstand. "Or you can research our next target."

"I can't help but notice the lack of a 'we' in that sentence." But he'd already gone back to his show. Chloe sighed as loudly as she could, picked up her phone, and began scrolling through her internet alerts, mostly new posts on sites that focused on strange and mysterious happenings. Even years into it, she sometimes had a tough time sifting the actual cases from the BS, the one true ghost or creature in the list of "30 Bizarre and Unexplained Phenomena that Will Keep You Up at Night."

The emails about her day job clients were always getting buried.

"Anything good?" Ramses asked.

"Good, maybe, but here's one that's definitely close. A very small town outside Waxahachie. A flying creature. People in the area are calling it everything from a huge owl to a giant bat to the Mothman going south for the winter."

"Ah, the Mothman." He smiled fondly. "I remember that one with your mother. Think this is another griffin?"

"Let's hope so." She knew where she was with a griffin. "Or nothing at all. That would be even better."

"Oh yes. So we have a nice vacation in scenic Middle-of-Nowhere."

"Ha. I don't know. I could have some time to work on tech journals, a leisurely dinner, a warm bath, and be in bed by ten." God, she was too young for that to sound as good as it did.

Ramses gave her a flat look, one that said even he was too young for that to sound good. "And there's always figuring out why we've had so many new sightings. As perplexed as Goodspeed seemed by his surroundings, I'm certain he was summoned."

So was Chloe. But so far, no spell or fellow monster-hunter had revealed the key to why there'd been so many ghosts and beasties lately. And if her mother had the answer, she hadn't said.

Not that Chloe had really asked. Please don't point it out, she thought.

"You know," Ramses said, "your mother might—"

"Ugh. Yeah." But she'd been trying to lean on her mother as little as possible. She was still mourning Jamie, the loss of her powers and purpose, and her marriage.

Plus, there was the little fact that Chloe didn't want to hear what a shit job she was doing. Not that her mother ever said that, not in so many words.

Double ugh. Now she couldn't sit still. She jumped up and started gathering her things and stuffing them in the battered blue suitcase she'd had since 2003, before they'd started putting four wheels on the damn things, but it still worked, and the voice of her father that she carried in her head wouldn't let her simply abandon it.

God. Maybe she should call her dad, too. How long had it been? The thought was enough to send pain oozing through her lower intestine. And she fought monsters, for fuck's sake.

With a huff, she left off packing and grabbed her phone again, pointedly not looking at Ramses, even though he was no doubt pointedly not looking at her. She ducked out the door and stood on the warm walkway in front of her room.

The lesser of two evils first. At least her mom would never put on the type of brittle cheeriness that her dad favored. And she was never far from her phone.

Her mom answered on the second ring. "What's wrong?"

Nothing like the, "Hey, kiddo," of her dad's habitual greetings. But their relationship went smoother when they kept it all business. Her mom never said so, but Chloe knew she hated being on the periphery of "the family gift." And she had to miss Ramses, too, though she'd doubtlessly rather try to eat her own face than admit such a thing. "Um, nothing urgent. I was just wondering if you had any more thoughts about, you know, the uptick in, um, monster stuff?" Yeah, that was some confident, ghost-banishing shit right there.

Her mom sighed. "I've been watching the internet. I've never seen so many reports."

Chloe froze in stunned surprise. If her mother didn't know what was going on, then Jamie probably wouldn't have—

Damn, she had to get a grip.

"Maybe we should find an oracle or something," her mother said. "I think there's supposed to be one near Memphis." Though she sounded like she'd rather eat lemons than rely on any "magical bullshit" for help.

Other than Ramses, of course. It had to have felt like he'd died on her just like Jamie had, though he'd been dead a *long* time.

Chloe rubbed her temples. "Maybe."

"But I don't like it. Neither did your sister."

Aha, it only took four seconds to mention Jamie this time. "I know… and oracles are fucking creepy, Mom." Deeply professional, that was.

"Well, if we want to find out what's going on, we might need a guide. Ramses is limited on where he can go and what he can tell us."

"Lucky he isn't out here to hear you."

"Tell me about it." They shared a laugh, but there was an undercurrent of sadness. Her mom was alone most of these days.

"Did you read about the Waxahachie case? Looks promising," Chloe said, sticking to business, but whether she did because it made sense, because she rarely defied her mom, or because of guilt, she couldn't say. "It's not far from here, so I can get on it."

"Good girl."

Dependable. Right. And she was back to fighting her own damn feelings again.

"You be careful, you hear?" her mom said.

Chloe swayed back around to feeling loved. When it came to her mom, she suspected her brain would always be spinning like a compass needle at the North Pole. "I will." She played with the drawstring on her yoga pants when silence fell between them like a steel wall. She started to say, "Well," right as her mom said, "I," and they both chuckled awkwardly.

When they spoke again at the same time, Chloe slipped in the word, "love," and thought she heard it in turn before her mom said, "Good luck."

Like a moron, Chloe said, "You too." She hung up rather than bask in her idiocy.

"What did she say?" Ramses asked when she came back in. "Consult an oracle?"

She glared. "You could have just suggested it yourself, you know."

"You wouldn't have listened to me." He sounded half-indignant, with more than a hint of bruised feelings.

"I know I should listen to you," she said, hoping she sounded conciliatory and not like she was laughing at him. "You've been around for thousands of years."

"All that experience—"

"Wasted on mere mortals."

His mouth twisted wryly. "I am completely unappreciated in death."

She rolled her eyes. "I appreciate you all the time. I'd buy you a diamond tiara if you could wear it."

He stood and stared her down, the crown of Egypt manifesting on his head, and she knew she'd gone a bit too far. She'd be very dead without his help. More than that, if he hadn't been guiding her family for generations, she would have never existed.

As he turned away, crown still in place, she said, "You know, the Houston Museum has your exhibit on right now." She always tracked its travels.

He shrugged, and she knew exactly what he was thinking as if he was possessing her.

"I'm not trying to placate you," she added.

He snorted. "Like offering some child a treat."

"I just thought it was cool that they've got a new set of short films with better CGI, and a very realistic model made from scans of your mummy. I really want to see it. You might get a kick out of it. Maybe after the next case?"

He glanced over his shoulder, looking thoughtful, no doubt wavering between affront at being mollified and maybe touched that she'd put some time and research into it. "That could be amusing." The crown faded back to the striped, cloth nemes he wore most of the time.

She smiled, genuinely relieved. He'd bound his spirit to her family generations ago in order to follow them wherever they were and for ease in possession, but he could still come and go as he liked. She knew he'd never abandon her in battle, but she'd be terribly lonely if he only showed up for that.

And her mom didn't even have that anymore.

What did I tell you, asshole brain?

Moreover, she didn't actually want to hurt Ramses's feelings.

That's better.

"Thanks for putting up with my moods," she said.

He smiled, his eyes saying all was forgiven. What would it have been like to be in his company when he was alive, to have him as her pharaoh, to have been one of his many children?

He tilted his head. "Why so sad?"

She sighed, hoping her expressions didn't make her an open book to everyone. "Not really sad, just thoughtful. Thankful."

He put his spectral arms around her, and she could feel the tingle of his energy in place of warmth and pressure. "I'll always be here for you."

At least until she got too old, then she'd have to choose a protégé from her extended family to take over. And that thought just made it easier to kick that decision farther down the road.

CHAPTER FIVE

The problem with hunting mythic creatures instead of ghosts was the lack of a starting place. Ghostly activity could always be traced to a statue or monument or other 3D representation of the ghosts themselves. But with creatures, Chloe had to sort through a ton of bullshit just to get started.

Internet rumor had led her to a tiny farm town just south of Waxahachie—itself a town of around fifty thousand south of Dallas—but after she parked her beat-up 2013 Camry in the parking lot of a Waffle Hut, she sighed and gave a lazy flick through the online journal that contained the clues she'd managed to glean so far:

Flying monster seen at night.

County Road 276, a length of road inhabited mostly by cows.

Witnesses had been near this Waffle Hut.

The first was no help at all. The second sounded promising, but the road was too long to stake out all at once, even between her and Ramses. The third was the most promising, and she'd only managed to pick it out in a blurry photograph of the monster in question, so out of focus, it could have been anything from a griffin to the Flying Spaghetti Monster. The Waffle Hut in the distance close to a freeway had been clearer.

So under the guise of an intrepid reporter, she would start asking questions here. She'd emailed the author of the clickbait article, asking some follow-up questions but hadn't said why she'd wanted to know. It hadn't helped. The author had seemed more interested in getting info from her, asking if she'd seen something similar, talking about reposting rights, and so on. Chloe hadn't bothered to reply.

At two p.m., the Waffle Hut was mostly dead, the lunch rush over, and the early dinner rush of old folks yet to begin. Chloe chose a table close to the server's station, which the cute blonde in the brown uniform seemed to appreciate if the grin was any indication.

"I wish I could eat," Ramses said after Chloe had ordered a soda. "Breakfast food looks so decadent." He scanned the pictures on the menu pinned under the clear plastic tablecloth.

"Not for me," she muttered, not looking at him. "It's either too sweet or too salty." She ordered a club sandwich when her soda arrived, then took out her phone and pretended to dial before she held it to her ear so she and Ramses could talk without attracting attention. Still, she kept her voice low. "I don't suppose you feel anything here in the Hut, and we can clear this up quickly and leave?"

"Nope. If the server is hiding under a glamour, I'd sense it, and I don't feel any ghosts hovering around in the in-between places separating the mortal realms from the underworlds."

She sighed and rubbed her neck. "Any thoughts?"

"Only about breakfast." He toyed with the end of his striped nemes. "How exactly does one stuff French toast? Is that just a clever name for a sandwich?"

She snorted a laugh. "If you'd ever tried my cooking, you wouldn't ask me food questions."

"Oh yes. I've seen the evidence."

She almost threw her napkin at him before remembering that she'd just be throwing trash on the floor to anyone watching. "Shut up."

He looked up at her, eyes narrowed. "Why are you so touchy?"

"I don't know." Her gloomy thoughts from earlier hadn't entirely left her, but more than that, the feeling that something sinister was at the heart of all her latest hunts had grown now that the seed had been planted. She felt like hundreds of invisible eyeballs were trained on her. But Ramses was right. They would both sense it if any creature was using magic to hide from their sight; the powers that infused their family line saw to that. And Ramses could sense a haunting even when the ghosts wouldn't show themselves. Still, she felt like squirming in her seat. "Maybe because the cell bill is due soon, and I still need to complete a few day-job contracts to cover it."

He gave her a sympathetic look, but she could almost hear what he no doubt wanted to say: that he and her ancestors had hunted just fine before cell phones, and she could do so, too. Thankfully, he didn't actually say it. She did not want to try to do this job without roaming data.

"There do seem to be more recent sightings, not just here in the south but around the world," he said. "Some seem deliberately put in our path."

"How?"

He shrugged. "Just a feeling. It has to marinate more to become an idea."

She rubbed the bridge of her nose and fought the urge to press her shoulder blades closer together. "Makes me wish we could roam wider in our work. Or that we had more contacts. I know my mom knows some scrupulous monster hunters, but lots of them are just after trophies or sell monster bits on the black market." She shivered. The purpose of banishments and killing monsters was to keep people safe and return spirits to their proper rest, not turn a profit.

"Well." He sat back and waved regally. "Not all are as noble as us, of course."

And just like that, Chloe was glad she hadn't thrown her napkin at him. "And even if we knew more critters were popping up around the world, that wouldn't tell us why. Maybe someone opened a gate of some kind, something like Pandora's box but for monsters and ghosts. God, that would suck."

He nodded. "But if it was something so simple, we could close it."

True. When her sandwich arrived, Chloe set her phone down, digging in while Ramses went back to commenting on the menu. When he glanced over her shoulder and stared at something, Chloe froze. "What?" she asked around her sandwich.

"Did you tell anyone but your mom that we were coming here?"

She set her food down and fought the urge to twist in her seat and gawk. "No. Well, the author of the article might have gotten...oh shit." She sighed as his eyebrows rose. "She's here, isn't she?"

"I never saw her picture, but someone has been staring at you since they walked in, and now they're talking to the server, and...yep, here she comes." He clucked in irritation as a cute redhead pulled his chair out and sat on top of him.

"You're Chloe, right? Who wrote me about my story?" She held out a hand. "Tabitha Milton."

Chloe shook her hand briefly as Ramses drifted to another seat. Tabitha might have been pretty, but in three sentences and a handshake, she already oozed too much enthusiasm and the kind of "up and at 'em" attitude that exhausted Chloe just by looking at her. She couldn't be any older than twenty, and her entire posture screamed, I am ready.

"How did you know?" Chloe asked. She didn't see any point in lying. A source was a source, after all.

"You're a new face around here. I gave it a guess." She nodded toward the door. "And I told Kylie to text if anyone but a local or a trucker stopped in."

Et tu, cute blond server? Chloe glanced over her shoulder, but Kylie didn't seem inclined to meet her eyes anymore. "Do you mind if I eat while we talk?" She wasn't about to let a good sandwich go to waste.

Tabitha waved as if shooing all good manners away. "You're a reporter, too, right? Who are you with? A paper or just a website?" Her green eyes got huge. "A TV station? From Dallas? Or, like, a national affiliate?" Her voice got higher with each guess until only squirrels had a chance of understanding.

"Sorry," Chloe said before Tabitha went out and spent any money on what must surely be her "big break." She didn't want to offer any place of employment that could be fact-checked, so she fell back on a lie she'd used many times: "I'm actually scouting locations and cases for a new web series on unexplained phenomena."

Tabitha's young face froze between expressions, as if her brain was too busy tabulating her chances for future fame to keep up. "Oh." She seemed to settle on shrewd. "You'll need a local to show you around, do interviews, that sort of thing." She put her palms flat on the table and leaned forward. "And I'm really good at acting scared." She looked into the distance with an expression of slightly constipated terror.

"I'm starting to like her," Ramses said.

Chloe resisted the urge to roll her eyes. "But if you're having to *act* scared, then there's nothing to the story?"

Tabitha sucked in her lip as if realizing she might have talked herself out of a fortune. "No, no, there is. I've seen it. I just thought, like, if you had to, you know, have some filler. Like in ghost shows." She went from terror to worry really quick, though the constipation was still there.

"I can't promise anything until I see what there is to see. Can you show me exactly where the creature appeared?"

"Sure can. You finish up. I'll go get some snacks, and we'll do a proper stakeout tonight."

"Whoa," Chloe said before she could dash off. "I only need you to show me on a map, maybe answer a few questions. I won't be filming anything this trip."

"That's fine. I can still be helpful. Like an assistant." Or a burr. Her smile seemed to add, you ain't getting rid of me.

She nearly ran out of the room. Chloe wiped her hands and spoke to her sandwich. "An audience, just what we need."

"I don't know. If she sees a real monster up close, it might scare her into leaving the 'unexplained phenomena' alone and going into something physically safer but still scary, like politics."

"And if she snaps a pic of us fighting a monster? Or of you moving something around invisibly? Or what if there's a ghost, and she gets possessed? Goddamn it, Ramses, what if the Southern Mothman eats her?"

He rubbed his chin. "Hmm, yes, there is that."

"We'll just have to get the info, pray for an unproductive evening, and try again tomorrow." Hooray. Maybe she would get more time to work the job that paid the bills.

Ramses crossed his arms and frowned. "And we'll hope that if anything spies us, it doesn't guess at our purpose and run away."

That was preferable to anyone being eaten.

CHAPTER SIX

S itting in the Camry, Chloe tried not to stare in open-mouthed shock as she watched Tabitha eating sour gummy candy and obscenely hot chips at the same damn time. It was her mouth, not to mention her stomach, and she could treat both as she liked, but something in Chloe's very soul rebelled at this diet. She felt really old all of a sudden, even though there were only five years or so between them.

But damn, what a difference five years made.

"What?" Tabitha asked around a mouthful of horror.

"Nothing." Chloe looked back out the windshield at a dark field, the first stop on the Southern Mothman tour. A rancher had supposedly spotted the monster in this area first and held it responsible for the mutilation of one of his cows. Tabitha had said the rancher put it down to aliens, and she seemed just as excited about that as she did about any of the hundred harebrained identities she'd come up with for the Southern Mothman.

God, Chloe had to stop thinking of it that way, or she'd end up blurting it out, and Tabitha would run with that name all the way to BuzzFeed.

"I think this is a bust," Chloe said. The only lights for miles sat atop distant poles, marking where the shitty pavement gave way to gravel driveways, the pretty orange sparkle of some kind of factory or refinery in the distance, and the steady glow of the freeway leading to the larger glow of Dallas.

And the blue light coming from Ramses as he wandered around the field. The ritual that bonded them didn't allow him to go far from her, at least while on the mortal plane, but he could see a little better at night and was searching for clues. If she had to leave quickly, he'd be pulled along with her. Which was kind of funny, but Chloe wasn't in the mood to laugh.

"Give it a few more minutes," Tabitha said as she jiggled one of the chip bags over her mouth, shaking in the crumbs. "What's your hurry?"

No hurry. I just want this evening to end before you get eaten. But as Tabitha slurped on another candy, Chloe reconsidered that a tiny bit.

Ramses walked back toward the car, his arms slightly out as if to signify that he hadn't found anything.

"I told you. I'm just a scout for the show. Empty fields don't make for good viewing."

Tabitha shrugged, the lights from the dashboard turning her face into a mass of slightly ghoulish shadows, fitting for her snack choices. "There's an abandoned barn where it's been seen a few times." She pointed down the road. "Let's try there."

Chloe took her time buckling her seat belt, waiting until Ramses got in the car. If he concentrated, he could stay in the back as easily as he could on a stationary chair. He'd once said he'd learned the knack after trying to ride a horse with one of her distant ancestors who'd ridden off and left him hovering in the air too many times for his dignity to allow. The ancestor had apparently laughed himself sick over it.

"Nothing," Ramses said. "No physical clues, no magic of any kind, except some stuff that feels far too ancient to be our current beastie."

Shit. She wanted to respond, talk it out, even just ask more about this ancient magic, but with Tabitha there, all she could do was nod slightly.

"How is our companion?" he asked.

She coughed around a snort. "How you doing for snacks, Tabitha?"

"Great." Her teeth gleamed in the meager light. "I've got some sour worms and gummy apricots and some ranch-flavored jalapeño chips if you want some."

Chloe looked at Ramses in the rearview mirror and widened her eyes, hoping that answered his question.

"Good gods," he said, frowning deeply. "Makes me glad I'm dead and can't smell it."

"No, thanks," Chloe said. "Just checking on you."

"Aw, aren't you sweet?" She crunched another chip and grinned. But there was something sly in her smile, too, something that said, "If you're trying to butter me up in order to leave me behind, you can forget it."

Fair enough. Chloe drove where directed, but this time, they would have to pull down a gravel road, park, and walk into a field that looked as bare as a silver lake in the moonlight.

"I'm not sure about this," Chloe said. "I'd rather scout in the daytime." Without you.

"The barn's farther in. You park under some trees off the gravel and then walk in," Tabitha said, pointing.

Chloe pulled over where the gravel met the pavement, preparing to turn around. "Then I definitely want to wait for daylight."

"But it's only been seen at dusk or at night," Tabitha said with a whine. "Come on, it's not bad. The owner of the field doesn't live around here, and people go to the barn to party all the time. It's easy to find."

Yes, more of an audience, exactly what she wanted on this expedition. She thought fast and settled on an excuse that had gotten her out of many a tight corner. "No, I'm sorry. You're not covered under my liability insurance, and they might even object to me taking avoidable risks." She turned the car and started back the way they'd come.

Tabitha glared. "You're not coming back here without me, are you?"

Chloe could have promised, but she really didn't like lying. "I'll have to see what my bosses say."

"Is that me?" Ramses asked, sounding amused that she couldn't object.

"But they can't argue about me coming with you tomorrow during the day," Tabitha said. "It'll be safe enough, then. I can give you some local history, and I know who owns the land. You'll need their permission to film there, right?" She crossed her arms as if she'd just closed the deal of a lifetime.

Which would have been true if Chloe was who she'd claimed to be. "I don't—"

"Wait," Ramses said from the back. "I saw something."

Chloe slowed. "Where?"

"Where's what?" Tabitha asked.

Shit. "I, um, saw a possum, I think, wondered...where that came from."

"Behind us," Ramses said, "heading into the suspect field. Far too large for local wildlife."

Tabitha was sitting as far forward as her seat belt would allow. "I don't see anything. Was it just a shadow, or did you see a...wait, did you see the creature?" She reached squirrel level decibels again with the final word.

"No, it was just a, a…" She looked at Ramses in the mirror.

"If you can linger a moment, I'll take a look," he said.

"You did see something," Tabitha said. She wrenched around in her seat, and Chloe knew she'd been caught staring. Tabitha grinned, seeming to grasp at the wrong straw entirely. Her belt was off and the car door open before Chloe could get a word out.

"Holy shit, Tabitha." Chloe jerked the car to the side of the road and stepped out. "Get back here."

Tabitha was nothing but a collection of shadows under the trees. Chloe heard the gravel crunch as she ran down the road. "Ramses, stay with her." As his blue glow ran after her, Chloe wished he could possess Tabitha and walk her out, but the only person he could possess was Chloe, part of their bond.

She threw open her trunk and grabbed her satchel, slinging it crossways around her body. She wished she had a trunkful of weapons like on a TV show, but she'd been pulled over one too many times to risk such things. And most mythical creatures wouldn't be defeated by guns and knives anyway. A person had to be smart with their ratios of salt or cold iron or silver, blessings or curses by various deities or spirits. Sometimes, she felt more like an alchemist than a monster hunter, though she did carry a knife for emergencies.

Using the flashlight app on her phone, she ran after Tabitha, cursing the gravel that skittered under her sneakers, the larger rocks that threatened to trip her up. Music played in the distance, a thumping bass, and she could see Ramses's glow ahead. He turned right sharply, and she kept her light angled that way, hoping she wouldn't miss where he'd gone.

When she saw two pickups, she realized she needn't have bothered. This had to be the impromptu parking lot the local teens used when sneaking out to the old barn. She ran past them, a stitch forming in her side before she even got to the barbed wire fence that separated the field from the road. A giant gap between two rows of wire spoke of many instances where someone had put their foot on the lower and pulled on the upper so another person could pass through. Chloe scooted through with only a stoop.

Ramses had probably run right through it. She could still see him in the distance, approaching a hulk of a barn with a small campfire burning behind it. Music and laughter filtered through the air, the sound cutting off as Tabitha called something. Good, maybe she was warning them away. Maybe they'd go with her, especially if they'd all heard about the slaughtered cow.

Chloe slowed, trying to catch her breath. She didn't want to arrive in the middle of a bunch of teenagers and have to lean on her knees and recover while they made fun of her. If there was something at the barn, maybe Ramses could distract it long enough to—

The night erupted in screams, and several forms leapt to their feet around the fire, scattering like flies. Inside the barn, something roared.

Chloe went cold, shuddering to a stop. That wasn't the Mothman. Not a griffin, either. It sounded like someone had combined the shriek of a large bird, the trill of a housecat, and the deep-throated call of a leopard, put it all in a metal bucket, and shaken it.

At least, that was how she'd thought of it when she'd first heard a recording her grandfather had made, the only time she'd heard the roar of a wyvern.

The only other time.

"Oh fuck, fuck, fuck." She ran again, yelling, "Run," over and over, hoping no one would question it. A griffin wouldn't notice people unless they pissed it off, preferring to eat cows, horses, and bison, but a goddamned wyvern? Legend said they were always hungry, always grouchy, and had a massive inferiority complex because they only had two legs like a bird and not the four granted to their cousins, the dragons. They hailed from the mountainous areas in Europe, ate everything they could and destroyed the rest, and everyone thought them extinct.

So what the fuckity fuck was one doing in Texas?

Chloe dashed to the side of the barn and put her back to it. She could still hear screaming and the strains of music disappearing into the night, but something was moving around inside the barn, too, something large. Good, that meant the wyvern wasn't chasing the kids. Bad, that meant she'd have to go in there and deal with it in close quarters.

Maybe it was tired. Or full. Two words that had never been associated with wyverns in any lore. Maybe it really liked the ruins of this barn, God knew why. The rough wood, worn and pitted by sun and time, snagged at Chloe's hair and clothes. Gaping holes pocked the second story, and she could see the metal beams of the roof silhouetted against the moon.

She breathed slowly as she stepped toward the rear of the barn and the fire, her nose full of the smell of old hay, wet tin, and ancient manure.

What did she even have to fight a wyvern with? Moments ago, she'd prided herself on her bag of herbs and thread and iron filings, but now all that seemed like Baby's First Magic Kit. Wyverns might be harmed by guns and knives, but their hide was thicker than a whale's and tougher than an alligator's. She would have needed a lightsaber to cut through one. Or a shoulder-mounted missile launcher.

Her grandfather had tricked one into eating a poisoned sheep carcass. Pity she didn't currently have one of those in her bag. Could a person DoorDash poisoned carcass?

Wyverns were said to be a little intelligent. Maybe she could convince it to bugger the hell off. Or at least come back later.

She peeked around the corner. The campfire was surrounded by bare earth, but the teens had laid blankets around that, and those were festooned with beer cans and snack bags. The door was missing from this side, leaving a massive hole framed by sheets of corrugated tin as broken and jagged as a dragon's smile.

Fitting.

Something huffed inside, followed by what sounded like a wheeze or a cough. Chloe couldn't believe a wyvern had simply wandered into this neck of the woods. Someone had to have brought it. Had it escaped? If it was sick, maybe they'd simply dumped it.

Bastards. If she ever got her hands on them…well, Ramses would kick their asses with her body, but she'd be egging him on from the inside.

"Chlo."

Her heart shot out of her mouth, and she leapt into the air as Ramses poked his head through the wall. She put a hand to her chest to stop the latest of many heart attacks and glared at him so hard, it hurt her face. Before she could unleash her fury, he put a finger to his lips.

Oh, sure, for now. But later, she was going to yell so hard.

"Come inside," he said. "Softly. It's sick."

She tiptoed into the rear of the barn. The roof on one side was mostly torn away, the second floor little more than a few boards crisscrossing a sliver of moonlight. A shape the size of a VW Bug stirred from a heap of old hay gathered at the back, hints of firelight glinting off dusky green scales. A sinewy neck lifted, revealing a reptilian head with short horns going back over the skull and large frills just behind the ear holes.

Chloe's terror fled as milky eyes blinked at a spot near where she stood, the nostrils flaring and streaming with snot. The scales seemed to be molting in great patches, and as it coughed again, she caught sight of yellowing broken teeth and the scent of old meat and musk.

Old, probably blind, it didn't seem like a threat to anyone. It had no doubt returned to the barn, its home for now, and had only roared to scare those damn kids off its lawn.

Slowly, Chloe backed up, out into the open again. The wyvern might be old and sick, but it could still snap her head off. She couldn't risk getting close out of pity.

Ramses followed, looking grim. "It's a bit sad."

"I know." She shook her head. "Here I was thinking we'd have to find a claymore or something so you could have this big epic battle, but, ugh."

He nodded. "I think it will die if we just wait a little while."

She raised her eyebrows. "Really?"

"I must confess, I don't know for sure," he said with a sigh. "There's not a zoologist alive who could tell us if it has ten years or ten minutes."

Chloe thought back to everything she'd heard about the wyvern since arriving here and everything she'd read about them in the past. This one had mangled a cow, sure, but a healthy wyvern wouldn't have left even a scrap of meat behind. And it hadn't killed—or even really bothered—anyone, except for scaring some teenagers. Simply being a tad annoying was definitely not in the average wyvern's MO.

"Will you think less of me if I say I want to walk away from this one?" she asked.

"Of course not." But he tilted his head, and she knew he was prompting her.

"And you know I won't."

His smile said he was proud, and she got a childish rush of pleasure at that. Her father had often expressed his pride, "for both my girls," but in her mom's eyes, Jamie had been the one to be prouder of, the one with the important job, the one who'd trained to carry on the monster-hunting, ghost-banishing legacy. But Ramses filled that gap in her heart a little.

"I don't think it's a danger to anyone right this minute," Chloe said. "But if someone decides to go in that barn and bother it?" She shrugged.

Ramses nodded. "Like young Tabitha. Not to mention, someone unscrupulous could follow the same trail we did, and they might make sure its final days are painful and humiliating as they either exploit it or attempt to study it."

And monsters like this were supposed to stay secret. The more people who knew, the more who'd go looking for the things and get their asses eaten.

"At the very least, we have to sedate and move it," she said. Then they'd have options.

"Looking past the problems of sedating such a creature, how on earth do we move it?"

"One thing at a time." Chloe turned to find Tabitha watching from the side of the barn and nearly leapt out of her skin again. "For fuck's sake, will you people stop doing that?"

"People?" Tabitha whispered. She took a few steps forward, but her eyes were wide, and she seemed to lean back as she walked, like someone sneaking up on a snake. "Who are you talking to?"

Well, shit. Didn't this round off the evening nicely?

Chapter Seven

Helen was forced to switch transportation once she reached Galveston. Riding a flying horse wouldn't work over land, even at night. Flying high enough to remain unseen was just too cold and onerous—not to mention dangerous with all the flight paths—so she sent Pegasus home, planning to return to the sanctuary via the nereids' boat.

She couldn't go alone on this trip, either. Strong as she was, she'd need a bit of help either convincing the creature currently living near Waxahachie to go with her or moving it once she'd incapacitated it. So along with renting a small moving truck, she'd brought along Ligeia, one of the sirens, who was often as annoyed by humans as Helen was, especially as she'd had to explain numerous times why she looked nothing like the Rossetti painting that bore her name and how she wouldn't be caught dead just standing naked in a jungle playing a musical instrument like some sad weirdo.

She currently had her bare webbed feet propped on the dash, their blue color seeming to fade into the sky beyond the windshield. She wore a hoodie over the crest-like fin that ran from her forehead back to her nape and the similar fins at her elbows and wrists. Her loose-fitting cargo pants covered the rest of her petite frame, the clothing almost swallowing her.

With a sigh, she sank farther in her seat and blew a huge pink bubble with her Hubba Bubba gum. "How far is it again?"

Helen fought her irritation, even when Ligeia smacked her gum and stared, her large blue-green eyes screaming, *I'm so bored.* She could no doubt lure many sailors to their doom with her pretty face, if she'd been interested in that sort of thing. Lately, she was more into body mods than anything else, sporting piercings in her septum, nostrils, lips, the frills of her ears, and her eyebrows. Gold tattoos done by an oni in the sanctuary covered her hands and the tops of her feet and probably everywhere else.

"I've already told you," Helen said. "You should have brought your e-reader."

Ligeia shrugged. "So talk to me," she said with only a little whine.

Gods, maybe she should have brought Maurice, after all. But she still hadn't quite forgiven him for losing his head at that poker game. And Ligeia had more going for her than just her ability to hypnotize. She was the only one in Helen's sanctuary who'd mastered the use of the tarnkappe, a helmet out of German folklore that made the wearer invisible and gave them ten times their normal strength. It sat under Ligeia's arm, a simple design, rounded at the top, unremarkable save for the fine golden chainmail that dangled from the back.

Ligeia's boredom wouldn't be cured by anyone else's stories. But Helen knew one surefire way to keep her happy. "Tell me the story of how you mastered that helmet," Helen said, trying to imbue her voice with excitement.

Ligeia perked up. "Really? Again?"

Three, two, one.

"I mean, it is a pretty bitchin' story. I guess I could tell it, like, one more time or whatever." Her grin and the tinge of purple in her cheeks belied her words, and she rushed into the story of how the Sphinx had been cataloging the artifacts collected in the sanctuary, and several people had tried the tarnkappe but couldn't handle the strength or freaked out at the invisibility. "And I was like, fine, if y'all can't handle it, I guess I'll try." She rolled her eyes and turned as sideways as the seat belt would allow. "And the Lamia, like, laughed at me, but Dani the hippogriff was like, 'Show 'em, Lig,' and I was like, fuck yeah, I will, and the Lamia said something about how people couldn't stand not seeing themselves in the mirror unless they were born invisible or something, and I was like, *pssh*, it ain't my fault y'all aren't comfy in your own skin, that y'all aren't deep enough to, like, accept the nothingness inside."

Helen hoped her chuckle would be put down as agreement. "Totally."

"Right? So I put it on, and right away, looked in the mirror, and I didn't see me, but I still was me. So I was like, boom, y'all, no probs, still sane, still me. What else you got? And the Sphinx asked me to move some stuff around, get a feel for the strength. And Dani was like, 'All right, Lig, you got it,' and I was like, hell, yes. You just gotta be careful.

Just like with the siren song. If you have a special talent, which I do, you have to be careful. So I was, and I got it, and now I can use it whenever and not smash anything I don't want to. Tried, tested, approved."

Helen offered a high-five, which was also approved, though the piercings in the webbing between Ligeia's fingers grated against her skin. "And now you've mastered three powers."

"Right?" She turned forward again and blew another bubble.

That story bought Helen a hundred miles of silence afterward. Luckily, Ligeia had lots of stories, and it didn't matter how many times Helen had heard them. Something about the excitement in Ligeia's speech drew her in every time.

And earned her blissful silence in between.

After the flight that morning and the drive—and a few stops for more gum—night was nearly falling by the time they reached the approximate location of the griffin. They pulled over at a gas station near the freeway, and Helen wished for the thousandth time that she could simply feel the presence of mythological creatures, but that wasn't a talent she possessed.

But that was what she had tools for. She grabbed her bag from the floor and carefully took out a velvet-covered box. Even Ligeia grew quiet with reverence as Helen opened it and lifted the silver necklace inside. A long, jagged sliver of bone served as its pendant, the tooth of Echidna, mother of monsters, stained with a bit of her blood. It swung back and forth like a pendulum, the stained tip glowing softly when it pointed at Ligeia. It was capable of pointing the way to any being or creature who could draw their family line all the way back to Echidna herself, which a griffin certainly could.

"Come on," Helen whispered as the tooth continued to tell her that someone with a monstrous bloodline was currently sharing the cab of the truck with her. "Tell me we haven't driven all this way for—"

The tooth slowed and added a gentle second location to its swing. Whatever they were after was either not very strong or still far away. Helen prayed for the first instance. One long soak in the tub last night hadn't been enough.

"Hell, yeah," Ligeia said. She held out a hand, and Helen hung the chain over her webbed fingers before she started up the truck again and followed the second point by the most direct route they could find.

"It's gotta be big," Ligeia said after they'd driven for nearly twenty minutes, having to turn around and try another path after several dead ends. "Since the tooth picked it up from all the way out by the freeway."

Helen nodded, her hopes for a quick expedition dashed, and now she had to concentrate on driving through the gloom on barely lit country roads. "I'm glad we brought the truck."

"What if this isn't, like, big enough?"

Then whatever they were hunting was larger than the Sphinx, maybe even as large as someone like Charybdis, and they'd have to call in more help as well as a larger truck. But she didn't want to show any uncertainty if she could help it. "Don't worry. I packed five large tranquilizer darts filled with carfentanil. We could keep several elephants sleeping for days if we had to."

Ligeia's smile flashed even in the dark cab.

Helen smiled back, though she was a bit worried, too. Still, she wouldn't let her calm facade crack, not even when the tooth began to pull harder in one direction, leading them down a gravel road near an abandoned car. She didn't even let her true worry show when two other cars roared past, nearly forcing them into a ditch.

"Damn," she said, braking hard but keeping control.

"Whoa," Ligeia said, craning her neck out the window. "What's their fucking hurry?"

"I think we're about to find out." They reached a makeshift parking lot seconds later. One car remained, and even in the truck's dim headlights, Helen could tell by the churned-up gravel that this was probably where the other cars had come from. "Time to put on the helmet, Lig."

With a nod, she did so, vanishing on the spot as they pulled to a stop. Helen lamented that she couldn't see through invisibility, though she could sometimes sense the unseen. But to truly see them required the blood of a particular Egyptian god, a pantheon she didn't know as well as some of the others.

Still, the chances that the creature they were hunting had the blood of that particular god running through their veins was so low, she'd never place a wager.

She slipped from the truck, took her rifle and the case of tranq darts out from behind her seat, and slung both across her body. All that stood between them and an open field was a sad-looking barbed wire fence. A relic of a barn stood in the distance, but to Helen's dismay, a campfire burned near the rear of it.

"Great," Ligeia said from her right. "Humans."

"Maybe not anymore," Helen whispered. "Remember the cars that blew past." They quickly helped each other through the fence, and Helen loaded the rifle. "Maybe all the humans were scared—"

Voices interrupted her in the distance. Shit. Two dark forms passed in front of the fire. Helen moved quickly, hoping no one would see her or Ligeia by the slight glow of the sliver of moon, but these two seemed focused on each other. Two young women, from what she could see when she pressed her back against the side of the barn.

"Let me explain," one was saying.

"You know what that thing is? What's going on? And who exactly were you talking to? Or do you often carry on one side of an entire conversation with yourself? Fuck, I don't know what to write down first. Maybe if I just record it all—"

No.

"No," the first woman said as if reading Helen's mind. She wrenched a phone out of the second woman's hands.

"Hey, freedom of the press."

By the gods, that was all they needed.

"That smell ain't no griffin," Ligeia whispered near Helen's shoulder.

As the women continued arguing, Helen tilted her nose up. It was a musty odor, one she'd either never smelled, or it had been so long, she'd forgotten. She cast her thoughts back, crossing creatures rapidly off her list before she hit on one.

"OMG, it's a wyvern," Ligeia said right as Helen thought, dragon.

She exhaled. Nearly as bad as a dragon. Still, she thanked the gods she'd been wrong. And that still left them a fucking wyvern to deal with. And two young humans who were too damn close to a wyvern for comfort. It had to be in the barn, so why wasn't it out here tearing everyone to pieces?

And there was something else prodding her senses, some magic in use perhaps. Not very likely to be the wyvern, but perhaps something that would help or hinder in sedating and moving it? She'd find out later. Right now, she had to move the humans along before they became wyvern chow.

She stepped into the light, the rifle up. "What the hell are you doing on my property?" she asked, bluffing for all she was worth.

The women turned with wide, disbelieving eyes. The pale, petite redhead who'd been barking all the questions stared at the gun, her mouth open as if she'd been petrified where she stood. The other seemed a little older, her skin darker like Helen's natural shade, and her tight jeans and T-shirt revealing an hourglass figure one could die for, highlighted by the satchel she wore across her body. She flicked her dark ponytail over one shoulder and gave the gun a cursory glance, brown eyes darting everywhere as if creating a strategy for a counterattack.

And she didn't seem the least bit afraid.

Impressive. But as always, Helen didn't have the time or inclination to get to know another human. "Go on," she said, waving the rifle. "Get outta here."

The redhead took a step away. The brunette took a deep breath and stood tall as if about to argue when a new voice said, "No one moves."

Helen glanced to the right as Fatma stepped around the other side of the barn, also with a gun in hand, though her pistol looked like it fired more than darts. Ali followed with a rifle that seemed more like Helen's, clearly there to take prisoners.

"This has got to be the most sought-after wyvern in the world," Ligeia whispered.

And Helen couldn't shoot any of them with the darts in her gun, not if she wanted them to survive. And she did. She hated having to kill anything, let alone a human, and part of her was actually happy to see Fatma alive and well. She didn't seem permanently scarred from their last encounter. And this new brunette had a cunning expression and a stubborn set to her shoulders that said she wasn't leaving without a fight.

All thoughts of a comfy bed and long baths vanished from Helen's thoughts. Finally, something truly interesting.

CHAPTER EIGHT

This night was just full of surprises. Chloe usually expected one or two unknowns, but now she had four, three armed, all staring, and by the look of the tranq rifles, both parties were after one sick old wyvern.

As if telling everyone to keep it down, the creature emitted a coughing half roar that managed to miss being scary and landed squarely in pathetic. Nobody even looked.

"Chloe?" Ramses said, and she knew he was asking permission to possess her. She nodded and tried not to react as he stepped into her. Her mind shifted to the side, letting him size up the situation.

The two newest-comers seemed wholly human, the black-haired woman pointing a pistol confidently between Chloe and Tabitha and the other interlopers, ready to shoot whoever acted first. The man—who looked so much like the black-haired woman he could have been her twin—kept his tranq rifle pointed at the sky. They began a tense, whispered conversation Chloe couldn't make out.

The other two were much more interesting. This woman was tall, willowy, her features slightly pointed, striking. When she'd first appeared, Chloe hadn't known where to look: the gun that was quite obviously another tranq rifle, or the firelight dancing off her brown hair, or maybe the athletic figure with the legs that seemed eight feet long. Her eyes flashed silver, hypnotic. It took a whole bushelful of energy to look away from her.

Except that her companion looked so out of place for a pasture in central Texas that they might as well have been at a neon-coated German sex club.

They had a slight glow, and Chloe could see the outline of the barn through their torso, though not as well as she could see through Ramses. No doubt they were invisible to most eyes but not hers. They wore baggy clothes, including a hood that rested about six inches above their blue head, and a helmet sat atop that. They either had the largest forehead in *The Guinness Book of Records*, or something else was going on up there.

"That's a siren," Ramses said in their shared mind.

She was caught between wonder and panic. "I've got the special earplugs in the second pocket of the bag."

When he twitched their hand in that direction, the black-haired woman's gun and attention jerked her way. "I said, don't move."

"Are we supposed to just stand here while you decide if you want to kill us?" the willowy woman asked. She pointed her rifle at the ground while her invisible companion crept toward the other couple.

"I suppose I could spare you the suspense and kill you now," the black-haired woman said with a wry smile. "Or wound you as payback for our last encounter."

The willowy woman smirked, but whatever their history, these two seemed more irked with each other—in an enemies-to-lovers story, they might have been making out by now—than actually antagonistic. "Get a room," Ramses said with Chloe's mouth.

"Oh my God, Ramses," she said in their mind. If she'd been in charge of the body, she'd have been blushing up a storm when everyone looked at her again.

"Well, you were thinking the same thing," he said. "While also feeling a little jealous at being left out, I might add."

Yep, she was definitely going to banish him later. "Shut. Up."

"What's going on?" Tabitha said, her voice barely a whisper. She shivered so hard, her red curls seemed to tremble, but there was still something hungry in her eyes, some reporter gene that spied a scoop. "Chloe?"

Ramses reached for her hand, and she took it eagerly, her skin clammy and cold. "Just repeat after me," Chloe told him, and with a sigh, he agreed.

"Look," they said. "I don't know what's going on with you... three." She'd nearly said "four," almost giving away that she could see the invisible person still inching toward the dark-haired duo. "But we're just innocent bystanders, totally willing to forget everything we've seen or heard in exchange for being allowed to walk away."

Tabitha made a noise of protest, but Ramses squeezed her fingers until she squealed. Chloe hoped she got the picture. They'd let these four thin themselves out and then come back for the wyvern.

The dark-haired couple had another whispered exchange, but the way the woman moved the gun in a shooing gesture lifted Chloe's spirits. Until Ramses looked again at the willowy woman. Attractive as the other one was, this one would be the hardest to walk away from. Stunning wasn't a description Chloe had ever used for a person; only a true work of art could rob someone of their senses, but this woman was godlike. If Chloe hadn't been wearing shoes, her socks might've popped right off.

And the goddess's stare was like a laser, pinning Chloe to the spot, stripping her to the bone and laying all her secrets as bare as a bobcat. Luckily, Ramses was in charge of the body, so she didn't have to suffer the humiliation of going weak in the knees. And everywhere else.

"She is very beautiful," he said in their mind.

The longer they stared, the more Chloe thought beautiful wasn't enough. Maybe an adequate adjective didn't exist.

"Focus, Chloe."

Right. They had a job to do. No time to get lost in those eyes, legs, cheekbones, lips…

"Your name is Chloe?" the willowy goddess said.

"Fuck, Ramses, she can read minds."

"Tabitha said it," he replied dryly. Aloud, he added, "Correct, lady, and you are?"

The goddess frowned slightly, probably because Ramses had nearly m'ladied her. "I am never living this night down," Chloe muttered.

"Helen," the goddess said, studying Chloe like a scientist with a microscope.

Ramses tensed. "She's reaching for something on her back."

"No talking," the black-haired woman snapped, focusing on them again. She gestured. "Get in the barn."

"No." Helen seemed even taller as she faced down the gun. "You can't put them in there with a wyvern."

Oof, that commanding tone. Chloe would have followed her into the pits of Tartarus.

"Seriously, Chloe?" Ramses said in their mind. "If we make it out alive, you are never facing this woman on your own."

The black-haired woman tilted her head as if bored. "You're choosing death instead?"

"We'll go in the barn," Ramses said aloud. They could outmaneuver a sick wyvern but not a bullet.

Helen took a step forward. "They'll be killed."

Ramses pulled Tabitha with them so Helen was between them and the gun. He made it to the opening in the barn when the invisible siren knocked the black-haired woman's gun arm into the air.

A shot cracked through the night sky. Helen drew something from behind her back, and Ramses threw Tabitha into the remains of a horse stall in the corner. He turned and rushed toward the wyvern, and Chloe lost sight of the battle outside. She heard another shot and several yells, trying to determine anything so she could feed Ramses the information while he focused on…whatever the hell he was up to.

"Ramses, what the fu—"

He ran up the wyvern's tail, put a hand on its back, and leapt over it. It grumbled, milky eyes searching the gloom, head turning toward them. With a sharp whistle, Ramses drew the hunting knife Chloe only ever used to cut rope and stuck it in the thin, molting skin of the wyvern's bony ass.

It shrieked, the bird and cougar sounds joined by several dozen paint cans rolling down a hill before it bolted upright and shot out the barn like its hair was on fire.

Ramses followed, knife in hand, pausing at the door as the wyvern trampled through the campfire, whirling and snarling and flapping its wings like a pissed-off chicken. Everyone outside dove for cover or backpedaled away. The crack of a tranq gun sounded from the left, the sound nearly lost in the roars. The wyvern flapped harder, taking to the air, but another crack came from the right, and it faltered, its roars fading.

Chloe caught another sound. Music? Her thoughts went to the teens who'd fled. But one roar had driven them off. Surely, they wouldn't be tempted back by more. No, it wasn't a radio. Someone was singing.

"Ramses, the siren."

He ducked back from the chaos outside and dug out the earplugs, a special pair designed by one of Chloe's ancestors. They were small loops of wax, but instead of blocking out all sound like those worn by Odysseus's crew, these were mixed with slippery elm powder and a touch of magic, canceling the siren song only.

When Ramses placed them just inside Chloe's ears, the music stopped so abruptly, she expected a record scratch. When they peeked outside again, the wyvern had slowed to the ground, wings twitching, the roars mutating to snores.

The dark-haired duo was sitting contentedly at the siren's feet, and nearby...

"Is that sword flying?" Chloe asked.

"I don't know," Ramses said. "I've never seen the like."

"I hate to do this to you twice." Helen walked past, eyes fixed on the sitting pair. "But you will keep wandering into my plans." She sighed. "Subdue."

The freaking flying sword flipped in midair, and the pommel cracked against the back of the black-haired woman's head, making her slump to the ground. It did the same to the man half a second later.

"You may as well come out," Helen said as the sword's grip settled in her palm.

Ramses held the hunting knife at the ready as he emerged, but how in the hell was he supposed to fight a flying sword?

"I'll make it up as I go," he said.

Yeah, that sounded really confident.

Helen gestured, and the siren's mouth stopped moving, though she was still invisible. Ramses kept from staring at her, not wanting to clue them in. Helen gave their shared body another intense look. "You seem different from when I first saw you. Is it magic or something else?" She tilted her head with that same laser gaze.

Ramses tensed. If he could catch her mid-ponder...

Helen started as if she'd been shocked. "It's a ghost. Possessing you. It's been so long since I've sensed one." She straightened, all the power in the world in one fantastic package. "Begone, spirit, cease riding this woman."

Okay, ew. "How does she know?" Chloe asked.

Ramses took a step. Helen brought the sword on guard. The siren advanced a few paces, but Helen held out a hand. "Chloe, if you can hear me, don't worry. I'm going to help you."

It was kind of sweet that she cared. And a wee bit insulting that she assumed Chloe couldn't take care of herself. Way too many feelings to sort out at the moment.

Helen began to mumble something in a language that sounded vaguely...Greek?

"Damn," Ramses said both aloud and in their head. "That's an exor—"

Helen released the sword in order to smack a fist down on her open palm. Golden light flowed from her in a wave, throwing Chloe backward and ripping Ramses from her body in one agonizing breath.

She landed hard, fought to breathe, the dull pain from hitting the ground nothing compared to the feeling of being separated by force. Her skin felt raw, beyond a sunburn, more like someone had flayed her alive. Agony danced along every nerve, sending spasms and cramps through the body she could no longer move. The scattered campfire, the wyvern, Helen walking slowly toward her; everything faded in and out like a strobe light.

Helen knelt at her side and placed a cool hand on her forehead. "Easy," she said softly, and the sound soothed some of the fire racing through Chloe's veins. "The pain will end soon. In the meantime, perhaps I can banish the ghost."

"N…no," Chloe wheezed. She managed to turn her head, grinding her cheek into the dirt.

Ramses's spectral form floundered a few feet away, his blue edges tattered. "Get…away from…her," he managed, his eyes glowing with rage as they fixed on Helen. He fought to rise but only floated above the ground like a wind-borne leaf. "I'm here…Chlo. Be right there."

"No…stay 'way," she managed, but the effort was enough to make her sob. Still, she'd say it a hundred times if it would save him. "Don't."

Helen frowned and wiped her tears with the back of one soft hand. "Shh. It'll pass soon. I'll find the ghost, don't worry."

Chloe looked past her as the siren approached. If she could just get through to one of them.

The siren frowned too and bent toward her. "Holy shit, Hel, she can see me."

Helen's gaze snapped to her. "What?"

The siren grinned, stretching her various piercings. "She totally sees me. She's got the blood of Isis."

CHAPTER NINE

The blood of Isis? Helen paused as she leaned over Chloe, the young woman she'd just knocked across the yard. Confusion overwhelmed her pity for a moment. She hadn't expected the exorcism to be so hard on the living person. Chloe and the ghost must have been very closely joined. For years, maybe.

But the ghost hadn't been possessing Chloe when Helen had first arrived. She'd have sworn to it. And if Chloe could see the invisible, that surely meant she could see unquiet spirits as well. Or could she do more than just see them?

Helen put a hand around the back of Chloe's neck and lifted her slightly. Some residual energy lingered in her body, making the contact between them practically hum. "Where is the ghost?"

Chloe shuddered and coughed, tears streaming down her face as her limbs twitched. Her dark eyes bored into Helen's, fearful, pained, but also a tad defiant.

Helen's admiration grew. "Did you allow it to possess you?"

"Y...yes, you can't...don't..." She closed her eyes and breathed deeply.

No wonder the exorcism had cost her so much. The shock to her system must have felt like having a limb torn away. "I'm sorry, Chloe. I didn't realize." She brought their faces closer. "But you shouldn't traffic with spirits. You might encounter one you can't get rid of on your own." At least, Helen assumed so.

Maybe Chloe's lineage helped her force the entities out of her body at will, but there were ghosts in the world who were more powerful than anything she could have encountered.

Helen's travels through Egypt and Persia came to mind. Her skin had hummed there, too, no doubt because of all the ghosts lingering around their statues and monuments.

A flush rose in Chloe's cheeks, and her eyes darted to Helen's lips. Interesting. If she was smitten, she might obey Helen's request to flee without any magic backing it up. And she had to admit, this close, Chloe was pretty smitten-worthy herself.

But the point was, Helen could send her off to safety, then take care of the ghost. If she could find it.

"Would a ghost succumb to your song?" she asked over her shoulder.

Ligeia blinked into view and tucked the tarnkappe under her arm. "I mean, I don't think so." She shrugged and barked a laugh. "I can't see invisible shit like she obviously can, though. I could have been, like, calling ghosts to me all the time and wouldn't know it."

And they didn't have anything with them to tackle a ghost besides the few spells Helen knew and the power of her godhood. And that felt a little wobbly after the exorcism.

"Please." Chloe grabbed Helen's arm, hauling herself a little more upright. Her full lips parted, dark hair dangling down her back as she strained upward as if begging for a kiss.

Behave, Helen told herself.

"Don't...hurt...him." Chloe fell back, forcing Helen to hold her more firmly. She smiled and seemed so happy to have gotten the words out, as if she'd accomplished a mission.

"Him?"

With another happy smile, Chloe's head turned slightly, her eyes trained on nothing. "Ramses."

The hair on Helen's neck stood up. Ramses? As in, one of the pharaohs? Could it be? "How—" She cried out as a shock rolled through her shoulder, and an acid feeling careened down her arm. She dropped Chloe and scuttled several feet away before falling, cradling her arm as it burned with liquid fire.

"What the hell?" Ligeia knelt at her side. "What happened?" When Helen could only hold her shoulder and groan, Ligeia ran her hands over it. "Lemme see so I can help."

But she wouldn't find anything. Helen knew this pain. The attack of a powerful spirit was like the agony of a kidney stone, not something a person could forget. Even without the blood of Isis, she could nearly see an outline kneeling next to Chloe, a faint glow that disappeared if she turned her head.

"Stand away, spirit," Helen said, marshaling her godhood again. She stood with Ligeia's help, wanting to save all her energy for another exorcism if necessary. "Whatever pact you have with this woman, if you possess her now, it could cause her irreparable harm. She's too weak."

"S'okay," Chloe said, waving weakly. "We're cool." She sounded a little drunk, no doubt the shock making her tired beyond measure.

"You're...friends?" Ligeia asked. "With a ghost?"

"Yes'm." Chloe's eyes fluttered closed, and she sagged as if sleeping.

The glow didn't seem to be moving into her, just hovering nearby. Whatever was going on with them, the problem seemed sorted for now. That just left what to do with Fatma, Ali, and a sleeping wyvern.

"Um, Hel?"

She turned, following Ligeia's pointing finger to the barn. The red-haired woman knelt in the shadows, cell phone trained in their direction. "Ah. I'd forgotten about her."

"If that's a live stream, we're kinda fucked."

Helen nodded, resigned to the evening going that direction no matter what. "Let's just hope this one doesn't have her own ghostly protector."

❖

"Chloe? Wake up. Open your eyes."

She wanted to tell Ramses to piss off or give her five more minutes or whatever it took to get him to shut up. He wasn't even supposed to be talking to her. He would bond to Jamie after their mother retired or died. Chloe might see him once in her life if he could expend the energy to appear, but mostly, she'd just have to guess that he was there, just like always.

Well, almost always. Her mother had battled a particularly dangerous ghost one time, and Chloe hadn't been able to sleep that night, terrified that other ghosts would come for revenge. "Honey, I'd know if any ghosts came near this apartment," her mother had said patiently yet firmly. She'd tried to explain the rules that ghosts had to follow, Jamie unhelpfully saying, "Duh," or rolling her eyes, but neither had said what Chloe had really wanted to hear: that it was all going to be okay.

"No ghost can beat Ramses, anyway," her mother had said after Chloe's third refusal to go to bed. She'd paused, head cocked, and Chloe had known that meant Ramses was speaking to her. "How about he spends the night in your room, watching over you?"

She'd realized later that an invisible dead person hanging out in her room to protect her from other invisible dead people should have done nothing to combat her terror, but Ramses had been a constant in her life—more than an imaginary friend but not quite a parent—around nearly as much as her hardworking father.

He had been reading books back then instead of watching so much TV, and she'd woken up several times from terrifying dreams only to relax at the sound of softly turning pages under the glow of her desk lamp. Once, when she'd awakened in tears, she'd turned to find a note on her nightstand that said, *Is okay Chlo Im here.*

The words had been clumsy, mismatched, and thoroughly lacking in punctuation, but Ramses had trouble holding a pen. She'd gone back to sleep with the note clutched in her hand.

She supposed she owed it to him to wake up now, even though she desperately needed sleep, and Jamie…

Was dead.

Chloe inhaled sharply, painfully, her eyes flying open to see Ramses's glowing form and smiling face. Right, yes, she had passed out in a field after being exorcized by a willowy goddess named Helen and a siren, both of whom seemed to want the wyvern Chloe and Ramses had been hunting in the first place.

Along with Tabitha the journalist and two well-armed unknowns.

"That's it, Chloe, come on," Ramses said, sounding like someone trying to get a baby to walk. "Keep your eyes open. You can do it. But try not to move too much." He gestured over his shoulder and leaned back so she could see.

Near the barn, the siren was messing with a cell phone, the helmet she'd been wearing at her feet. Helen was kneeling beside Tabitha's unmoving body.

"I hated to knock her out when she already has a head wound," Helen said.

"Yeah, but these two gave her that." The siren gestured vaguely in Chloe's direction but didn't look up. "When they threw her in the barn the first time. Probably, like, knocked her stupid or whatever, and that's why she didn't come when I sang."

Oops, sorry, Tabitha.

"I just hope she's not concussed," Helen said.

The siren rolled her eyes and turned her back to Chloe. Leaving the helmet unguarded. "C'mon, Hel, you hate humans. Why are you so interested?"

Chloe nodded toward the helmet, no doubt the source of the invisibility since Chloe couldn't see through her at the moment.

"Right." Ramses knelt by it, flexing his power gently and inching it toward Chloe's hand while she stretched. "Best if we steal it without them even noticing."

"I don't know," Helen said with a sigh. "I mean, it's not hate, really. I don't like them, but I don't want to cause them pain."

"*Pfft*, after all the pain they've caused us? Hello?"

Just you wait. Chloe nearly had it.

"I can't simply—" Helen turned, her eyes widening as she locked gazes with Chloe. "No!"

Well, time for plan B. Ramses used his energy to give the helmet a shove, sending it flying into Chloe's hands. She didn't think, only used the momentum to jam it on her head and scramble to her feet, hoping that neither Helen nor the siren could see invisible people.

❖

Helen lurched toward the tarnkappe with a cry, but Chloe vanished before she got there.

"OMG, that sneaky—"

Helen held up a hand to stop Ligeia and listened. She tried to feel the ghost's presence. If it was one of the Egyptian pharaohs, he was no doubt powerful. But why in the world was he here? Powerful spirits could sometimes travel to wherever there was a large collection of statues or other three-dimensional images of them, like museums, but she very much doubted that this field had its own Ramesseum.

There, to the right, near where Fatma and Ali lay unconscious. Well, if he wanted to possess them, they wouldn't get him anywhere. A ghost couldn't get an unconscious body to move. That meant he was out of luck with the redhead, too. Ligeia's magical nature made her immune, and Helen…

Gods, let him try. She'd let him in, then pull him to pieces with her godhood.

But he seemed attached to Chloe, had attacked Helen on her behalf. Hell, he could be serving as a distraction if he knew Helen could sense him. Then Chloe could get away. Or attack.

Helen drew her kladenet. "Guard." It hovered in a circle around her and Ligeia, twitching this way and that.

"What are we gonna do?" Ligeia whispered as she tongued her lip piercings.

Helen shook her head. Without the tarnkappe, they were never going to get the wyvern in the van. She eased her phone out of her pocket. Ligeia had already erased the footage on the redhead's phone. Luckily, the cell service out here was too shitty for live streaming. This mission could still be salvaged if Helen could get ahold of the Sphinx and have her send some help.

The wyvern stirred slightly.

"Shit, that's all we need." Helen glanced around. "Where did I drop the tranq—"

Ligeia's shove took her by surprise, sending her tripping over her own feet just as the wyvern hurtled toward her. She curled into a ball, but when the wyvern sailed overhead and crashed into the barn, she rolled away. The barn shuddered, letting out an ear-splitting shriek of tearing metal and snapping wood.

Helen ran for Fatma and Ali as one side of the barn gave way with a groan, falling to the side, the roof collapsing. She grabbed one ankle apiece and heaved, managing to get them out of the way before the wall crashed to the ground in a *whoosh* of air that sent up a cloud of ancient hay, dust, and manure. She put her hands on her knees, breathing hard as the remains of the barn settled in a hazy cloud, rattling and pinging.

And…snoring?

She came closer, trying to wave away the cloud. Yes, the wyvern sounded asleep inside the ruins. It must have been sick to sleep through that landing. Did it leap at her in its sleep?

No, of course not. Helen snorted a laugh. Chloe had to have figured out how to use the superhuman strength that the tarnkappe conveyed. "You're a clever one, Chloe."

"Would you call this thing off?" Ligeia cried. The kladenet was swiping at her before starting back toward Helen, then wandering near the barn before returning to swipe at Ligeia again. It was no doubt confused about who to guard or attack since Ligeia had pushed Helen, and the wyvern seemed no threat now.

Helen held out a hand. "To arms." The kladenet returned to her grip. "Thank you for pushing me out of the way, Lig."

"No probs. The Wonder Twins okay?"

"I think so."

"Great. Everyone's alive. Now what?"

Everyone? "Shit, the redhead." She pushed into the dust cloud, but the redhead was nowhere to be seen. Buried in the rubble? "But she was right here."

Unless she'd been moved, rescued while Helen was distracted. Again. She should have been angry, but that same sense of admiration filled her. Chloe was far more formidable than Helen had given her credit for. After lifetimes of being underestimated, she'd fallen into the same trap she'd sprung on many others.

It wouldn't happen next time.

And there would most certainly be a next time.

Chapter Ten

This fucking helmet was amazing. Chloe could still see herself; her inherited abilities always let her see invisible stuff, after all. But she hadn't expected the sheer power filling her limbs and begging to be used.

She'd lifted a fucking wyvern. On her own.

True, she'd only meant to wiggle it a bit, distract Helen and the siren. She'd managed that the first time she'd shifted it. She'd decided to try a little more, maybe stand it up so they'd come running. She hadn't even doubted that she could. With the helmet on, she could do anything. Apparently without even meaning to because she'd hurled the wyvern hard enough to bring down the barn, almost squashing Helen, the two unknown intruders, and Tabitha.

Still, Helen and the siren had seemed pretty damned distracted. And the resulting dust cloud had let Chloe sneak in, haul Tabitha over one shoulder like a sack of corn, and run like she had the devil on her heels.

Now, it had to look like Tabitha was flying through the air, doubled over like Superman after a night of tequila-Kryptonite shots. She hoped no one else was watching and that Helen and the siren were too far behind to see Tabitha clearly.

"Slow down," Ramses yelled from where he barely kept pace.

God, she'd never been as fast as him. That was squee-worthy alone. "The faster we go, the less chance we'll get caught."

"It'll be a wonder if Tabitha doesn't vomit down your back with the way she's bouncing on your shoulder."

Chloe slowed a little, trying to ignore the pull of the new strength. She could run like a deer, leap over trees, throw cars. Hell, she could have lifted the Waffle Hut and carried it down the freeway, bringing waffles to the masses.

"Chloe!"

"Right." She slowed again. They'd passed the makeshift parking lot by the gravel road, hoping to throw off any pursuit. They were now approaching the corner of the field that would let them onto the paved road where Chloe's car waited. She slid to a stop and grabbed the fence, wanting to lift it enough to pass Tabitha through instead of chucking her over the top. With this helmet, she might hurl her into the next county.

When she pulled, several of the fence posts sprang from the ground with a loud *broing*, the barbed wire curling between them, vibrating in the air. "Oops." She dropped it. "Didn't mean to do that."

Ramses walked through the downed fence and beckoned. "As soon as we get Tabitha in the car, you have to take that helmet off." He was right. She was more likely to bludgeon the masses to death with the Waffle Hut than feed them.

"Gently," she told herself when she reached the car. She opened the back door with her thumb and forefinger. "Now, slowly lower her to the seat."

But instead she tossed her hard enough to bounce off the upholstery and wind up in the floorboard.

Chloe stared for a moment. "Good enough." She took the helmet off and felt ten times heavier but just as relieved. That was too much power to have in one's repertoire without practice, worse than a bull in a china shop. A bull in a china world.

She hopped in the front with Ramses, threw the helmet onto the floor at his feet, and drove as fast as she dared down the dark country road. After a moment of silence, she and Ramses said, "What the fuck was that?" at the same time.

"A siren and a human working together?" Chloe added.

He shook his head. "That Helen must have god blood, might even be a demigod."

She snorted. "Yeah, right." When he didn't laugh, a chill passed through her, but she shook her head. "Come on, Ramses. We're fighting gods now? And I suppose you believed all that stuff about me having the blood of Isis? Descended from a god, *woo*." She wiggled her fingers at him.

He stared out the window and said nothing.

"Ramses?"

"I thought you knew, that your mother told you."

"What?" Was this just one of a thousand lessons Jamie had gotten instead? "But there's no way." She felt sick. And intrigued. But mostly sick, though that could have been from the off-gassing of Tabitha's remaining jalapeño ranch chips.

"Are you okay?" Ramses asked.

"Was anyone ever going to tell me?" She raised a hand before he could respond. "I thought our legacy was to hunt magic stuff, like we were born as an opposing force, but now you're telling me we're part of that magic?"

"Well, you also hunt ghosts while working with one."

"That"—she tried in vain to find an argument—"is not what we're talking about. How much of me is god, and how much is human?"

He rolled his eyes. "There are no DNA-testing kits with a godhood edition, sadly."

"Okay, the sarcasm is completely unappreciated right now." She took a deep breath. "Putting aside my own heritage for a moment, if Helen is a demigod, how the hell do we fight her? Find another demigod and ask them to do it for us?"

He stared at her now, face stoney.

"What?"

"Find *another* demigod?" When she shrugged, he pointed to himself. "Hello?"

"You're not...are you?"

His mouth fell open. "Seriously?"

"What? I know the Egyptians used to worship pharaohs like gods, but..." His affronted expression grew with his glow. "Really?"

He looked ahead at the road, his chest moving as if he was taking deep breaths that he no longer needed. The crown of Egypt replaced the cloth nemes on his head, the top of it poking through the roof of the car, but she didn't dare laugh while he was clearly calming himself down. An anger-fueled jolt of his power could fry the car's electrical system.

But that wasn't the only reason she wouldn't laugh at him. She hadn't meant to piss him off so much. Tears pricked her eyes, no doubt also from the fading of adrenaline and the aftershock of the exorcism, but there was more than enough guilt from having insulted her best friend.

Her only friend.

"I'm sorry, Ramses," she said, taking her own deep breaths so she didn't bawl like a baby and crash into a tree. "No one ever told me you're a demigod."

"I would have thought it evident," he said, his tone clipped.

She thought of everything she'd learned about his life, the countless books she'd read, even when she'd thought she'd never hear or see him. She still had his long-ago note, now a laminated bookmark. "I guess it should have been obvious with everything you accomplished in life. I just never thought, oh, he was able to do all that stuff because he's a demigod. It was more like, he was able to do it because he's Ramses, unstoppable as the tide. After all, a demigod could still sit on their ass and eat chips all day and not accomplish anything, right?"

His glow faded back to normal, the striped nemes once again adorning his head as he smiled softly. "Right."

He passed one spectral hand over hers on the steering wheel, making the hair on her arm stand up, a feeling she'd long associated with the comfort of having him around. "Thank you, Chloe. You're forgiven." He glanced over his shoulder. "And once we're rid of Tabitha, I suppose I should tell you exactly what it means to have the blood of Isis."

And exactly why her mother had kept it from her.

CHAPTER ELEVEN

After a few phone calls and more than a few favors called in, the wyvern was finally loaded into the moving truck, courtesy of a troll who lived about an hour away and supported himself via an Etsy shop. He made pretty good money selling carvings made from the pieces of his rocky body that occasionally dropped off. Helen had to put in quite a few orders before he'd even agreed to drive out to meet her. Now he'd come and gone, and she would have to find somewhere for over one hundred figurines detailing the bulk of the cast from *The Lord of the Rings* trilogy.

Still, it was worth it to get the hell out of this field. But not worth the loss of the tarnkappe.

"I'm sorry," Ligeia said again, no doubt reading Helen's expression in the dim light of the rapidly dying campfire.

She shook her head, staring at Fatma and Ali and wondering what to do with them. "I know. It's all right."

"Ugh, you keep saying that, but it's not true. You should have let me chase that woman with the ghost."

"She was gone before we could see what direction she'd taken Tabitha in."

Ligeia blew an obnoxiously huge pink bubble, the pop echoing. "I'm still sorry, whatever." After a moment, she added, "Are we gonna, like, go or…"

"These two seem well-informed about paranormal goings-on. I have a feeling they'll keep dogging my steps if I don't do something."

"Like?" Ligeia dragged a thumb across her throat. "I mean, it's probably for the best."

"Oh yes? Well, go ahead." She moved out of the way, too tired to lecture and in no mood for murder.

"Me?" Ligeia took a step back. "No way."

"Why do you care if they live or die?" Helen asked, using one of Ligeia's earlier questions against her.

The tattoos on her hands glimmered gold as she crossed her arms and rolled her eyes. "Okay, I get it. None of us are mad-dog killers anymore. How many times do I have to say whatever? Life is precious, blah blah. But what do you want to do with them?"

"Take them with us," Helen said, the decision easy compared to the alternatives. "They can ride in the back with the sleeping wyvern. Maybe that will make them more inclined to talk when they wake up."

❖

The cargo area of the moving van stayed quieter much longer than Helen expected. After Fairfield, she was starting to suspect that Fatma and Ali were more injured than she'd realized, and guilt persuaded her to pull over in an abandoned weigh station to check.

Ligeia didn't comment, but her side-eye spoke volumes, all with the title: *Helen's Gone Soft on Humans.*

Worse still, Helen couldn't recall exactly when that had happened. She'd been betrayed by them, disrespected, her entire history morphed until she was nothing more than a pawn of gods and men. And she'd killed more than a few humans in defense of her sanctuary and its denizens. She'd sunk whole shiploads without batting an eye, and now here she was, checking on two she didn't even know.

Maybe she was getting soft.

She paused before opening the back of the truck. Instead of checking on these two, perhaps even letting them go, she could slit their throats. Her stomach churned at the thought, and she snorted at herself. She had no desire to add to the bloodshed in the world. In fact, she was willing to go quite out of her way to avoid it.

Case in point.

As soon as she lifted the door, two voices spoke over each other in a sort of whisper-yell:

"Let us out of here."

"The wyvern could wake up."

"You have no right—"

"I demand—"

Helen began to lower the door again. If they were healthy enough to bitch at her, they were probably fine.

"Wait, please." Fatma's voice, a tad more conciliatory. "We know who you are."

Interesting. Well, if they felt like talking. She lifted the door again, encouraged by the silence that greeted her. Except for the wyvern's snoring, of course. "And who am I?"

Fatma and Ali were sitting against the wall, their hands and feet bound in front of them with cord from the creature-wrangling kit Helen had brought. She and Ligeia had laid them on a moving blanket at first, and now, besides the purple bruises near their temples, they seemed no worse for wear.

Helen handed them a bottle of water, and after both had taken a few sips, they glanced behind her, but they'd discover nothing but darkness, even with the dim streetlight overhead. Dawn was still a few hours off, and the freeway was largely silent at that time of night.

"You run some kind of zoo," Fatma said, disgust lacing her tone.

Helen clenched her jaw and fought the urge to argue. She didn't want to just hand over information. But a zoo? "Go on."

Fatma glared. "Sick old animals deserve better than that."

"And antiquities should stay in their countries of origin," Ali added.

Very interesting. And she agreed for the most part. But magical antiquities did not belong in human hands. "And here I thought you were common smugglers. I didn't know you had convictions. Beyond the criminal, anyway."

"Are you going to lock this wyvern in a cage so your rich friends can gawk as it dies?" Fatma asked.

"Yes, because I'm friends with Satan himself," she said flatly. "I don't think our intentions are as misaligned as they appear. The wyvern will be looked after and gawked at by no one."

They glanced at each other and said nothing.

"What were you going to use the ambrosia for?" Helen asked. "You and your dealer with the fairy blood?"

Ali smirked. "To tempt people like you, follow you, and raid your magical hoards."

Recalling the brief confrontation with Fatma in the alley behind the dry cleaners, Helen put on her own smirk. "Not exactly a success on your part, then."

Fatma looked a bit sheepish. "I didn't realize you were…" She mashed her lips together.

"Anyone important? Yeah, that's kind of the point of a disguise." But did it still grate? Oh hell yes. Worse, now she liked these two a little, even if they didn't have nearly enough facts to be tinkering in the realms of the paranormal. But it wasn't her job to educate them. "If I ask you to stop interfering with me, is there a chance that will work?"

Ali had the savviness to at least appear to think it over, but Fatma kept her signature glare.

Well, that was it. Helen still didn't want to kill them, but if they weren't going to at least lie about leaving her alone, she wasn't going to help them, either. It was time to cut them loose with their phones and a warning that if she ever saw them again, she would reevaluate the whole no-murder thing. She cut them free, then waved them down and away from the truck so she could close the door.

They spoke quietly to each other, pausing when Helen handed back their phones. Now for the threat…but nothing came to mind. No one Helen had met that evening had come across as a trademarked Bad Guy. And if it had been Chloe standing there, Helen might have even said something like, "It's not a zoo. It's a sanctuary."

When those words actually came out, she bit her lip, not meaning to speak aloud. But now that she had, she surprisingly wasn't sorry about it.

"What?" Ali asked.

Fatma's frown turned confused. "But we heard—"

"I know the rumors. Hell, I started many of them, but since you seem like you might be on the ethical side of this business, I thought you should know that my efforts go into creating a retirement village for creatures who aren't exactly welcome in the world anymore."

"Why should we believe you?" Fatma asked.

"Believe it or not, I don't care." She started toward the driver's side of the truck. "But if I was some evil Mommy Fortuna, you'd be dead several times over."

"And what of the artifacts like that one?" Ali asked, pointing at the kladenet.

"They are not for human hands."

"Except yours, of course," Fatma said, crossing her arms and sporting a smirk identical to Ali's. "Fucking hypocrite."

That was the line. Helen pushed through her fatigue and summoned her godhood, letting it flow beneath her skin, lighting her up as if she had molten gold in her veins. Fatma's and Ali's shocked expressions grew brighter as they bathed in her light.

They took a step back, faces shifting from surprise to awe.

Better. Helen climbed into the truck, letting her godhood settle but not before catching a glimpse of her blazing eyes in the side mirror. *Still got it.* She drove back to the freeway, feeling quite smug, even if the flex was quickly giving her a headache.

"Feel better?" Ligeia asked.

"Much, thank you."

Ligeia snorted a laugh and put her feet on the dash as she began to fiddle with the radio.

Helen smiled to herself but had to wonder how that encounter would have gone if the intriguing Chloe had been there instead. A disturbing tingle went through her at the thought, surprising her. They'd barely interacted, but Helen's desire to see her again had crossed the border of "might be nice" and was on the disturbing cusp of "really, really want to."

And why? Had she been disappointed so many times she was now in love with the feeling? She hadn't been bitten in the ass enough and wanted another wound?

More alarming still, was she drawn to humans because she was seeking a connection with someone she didn't know as well as the back of her hand, someone she hadn't spent centuries with in her sanctuary? She'd told Fatma and Ali more than she'd intended. If Chloe had been there, who knew what information Helen would have blurted out?

She shook her head and focused on the road, determined not to think of any human as intriguing. The only adjective they needed? Dangerous.

❖

"It's basically what you've already guessed." Ramses walked up and down the waiting room in the hospital. "The goddess Isis is one of your ancestors, so to speak."

They'd brought Tabitha in just to be safe, saying she'd gotten hurt when a barn had collapsed. One of the nurses had even heard of the teenage hangout, lending credence to Chloe's story of hijinks gone awry, though the nurse had also given her a look suggesting she'd passed her hijinks days long ago.

The nerve. It hadn't been that long ago. Must have been the job aging her. She kept her phone pressed to her ear and said, "You make it sound like Isis was just a traveler who showed up in town one day and decided to warm the bed of a local."

He tilted his head back and forth. "Nothing quite so human. We say someone has the blood of a god, but it's really more like an ancestor received an infusion of godly power, usually while pregnant or shortly before impregnating someone, and the result was a demigod, with several subsequent generations sharing a decreasing fraction of power."

"Until you're left with a small gift like being able to see the invisible." Chloe shook her head. "If I'm a demigod, I should have cooler abilities."

He gave her a wry smile. "Isis was very long ago for our family. Now our gift can only be carried by one relative at a time. And it's more than just seeing the unseen. Your senses are more in tune with the paranormal—"

"I know, I know." Chloe sighed, feeling like she'd had one of the longest nights in years. She wondered how many other demigods were ready for bed well before midnight. Though the clock above the nurses' station read one a.m., and she was still wide awake. *Still young, baby.* "I was just lamenting that I didn't get fire breath or something."

He sat next to her, hovering slightly above the seat. "Take up Tabitha's diet, and you might."

She chuckled, then glanced around to make sure no one was paying her too much attention. "I'm too far removed from Isis to even call myself a demigod, aren't I? Especially if you think Helen is one. I can't do nearly the things she can." Like exuding beauty and grace and a kick-ass confidence that made Chloe want to follow her around like a lovesick idiot.

"She did seem to have inner power to tap into. That exorcism spell." He rubbed his neck.

Chloe nodded. She was still having the occasional muscle spasm, too. And a few brain-pickling jolts of lust, but that had nothing to do with any spell. "Why didn't Mom tell me? I mean, it's a bit jarring to find out I have a god in the old family tree, but I'm not cut up about it."

He sighed and slouched, sticking out his long legs. Chloe fought not to flinch when a nurse walked through them. "We had an idea that the knowledge would make you both reckless, that you'd think having god blood made you immortal. She did promise to tell you one day, and I hoped—"

"Wait." She coughed and had to remind herself to keep her phone up and her voice low. "Make us both reckless? She didn't tell Jamie, either?"

"Not as far as I know."

What the hell did that mean? That Chloe finally knew something about this job that Jamie hadn't? Of course, Chloe had found out from a random siren, so it wasn't like her mother had favored her.

God, she was going to have to call her mom. Again.

And what else could having the blood of Isis do for her besides make her able to see invisible stuff?

When a nurse came out to tell her that Tabitha only had a minor concussion and could go home soon, Chloe couldn't put it off any longer. She and Ramses headed out, leaving it to the hospital to call Tabitha's family or the cute girl from the Waffle Hut to come get her. Still, Chloe told herself she could wait until the hotel, at least.

Until her phone chimed while she was driving. "If that's Mom, I don't think she lost all the family's psychic gifts when she temporarily..."

Shit, she really thought she'd have been able to say died while making a joke, but she guessed not.

Ramses bent to peer at the phone where it sat in the cupholder. "It's an alert on your browser." His finger hovered over the screen, a speck of power letting him manipulate the apps. "Well, well, looks like my exhibit won't be the only thing we see in Houston. We've got another ghost. Maybe two, by the looks of things. But we can head out tomorrow after we check on the wyvern."

"You don't think they took it with them?"

"Only one way to make sure."

"What the hell do they even want it for? At least if they're busy with it, they won't show up in Houston. No guns crashing our banishment or sirens or demigods named...Helen," she whispered, the name tumbling together with all her lessons on mythology. "Holy shit."

Ramses glanced at the nearly abandoned freeway as if Helen might appear. "Let's hope she doesn't show up again. You couldn't seem to keep your head last time."

She ignored that, her mind still whirling. "Helen, Ramses. Demigod. Daughter of Zeus. Her mother was either Leda or freaking Nemesis." When he said nothing, she added, "Trojan War? Golden apple, all that jazz?"

He stared at her blankly; he'd never been one to pay attention to myths that didn't involve monsters. Or himself. "Helen...of Troy?"

"Yes."

He nodded. *The Iliad* and *Odyssey*. They had a sorceress, a cyclops, some gods, Scylla, that other sea monster—"

"Charybdis."

"And sirens. I wonder if Helen and that siren have been friends all this time."

"No, Helen wasn't on the boat that…" Chloe sighed. "Look, who gives a shit? It's Helen. The Helen. Face that launched a thousand ships." And Chloe could believe that now. The face, the body, the presence, the sheer chutzpah. Chloe wouldn't have gone to war for much, but damn. "God, I threw a wyvern at her. You told her and that woman to get a room. We were so rude."

Ramses gave her a flat look. "Being rude? That's the part that worries you?"

"She is beyond famous. She is an actual legend." She put a hand to her forehead and rubbed at the headache that had been dogging her all night. Thank goodness they were headed to the hotel. She could die peacefully of embarrassment there.

"Ooo," Ramses said, "maybe we can get her autograph next time she interferes in our affairs. Or make her some cupcakes."

"Look—"

"Next time we see her, wait until she's foiling our plans, then write her a sonnet."

"I don't—"

"Propose on the spot."

"Okay," she yelled. "I get it. She's dangerous, especially if she's going to keep crashing our party with sirens and tranquilizer guns." She held up a hand when he opened his mouth. "And whatever magic forced us apart."

He nodded. "Promise me that any research you do about her will be purely for defensive purposes."

She nodded back, happy he couldn't read her mind at the moment. Freaking Helen of freaking Troy. Yeah, Chloe was going to research the hell out of her. And she wouldn't blame herself if defense wasn't the first thing on her mind.

Chapter Twelve

Staring at her phone for fifteen minutes before making a call was part of the process, or so Chloe told herself. When she'd woken up a few moments ago, there had been too many "hates" to start the day with: she hated talking on the phone, hated talking to her mom, hated talking about stuff she should have been taught, Jamie or no Jamie. She deserved to know her roots, even if, like many Americans, those roots were sort of everywhere.

So with more than a little bitterness, she typed, *Blood of Isis, huh?* in a text to her mom and hit send.

After a moment passed with no reply, she figured she had time to pee. She'd crashed immediately when they'd gotten in around two a.m., but her dreams had been absorbed by the fact that she was descended from an actual god and seemed doomed to have another demigod as an adversary, though this one was a lot closer to the source.

And this one was also freaking Helen of freaking Troy. Whom she'd quite like to—

"Are you going to shower?" Ramses asked from where he sat on the bed watching TV.

"I thought my mom would respond quicker than this."

"She didn't answer?"

Chloe picked at the edge of the duvet cover with her toes. "Texted," she said, trying for nonchalant. She felt his look. Her mother was notorious about not texting back, but surely *blood of Isis* would have her calling right away.

She could still feel his look.

"Fine, ugh." She sat on the edge of the bed and dialed, hoping she'd at least distracted him from his five-millionth show. When the call went unanswered, she hung up and tossed her phone on the covers. "She's either out or in the bathroom or something." She fled for her own bathroom. Calling her mom and not getting an answer was one-tenth as stressful as actually speaking to her, but it was still stress.

Though emerging from the shower to discover that her mom still hadn't responded was more stressful still. Ever since Chloe had taken over the family duties, her mom had never waited this long to return a missed call.

The image of the EMTs working to bring her back from the dead flashed in Chloe's mind. Along with Jamie, all covered as if to shield her from the cold. "Would you know if Mom…" Again, she couldn't say it.

Luckily, with Ramses, she didn't need to. "No," he said quietly, this look feeling a lot kinder as he smiled. "Not since the connection passed to you. But I'm sure she's okay."

"Yeah." A comforting lie was better than nothing. She thought about calling her dad, but he hadn't spoken to Mom much since they'd split. He would be sure she was okay, too. "Let's get on the road."

She packed quickly, could have done it blind. Ramses hung around while she packed where he sometimes vanished to wherever he went, only reappearing when Chloe reached their destination. When he showed no signs of leaving, it was time to give him a look.

"What?" he asked, the picture of innocence.

"You don't have to…hover," she said, absurdly proud of the pun.

He rolled his eyes. "So you've decided to make me regret doing so?"

She shrugged, still pleased.

"I just thought I'd stick around, that's all."

"Well, you don't have to."

"I know."

"I'm fine."

"Duly noted."

"Okay." But when she had the key in the ignition, fear crept over her like an oily slug, the anxiety of too many unknowns converging. "Of course, you are welcome to stay."

"Thank you."

"I mean, good company and all."

"Quite. You too."

"Thanks."

"Of course."

"Right." She tapped the steering wheel for a few seconds, hating the tiny talk, hating her fear. "It won't be really taxing for you, will it? Like, sap the energy you can use later?"

"No, Chloe," he said softly. His head was bare again, a sure sign of him feeling paternal, and she wished for the umpteenth time that she could hug him. "Chlo," he said after a few moments. "Drive the damned car, would you?"

She barked a laugh, shaken out of her melancholy. "Houston, here we come."

❖

A quick stop by the ruined barn proved that the wyvern was indeed gone. Maybe it would have an easy life from here on out. Or at least a short one. No matter who'd wound up with it, Chloe and Ramses couldn't linger.

When they reached Houston, they decided to save the exhibit for last and check out rumors of a local ghost haunting a comic book store, of all things. In the afternoon, it was mostly dead, one bored-looking employee behind the glass counter, and a few browsing the rows of comic books or the shelves full of collectibles. And everyone she could see looked very much alive. Great, this was probably another wild-goose chase, one of many Chloe had experienced in this job. She supposed she should count her blessings after the busy few days they'd had, but doing nothing gave her mind room to wander. About bills, Helen of freaking Troy, the fact that her mom still hadn't called back.

Chloe took her phone from her pocket and stared, tempted to drive straight to her mom's house in Austin, but she knew she couldn't drag Ramses all the way here and not go to his exhibit. He asked very little for the amount of shit he put up with.

"They have a scale model of me," he called excitedly from where he peered at one of the glass cases. "We have to get this, Chlo."

She fought the urge to smirk and leaned down to examine a very detailed twelve-inch-tall model labeled *Ramses II*, though many of his features were off, and the bulging muscles on his arms and torso rivaled the most flattering statues. When she saw the price tag, she choked on her smile. "It's almost two hundred bucks," she said out the side of her mouth.

His expression crumbled like a kid who'd been told Santa wasn't real. "We can't afford that, can we?"

"Not unless you want to cancel a bunch of streaming services for a month."

When he sighed, she nearly threw her credit card on the counter anyway, but he waved it off and sniffed, drawing himself up. "It's not very accurate anyway."

"Right." She hoped she didn't sound too relieved. "Though I do wonder if you could appear around your action figure like you can a statue."

"Model," he said, not breaking eye contact.

For heaven's sake, do not laugh. "Model. Though you are a superhero."

He shrugged and smiled, seemingly mollified.

"And it begs the question, could that be why a ghost is here?" Chloe took another look around, slower this time. The ghost could simply be choosing to be elsewhere at the moment. Nothing seemed disrupted, and her brief internet search hadn't turned up stories of anyone being hurt, just merchandise sometimes rearranged when the store opened in the mornings. If they did have a ghost, it was very benign and likely hadn't been summoned. Those were always ornery as hell. Like Goodspeed.

But she'd take anything at the moment to avoid worrying about her mom. She leaned on the counter near the employee. "Hey there, I heard a rumor this place was haunted."

He sighed, straightened from scrolling on his phone, and muttered something about tourists. "Yeah, I guess." He ran a hand through his blond hair and made studious eye contact with a spot just above her head. "Weird stuff happens sometimes."

"Like what?" She tried smiling brightly, hoping an interested audience would break through his indifference, especially if she played cute.

He yawned, clearly not biting. Either she'd lost all her natural charm, or he simply didn't care. Her pride told her it had to be the latter.

And she wasn't in the mood to try more flirting. She headed for the door. They could come back tonight after the exhibit and see if the ghost was in a mood to show itself. A comic book store shouldn't have much security.

She hoped.

"Wait," Ramses said, ducking into an aisle of board games.

She followed, really hoping he hadn't spied something else about himself, though if it didn't cost much—

"Someone powerful," he muttered, glancing back the way they'd come.

Chloe rubbed her neck and used the motion to look but only saw the same three people who'd been there the whole time. "Which one?"

"Coming in the door."

She pressed her back into the games, hoping to remain unseen until she got a look at the newcomer, wondering if they were tied to the ghostly rumors.

When Helen walked through the door, Chloe had to throw a hand over her mouth to keep from shouting or squealing or just dissolving on the spot.

❖

Helen was exhausted, never mind the hours she and Ligeia had spent sleeping at a truck stop just north of Houston. Dealing with the wyvern and then Fatma and Ali had taken much longer than she'd guessed, so they'd been forced to stop for a bit of shut-eye.

They'd woken up just after four when a wandering truck driver had peeked in the windows and asked if they were up for a little late-night delight.

Ligeia had sung him into oblivion. Helen hoped he was still somewhere in that parking lot, sucking his thumb and rocking back and forth.

Traffic through Houston had been proving its usual crawl when the Sphinx called. Helen put her on speakerphone after they said their hellos: "My friend Colin is having trouble with a ghost in his shop," the Sphinx said. "It's been fairly quiet until now, but lately, it's been rearranging his stock in the middle of the night, and it scared some customers."

"And?" Helen asked, fatigue making her snappy.

"I told him you could look into it, seeing as you're nearby. Don't you know a spell to banish ghosts?"

Ligeia pursed her lips. "Funny, we just had a run-in with a ghost."

"Really? With the wyvern?"

Helen held up a hand to stop everyone talking at once. "It's a long story. How good of a friend is this Colin?"

"Well, I mean, he is a good Houston contact."

"That doesn't answer my question."

"And he knows a lot of people."

"And…"

The Sphinx sighed.

Ligeia snapped her gum and grinned. "And she might have dropped your name more than a few times and now wants to impress her friend with how awesome you are."

Flattering, but…

"Pretty please," the Sphinx said. "I'll be your best friend."

Helen had to laugh. "Tell him to have a cup of coffee waiting." She disconnected.

Ligeia poked her in the arm. "Softy."

"Yeah," Helen said with a sigh. "I remembered how to exorcize a ghost, but I don't exactly remember how to banish one."

Ligeia waved boredly. "Just, like, flex and it'll run for the ghost hills."

That would be a nice ego boost. "Fine, but you'll have to wait in the van."

When they arrived at the shop, Helen went in alone, taking off her sunglasses inside. The man behind the counter nearly sprang over, his face alight with a grin. "Colin?" she asked.

He nodded like a bobblehead. "Gosh, I'm so happy to meet you. S has told me so much. It's an honor." He bent as he gushed and produced a tall to-go cup from behind the counter. "Coffee as requested. It's a caramel latte. S told me that's your favorite."

Ego boost indeed. She sipped it gratefully. Magic prickled her skin, no doubt Colin's glamour. "What can I do for you?" She lowered her voice as she leaned closer. "With magic like yours, I don't know why you'd need mine." She added a wink, enjoying the way he grinned and squealed, holding his arms up close to his chest. Good to know her celebrity still counted in some circles.

"Oh, S really shouldn't have bothered you, but I'm so glad she did. It's Basil, our ghost."

She blinked. "The ghost has a name?"

"He's been really upset lately, like, big time. Some disruption in the ether is making him act out." His voice dropped to a whisper. "You've heard about the new queen of the Greek Underworld?"

Helen nodded. "The one who was human."

"Well, my friend's cousin knows the fiancée of a banshee who's met a hierophant, and he thinks the new queen might have weakened the walls between the worlds enough that it's affecting ghosts in this one." He put out a hand as if it held up all those people and their rumors before putting up the other hand. "And my boyfriend's aunt's ex-husband learned from two people in a satyr's thruple that someone is summoning ghosts around the globe for some kind of, I don't know, ghost army or something."

Helen tried to wrap her head around all that. "And your ghost is... part of the army?"

He snorted a laugh. "Basil? Hardly. I mean, I guess he could have been at one time or another. We've never actually, you know, met." He gave another vague wave. "I don't even know what his name was when he was alive. I just call him Basil after Basil Rathbone, you know, the actor who played Sherlock Holmes about a million years ago. Such a cutie. Anyway, Basil's been here as long as I have, but he's always been as gentle as a lamb, and he is a *wizard* at alphabetizing all the comics and zines. But he's been putting things out of order lately, and he almost knocked a customer on the head the other day when he shifted the red dragon mini I keep only for display."

Helen followed his finger to a model of a dragon—that looked far from mini—that perched over one of the aisles, forever glaring at the patrons below. She was not awake enough for all this. She should have made Ligeia come in with her hoodie pulled low. They both spoke almost too fast to follow. "So you want Basil...removed?"

"Um, no." He seemed shocked, maybe even a little pissed. "Just, you know, calmed."

If she couldn't remember a spell to banish ghosts, she sure as hell couldn't remember one to calm them down. "Have you tried a séance?" She was only half kidding.

He seemed thoughtful. "You think that might work?"

Hallelujah, a way out. "Yep." She kept her face serious through a Herculean effort.

"Well, great." He beamed again. "Now while you're here..." He paused, looking sheepish.

Helen barely kept herself from swearing and took a gulp of coffee, hoping Colin wasn't going to ask for more than an autograph. She really didn't have it in her to hear more about a ghost who'd done nothing more than mix up some books and knock a figurine off a shelf. And she really, *really* didn't want to meet him. "Yes?"

"Well, I don't want to hold you up, but I thought you should also know about the new ghost in the apartment complex behind here that tried to kill several people a few days ago. People keep coming in and asking about it after some internet rumor, and I think they're confusing it with poor Basil."

Helen just kept from crushing her cup. "New ghost."

"Uh-huh."

"Tried to kill people."

"Mmm."

Helen sucked her top lip in and bit it hard enough to keep from screaming. "Don't you think you should have led with that, Colin?"

He looked a little alarmed. Not enough, but Helen would take what she could get. "You think that might be what's upsetting Basil?"

Spoke too soon. If it wasn't about Basil, Colin clearly didn't give a shit. "Tell me about this other ghost."

As he spoke, Helen's mind wandered. Partly from fatigue, but she also didn't know what to do about either of Colin's ghostly problems. Her limited experience with the unquiet dead lay far in her past.

Mostly.

Chloe appeared in her mind's eye again, and she didn't even have the energy to be pissed off at herself. What was that strange energy Helen had felt between them? The energy of the ghostly pharaoh or perhaps the magic that bound him and Chloe together? Helen hadn't been around another demigod in a very long time. She'd forgotten just how powerful the pull between gods could be, and since she'd once felt a similar twinge in Egypt, it made sense that—

"...you know?" Colin asked.

"Totally," Helen answered on auto-pilot. Something about a pharaoh's energy didn't fully explain what she'd experienced in Chloe's presence. Maybe it was Chloe's innate magic. Or maybe it was just...her.

Helen sighed. Gods, what was she doing? She had been down this road too many times.

"*So.*" Colin drew the word out, staring expectantly.

Helen shook herself. "Right. I'm on it." Hoping she'd just agreed to take care of the ghost and nothing else, she lightly slapped the counter and walked away, hoping to banish her disturbing thoughts here, too.

Chapter Thirteen

Ramses repeated everything Colin the cashier and Helen said as they said it, only loud enough for Chloe to hear where she hid between the aisles. She could have done without the list of relatives and friends and thruples, but it was good to know they were in the wrong damn place for the really dangerous ghost. The article she'd found had obviously confused the two hauntings as much as Colin claimed.

And now she had their real target. But what the hell was Helen doing here investigating it? If Helen of Troy was a regular ghost hunter, Chloe would have heard about it by now. Unless it was yet another thing her mom had never told her.

She supposed they could just leave Helen to it, be on their way to the museum, but when she left, Ramses returned to Chloe's side and said, "She didn't seem that confident about dealing with a ghost."

So she wasn't normally in the business. "Sounds like she knows this guy or knows someone who does." She inclined her head toward Colin the cashier. "Someone calling in a favor?"

He shrugged. "We can't let it go."

She sighed. "Not when people might get hurt. Even if Helen looks into it, we have to make sure she does the job right." She sidled close to the door and peeked out. Helen was crossing the sidewalk to the larger parking lot of the gas station next door. Chloe slipped out while her back was turned and hurried to her car.

Helen climbed into a U-Haul and spoke to someone Chloe couldn't make out in the shadows. "That's probably the siren."

Before Ramses could even suggest following them and eavesdropping again, the U-Haul pulled out of the gas station. Chloe let out a breath, though she couldn't decide if she was relieved or disappointed. Either way, Helen was gone, and that would make this whole operation much easier.

They pulled the car into the street behind the comic shop, parking on the curb down from the metal gate that guarded the entrance of the small apartment complex. Chloe slipped her bag over her shoulders and walked through the open pedestrian entrance. She didn't have any info on this ghost, but she was used to operating on rumors and innuendo that proved false most of the time. Like Southern Mothmen who turned out to be wyverns.

"I really hope this isn't another case of mistaken identity," she muttered as she looked around, hoping to appear like someone apartment hunting. "And it's really an army of zombies and not a ghost."

"Armies of zombies only exist in fiction," Ramses said before frowning. "I think. Anyway, could an army of the undead be confused with Basil the alphabetizing ghost?"

"Depends on what else Basil gets up to in his spare time."

"I wonder who it really is in that shop, what figurine is holding them there." He sounded a bit maudlin, and she wondered if he was thinking of his time wandering the desert before he'd decided to bond himself to one of his descendants. By the time his statues had been on display around the world, he'd been part of Chloe's family for years.

"Do you want me to banish that ghost, too?"

He was silent for a few moments. "Nah. For all I know, they may be deliriously happy. If we get rid of this ghost, that one may even go back to normal."

"And maybe they'll convince Colin to give us a discount on that slightly inaccurate Ramses figure."

He lifted his eyebrows as if to say anything was possible. "Yes, they didn't quite get my nose right."

And the biceps as big as most people's thighs, but she didn't mention that.

Chloe asked for leasing info at the office, then loitered a bit, looking lost and thoughtful until she could quiz a few residents on what living in the complex was like, acting like she was thinking of moving there but hoping for a little ghostly gossip.

Mailbox woes, crowded parking, a pool that was always closed, and a dishwasher that still hadn't been replaced. She didn't think much of it as a place to live until someone said, "Oh, and the tree that tries to murder people."

That was better.

"Murder tree?" she asked.

The older woman she was talking to jerked one thumb over her shoulder. "Dropped a limb on someone a few days back without a gust of wind. And the kids in 5E have said they've seen the limbs moving all the time, no matter the weather, says the tree knocked one of them out on their ass, but I think they've seen *Poltergeist* too many times."

Thank God for ghost movies. They kept people from thinking the paranormal could ever be real. "Weird."

"Don't let it put you off. It's not a bad place, and the rent's reasonable. And that kid only broke an arm. The man the limb fell on just had a mild concussion."

Only. Just. They were lucky they weren't dead, but Chloe smiled, hoping it didn't look too wooden. "Thanks."

The woman gave another shrug as if she cared about being thanked as much as she cared about a tree almost killing people.

Ramses was already on his way toward the tree. Chloe followed, though she couldn't see anything in the old oak's branches. If there was a ghost, he was staying hidden for the moment.

"Some sort of magic was done here," Ramses said as he knelt on the ground. "And not long ago." He looked up. "The trail extends up the tree." He walked up the side as easily as he walked up the ground.

Chloe maneuvered closer to the fence that surrounded the complex, trying to remain slightly less conspicuous as she watched her invisible friend, though she had to shade her eyes from the sun.

"There's something lodged in one of these branches," Ramses called. "Can you shake it loose?"

"Not without causing the branch to move significantly. I might also damage the tree."

Chloe wasn't much in the mood to protect the tree along with everything else. "Fuck. I really don't want to climb up there, Ramses." She tried to keep her voice low but noticed one of the apartment residents staring at her from where he was walking a dog by the mailbox.

"Just rehearsing a play," she said stupidly, her cheeks burning. "About...the pyramids."

He frowned and stared as he pulled his dog in the opposite direction.

"Smooth," Ramses said from Chloe's back.

At least she was too embarrassed to jump out of her skin. "Please don't do that."

"Appear beside you, or ask you to climb trees?"

"Either."

"Can't, I'm afraid. It's a small figurine of some sort, undoubtedly the cause of our ghostly activity, and it will take more nimble hands than mine to remove it. Living hands. Unless you want me to try a powerful enough jolt that I risk setting the tree alight."

"Tempting." She put her hands on her hips and sighed. "And moving it might provoke the ghost into showing itself. Do we risk doing it in daylight?"

"Better to be thought odd in the day than try to fumble your way up there at night, especially since the ghost seems to be absent at the moment."

"I'm not afraid of the ghost, not with you around."

He smiled and nodded benevolently.

"I suppose having a ghost companion would make finding other ghosts easier," a familiar voice said behind them.

Helen. Where the hell had she come from? "I thought you could sense her coming," she said quietly, not turning.

"I've been a little preoccupied, Chloe," Ramses said.

She turned slowly. "Hi." She drew out the I, trying to sound unconcerned, cheerful even.

"I suppose I shouldn't be surprised." Helen's hair gleamed, falling over her shoulder in perfect waves even after a long night in an abandoned pasture. Her eyes looked more light brown in the day, maybe even hazel. And she smiled wryly, a look Chloe much preferred over the pissed-off expressions of the night before. "If I heard of nearby ghosts, why wouldn't the woman who has her very own ghostly guide? Tell me, do you investigate ghosts as well as wyverns?"

"Maybe," Chloe said, trying not to drool. "I didn't know the wyvern was there, or I would have been better prepared."

"Don't defend yourself," Ramses said. "It puts you off your footing in an argument."

Funny, this didn't feel like an argument. Was it a trick of the light, or did Helen give her a quick once-over? Helen of freaking Troy was checking her out.

"Are you a reporter like your friend the redhead? How is she, by the way?"

"She'll mend, and I'm not a reporter." Though, damn, that would have made a good cover. She'd used it often enough. But she didn't want to lie. Was having a hard time not shouting the truth, like, *I would really like your phone number.* Or *please go out with me.* Or *can we just forget talking and make out?* "I banish ghosts." She tried to say it off-hand, like it wasn't a really awesome job. She'd never gotten to use it to impress anyone before, but she figured Helen of freaking Troy was already well-acquainted with the paranormal.

"Just ghosts?" She tilted her head coyly.

Chloe shrugged. "Mostly. Occasionally, there's more dangerous stuff."

"Chloe," Ramses said in a warning tone.

"Like wyverns?" Helen asked, perfectly shaped eyebrows rising.

"Shut up, Chloe."

But he didn't know what it felt like to have a goddess so interested, so impressed with her, leaning forward as if she didn't want to miss a single word. "Well—" She yelped as Ramses shocked her arm. "What the hell?"

He glared at her. Helen's expression had shifted from eager anticipation to wariness in the blink of an eye. Something was off. "She's leading you on."

"Really?" Chloe said aloud, strangely hurt. "You were pretending to be interested to get me to, what, spill my guts?"

Helen blinked, clearly taken aback and maybe even a little guilty before she shook her head. "You're a *monster* hunter, aren't you? A killer?"

No one had ever called her a killer before. That hurt, too. "I protect people, yeah."

"From sick old creatures who never did anyone any harm?"

"I didn't know…" Chloe curled her hands into fists, remembering what Ramses said about defending oneself. "You don't know that sick old wyvern never harmed anyone. And I didn't hurt it, either."

"You stabbed it and threw it into a barn."

"That…well…yeah, but that was so we could get away from all the guns." She pointed at Helen in victory. "We don't shoot anything, so there."

Helen sneered. "You're coming at me for using tranqs?" She waved. "Doesn't matter. I don't need to defend my actions to you."

"That's all you should have said," Ramses added.

"Ditto," Chloe said, mostly for his benefit. She pointed behind Helen. "And I don't need your help. So there's the door. Unless you want to try to tranq a ghost that *has* hurt people."

"You can't dismiss me."

"Surely you have someone else to flirt with so you can get information out of them."

Helen drew back, affronted. "I was not flirting." But her bronzed cheeks went a little darker. "I was feigning a slight interest to prompt a killer to confess."

"Oh, bullshit. You gave me one of these." She made a show of looking her up and down.

Helen's mouth worked, but she couldn't seem to find anything to say.

Was she really that flustered? Holy shit, maybe that once-over had nothing to do with pumping Chloe for info.

No, no way, it was Helen of freaking Troy. She couldn't actually be interested in some mere mortal. Still, a pull began in Chloe's chest, an even more powerful attraction, like Helen was the lodestone Chloe had spent a lifetime searching for before she even knew it existed.

And she wasn't any *mere* mortal. She had god blood in her veins. "I have a job to do," she said more calmly. "Or more people could get hurt. I think I…know who you are."

Helen leaned back slightly as if fearing an explosion.

The word Troy was on the tip of Chloe's tongue, but something in those wary eyes made her hold it back. Maybe there were too many ears around. "And I'm really honored to meet you." That was true, and it seemed to soften Helen's stance a bit. "Normally, I'd have so many questions, but this doesn't seem like the time or place." *And I'm still pissed at you for calling me a killer.*

And a bit too turned on for rational thought.

"You must be busy lately," Helen said.

Chloe nodded. "You've heard of the extra paranormal stuff, too, huh? Seems like either lots of people are taking up the shit hobby of summoning ghosts, or a few are having a real spree."

That earned her a little smile. "I have heard that the veil between worlds has weakened."

"That stuff your friend at the shop was talking about," Chloe blurted, trying to think back through everything that had been said.

"Oh, Chloe." Ramses walked a few steps away, shaking his head as if she'd just missed the winning goal because she'd done something stupid.

And Helen was now glaring.

Because you just admitted to eavesdropping on her, asshole. "Oh shit." Chloe put a hand over her mouth, but it was far too late.

"So you were following me?" Helen asked. "You're not getting your hands on that wyvern." She drew herself up until she loomed like a coming storm front. "And I want my tarnkappe back."

"I didn't take your—"

"The helmet," Ramses said.

"—anything that I'm willing to give back to you right now," she finished stupidly. "And you can have the wyvern. You keep it away from people, and we won't have a problem."

Helen rolled her eyes so hard, she surely risked a strain. "By people, you mean humans, the only ones who really matter."

"Anyone it could hurt," Chloe said from between her teeth.

"In its condition, it couldn't hurt a fly."

"That's not true, and you know it."

Ramses cleared his throat. "You're starting to attract attention."

Chloe didn't care who was gawking this time. She kept her glare on Helen, wishing she wasn't so easy to keep looking at. Helen glared, too, but there was something in the way her shoulders heaved, her mouth slightly parted, that gave Chloe the feeling that she wasn't wholly angry. The little glance she gave Chloe's lips said a part of her was turned on.

Helen of freaking Troy was into her.

What were the fucking odds?

Chloe suppressed the urge to squeal. Just. She licked her bottom lip, not quite sure what she wanted to happen. Helen took a half step closer, and part of Chloe's brain exploded. Was she about to make out with a pissed-off Helen of freaking Troy right beneath a haunted tree in an apartment complex in Houston that neither of them lived in?

The world was a strange place indeed.

Helen shook her head again as if emerging from a trance. She glanced to the side before taking a step back and smoothing down her already impeccable shirt. Chloe followed her glance to find a kid watching them from the mailbox while eating a small bag of chips. She swallowed the urge to dare him to take a picture. Her luck, he'd put it up on the internet, and her mother would find out she'd been fraternizing with demigoddesses. Fuck, that would be a world of hurt crashing onto her shoulders.

"I'm going to focus on the ghost now," she said quietly.

To her surprise, Helen nodded but only once. "And I have no wish to see any innocent being hurt." But her look said she included much more than humans in that one, no matter how un-innocent they were.

"Is that you offering to help?" She didn't need it, but she also didn't really want Helen to go.

"I'm guessing your ghostly companion spotted something in the limbs of the tree?"

Chloe wanted to believe this was a genuine offer of aid, but her confidence was still a bit bruised from the feigned attention earlier. "I gotta climb it and look." When Helen stared, clearly waiting, Chloe's ears burned. She hadn't climbed a tree in years and didn't want her latest attempt witnessed by the most beautiful woman she'd ever seen. "You can, uh, you can take off. I'll be fine."

Helen smirked but quickly ducked her head and looked a lot less amused when she raised it. "Once you remove whatever's up there, the ghost will vanish?"

"No, the ghost would be forced to follow it and would just move to another figurine or statue if I destroyed this one. That's not a real solution," she added before Helen could suggest it. "A ghost that's summoned can be out of its mind with confusion and anger once it shows itself. Best to put it back to rest."

Helen held her gaze for a long moment, and Chloe resisted the urge to shuffle her feet. "Put it to rest," she said softly, sounding as if she admired that idea.

Even though she should have doubted the genuineness of that admiration, Chloe didn't. The feeling warmed her way more than it should.

"How do you put it to rest?"

Chloe waved vaguely at her bag, not wanting to get into specifics, especially if it might set off another yelling match.

"I feel like I can trust you, Chloe, at least in this."

Her name on those lips? She could've swooned. "To banish ghosts? Hell yes."

That earned her another small smile. She turned as if to go. "But our discussion about the creatures of the world is to be continued."

Whenever you want, babe. But she couldn't muster the courage to say it, could only wave dumbly as Helen left.

Chapter Fourteen

Ramses was conspicuously silent as Chloe removed the figurine from the tree. It proved to be of a woman in a dress from the early nineteenth century, though Chloe didn't recognize her. As she'd hoped, moving the figurine prompted the ghost to show herself. Her ringlets and clothing reminded Chloe of Ada Lovelace, and she hoped to God this wasn't her. Especially after Ramses tackled her into the bushes while she growled like an animal, her eyes wide, teeth bared. She had to have been summoned very recently to be so out of her head.

Chloe banished her quickly, hoping the kid with the chips hadn't wandered into the shrubbery to watch.

Afterward, Ramses stayed silent on the way to the museum. It closed at six, but they had just enough time to take a tour of his exhibit and find someplace to hide and wait for their second ghostly target.

"I know you're dying to say something," Chloe said as they parked.

"You already know what I'm going to say. If she doesn't approve of what we do, that makes her our adversary." He gave her a look down his nose.

"And I shouldn't be…admiring her."

He snorted. "Wanting to admire her naked, sure."

"Oh my freaking God, Ramses." Though now that she'd started to imagine it…

He only snorted again.

Inside the museum, he loved the editions to his exhibit as much as Chloe knew he would. He beamed at the short films highlighting various battles and accomplishments, and as usual, he teared up at the little bits about his children and wives, especially his beloved Nefertari. He never spoke about her, and Chloe had been warned never to ask. It was one of the few tips about getting along with him that her mother had shared.

Speaking of. Chloe checked her phone again, but her mother still hadn't called or texted. Chloe had finally texted again, saying she wasn't angry, but they did need to talk. Still nothing. Her last text had been an appeal to just acknowledge that she was all right, but again, nothing.

The minute they were done here, Chloe was going straight back to Austin to check on her, ghosts, monsters, or demigods be damned.

So to speak.

Ramses wore a happy smile as they wandered the rest of the museum looking for any ghostly activity. "Do you sense anything in here?" she asked as they paused near the dinosaurs. She ducked her head as she spoke, not wanting to walk around all day with her phone next to her ear.

"No. Did you notice the error that one video made about chariot combat? On the whole, I was quite pleased, of course, and I suppose some inaccuracies are unavoidable, but maybe you could write a letter suggesting a few changes."

That wasn't going to happen, but it also wasn't like he would have listened if she'd objected.

"I remember driving over this one patch of road between cities. It was so rocky, I thought I was going to vomit from the vibrations alone." He barked a laugh. "I had it fixed, and now people think I improved the infrastructure for altruistic or military reasons, both a bit true, but I really did it so I wouldn't be heaving my guts out when I passed that way again."

Chloe chuckled along with him, but she was starting to get impatient for this ghost to appear so she could find out where her mom was or just begin to sort all the tumultuous emotions brewing in her like a thunderstorm. When closing time rolled around, she was tempted to just leave and hurry back to Austin, but her mother would much rather she do her duty, she was sure.

Ramses short-circuited the electronic lock on one of the Staff Only doors, and Chloe hid behind a lot of boxed-up artifacts, mainly taxidermic animals, by the look of it, until everyone except security went home. Luckily, security relied almost solely on cameras.

Too bad for them, Chloe thought as the overhead lights flickered and died. Ramses would be taking a stroll through the computers and consoles, killing the camera feeds. And the lights, apparently, since red emergency lights switched on in their place.

Of course, now they had to search for ghosts in an empty museum that looked as if it had been painted with blood. Nothing like a horrific hellscape to make ghost hunting less terrifying. The occasional flashlight-wielding guard was almost a relief, even if Chloe had to duck and hide.

Having Ramses at her side made it less spooky, thank goodness, though his sudden appearance made her leap into the air again. "Which way first?" he asked.

The article Chloe had gotten an alert about hadn't mentioned a specific part of the museum, only reporting on strange noises and theorizing about grisly crimes committed on the spot, perhaps a ghastly battle, all the usual nonsense. "It has to be somewhere with a lot of statues," she said. "The regular Egyptian exhibit is a good bet. Our summoner probably thought they won the jackpot. They wouldn't even have to sneak a figurine in."

She hoped like hell that the ghost wasn't anyone in Ramses's family, though most of the statues in his exhibit were of him. Hell, most of the statues in Egypt seemed to be of him. Maybe they'd get lucky and find nothing but a waste of time and have a nice, creepy walk through a museum bathed in red light like a vision of Tartarus.

Fun. Made even more so by the fact that Chloe's mom still wasn't answering her damned phone.

They took another few passes through the Egyptian wing, and Chloe was resigning herself to the fact that they might have to wait for the witching hour when she spotted a flash of light from Ramses's exhibit.

Oh shit.

He didn't speak as they turned in that direction, and it seemed almost inevitable when a dark-haired woman in a pleated white gown walked through the central room. She wore the bird-shaped crown of an Egyptian queen, and her dark skin gleamed even through her ghostly glow.

"Fuck," Chloe whispered. She didn't need to see the beautiful face, clothes, or crown to know who this was or why this mission was so screwed or that Ramses was going to tear the summoner to little pieces. She only thanked God that this ghost wasn't foaming at the mouth like the last one.

"Nefertari," Ramses whispered.

She blinked as if she didn't quite hear him, her eyes on Chloe. The dead were often confused, but she didn't seem angry or even that unsettled for a summoned ghost. Chloe's bullshit meter pinged. This couldn't be what she'd always thought of as a natural haunting. All the times she'd seen this exhibit, and Nefertari only showed up at one of her statues now?

Ramses stepped forward, tears in his eyes. Chloe put an arm out, even though he could walk right through her if he wanted. He stopped and gave her a pleading look.

"She has to have been summoned," Chloe said. "If she was just a wandering spirit, we would have encountered her before now, but look at her. Where's the anger?"

He looked pained before turning thoughtful, then dark blue with rage. "Who would dare?"

Whoever had summoned her wanted to hurt Ramses for sure, but their reasons didn't matter. They were gonna pay big time.

Though something still felt off, Chloe took a few steps closer and decided to play along. "O Queen, who has summoned you from the realm of Osiris?" It was best to lay it on thick with ghosts when one wanted answers, and Nefertari didn't seem inclined to flee or attack. Chloe slipped a hand into her satchel and gripped the baggie of salt and cayenne, ready just in case.

Nefertari cocked her head, delicate brows furrowed. "I await my king."

"I'm here, my love," Ramses said, his voice thick.

Nefertari still didn't look at him. *What the hell?* "He has forsaken me."

"Never, never." He took another step.

Chloe frowned. It was like she couldn't hear him. Or even see him, but ghosts could see one another. They didn't need the god blood that a living person apparently did.

Or a living *creature.*

A living trap.

Chloe chucked the salt and cayenne at Ramses's feet, freezing him in place.

"Chloe," he barked.

She stepped in front of him and glanced at the museum case, the wall, the floor. There, the pattern in the carpet seemed different in one spot, like something added to trap a ghost since there only seemed to be one here. "Who are you?" she said, taking hold of the hunting knife that had recently stabbed a wyvern's ass, but she didn't draw it, not yet. "You're not Nefertari, not a ghost at all."

The faux ghost rolled her eyes. "Don't tell me you didn't even bring your ghost friend." She waved toward where the salt and cayenne had settled on the carpet. "Or does he have something to do with your little spice explosion?"

"An imposter?" Ramses said, his tone freezing the air. "Thrice damned, pox-ridden daughter of licentious pigs! I'll—"

"It's just me," Chloe said, fighting the urge to yell over a litany of insults no one but she could hear. "Why did you lure me here?" She put her hand on her hip, hoping to radiate bravado, maybe get this fake ghost to come out from whatever ghost-harming spell they were currently standing behind. "Well?"

"Oh, for fuck's sake." The faux ghost sighed extravagantly and leaned on the info panel of a small selection of shabtis. "She's gonna be so mad that you didn't fall for the trap."

"Who?"

"Oh well, time for plan B. If she can't have the ghost, she can at least have you." She shook her hair, and her form blurred, shifting like molasses, the glow disappearing as the blur settled into the handsomest man Chloe had ever seen. He should have been featured in the dictionary as such, and not just for his face. His sculpted chest couldn't have been more hypnotic if he'd had pocket watches swinging from his nipples. The rest of him was as perfect, and she could swear to that because he stood as bare as a bullfrog.

He licked his lips and held out a hand. "That's right, darlin'. Drink it all in. Come with me, and I'll fulfill your every desire. If your ghost is on the way, we can await his arrival in whatever way pleases you most." Something roiled out from him, a fascinating collection of delectable scents and a gentle breeze that seemed to carry an enticing hint of desire.

Too bad men had never done anything for her. Overall, it seemed a rather old-fashioned ploy. But she could play his game for answers. She could even take a few tips from Helen's earlier performance.

Thinking about Helen made it easier to open her mouth as if in awe, hoping the red light let her appear flushed and appropriately dampened. "Oh, but I…I mustn't. I don't even know you."

His crooked smile had probably laid many people at his feet. "Then let's get to know each other better." He took the smallest step toward her, still not clearing the marks on the floor, and the fog of scents got thicker. "I'll start. I'm a friendly incubus, irresistible to humans. And you're Chloe, irresistible to me." His eyes burned like stars gone nova.

It was a good show, nothing to raise her temperature, but she couldn't help a certain fascination. She breathed easier when Ramses said, "Just step out of that magic trap, hell spawn."

Chloe backed up a step, into Ramses, knowing he'd get the hint to possess her as soon as the incubus came within reach. She put a hand to her chest and tried to look as though it was taking all her will to resist. "No, this is a trick. You don't want me, you can't. You're so gorgeous." *Barf.* "And I'm—"

"Beautiful," he said, moving a hair closer, his power pulling at her like something akin to gravity, though the flattery was definitely helping her stay in place. "You're breathtaking. I can show you such wondrous heights, Chloe, so much ecstasy."

One more step.

Chloe swayed, keeping her eyes on his hand as if she might succumb at any moment. "You can?"

"And will. Take my hand, darlin'."

"I…"

"Take it."

"If she won't, I will." Ramses merged with her seamlessly just as the incubus's hand passed over the magical marks on the carpet. He grabbed the incubus's wrist and yanked him closer with one powerful pull.

"Hi, I'm Ramses," he said with Chloe's mouth as they stared into an admittedly startling pair of green eyes that were currently very wide. "And I'd like to speak to you about impersonating my wife." He spun, and in one smooth motion, he launched the incubus over Chloe's shoulder to land on the carpet with an *oomph.*

The incubus groaned, half curling into a ball.

"Careful," Chloe said in their mind as Ramses grabbed the incubus's ankles and dragged him farther from the magical trap. "If he made those marks, he has more powers than just shapeshifting and that lust thingy."

"I don't dare ask where he's keeping his magic kit at the moment." Ramses knelt on his chest and held the hunting knife to his throat. "Who are you working with?"

"No one," the incubus said through gasps.

"You said 'she' was going to be mad. Who?"

"I…can't."

"I disagree." Ramses cut him lightly, just shy of the jugular, and black blood dribbled to the floor. Chloe would have winced if she'd had control of her face. "Give me a name."

"No, she'll—"

"Slit your throat? You'd rather I do it? Very well."

"Wait, please." His beautiful eyes were wide, terrified.

"The name."

Chloe focused on the other sounds in the room as the incubus panted. Someone might try to creep up on them while this bastard stalled. Nothing. But they couldn't stay here forever. "Maybe he's connected to the two people who showed up at the barn, the ones who looked like siblings." Or Helen, but she couldn't say that.

"Are you working for the twins?" Ramses asked, clearly wanting the incubus to either correct him or fill in any gaps in their knowledge.

"Twins…yes."

"The blondes?"

"Yes, they're—"

Another cut appeared on his neck, Ramses moving Chloe's hand faster than she ever could. "That's the only lie you'll get."

"I don't know her name."

"Describe her."

His expression grew more afraid, though Chloe wouldn't have thought that possible. "She only speaks through the Lamia, whose terrible power is nothing compared to her mistress, or so I've heard."

If Helen had some terrifying power, surely she would have used it during the whole wyvern debacle instead of letting Chloe get away with a magic helmet. But who else but a demigod could control an incubus and a child-eating, blood-sucking, snake monster like a lamia, the only lamia left from the sound of it.

"And you don't know this mistress's name?" Ramses asked, skepticism dripping from every syllable.

"No." He sagged and seemed like the most pathetic person in the world. "And now I've betrayed her like a coward. You better just kill me."

Chloe would have winced again. "I feel a little sorry for the shitty sex demon."

"I don't," Ramses said both aloud and in their mind. "And if he wants oblivion, we'll let him live for this nightmare mistress to devour." He stepped out of Chloe's body, and she stood, shivering at the cruel satisfaction in his tone.

The incubus stood, too, wiping at the cuts on his neck. "Ramses, I—"

"That's not my name right now," Chloe said. "And you better watch your mouth when you're talking to him, or I'll shove my foot so far up your ass, you'll taste my sneaker." The incubus stared as if she had two heads, but she waved his shock away. "Did you make that ghost trap?"

He nodded. "The Lamia told me how before she ordered me to come here. Over the phone," he added quickly. "I didn't see her or anyone else when I was summoned. It was dark."

"Is she nearby?" Chloe glanced around. She did not want to deal with another monster right now.

"Not that I know of."

"So what were you supposed to do with Ramses or me if you caught us?"

"Use one of the guard's phones to call her. Keep you occupied until she got here." He offered a half leer. "I don't have to check in right away if you want."

"Nah," she said, and that seemed to wound him, but she didn't give a shit. She wasn't waiting around for a lamia or her nightmarish boss. A wyvern had made her current kit look weak. She needed some serious firepower to tackle something even stronger.

Like freaking demons. Though this one didn't seem inclined to leap at her. He just stood there looking awkward. "Are you going to kill me?" he asked softly. "Or banish me?" That was even quieter, like it was the worse choice, though she didn't know how that could be.

"You're not worth the trouble."

Ramses said, "Ha," and followed her out of the exhibit. They needed to find a more discreet exit than the emergency doors.

"Seriously?" the incubus asked as he followed.

"Sounds like the people you work for will take care of you."

"That's really rude, Not-Ramses-Maybe-Chloe, not gonna lie."

"We don't give a shit what you think, Not-Nefertari."

He hugged his elbows as he kept pace, looking a little sheepish. "I admit, that was an asshole move."

"Probably the most honest thing he's ever said," Ramses muttered.

"Look." Chloe paused at the next corner. "Run away, naked demon. Maybe your horrific boss monster won't find you if you hide on the other side of the world."

"The Lamia says she has spies everywhere."

That would explain how Helen had known where the wyvern was, if indeed she was this unseen leader. "I don't care what you do, just go away." But irritatingly, he followed her through an employee exit and out the back of the museum. "Do you need Ramses to kick your ass again?"

"Gladly," Ramses said.

The incubus did that blurry jelly thing and settled as a slightly less handsome man wearing jeans, a T-shirt, and sneakers. "By ancient law, since you spared my life, you're responsible for me."

She snorted and rolled her eyes as she headed toward the pay lot where she'd parked. "Lucky for me, that particular law ain't in the Texas Constitution."

"No, it's far older than that," he said as he jogged to keep up. "I can be helpful."

"Sure, until your mistress shows up. Then you'll turn on us so fast, our heads will spin like one of your forefathers in *The Exorcist*."

"I won't. I promise."

Ramses laughed darkly. "Do we really need to look up demon promises in the dictionary?"

No, they did not. Chloe tried her hardest to ignore the incubus and hurry toward her car. She didn't fear the deserted streets as long as she had Ramses and her magic—and a lust demon, apparently—but she still wanted to get on the road. She'd never been happier to see her crappy old car.

Right up to the point where it exploded.

Chapter Fifteen

Strangely enough, Chloe blamed herself for not predicting that her evening would include Helen of freaking Troy, Nefertari, a sex demon, a lamia, and her car in flames.

Or Ramses knocking said sex demon on top of her as soon as the car exploded. "Sorry," Ramses said. "I thought he might make a good meat shield, at least."

Chloe struggled to her feet past the incubus, who was swearing and demanding to know what had just happened. She wished she had an answer. Her little car, on fire, after all they'd been through together? "What? How?"

"I'm headed in." Ramses marched toward the flaming wreck.

"Be careful," Chloe said weakly. Flames and smoke shouldn't hurt him, but she hadn't thought her car would explode, either.

"Thank you," the incubus said, "though your warning came a little late."

She glared. "I wasn't talking to you."

He jammed his hands inside pockets that hadn't existed until he'd made them. Either he could pull clothing out of the ether, or he was always naked under a glamour. Ugh, she did not have the brain power to ponder that right now.

"Damian," he said. When she stared, he pointed to himself. "My name. Not that you asked."

The hurt in his voice shot right under her skin. "Oh, I'm sorry. I should be more sympathetic since your car just blew up."

He rolled his eyes. "And I am so surprised that you pissed someone off enough to do that. Lack of manners, perhaps?"

"You wanna see pissed off?" she said, unsure what she was going to do, but it was gonna be violent.

"Manners cost nothing." He backed up a few steps "As my mother always said."

"Your mom the demon?"

"She had high ambitions for me in the demon court." He put a small tree between them. "Why do you think she named me Damian? Not just because she's a movie buff."

Chloe's anger began to dip into bizarre confusion. "What the hell are you even talking about?"

He pointed at her and grinned. "I'm distracting you from your grief. See?" He pointed to himself again. "Useful." He looked so proud, she wanted to kick his ass harder. Especially as he'd distracted her from something she definitely should have been paying attention to.

She dipped into her bag for a small bottle of anise oil, plucked out the cork, and flicked it at him. He stumbled back with a cry of pain. Good. She'd always heard that anise repelled demons, but she'd never gotten to—

"Chloe."

She nearly fainted when Ramses appeared next to her. "You have to stop doing that when I'm already rattled."

He waved as if dismissing her objection. "There's very little left. The magic helmet's over there, dented but intact."

Chloe followed him to it and tried to think straight. "Could you tell what happened? And please don't just say my car exploded."

He gave her a flat look. "Sorry, I don't have my CSI kit handy. Someone is either trying to scare you or kill you. They didn't leave any calling card that I could see."

She didn't know what to do, how to feel. There were way too many options. She picked up the dented helmet and considered putting it on, but it wouldn't make what had happened disappear. If someone did pop out and take responsibility, she could rip their face off, but in the long run, that probably wouldn't help.

At least her personal items were all in her magic kit. Except the insurance info in the glove box, a few CDs, and about a buck-fifty in change. Well, that was probably scattered around a few blocks if she wanted to look.

"The police will be on the way," Ramses said.

That was usually their cue to leave, but the cops would no doubt find out it was her car sooner or later, and leaving would raise too many questions. And right now, pleading ignorance was the absolute truth.

Damian came out of hiding just before the police arrived, and Chloe was forced to acknowledge him. She wanted to disavow like crazy—or maybe have him arrested—but one of the primary goals of her family was to keep paranormal shit a secret. Plus, small displays of his power seemed to speed the process along. With or without attraction, people seemed to want to believe whatever he said when he used his magic. Chloe was thankful her god blood seemed to give her some immunity. Or maybe that was her finely tuned bullshit detector.

It was just a bonus that he could hide her magic kit and the helmet with glamour. Maybe he was a little useful. A tiny bit. Microscopically so.

Even with his power—or because of it—the cops seemed to believe Chloe had been wandering the museum district looking for a hookup and had picked Damian up. Their mouths didn't exactly say it, but the double entendres flew fast through the conversation, and the looks going around spoke volumes. She fought the urge to grind her teeth and deny everything.

After several rounds of questions, the cops sent her off with guarantees that they'd be in touch.

Chloe walked away in the pre-dawn with Damian on one side and Ramses on the other. At least one cop smirked after them, and she wondered how much harder he would have grinned if he could have seen both her escorts.

"What are you going to do?" Damian asked.

"Find a way to Austin." And discover what had happened to her mom. She got her phone out and saw she'd have to charge it soon.

Fate made it ring at that moment, "Mom" displayed on the screen.

❖

Traffic was heavier than expected on the way into Galveston. After their pitstop in Houston, it was almost evening when they finally arrived at the marina, though Helen couldn't exactly be sorry to have seen Chloe again so soon.

No, stop right there.

That strange pull between them had been stronger than ever, so much so that Helen had nearly kissed Chloe in front of the ghost pharaoh and who knew how many watching humans. Beyond embarrassing, it was a stupendously bad idea. Could she blame the pharaoh's magic for that?

By all the gods, she could try.

Her attraction couldn't be this strong simply because Chloe was beautiful, though she was. Helen could have spent many hours fantasizing about that body. No, the hum that passed between them, like standing too near a power line? That wasn't due to Chloe's looks or brains or abilities, admirable as they were. And it certainly wasn't a member of the ancient dead.

The blood of Isis? Helen had met actual gods, for Hera's sake, and she'd never felt anything quite like this.

Except maybe that feeling in Egypt, after Menelaus, before Psamathe. At the time, she'd been too emotionally raw to pursue it, but—

"There they are," Ligeia said, shaking Helen from her reverie.

A group of nereids waited by the pier, and Ligeia waved as she climbed out of the truck. At this time of day, there was barely anyone there, and Helen was happy to find everything in readiness to transport the wyvern to the sanctuary.

"I really need to tell the Sphinx how much I appreciate her," Helen said as the team of nereids loaded the tarp-covered wyvern onto the sanctuary's yacht.

"You bring her weed. She doesn't want, like, anything else."

"True." And Helen really wanted to hurry home. She'd add "shitload of cake for the Sphinx" to her next grocery list.

Ligeia pulled her hood up for the short walk to the pier. The yacht had been moored pretty far from the other craft because of its size, but a gang of women muscling something huge onto it seemed to be garnering some attention. Most of the nereids appeared human from a distance—having left off their coral crowns and white robes for board shorts and sports bras—except for those whose coloring tended toward gray and blue. They'd helpfully donned caftans. Their strength should be put down to the fact that there were currently twenty of them and not the fact that they could lift any of the watching humans with one hand.

"It's heavier than it looks," one of them said at the yacht. Her voice was lyrical, singsong almost, with a slight echoing quality as if she was underwater. Helen was grateful for the coral pin sticking through the strap of her sports bra, declaring her to be Maera, current elected leader of the nereids. At least she wasn't Psamathe, the nereid who'd led Menelaus to Helen's door after—

And we're not thinking about that.

Good thing, too. She'd nearly crushed her water bottle. "Thank you for volunteering to transfer it."

Maera nodded. "It's a good break from the sanctuary. And we got to visit some naiad cousins nearby."

"Hear anything interesting?"

"About potential residents for the sanctuary?" She shrugged. "No. Though a passing pod of dolphins heard about a large group of humans who seemed interested in 'the paranormal.'" She rolled her eyes. "But they were light on details."

"Hmm." A group like Fatma's, who thought they were doing the rare creatures of the world a good turn? Or something more sinister? And was the mysterious Chloe part of it with her ghost?

And did Helen need to stop obsessing?

Absolutely yes. "We'll have to keep our ears open."

Helen phoned the moving company to come pick up their truck. The nereids then set sail, steering into the Gulf. The journey to the sanctuary would have taken more than twenty hours on a regular boat, but once they were safely away from shore, most of the nereids leapt overboard. Their magic sped up the currents, carrying the ship faster than it could ever go by engine alone.

They arrived in the Caribbean in around twelve hours. Still dark, but dawn wasn't far off. Despite the hour, the Sphinx met them at the dock, a worried look on her face.

"What's wrong?" Helen jogged toward the boathouse where the Sphinx kept the large gadgets she used to operate the island's technical equipment.

"Hello to you, too," the Sphinx said.

Helen rubbed her temples. "You wouldn't have come down here wearing that look if there wasn't something to worry about."

After a long sigh, the Sphinx nodded inland, and Helen followed her up the shore. "Our smuggler contacts reported a gang of paranormal hunters in the area."

"The nereids heard something similar, and I've been told there are more hauntings in the States lately." She shook off the mental image of Chloe and her fuck-you stare. "Maybe the humans are mounting a defense against the ghosts."

"Whatever they're doing, they're doing it out this way, too. Lots of boats in the area that don't seem put off by the warning buoys, and with the way some of them have been hanging around, they might be able to see through the glamour."

Like Chloe with her blood of Isis. She'd claimed to know who Helen was. Did she know what cause Helen had dedicated her life to?

Maybe she hadn't been interested in the wyvern anymore because she knew she could kill it when she attacked the sanctuary. Helen didn't want to believe it, but… "How close have they gotten?"

"A few miles. I've started regular patrols, but everyone's edgy, and I think some of our…less-agreeable residents might take advantage of any chaos."

Like the Lamia, always looking to make trouble. Helen acknowledged that some of the sanctuary's residents deserved their bad reputations, but she'd never let them be put down like animals.

"We'll keep watch through the night," the Sphinx said, her voice kind. "Get some sleep. I've got a place all ready for the wyvern."

Helen put a hand on her paw. "You're a treasure. I'm going to buy you so much cake."

The Sphinx leaned back with a surprised chuckle. "I mean, I won't say no."

Helen dragged herself up the slight incline from the beach, into the dense foliage of the island, and then along the path to her house. It had been a long couple of days, and she ached for bed, even if her worries wouldn't leave her.

She'd met far too many humans in the past few days, and someone staking out her sanctuary now couldn't be a coincidence. She only felt a little guilty at the hope that Chloe wasn't a member of this latest batch. But she'd never be able to investigate the strange pull between them if they were destined to be enemies.

❖

On the phone, Chloe's mom said, "Oh thank God," at the same time she did, and she was struck by how much her mom had taught her, if only by accident.

Before Chloe had the chance to ask what had happened, report on her own night, or even blurt out anything about gods in the family tree, her mother asked, "Are you safe?" and that panicky note of parental love killed all her resentment.

"My car blew up," she said, hating the tears in her voice but unable to stop them.

"Do you need a hug?" Damian asked quietly.

She held up a hand to stop him and whispered, "I will banish your ass so fast."

He stopped, arms raised as if the offer still stood, and winked. "Stopped you crying, though, right? Use. Full."

"Shut up."

Her mom stopped a barrage of questions in a stunned silence Chloe could feel even over the phone.

"God, no, not you, Mom. I was talking to Damian. He's an incubus." After a beat of silence, there went a different set of questions.

"Sorry, Mom, there's too much to tell in one sitting. Can you get me a ride?"

"David's in Houston right now. I'll call him." But she didn't hang up, as if she was afraid of cutting contact.

Lord, if only Chloe *could* hug someone right now. "Thanks, Mom." She bit her lip, fighting those freaking tears again. "I'm okay. Ramses is with me. We'll be fine."

"Good. Okay. Good." Repeating herself was a sure sign she was frazzled, but she hung up at last, and twenty minutes later, David, one of her mom's old contacts who'd gone on the occasional paranormal hunt with her, showed up in a small electric car barely big enough for the two of them plus a demon and a ghost.

"Hey, Chlo," he said as he got out to hug her. She barely kept herself from leaning into his tall frame. He was only about fifteen years older than her, more like a favorite uncle than a father figure, though she'd known him since early childhood. He smiled down at her, his pale face creased in concern. "Your mom said you had a bit of trouble."

"That's putting it mildly."

He shook Damian's hand after Chloe made introductions, and she could have blessed his heart a thousand times for holding off on the questions until he'd gotten them breakfast from a drive-thru and begun the three-hour drive to Austin.

Chloe charged her phone in the car, called her mom back, and filled in her and David at the same time. They had some news to share, too: seemed like Chloe wasn't the only paranormal investigator who'd been targeted last night, wasn't even the only one the assailants knew by name. For most of the night, Chloe's mom had been helping an old friend who'd been injured outside San Antonio, where she'd also continued the bad habit of leaving her phone in her car. Hence the unanswered calls and texts. Chloe nearly snapped at her for it, but she sounded too freaked out for Chloe to really be angry.

"It sounds like some kind of, I don't know, creature cabal," her mom said. "No one knows who's at the head of it, but they clearly have some powerful magic at their disposal if they're summoning ghosts and making traps."

And blowing up cars, though Chloe supposed they wouldn't need magic for that. She stayed silent, pondering. She'd already shared everything Damian had said. After a glance at the back seat, she regretted that a little. She'd hoped to kick him out of the car at some point, but her mother had insisted she bring him home as "the best lead we have."

He sat beside Ramses, working on his third slushie of the ride. The only reason Chloe could take his nonstop slurping was because she knew her mom wouldn't actually trust him. She'd extract the info they needed one way or another.

Ugh, though. The thought of torture made her queasy.

Or it had for the first two slushies.

After another promise to be careful, Chloe hung up with her mom, and the car was silent for a few moments, everyone seemingly lost in their own thoughts.

"I wonder if I could possess a demon," Ramses said, eyeing Damian dangerously, probably because of the slurping. "I could make him leap out of the car."

Chloe grinned at him in the visor mirror.

Damian caught her look. "What?" He glanced to his right. "Did the ghost say something about me?"

He was sharp, she'd give him that. But… "Not everything is about you."

Though David couldn't see Ramses either, he seemed to guess at what was going on and shook his head. "We don't have to be mean, Chloe."

"Thank you," Damian said pointedly. "Nice to know someone in your circle has manners."

"Ramses can throw you out of the car," Chloe snapped.

Damian crossed his arms and pouted out the window. At least he was quiet.

❖

When they arrived in Austin, Chloe let herself sag against her mom as they hugged hello. She wanted nothing more than to sleep for a few hours, but more of her mom's old contacts had descended on the apartment that morning. Chloe hadn't kept up with many of them after inheriting the family powers. She'd never gotten to know them like Jamie had, as a horde of honorary aunts and uncles, except for David. She leaned on her mom for information as needed, using her as a go-between to her old life and Chloe's new one.

Being surrounded by them felt like being the kid sister again. That burned. She was the one with the goddess-given power, the one connected to Ramses, but they ignored her as they stood around her mom's dinette table, gesturing at a map and placing markers as they gleaned info from cell phones and argued and theorized, Chloe's mother at their head.

"Get in there," Ramses said in Chloe's ear as she loitered near the sliding door to the small balcony.

The way she was feeling, he might as well have told her to leap into an alligator pit. "I can't just, well, I mean, they're…" Scary? Intimidating? They stood shoulder to shoulder, all well-worn jeans and old band T-shirts and leather jackets that had seen better days. Hunting creatures for no other reason than the good of mankind was not a lucrative business—unless one dealt on the black market—and their weathered appearances made her feel even less like she belonged. That and the fact that she was younger than all of them by at least a decade.

"Chlo, you see more paranormal stuff in one day than they do in weeks. You have the blood of a god. You brought home a demon, for the gods' sake."

A demon who was currently imprisoned in the guest bath. Maybe she should haul him out? She tried to feel the sense of pride that followed a mission, but this one hadn't really been successful, had it? She'd abandoned the wyvern and lost her car and scored a magic helmet and an incubus. Childhood insecurities stuck to her like a staticky balloon, and she couldn't just—

Ramses gave her a small shock, and she gasped much louder than she'd meant to, startled more than hurt.

And everyone turned to look.

CHAPTER SIXTEEN

Rumors and alerts came fast and thick, possible sightings of magic swords and griffins and fairies and more ghosts. Helen couldn't help thinking of what Fatma and Ali had said about using the ambrosia to lure out monster hunters. This could be more of the same, she supposed. After being abandoned in the middle of nowhere, they might have redoubled their efforts to catch smugglers and traffickers.

No, something seemed more sinister, like the sudden interest in the sanctuary. Someone was targeting her, trying to lure her out. Someone on the inside? That pointed to one obvious source.

The Lamia.

As usual, Helen heard the Xbox even outside the crypt. The Lamia was one of the few intelligent beings who hadn't come to the sanctuary willingly, forcing Helen to take her prisoner. For her own good, of course, and the good of the world.

The Lamia insisted on living in this stone mausoleum, all decaying statues and moss, instead of the home she'd been offered. If she was going to spend the rest of her days in prison, she'd said, she might as well pretend she was already dead.

Helen knocked as loudly as she could. Also as usual, she got no answer. She cracked open the heavy wooden door. "Lamia?" If she had another name besides her species, Helen didn't know it. She claimed to be the only one of her kind and always used "the" when referring to herself.

"Why even pretend I have privacy?" she called over the sound of her video games.

Gods, that petulant teenage tone. "I'm coming in." Helen followed the sound of a sigh monumental enough to be heard even above the action of the latest first-person shooter.

The foyer of the crypt was small, decorated with one important coffin, the shiny wood topped with a fringed throw and a lamp. Beyond the two columns at the back, the space opened into a larger stone room, one with a worn sofa, TV, a few bookshelves, and a small kitchenette. The chandelier bore a skeleton motif, tying into the niches along the wall, each with its own skull. Helen didn't have the stomach to ask if any of them were real. Too many were disturbingly small.

The Lamia stretched along the sofa, the lower half of her body coiled around several cushions, snake scales glinting in the light like puddles of gasoline. Her top half was as beautiful as always, even with the green skin. She set her controller down and twirled a long strand of midnight blue hair around one well-manicured finger. "To what do I owe the displeasure?" Her smile was mocking, sharp teeth glinting while she batted gold, reptilian eyes.

"Have you heard the rumors about people watching the island?"

The Lamia rose fluidly. She wore nothing but jewelry, including a gold chain around her waist where her two halves met. She always knew how to best showcase her well-muscled—and well-endowed—torso. "Cup of tea?"

"Sure."

The Lamia slithered to the kitchenette, Helen followed, fighting the urge to cross her arms. Everything was a dance in this crypt, and impatience would cost her.

After much rattling of cups and the hiss of the electric kettle, the Lamia finally spoke again. "Something goes wrong here, and I'm your first visit, as usual."

"So something is wrong."

The Lamia smiled over one shoulder. "So I am your first visit."

Touché.

"I have heard some chatter, yes, and as usual, it has nothing to do with me." The Lamia lifted her right hand, showing off the magical golden cuff that kept her from transforming into her even more dangerous form or leaving the island. "Still serving my sentence for existing."

For murdering gods who knew how many humans. "Those villagers nearly killed you before I found you."

The Lamia handed over a cup of tea and thumped the milk and sugar onto the bar separating them before serving herself. "And you thought you'd save them the trouble and kill me with boredom."

No, no, no. She would not be dragged through all this again. "I'm here to talk about the future, not the past."

"You're letting me go?"

"I can't—"

"Then I really don't see what we have to say to each other." She sipped her tea contentedly.

Helen just kept from swearing. Or throwing things. Or both. "And what will you do if a group of humans attacks the island?"

"Defend myself most vigorously," the Lamia said over her cup. She coiled her tail around like a stool and leaned back on it.

"Until they eventually kill you and everyone else?"

The Lamia shrugged, her expression as inscrutable as the Sphinx's was reputed to be, though Helen had a much easier time reading the Sphinx. She should have known that mentioning the welfare of others would get no reaction here.

Although.

"And what of Melusine?"

The Lamia went as stiff as one of Medusa's enemies. Aha, the name of her old flame could still get to her. They'd shared hundreds of years wandering the world, both reptilian in nature, both beautiful women with bad reputations, but Melusine had curbed some of the Lamia's more murderous desires. Until she'd grown tired of living but wasn't quite ready to seek death. She lay sleeping and dreaming in that coffin in the foyer, the throw and lamp atop it a sign of how angry the Lamia still was with her.

Though the coffin remained polished to a high shine.

The Lamia breathed out slowly, nostrils flaring. "Did you ever speak to Psamathe after she fucked you over?"

Touché again. "If Melusine ever wakes, perhaps we should introduce them."

That got the ghost of a smile. "You do like starting wars, don't you?"

Helen had to return the smile even as a millennia's worth of irritation stirred in her. "You honestly wouldn't give a damn if everyone here died, and this place burned to the ground, would you? Is there anything or anyone you'd risk being mildly helpful for?"

"Besides my freedom?"

Helen was about to retort, but the same reasons she'd given a hundred times died in her mouth. Had the Lamia just given her an actual answer? Had she made some sort of deal with outsiders for her freedom?

Or was she merely being an asshole like usual?

"What if I did release you?" Helen asked.

A blue eyebrow twitched. It felt like a victory parade with a full marching band.

"We could swear a deal on the River Styx, one that could never be broken lest we be banished to the underworld without even dying." It had been a long time since she'd sworn an oath, but it might work. "I let you leave, and you swear to stay close and guard the sanctuary."

"Sanctuary," she muttered with a humorless laugh. But she sipped her tea, eyes on the floor, clearly thinking. "The guardian Lamia?" she asked with a double helping of sarcasm.

"Why not? After thousands of years, you have to be bored of the same murderous routine." Melusine certainly had been, but Helen wasn't about to bring her up again if they were making progress.

"You'd be surprised how much life that idea still has in it." She flashed a fang, no doubt proud of the pun. "And why would you trust that I wouldn't exploit every loophole in such an oath?"

"I could always find a priest of Thoth to look it over." No lawyer in the world could hold a candle to a servant of the Egyptian god of scribes.

"Where?"

Well, that was the question. Chloe and her pharaoh sprang to mind. Surely, such a powerful spirit had some connection to the afterlife that awaited him. "Are you interested?"

The Lamia paused, a sign that some small part of the conversation intrigued her. "Yes."

A straight answer at last. Helen had to clench a fist to keep from crowing. "As a gesture of goodwill, can you tell me anything about these people who seem too interested in our island?"

"No."

Couldn't or wouldn't, she'd never say. But if she was in on some scheme to destroy the sanctuary, maybe she'd slow them down now in order to see if Helen was serious about her proposal. "I'll take my leave."

"Why don't you ask one of your pet humans?"

Chloe again flashed across Helen's mind. Perhaps daughters of Isis had the power to particularly stick in one's consciousness. "Like whom?"

The Lamia snorted a laugh as if to say she wouldn't fall for any trick that might expose how much she did or didn't know. "I can't tell them apart."

"Then how do you know I have more than one?"

Another elegant shrug. "Just a suggestion."

Helen left before she rolled her eyes, as usual having more questions than answers after a visit to this crypt. She'd ask the Sphinx to do another sweep for communication devices in the Lamia's lair. Then she'd give some serious thought to the bargain she'd made up on the fly.

And make doubly sure that their least intelligent but most destructive residents were as safely asleep as Melusine.

Chapter Seventeen

Chloe's story came out in a rush: fighting a wyvern and meeting Helen of Troy and stealing a magic helmet and somehow getting attached to an incubus who'd been trying to capture Ramses by impersonating his queen.

It all sounded made up by a particularly imaginative child, and her ears burned through the whole thing.

Luckily, no one smirked or raised an eyebrow. Maybe they were listening, trusting her. Maybe she'd erred in not keeping up with her mother's network. Jamie wouldn't have been embarrassed to speak in front of this crowd, after all. Chloe finished with her chin up.

Until they stared, clearly waiting for her conclusions or thoughts on what to do next. Embarrassment came back like a wave, threatening to knock her off her feet. "Um, yeah. We'll have to do something about that, I think."

Smooth.

"Stick the landing," Ramses said softly, as if they might hear.

Easy for him to say. "Uh, thoughts?"

Extra smooth.

Her mom leapt into the gap. "Someone gave these people your name. This Helen?"

Chloe's neck tingled, a bolt of anger. *This* Helen? As if Chloe had to be wrong about her identity. And no one so hot could be a part of any plan to murder her.

God, she hoped not.

"What about the rest of us?" Jillian, one of her mom's oldest friends, asked. Her salt-and-pepper hair was pulled back under a bandana, effortlessly cool. "No one dropped our names at the wyvern barn."

"I've heard of the dark-haired humans who showed up with guns," David said, rubbing his chin. "Sounds like Fatma and Ali Kareem. Siblings, artifact hunters, though it's unusual to find them going after living things. They're all about returning antiquities to their countries of origin."

Everyone fell into a debate about who might know what, and Chloe was about to succumb to her insecurities again, but her mother was staring at her. She had a small smile, and despite her obvious doubts about Helen's Troy-ness, she seemed…

Proud?

Happiness bloomed in Chloe like spring, and she could have carried the entire apartment on her back without the helmet.

"I think it's time to find out what else our demon knows," her mom said.

Everyone hushed at the sound of her voice, and Chloe wondered if she'd ever achieve that gravitas. Even if she did, would people listen to her like that?

Well, they were all staring at her again. Right. She could do this. "Cool," she said stupidly. "I'm immune to him, so I should be the, um." She cleared her throat. "Yeah."

Jillian took a huge knife from her belt. "Here. In case he needs extra persuading."

Chloe swallowed a rush of bile. Torture had sounded justified in her imagination, but she was not cutting bits off anyone in real life. "Um, no, thanks." She patted her bag. "I've got plenty of persuasion between me and Ramses." And she'd fixed up something special just for demons.

With a shrug, Jillian put the knife away. "Holler if you need help, kiddo."

Trying not to smart at the nickname, Chloe fled to the guest bath. Strange how the idea of speaking to a demon felt infinitely easier than talking to people she'd known since childhood.

When Damian stood from where he'd been sitting on the closed toilet, his tanned face anxious, Chloe's confidence rushed back, leaving her a bit giddy. "It's your lucky day," she said. "They've decided you can be useful."

He sighed and sagged, his relief almost tangible. "Good. Thanks. My mom would kill me if I was banished so quickly after my first job up top."

"No problem." If he wanted to feel indebted to her, she intended to let him. "We need info if you want to stay un-banished."

"Do with me as you will." He spread his arms and added a wink.

She wanted to *tsk* but had a sudden doubt. What if this was what she was supposed to do: dismiss him, underestimate him. His realm was known as a place of deception. And that was a game she was too tired to play right now. "Why are you being so helpful? And don't give me any bullshit about not wanting to disappoint anyone or staying up here. You could have stayed safe just by going your own way in Houston."

"I told you. My employers—"

"Don't sound like people who'd hire a pushover."

His dark eyes flashed red, a bit of demon coming through. "They didn't think you'd be immune to me, obviously."

"Why not? They know my name, know about Ramses. They did some of their homework. Why put all their eggs in one ineffectual basket like you?"

Ramses chuckled from where he stood at Damian's shoulder. "Get him, Chloe."

Damian frowned, his body tense as a wire. Chloe slipped a hand in her bag, right into the glove she had waiting. She wasn't worried about him hurting her. Ramses could possess her in an instant, and the crowd in the living room could handle one demon.

But no one would have to save her with the tricks she had up her sleeve.

"Insulting my kind is not a good idea." Damian's voice was quiet, gravelly, and Chloe wondered if his helpful, slushie-loving side was just another type of seduction designed to make her sympathetic, to cast herself in the big sister role if she wouldn't play the ardent lover.

But Chloe hadn't forgotten anything she'd learned about the life that had been thrust upon her. To get to a demon's core, a person only had to poke their ego. "Why can't I insult you, pathetic as you are? You're dependent on me now, right? On the lam from your employers, can't run home to Mom. By those ancient laws you referenced before, I'm responsible for you, but you're also my servant."

Ramses moved to Chloe's side as Damian's eyes lost the white and iris, consumed by scarlet light. "I am no one's servant."

"Well, at least I didn't say you're my bitc—"

His human mask dropped, power roiling from his heartbreakingly beautiful body, crimson skin shining, bat wings nearly filling the room behind him. He bared gleaming white teeth and leaned forward.

Chloe couldn't help a smirk as she drew out an iron pentacle dripping with anise oil and held it aloft in her gloved hand. Damian drew back, hissing, maybe from the oil or the holy pagan symbol or the cold iron it was made from.

She advanced, Ramses at her side, crackling with power that seemed to fill the room with ozone. "Who are you?" she demanded.

He tripped over the lip of the shallow tub and toppled, arms flailing, wings folding behind him in a painful-looking tangle. He caught the shower curtain and pulled half of it down across his chest, the dolphins leaping across it sitting sadly in his lap. "D…Damian."

So he'd given his real name, or at least the one he was allowed to give outside his home plane. Another bit of cockiness? "Who do you work for?"

"The Lamia."

"And?" She stepped closer, the pentacle cutting through his power like a knife.

He lifted a hand to shield his eyes. "The…I…"

"Who?"

"I don't know," he screamed.

And burst into tears.

Chloe stepped back, stunned. "What the hell?" Another trick? She lifted the pentacle higher, but her heart wasn't in it, couldn't be with a demon sobbing in her mom's guest tub.

"Are you satisfied?" Damian asked, blubbering wet, snotty tears. He still looked cute but sad, like a soggy kitten. "These people summoned me and told me what to do and say, but I don't know who they are, and I think they set me up to fail for some reason, and I'm only now realizing it, and I'm pathetic just like you said. Okay?" The words came out in a rush, getting higher as he went. He took a shuddering breath and managed several octaves more. "And they knew that!" He curled in on himself, weeping, one wing falling half over his black hair.

"Oh." Chloe looked to Ramses, but he mashed his lips together, eyes wide, looking as embarrassed as she felt. "Uh." Damian was either a really good actor or he actually was, well, pathetic. She glanced at the pentacle. He shouldn't have been able to lie in front of a holy symbol and oil and iron. "Hey, bud, it's okay," she said slowly, feeling awkward as hell.

He hiccupped. "No, it's not. Just banish me already so I can go home and face humiliation." He sighed as if the world sat atop him along with the leaping dolphins. "I can't tell you anything, and I'm useless as a..." He lifted his arms, dropped them. "I can't even think of anything." He dissolved into tears again.

"A hat in a hurricane?" Chloe supplied, desperate to defuse the tension.

"Condoms in the Vatican?" Ramses said.

Chloe snorted, repeating that one as she chuckled. "A raincoat for an alligator?"

"Oh, sure," Damian cried over their mirth. "Laugh it up, you soulless harpy."

Chloe put a hand on her hip. God, it had been a weird couple of days, even for her. "Hush. Your 'employers' can't get at you in an apartment full of monster fighters. And you're not banished. Yet."

He hiccupped again and stared as if she had hope shining from every pore. "You're not going to?"

She sat on the toilet lid, hoping she wasn't going to regret this. "Tell me everything from the beginning."

Chapter Eighteen

The nereids seemed to have new info by the hour, mostly gleaned from passing whales or dolphins, but it was difficult to sort fact from fiction. Different whale species had far-ranging personalities: humpbacks were optimists who tried to see the good in everyone; orcas were pranksters; sperm whales were braggarts, easily goaded; and narwhals hated everyone until their loyalty was won, and then they would follow a friend into hell.

Those were just to name a few. Dolphins had their own spin on events, and even the nereids couldn't always unearth the unvarnished truth.

Helen had her head in her hands as she sifted through reports in her large solarium. It was like her world had decided to go insane overnight. When someone cleared her throat, she didn't want to look up, but everyone was relying on her to—

Psamathe stood in front of the coffee table, her skin and hair shining like a lustrous pearl, beautiful as the day she'd betrayed Helen's location to Menelaus and led dozens of humans to her door.

Catapulted back in time, Helen could feel her heart sinking just like when the sails of her husband's fleet had come into view in Egypt. She'd sent a glamour-made copy of herself to Troy, using the opportunity to flee a marriage that had become bondage. In Egypt, she'd felt a pull that reminded her now of Chloe, but she hadn't explored it then, figured it must have been leading her to Psamathe, passionate and wild, a hurricane of emotions. They'd fought like tempests before crashing back together, over and over, but they couldn't decide what their immediate future held, a stupid question for beings who were practically immortal.

Psamathe had wanted the pledge of a lifetime of love, and Helen hadn't been able to give it, not again, not so soon after Menelaus, himself a demigod. She'd found his immunity to her seductive powers attractive at one time, a sign that he'd truly loved her. But, no, he'd only wanted to own her, and ultimately, Psamathe had wanted the same.

Helen pushed to her feet, her memories beating inside her brain like a hammer. For the first time in her life, she wished the Lamia was beside her. Maybe she would have dragged Psamathe off to Melusine's coffin, after all.

Psamathe lifted one long, slender hand. "Before you tell me to get out—"

"Get out."

With a deep breath, Psamathe crossed her arms over her silken shift. Irritation replaced some of the trepidation in her turquoise gaze.

Helen's heart surged, all the anger she'd claimed to have dealt with boiling over and naming her a liar. "Leave." She didn't recognize the ragged voice as her own.

"The other nereids are busy, but we had to tell you—"

"Tell the Sphinx."

"I couldn't find—"

"No excuses." Helen's godhood rose, flooding the solarium with golden light. "Go."

But Psamathe fell to her knees, the power clearly stealing her air. If only Helen could have done this to her before she'd had a chance to send a message to Menelaus. If only Helen's power had worked against him like this.

Psamathe had known it wouldn't, had counted on it. She'd wanted Menelaus to drag Helen away, wanted to see her humiliated, thinking that a just revenge for Helen's reluctance to tie their futures together.

No matter what it meant for the sanctuary, in this moment, Helen was not going to let her forget what she'd done.

But if she wanted Psamathe to leave, she'd have to curb her power.

No, not this time. "Crawl," she said, her voice a jagged shard. "If you can't run."

"Remora Island," Psamathe cried. "A human encampment. We tracked one of their boats."

Ah, she still cared about the sanctuary enough to pass on information under a barrage of Helen's power. Maybe she had learned how to think of others in the last few millennia. It was almost enough to turn Helen's power down.

Almost. "Go."

Psamathe got her feet under her enough to scuttle for the door before she ran.

Helen slumped onto the divan, her power leaving her as if through a drain in her soul. She balled her hands, past and present anger and frustration colliding into a knot of tar in her chest. Fighting to breathe, she vowed that she wouldn't weep.

She. Would. Not.

"Whoa." The Sphinx's cry saved her from the tears marching inexorably up her throat. "You okay, Hel?"

She exhaled slowly, her limbs like lead. Stupid to use what power remained to her so frivolously. "Psamathe was here. After having to spar with the Lamia, it was too much."

"Wait, Psamathe?"

"Please don't say her name."

The Sphinx tucked her legs under her and sat like a housecat. "I'll have a word with Maera. Ps—some nereids shouldn't be anywhere near this house."

Helen took another deep breath and another, counting her heartbeats, feeling a bit ashamed now, both of her display and the gossip that would spread through the nereids like oil on the surface of the waves, then be carried around the world by every mammal in the ocean. "It has been a long time," she said, blaming her aching throat for the way her voice wavered.

"Not fucking long enough." The Sphinx's eyes blazed. "Give the word, Hel, and I will skin that traitorous fish alive."

Helen's anger abated, both at her circumstances and herself. "I can always count on you. Thanks."

"Don't mention it." She nudged Helen's leg gently with one enormous paw. "I swept the Lamia's crypt. No phones, no radios. The only electronics are some appliances, lamps, her TV, and her game console."

Forcing her tired brain to work, Helen considered those. "Could she be talking to someone through the console?"

The Sphinx tilted her head, dark eyes crinkling. "Like, 'Hey, gamers, I'm actually a legendary Lamia, and I need some conspirators to help me destroy a sanctuary for mythical creatures run by a well-known demigod'?"

Helen didn't have the energy to smile. "No?"

"Eh, it could work." The Sphinx chuckled. "I guess she could work up to it, but how would anyone believe her?"

Helen didn't know, didn't really know how communication worked over a console. "I need to get out there, to Remora Island where these humans might be hiding."

"These humans being the bomb-toting bastards circling our sanctuary?"

"You don't know that they have bombs."

The Sphinx rolled her eyes. "I'm not sure of their legitimacy, either, but I'm willing to place a bet. Helen, you're not going out to fight them yourself."

Helen's ego flared, a bit of anger left, after all. "I'm not helpless."

"Or bulletproof."

"We have weapons and defenses."

"That we should use from the cover of our island."

"Sphinx." Helen rubbed the bridge of her nose, trying to think and feel past the fatigue. "If we launch an attack from here, they'll retaliate. I won't give them an excuse to hurt anyone."

"Now you're not even counting yourself as anyone?" The Sphinx frowned hard, though her body had gone as still as her namesake statue.

"You know what I mean," Helen said, loving her even while thoroughly irritated by her.

"If you die, Hel—"

With a groan, Helen pushed back into the cushions. "What will happen to the sanctuary? Sorry, that guilt trip is not going to work. I know you're trying to protect me."

"Doesn't make it any less true." The Sphinx's voice finally rose as she stood, cutting as imposing a figure as she had in ancient Thebes.

But Helen was too tired to be anywhere near intimidated. "Please verify with Maera that the Remora Island tip is true. I'll head over in the morning." She held up a hand when the Sphinx took a deep breath. "Just to reconnoiter, I promise."

"By yourself?"

"Well, I'll need some help getting there."

The Sphinx settled again, a gleam in her eyes. "Of course."

Helen frowned. The Sphinx's craftiness hadn't deserted her any more than her ability to be impressive. "You have someone in mind."

"You'll need to go by sea, stealthily, no Pegasus. Maera and a few nereids, perhaps Ligeia. Nothing beats the combination of strength and hypnotic powers."

It sounded reasonable. So far.

"And a fey presence to keep you under the cover of glamour."

"Okay," Helen said slowly. Invisible allies were always appreciated, but this sounded like more than she wanted. "Anyone else? Navy SEALS? Brass band?"

"You need backup, or you can't go. I will sit on you if I have to."

And she would. And the power remaining to Helen might not be enough to shift her. She would have to use that just to breathe. "Nereids, Ligeia, fey. Fine. They're all very capable."

The Sphinx flashed a bright smile. "Capable enough to go without you."

"Not happening." Helen narrowed her eyes. "I'll sit on you, too."

The Sphinx returned her look. "Bring it on, sis."

Helen couldn't help a smile. "Or I can cut off your weed supply."

"Oh, such an asshole move. And may I point out, my supply will also be cut off if you die."

"Aha, now I see what you're worried about."

They both chuckled. Helen was full of shit, and the Sphinx knew it, just as Helen knew the same about her. Affection filled the air between them like the warmest blanket.

"I'll be careful," Helen said softly. She'd never throw her life away.

"You bet your ass you will." The Sphinx smiled resignedly, clearly knowing that no lives would be thrown anywhere, but she also knew that Helen would sacrifice herself for the sanctuary if it came to that. And Helen would also do everything in her power to make sure it didn't.

Chapter Nineteen

D amian seemed determined to prove his usefulness by giving an extremely detailed account of how he was summoned and what he could glean from the dark, haze-filled ritual. "I swear two of the voices were female. There may have been others, but no one else spoke."

"But you talked to someone over the phone who claimed to be a Lamia and told you some all-powerful person was at the heart of the orders?"

"Most of that I overheard." He perched on the edge of the tub, his human guise firmly in place, and his glamour clothing back on. Chloe found herself hoping it was real clothing even more now. Otherwise, his ass would be freezing.

Not that she cared. She shook the thought away. "And you assumed this powerful person was…"

"Dunno." His gaze went far away. "It was warm where they first summoned me. Humid."

"Houston?"

"No, no, I felt the magical shift in energies as they sent me there. The original place felt more…tropical. Closer to equatorial ley lines."

Leaning against the wall, arms crossed, Ramses scoffed. "What does a minor demon who's never been summoned to this realm know of its climate or magical resonance?"

Chloe repeated the question, though with a bit more tact.

Still, Damian scowled at the bathroom as if sensing Ramses's scorn. "Every demon studies this realm. One doesn't acquire true power in Hell until one causes a bit of mischief up here."

"Mischief?" Ramses straightened, power flaring. He clearly hadn't forgiven Damian for the whole Nefertari incident.

Chloe held up a hand. "Settle down."

Damian's wide-eyed gaze darted around the room this time. "What is it? What's he doing?"

"Just...shush," Chloe told him. She gave Ramses a look, and his power slackened a little. She was skeptical of Damian's info, too. After his tearful confession, his eagerness grated a little, and someone so obviously desperate to prove his worth might invent more than report. "You're sure about this whole ley line thing?"

"Definitely."

She waited.

He blinked. "Probably."

She rubbed her chin and thought. Some creatures were sensitive to ley lines, the invisible strings of power that were said to circle the earth, and some could use the lines to enhance their abilities. Anyone who wanted to summon a demon would be a fool not to seek out every magical enhancement they could find.

"If I showed you a map of ley lines, do you think you could pick it out?" When he opened his mouth, she held up a hand. "Think about it first. Your life doesn't depend on just one question."

He dipped his chin. "Well...I think I'd have to feel it to be sure, but it was powerful. Ley lines pass through multiple planes of existence, and I'm sure I've felt this one before. It's powerful."

Those running near the equator would certainly qualify. Chloe put her head back and sighed. "There's a whole lot of world near the equator. And a lot of it is hot and humid. What about this spell they cast to send you to Houston? Could you tell how far you traveled?"

Again, he seemed to want to leap to an answer. Again, she urged him to shut his yap and think for a minute. That feeling of schooling a little brother came rushing back to her, and she hoped like hell that he wasn't a trap. Both for her own sake and because, against her better judgment, she liked him. She didn't want to keep him around forever—certain Ramses would peel his skin off eventually—but she could stand working with him for a little longer.

"I got the feeling that it was around the same time of day."

"How do you know?" Chloe asked before Ramses could. "You were summoned in a dark room and never left it."

He shrugged. "I sensed it."

Some innate power? A demon instinct? There was too much they just didn't know.

Damian said that he'd reappeared in some back room of the museum in the middle of the night, and that he'd been camping back there for a week and a half, using glamour to hide and haunting the exhibits enough to start internet rumors about ghosts.

It seemed like a long shot, but it had worked in the end. Chloe's mom's friends had confirmed that these sorts of traps were popping up all over, some sounding as personal as the attack on Chloe and Ramses. She wondered if there were other traps out there waiting for them that hadn't gone off yet, contingencies in case the Houston one failed. That plan did seem sloppier than some of the others.

Unless it had been designed to be.

And Damian was a plant.

"Ugh." Chloe stood and put a hand to her forehead. She could talk herself in circles all day. "I need to think about this, need to talk to the others." She stretched her neck. "Need to get some sleep." Eyes closed, she put a hand up in Damian's direction. "If you offer to give me a massage, so help me God—"

"I won't," he said quickly. "I wasn't." But when she looked, he seemed sheepish and shrugged again. "What can I say? I gotta be me."

She snorted. "Maybe one of the others will take you up on that."

He brightened ridiculously. "Really? You think so? Ask them. I promise, they won't regret it," he called as she left and shut the door behind her.

Ramses passed through it to stand beside her in the hall. She tilted her head toward the guest bedroom, wanting to talk with him before she filled in everyone else. "You don't believe him," he said when they were alone.

"Not entirely. But you saw the same display as me. Think he could act that well before the pentacle and your power?"

He sighed. "I've only ever fought a handful of demons, and not one of his kind." He worried his lip. "And the pentacle may have helped, but the real power comes from you. From us. Don't forget that."

She squinted. "You mean, stuff like that works better when we're using it?"

"Perhaps. But it's the bloodline that counts. The tools are mostly"— he waved vaguely—"window dressing."

Her world tilted slightly off its axis. "I'm sorry, what?" All the drills her mother had made her go through, all the pages of memorization, the crash course she'd taken in herbs and lore and various pharmacopeia.

"What are you saying? The rowan branches, the pentacle, the salt and cayenne, the nails?"

"Helpful, most of them. And some regular humans have used them quite successfully. Salt and cayenne against ghosts, cold iron against fey and demons, but a regular human couldn't manage the feats you can."

Disbelief warred with anger and a deep dread, all of it magnified by the lead ass of fatigue. She couldn't decide whether to feel proud or like a giant fraud. "I could have been doing banishing and all this shit with no tools at all? What the fuck, Ramses?"

He looked a little sheepish as he shrugged. "What? I thought you'd be pleased."

"Oh, sure, turn my world upside down and be pleased." She rubbed her hands down her face. "Why are you telling me this now?"

"I was hoping to give you a boost of confidence, but..." His smile was full-on embarrassed. "That was obviously my bad. You can still use the tools," he said, desperately cheerful. "They do help with focus. You can question Damian again with the pentacle showing. That might work better. Who knows?"

If the contents of her magic bag were a fat lot of window dressing, she could question him while holding a goddamned spatula, and it would do the same amount of good. But Ramses looked contrite enough, and she couldn't say any of that out loud. Instead, she snorted. "You really want to watch him bawl again?"

"No, that was too pitiful. Even after what he did." He fell backward to hover just over the bed and laced his hands over his bare stomach. The striped nemes on his head gave way to his hair, a sure sign of the king giving way to the more human side. "And I know you've been having the same thoughts as me about whether he's bluffing and if he suspects that we know and what we can do if we know he suspects that we know..."

She chuckled tiredly and sat on the quilt-covered hope chest at the foot of the bed. "Yeah." God, she really just wanted a few hours sleep, but the others were out there waiting for her and—

No, they weren't waiting for her as much as they were waiting for something to do.

"Hell," she said, laughing, her mood lifting a bit. "We don't have to think this through by ourselves for once." She stood but paused. "Do they know about the whole window dressing thing?"

"Your mom does. I don't know if she told the others." He rose to his feet in the middle of the bed. "I'm sorry I blurted it out like that, Chlo."

"Don't worry, I'm not going to drop Hulu or anything." But she smiled so he'd know she'd never really stay mad at him.

For long, anyway. She couldn't help seeing all her powerful tools as junk now. Still, she wouldn't be leaving them behind anytime soon. No matter what else they did, they helped her focus.

As Chloe delivered the rundown in the living room, her mom's friends migrated back to the table and the maps and books. She tried to pool all the confidence that Ramses insisted she had somewhere inside, and childhood insecurities felt easier to ignore in the face of fatigue. That, and she felt a lot more take-charge and kick-ass as they flipped through books or took to the internet at her request.

That gleam of pride was still in her mother's eye, too, and Chloe nearly leapt over the table and hugged her when she said, "Good work, Chlo. Go get some rest."

Earlier, she might have taken that as a dismissal to "let the grown-ups talk," but now it sounded more like she wanted their best fighter to get enough sleep before the big tournament.

She paused before leaving. "Oh, and Damian said that if anyone wants any, uh, company, he'd welcome the chance to, you know, show you what he can do." God, her exhaustion was overriding any sense that life ever gave her. But she'd told him she'd ask. Embarrassment threatened to override her other feelings, and she had to stare at the wall, cheeks burning. "You'd have to protect yourselves, but ah…"

Nope, that sounded too much like she was about to start handing out contraceptives to people her mother's age.

She donned her glove again, pulled the pentacle out and laid both on the glass cabinet that housed her mom's Cats of the World collection. "I'm just gonna leave these here in case…yeah." She fled to the guest bedroom, nearly slamming the door behind her. She ignored Ramses's amused look as she flopped on the bed this time and tried to hurry herself to sleep.

CHAPTER TWENTY

Helen took a cup of coffee and a pastry into the solarium in the morning and tried not to yawn her head off. A text from the Sphinx said it had been sent at six in the damned morning. No matter how late Helen went to bed, the Sphinx always managed to get up before her. She hoped it was some ingrained habit to rise with the dawn and not a sign that the Sphinx's arthritis was worse in the morning.

The Lamia said to tell you, "I accept," the text said. *What the hell did you offer her?*

Helen drummed her fingers on the arm of the sofa before she replied. *That I would set her free if she swore an oath to protect the sanctuary.*

A moment later, three little dots appeared as the Sphinx was responding. They vanished, only to reappear a second later before vanishing again.

Helen rolled her eyes. *You don't have to delete all your bad language,* she typed.

Fuck.

That's better.

What the actual fucking fuck are you thinking, Hel?

She started to respond, then slipped the phone in her pocket, wanting to gather her thoughts before responding to every worry she'd already had. She messaged Maera to gather five nereids—*not* Psamathe—and meet her at the solarium at ten. She sent a similar message to Ligeia and Maurice, inviting them on the little adventure to Remora Island, a supposed gathering place of the humans who seemed to be taking a sudden interest in the sanctuary.

By the time she switched back over to the Sphinx's texts, seven were waiting for her:

That is a bad idea on so many goddamned levels. Do I have to spell them out for you?

Number one, she'll betray you. Two, she'll betray you. And three, she will fucking betray you!!!

Are you not texting back because you know I'm right?

She's the Lamia, Helen. Betrayal is in her bones.

You better answer, or I'm coming over there.

Hello? Did you go hang out with your new best friend, and she fucking betrayed you and ate you?

I swear by Osiris, if I get there and you haven't been eaten...

Helen sighed and was halfway through texting back when there was a loud knock on the solarium door. A large shadow stood outside, one paw raised. The Sphinx only knocked with one claw, but it was more than enough to make every pane of glass rattle.

Helen gripped her phone and thought about pretending she'd already left, but she would have to face this music sooner or later. She hit the switch, and the section of wall began to retract, revealing the Sphinx's scowling face.

"I was writing Maera and the others and didn't see your new texts," Helen said before the Sphinx could start. "I haven't been eaten, and the Lamia is not my new best friend."

The Sphinx raised her brows.

"And yes, I fully expect her to betray me."

The Sphinx sat on her hind legs, her tail wrapped around her front paws like a housecat awaiting—no, demanding—a treat.

"Any agreement between us will be looked over by a priest of Thoth."

The Sphinx tilted her head back, frowning and regarding Helen as she might a particularly troublesome problem. But at least she wasn't yelling. "And where will you find one?"

"I hoped you'd know one."

"So you did plan on telling me about this?"

"Of course. Besides the uber lawyer, you're the only one I'd trust to read such an agreement." And if they were dipping their toes into the Egyptian afterlife, maybe they could ask Chloe's pharaoh.

And Chloe, of course, not that Helen had been thinking about her a lot, like as she went to sleep. And in her dreams. And just a tad when she woke up.

The Sphinx didn't lie down, but her chin did inch a few degrees lower. "I might know some people."

Helen smiled. Victory.

"But you shouldn't have agreed to anything with her."

"I didn't. It was only a proposition, nothing she can hold me to." She tucked one leg under her on the sofa. "But if we could pull this off, Sphinx."

"Then the sanctuary will be safe, but the seas around us will be red with human blood?"

"Let's focus on the positive. The sanctuary would be safe." The Sphinx shook her head as if she might argue, but Helen leapt ahead before she could. "And it's a conversation for the future, anyway. Today is about recon."

❖

Chloe woke from dreams of Helen, no doubt after getting in a little research on her phone before she'd drifted off. The more she'd read, the more her admiration had grown, and the more Helen seemed yet another woman maligned by myth, doomed to have "of Troy" follow her for all eternity. If she turned out to be the bad guy, life was gonna suck so hard.

The fact that someone like Helen could find Chloe even passing interesting? Part of her was beyond flattered and wanted to jump at the chance if given one. Another part worried that Ramses was right, that she and Helen might find themselves on opposite sides of the ol' supernatural conflict again. A third part, a nasty little fucker that wanted her self-esteem to be lower than pond scum, said that any interest Helen had ever shown was a goddamned lie, no matter the evidence of Chloe's own eyes.

Too bad the third part was in charge of her dreams, and any sexy times she might have enjoyed had been interrupted by monsters and school bullies and the traumatic memory of the day she'd gotten lost in Target.

She shook off the grim thoughts and stumbled to the living room to find that her mom and friends had not been idle. After making a study of ley lines, they'd narrowed the choices of where Damian was summoned. The good news? They were down to three possibilities. The bad? They were all in or near the freaking Caribbean, over a thousand miles away.

Well, Chloe had wanted to combine a work trip with a vacation, and the Caribbean sure beat Nowhere, Texas. But how to get there? And fast. There had been several more attacks on folks who fought against the paranormal, and Chloe was anxious to follow any leads before someone else got hurt.

Everyone mulled over the question, and an uneasy silence descended in her mom's apartment. Chloe had strategically refused to notice that the pentacle had been moved and tried hard not to think about why, but as the silence stretched on, she eyed everyone around the table. Who was the likeliest to have availed themselves of Damian's skills? She tried to imagine someone her mother's age—

Nope.

Could it have been her mom who—

I said, nope.

Did David look a little more invigorated than the others?

Nope, nope, nope.

"There's a dealer in San Angelo who claims to have part of the golden fleece. Doesn't it give someone power over the wind?" David asked, prompting Chloe's brain to continue processing the notion that a few hours with Damian could jumpstart the mind.

Or other parts.

Oh, fuck you, Brain of Asshole-ishness.

Derisive snorts sounded from every corner, interrupting her thoughts. "We've all heard that rumor," Chloe's mom said.

"It's total bullshit," Jillian added. "But a ship is a better idea than a plane. We'll never get the gear we need through security on a commercial airline."

The window dressing gear? Chloe kept her mouth shut but sneaked a look at Ramses. He shrugged. If they relied on the tools, they had to be good for something, right?

"Well, unless someone knows anyone with a private plane," David said, "a boat is our only option."

Snorts abounded again. None of them were private plane folk.

But Chloe might know someone who had fast transportation. Fatma and Ali were renowned for traveling the world collecting magical artifacts; they had to have a way to move them. Maybe they even used some of them for that very same purpose.

"Let's bring in Fatma and Ali Kareem," she said.

Her mother blinked at her, and Chloe felt the weight of all the eyes in the room. They were a tight network, and no one new had been brought in for a long time. Even Chloe's skin itched at the idea of revealing who she was, what she did. The secret was paramount.

But sometimes, shit needed to change.

After a few beats, her mother beckoned her into the hall while the others began sorting through information again, looking for contact numbers. "Are you sure about this?" her mom asked.

Chloe fought the urge to bristle and bluster as the child inside her wanted to. In a flash, she hit upon an answer that would explain her reasoning and check all her mom's boxes. "It's about time I started building my own network, right?"

As she suspected, that changed the tune; her mom brightened and nodded thoughtfully.

"And it's not like the whole paranormal world is a secret to them. We might not always be on the same side, but in this instance, I think we'd make good allies."

Even if it turned out that Helen was the enemy here? The idea made her a little queasy. She still couldn't see the same woman who'd "freed" her from Ramses and then knelt over her with a warm, caring expression as someone who'd orchestrate calculated attacks on various humans. Like blowing up their fucking cars.

Then again, she didn't really know Helen, not beyond the myths and stories. Perhaps she was as capricious as the wind, though that image did not gel with the one in her mind of the protective goddess who could command a room—or a field—with her presence alone. With those heaving shoulders or the way she'd looked at Chloe's lips. Beautiful, powerful—

"Chlo?"

With the ability to reach across miles and embarrass Chloe in front of her mom. "Hmm?"

Her mother gave her a calculating look, one that seemed able to invade her thoughts and riffle through her memories. "Are you worried about the Kareem siblings? Do we even know if they survived meeting this Helen?"

Oh thank God. Right subject, wrong emotion. "Uh, something like that."

Her mom nodded. "Well, if this Helen—"

"Mom, stop saying 'this' Helen. She was, is, named Helen."

"Sure, but I don't know—"

"Helen of Troy. You didn't see her, feel her power. She's a demigod, maybe even more than that, like, two-thirds god."

Her mom still didn't seem convinced.

And there went those childish emotions again. The urge to stomp her feet, hands ramrod straight at her sides, and demand to be listened to. It wasn't right. It wasn't fair.

It wasn't what Jamie would do.

"You weren't there," Chloe said, thinking only to reiterate, but part of her knew those words would land in a different way, one that said: *your power is mine now, along with your best friend.*

Her mom's face contorted just as Chloe's regret took hold, magnified by that look of shock and hurt.

"I'm sorry, Mom."

"No, I am. I should have continued to go with you on your missions, I should have insisted."

"No, that's not what I—"

"I just couldn't." She took a deep breath. "After Jamie…"

The ultimate trump card. Chloe's shame built to tsunami levels and washed her confidence away.

"Say something," Ramses prompted from behind her.

Chloe fought the urge to spin around even as her heart lodged briefly between her ears. "What?"

Her mom closed her eyes as if bracing herself to repeat what she'd said, but Ramses spoke before she could. "You're not asking her to babysit you, Chloe, you're asking her to trust you."

Yeah, now that she thought on her mom's words… "Are you saying that if you'd been there, you would have proven she's not Helen of Troy? That you would have naturally known more than me?"

Her mom's eyes flew open. "What? No."

"Then you should trust my judgment." Chloe was on a roll, and her childish self watched with equal measures fear and glee. "When you meet her, you'll see, but for now, you're just gonna have to take my word for it." There, casting the die at last, daring her to argue, to bring Jamie up again, to once again say that Chloe would clearly never understand.

Her mother nodded, the move slight enough that Chloe wasn't sure if she'd imagined it. "Okay. You're right. I'm sorry."

It didn't seem like a wholly sincere apology, but for right now, it was enough.

❖

After what seemed like hours of back and forth, Fatma and Ali finally agreed to meet Chloe at Galveston, even though the only thing they promised was that they'd have questions that Chloe needed to answer. She'd decided to hold nothing back, except any limits to her power. They didn't need to know anything she couldn't do.

And the fact that many of the tools she used were apparently BS. She still couldn't reconcile that one with her own history.

Fatma and Ali claimed to have a very fast boat, but Chloe bet they'd only let her use it if they were happy with the answers she gave them. As it stood, they were waiting on the beach down the street from a marina when Chloe arrived with her carful of helpers.

Whether her mom would come with her was never in question. She'd insisted before anyone had asked. Chloe was salty at first, but if this enemy was as organized as they thought, some extra firepower wouldn't hurt, even if she had doubts. Thank God the only others to tag along were David and Jillian.

And Damian, of course.

"Why is he coming?" Ramses had asked with a bit of a whine.

"He might come in handy. He has the best feel for where we're going, and most importantly, we have no way to keep him locked up while we're gone."

"How about we, I don't know, banish him?"

She'd had the same thought. But… "I said I wouldn't."

He'd given her a look that said he was sympathetic, frustrated, and somewhat proud, all at the same time. "Chloe."

She'd had a thousand responses, many petulant, some angry and insistent, but that was the quickest way to make his crown come out, so she'd settled for resigned. "We'll keep an eye on him. At the first sign of betrayal, we shove his ass into the sea."

That had seemed to calm him a little.

The Kareem siblings stood the same way: arms crossed and one leg cocked slightly sideways, a similar scowl in place. Chloe fought not to snort, wondering if they realized. It was amusing enough that she waved instead of returning the dark look. Ali rolled his eyes while Fatma's frown deepened.

"They ought to be careful," Ramses said, "or their faces will stick like that."

Chloe sputtered, "Don't make me laugh," through a smile. To her surprise, her mother and friends hung back, and the realization almost made her stumble.

Don't embarrass yourself. You're the one with the power.

Right. Confidence. Shoulders back, capable smile. "Hey, y'all. I'm Chloe." Too friendly. She needed to dial back her accent by about twenty percent.

"We know your name, and you know ours," Fatma said.

"Great, we're off to a good start." She hoped they took it as half-sarcastic as she meant it. "I'm guessing y'all don't want to waste time asking about where we grew up and such."

Their answer was their usual pissed-off look.

"You have questions?" Chloe gestured toward a nearby bench that overlooked the beach. "Let's get to it."

They followed, but neither sat. She did, scooting a bit away so she didn't have to crane her neck. Ramses sat between her and them, his arms crossed as if he could reflect their negative energy right back at them.

As they stared, Chloe looked between them, waiting for the first question, but the moment stretched on. The Kareems glanced at each other. Maybe they hadn't worked out who was going to ask what. Or maybe they didn't expect to even have the chance. Did they think she'd show up tossing grenades or something?

Laughing still seemed like the wrong thing to do, so with a sigh, she leaned forward. "A long time ago, one of my ancestors discovered they had this power..."

She went on to relate her history as Ramses had told it to her. The bits before one of her ancestors had discovered him in the desert remained a bit of a mystery, but it was still hundreds of years to draw on. She left out being the blood of Isis and downplayed much of what Ramses could do so if he had to possess her or attack them, they wouldn't know what was coming.

"We mostly deal with ghosts," Chloe said after she'd wrapped up the history. "I don't know how familiar you are. The spirits we banish aren't like Ramses. Especially the recently summoned ones. They're extremely pissed off and confused, like they didn't bring their whole mind when they were called back. So we put them to rest."

"And the creatures?" Fatma asked with one eyebrow up. She'd finally perched on the edge of the steel bench. Ali leaned on the back of it, occasionally glancing down as if willing her to move over a bit and let him sit, too, but she stayed stubbornly in place.

"If they're not endangering human life, we don't usually even find out about them."

Fatma snorted and rolled her eyes and muttered something like, "Oh, yes, because human life is paramount."

Chloe bristled, but Ramses mumbled, "We can't change the past," and she knew he was warning her not to get into an argument like she had with Helen.

She bit her lip and glanced toward where her mom, David, Jillian, and Damian had gotten a small table at an outdoor café across the road. They watched her unabashedly over drinks. She wished she'd thought to have this conversation in comfort, but a bustling café was no place for privacy.

"If you have any alternatives going forward, I'd love to hear them," she said, hoping to move the conversation on.

"Perhaps," Fatma said. "Once we're sure you're not going to use these 'alternatives' as a way to gather all the creatures together and slaughter them."

"She's just trying to goad you," Ramses said.

No shit. But Chloe wasn't just going to sit and take all the venom dripping from those fangs. "Do you want to come up with solutions, or are you just looking for someone to yell at?"

Fatma opened her mouth, face further contorting into anger, but Ali nudged her, and she closed her mouth with a *tsk*. "What do you want from us?" he asked.

She repeated a lot of stuff she'd said on the phone: the traps, the attempt to steal Ramses, the evidence that someone was summoning ghosts or gathering creatures for concerted attacks. When they didn't mention Helen, she didn't either. Instead, she tried to stress the fact that she didn't know who might be involved; a Lamia had been mentioned, but they couldn't be sure humans weren't at the heart of this, using creatures or artifacts to get what they wanted.

"And now we know where they might be," she said, waving a map. "We just need help getting there."

Fatma nodded at the map, one hand out.

Chloe shook her head. "I'm sorry. I'm not giving y'all the chance to leave us behind."

If Fatma's chin came up any more, she'd be looking at the sky. "Because then some of these creatures might live?"

"If any creature's being used against its will, you can haul it off to Bora Bora for all I care," Chloe snapped. "If it ain't hurting people, it's fine by me."

Fatma's expression twisted several times, and Chloe would have placed a bet that she had been hoping for a response like, "Hell, no, we're gonna fry and eat every one of them critters," so she could stomp off in righteous anger.

"And the artifacts?" Ali asked. "If the goddess Helen is at the heart of this, she seems to possess more than a few."

So they knew Helen was more than human, too. She let it go for now, though a few pleasant memories did drift through her.

Focus.

"We'll have to play it by ear. If you have somewhere where you keep this stuff that no one can get to, I'm all for it. I know you like to send things back to their countries of origin, so maybe you have caches everywhere? Like museums?" She looked between them.

They glanced at each other, but they looked thoughtful and not so damned angry. Until Fatma turned back to her, of course. "And Ramses?"

Chloe shook her head. "What about him?"

"You'll let him go?"

"Let me go?" He shot to his feet. "Let me go?" The crown of Egypt appeared on his head again, and the hair on Chloe's arms stood as if a helluva storm was rolling in off the Gulf. "They think me your prisoner? Me?"

So much for not showing the extent of his power. The Kareems glanced around. Their hair moved as if tossed on the wind, but the breeze off the ocean was mild. It was only Ramses's crackling energy that made it seem like a storm was brewing on a mildly overcast day.

Chloe held her hands out. "He is so not my prisoner," she said hurriedly. "He stays with my family because he wants to, and he has dedicated his afterlife to helping people. He could leave anytime, really. If you know what's good for you, you'll apologize. Now."

They stared at her like she'd lost her mind, but they surely couldn't deny the building energy. "I'm sorry," Ali finally cried, glancing around. "I didn't know, we didn't know that you could hear us or that you were not a prisoner, and we apologize, King Ramses."

The energy died a little, but he still glared at them with the crackling eyes of a god.

"There's not a more powerful ghost in the world," Chloe said, irritated on his behalf even as she hoped he'd calm down. "Even if the trap in Houston had succeeded, they'd have found they'd caught a lion in a rabbit snare."

His power dimmed to its normal background hum, and the striped nemes replaced the crown on his head, but she could still catch a glimpse of it from the corner of her eye as he gave her a satisfied nod.

Fatma and Ali seemed sufficiently cowed, like fright had pushed their ever-present anger to a muted level. "I should have known better," Fatma said quietly.

Ramses nodded again.

Chloe took a deep breath. "Do you have more questions, or should we get going? Because I'm betting that no matter what, you're going to insist on coming with us?"

"Of course," Fatma said, but she seemed to almost smile as she gave Chloe an exasperated look. It wasn't exactly a friendly smile, but Chloe wouldn't be choosy.

"And you said you had a faster than normal boat?"

Ali nodded. "We have a piece of the golden fleece to help control the wind."

Chloe had to chuckle. David would be saying, "I told you so," for years to come.

CHAPTER TWENTY-ONE

The trouble with Remora Island was that the dense foliage extended nearly to the water, impossible to see through. But a long speedboat had been anchored just offshore, along with what looked like a modified fishing boat that had seen better days. No one stirred aboard them, not that Helen could see through her binoculars as she bobbed in the water with four nereids.

Ligeia swum in lazy circles around her, clad in nothing but her skin, and the sun glinted off her blue scales and golden tattoos. "See anything?"

"No." And it was getting toward afternoon. Helen didn't want to go stumbling through enemy territory at dusk. "Maurice, do you feel any glamour?"

His weight shifted on top of her head. He'd flown from the sanctuary instead of swimming, perching on Helen now and again as the nereids brought her up for air. They could swim nearly as fast as he could fly, so they'd made good time, though Helen could feel the parts of her not covered by her short-sleeved wet suit starting to prune.

"Nope," he said. "Not from this distance, anyway."

Shit. They'd have to get closer. They swam down the shore from the boats and came in near some rocks and a steep ledge rather than the beach. Ligeia, Maurice, and Maera clambered up with Helen while the rest stayed in the waves, kicking out a bit, readying a whale song in case they spotted anyone.

It was hot and muggy inside the trees, and every inch was alive with bird and insect calls. Helen waved for Maera to stay near the shore and relay any signal if necessary. She could leap in the water with the landing party and pull them away faster than anyone could follow, but she'd dry out on land for any length of time.

Inside the trees, Maurice settled on Helen's shoulder, muttering under his breath as he extended his glamour around her and Ligeia, rendering them invisible for a short time, at least to outside eyes. Taking them under his magic took a lot out of him, and he wouldn't be able to do much more than concentrate, but this way, they could move quickly and not have to worry about anyone spotting them.

Helen scoffed. The Sphinx shouldn't have worried.; they moved like a well-oiled spying machine.

Helen headed in the direction of the boats and spotted several little trails. Someone had broken through the foliage. She followed the clearest, her ears straining. Voices and a low electrical hum made her slow. She drew the kladenet before creeping ahead. Through a break in the bushes, she spotted something beige, metal.

A small clearing past the broken bushes looked ragged, the plants still oozing sap as if someone had hacked them from existence no more than a few days ago. Three portable buildings stood under the hot sun, one draped in ivy as if it had been there much longer. Two generators hummed outside the newer buildings, and a larger trail snaked through the trees on the other side of the clearing.

Helen bit her lip. Why would they make two trails? Why not walk along the one that had clearly been carved for the buildings? It screamed *suspicious* if not *trap*.

Loud voices came from one of the newer buildings, along with the faint sounds of music: TV noise rather than conversation. Damn. She'd been hoping to find someone talking, discover a little more than the obvious fact that someone was here.

Would the Sphinx kill her if she went closer? If she peeked in the windows?

"How much glamour do you have left?" she asked softly.

"Maybe an hour." But the strain in Maurice's voice said it was a little less.

If she was going to do something, it had to be now. "Come on." She strode toward the nearest building, the oldest, and paused beside a window, finding it too covered in dirt to see through. She hurried toward one of the newer ones. The curtains hung open in the center, so she rose on tiptoe to peek inside.

Boxes and crates filled one side of the room, leaving only enough space for a ratty old armchair. Someone sat in it, their face hidden behind a graphic novel held in two pale hands. They wore cargo pants and thick-soled boots and had a pistol strapped to one thigh. A longer rifle leaned against the crate beside them, and they had their feet propped on a box. At least this one wasn't worried about intruders. Or much of anything.

Were the boxes full of more weapons like the rifle? None had markings or labels, and she dearly wanted to get a closer look. She sneaked to the other building. The glare of a TV bounced off the blinds. Perhaps it was as sparsely guarded as the other one.

She led the way back into the trees. "Drop the glamour."

With a sigh, Maurice did so, though he remained invisible, his natural magic always in place unless he chose to lower it.

"Well, boss?" Ligeia asked.

"I don't sense any magic, do you?"

"Gimmie a minute to catch my breath," Maurice muttered.

Ligeia shrugged but sensing spells or glamour had never been one of her talents.

"Nothing," Maurice said. After a beat, he added, "But then again, some of these fey-human glamours…"

"Yeah." Like the dealer's glamour that he'd missed at the poker game. That had put them in a pickle, even though no one there had an automatic rifle. "But if they have human blood at all, Ligeia's song should work."

"Should? That's, like, some nice confidence, *boss*."

Helen gave her a flat look. "Think you can get through the walls and the sound of that TV?"

Ligeia snapped her gum and returned the dark glance. "I've gotten through all the decks on a cruise ship, baby."

Excellent. "Show me."

Ligeia rolled her eyes but turned toward the clearing and started to sing. Loudly. Helen winced from the noise but waited for all the doors to come popping open.

❖

The Kareems weren't lying about having a fast boat. The wind shear was so great, Chloe felt like her face was going to slough off, so she finally went inside the bridge with the others. Luckily, Ali and Fatma had made some modifications to the yacht so their piece of the golden fleece wouldn't tear the boat to pieces either.

The fleece had been draped over the console, as shiny gold as lamé, though the texture was a bit lumpy, and it felt scratchy and cold to the touch. Definitely not sweater ready. Tiny bronze clips held it in place, and wires led from those into the console itself. It seemed a fascinating mix of magic and technology. Chloe would have loved the chance to study it, but Ali stood over it with a wary eye and didn't seem in the mood for conversation.

When the boat made it out of the Gulf of Mexico in what seemed like an hour, maybe a little less, David gave Jillian and Chloe's mom a very smug look but was kind enough to say nothing.

The first island on their map proved a bust, and traipsing around it felt like wasting time, but Damian wasn't sure about the quality of the air or the ley lines being exactly as he remembered and needed to get a "feel for the whole place."

By the tenth mosquito bite, Chloe could have banished him on the spot.

At the second island, he didn't even get off the boat, saying this air definitely wasn't right. Chloe's mom and the others seemed skeptical, but she was more than willing to take his word for it, leaving it to the others to take a short look around while she stayed safely in the air-conditioning.

By the time they were on their way to the third island, her nerves returned. If this one was in wild-goose territory, too, this whole trip had been a fuckup. And it had been her idea. Of course, the alternative wasn't exactly pleasant: finding the people behind the traps and getting pulled into a big ol' fight.

Chloe moved below into the yacht, taking a seat at the four-person table built into the wall while her mother, David, and Jillian looked through their equipment. Fatma and Damian had stayed up on the bridge with Ali. Chloe hadn't told them he was a demon, but she was certain they suspected he wasn't human. She had her pentacle ready to go in case he decided to prove them right.

Ramses sat beside her, turned as if to keep an eye on the stairs. He seemed worried, too, his leg bouncing up and down, fingers nervously playing with the edges of his pleated kilt as he kept casting glances at the piles of equipment.

"Nervous about the window dressing?" she asked at last, speaking low and hoping the others wouldn't hear. "You're twitching like a wet cat."

He didn't bark back at her, a bad sign. "Now that I've said it aloud, I don't like how much they seem to be relying on all that…stuff." His mouth twitched as if he'd rather have said, "garbage."

She shrugged. "It's what we've got." She'd almost said it was what *they* had, those without the godly gifts, but she wasn't ready to let go of all her paranormal trappings yet.

"No, the real power we have is you and me." He waved vaguely. "Not to brag."

Though he totally was. "And if we get into a bind, we might have to rely on everyone else and their junk."

He shook his head, his leg bouncing harder. "I shouldn't have told you. It's just made me nervous, too."

Her nerves went to a hundred, but she tried to laugh it off. "Come on, I'm just teasing." A bit. Some. Barely any at all. "You don't usually get nervous before a fight. Is it more than just the supplies?" She frowned. "Please don't give me some speech about dying."

"I'm not going to."

"Or reminding me that you love me—"

"I do, but that's not it."

She sighed. "Let's have it, then."

He shook his head. "All my instincts say something isn't right, but I don't know what." When he looked up, his smile was kindly. "But there's nothing we can do except keep moving forward."

Very inspirational. If he'd made that speech in front of his army, they would've gone home. But she wanted him to feel better as much as she wanted to feel better, too. "Well, we've got the helmet now, so strength won't be a problem."

"Right. Of course." His reassuring smile had all the weight of a feather punching bag.

Chloe felt wooden as she glanced at her mom, David, and Jillian and all the gear they took so much care of, all the stuff that might let them down now that her mom didn't have any power. Had she even tried going after any ghosts or monsters since she'd lost it? Not without Chloe. What if they got separated? If her mom charged in without her?

"I'm sorry, Chloe," Ramses said again. "I shouldn't have—"

Man, she was tired of hearing that. "It's done, Ramses, and it wasn't like you lied. I know my belief isn't actually going to change whether or not iron or salt or turning my clothes inside out actually affects the creatures we come up against. And you and Mom were right in that they do help me focus. We're good." For the millionth time, it would have felt so good to be able to touch him. "Solid. Always."

He nodded proudly. "Use all the focuses you want. Our enemy may have their own trinkets, but they don't have our power."

Damn straight. No need to point out that they might have different powers all their own.

She wandered back through the galley into a narrow hall, trying to walk away from her head for a bit, but as her grandpa had once said, it always came with her. She wished she could go pace the deck, but she didn't feel like having to staple her face back on later.

When she felt a hand on her back, she just kept from yelping, ready to growl at Ramses again for scaring her, but that warm touch couldn't be his.

Her mom's scowl greeted her. "Where's your head at, Chloe? Because it certainly doesn't look like it's in the game."

The game. Yeah, it really felt like that at the moment. "Blood of Isis, Mom, ever hear of it?"

Her mother drew back as if shocked. "Ramses told you."

"Well, it sure as shit wasn't you."

To her surprise, her mother leaned against the wall, her expression sad but serious. "What did he say?"

"Oh, you know, the usual, descended from a god, special powers." All the tools she'd ever relied on being mostly for show, but she couldn't say that to her mom now, not when she wasn't sure exactly what Ramses had told both of them, not right before they got in a fight.

Her mom *tsked.* "I didn't want you to rely too much on the bloodline. It's the combination of blood and gear that's the key, and your heritage is going to help you whether you use it or not. The rest takes finesse, practice."

Chloe held up a hand. "I remember." God, she'd heard it all often enough. "He thought the god stuff might boost my confidence." Even though her mom was saying almost the opposite. They couldn't both be right, could they? "But that he told me feels like you wanted to leave me out again."

"What do you mean?"

Chloe waved around and wished she could gesture at the entire world. "You and Jamie. All of this. Me and Dad were always outside looking in."

Her mom went still. Fuck. She should not have mentioned her dad.

"I did my best, Chloe." Her voice was only a bit pissed, maybe even a little guilty. Maybe she knew she'd left Chloe out in the cold more than once.

"I know." But she did not need to talk her mom off the ledge when she also needed comfort.

David poked his head into the hall. "We're here."

Chloe nodded. All the things left unsaid would have to stay that way for now.

❖

For a moment, all was as still as it had been, save for the sounds of the TV and Ligeia's song. Helen could imagine any guards lounging inside sitting up as they heard something. They'd pause, not knowing what the noise was, and turn down the TV, and by the time they realized it was a voice singing, they'd be trapped by Ligeia's power.

The doors thumped open as if on cue, a guard clomping down the wooden steps from one building, and three filing from another to fall at Ligeia's feet. They were all dressed similarly, though nothing in the nondescript, professional-looking clothing could be called a uniform, and with their varying skin tones, she wouldn't have pegged them as all being from the same region. Mercenaries, perhaps.

All information she'd figure out later. She hurried into the dark room with the crates, fumbling for a switch, but the overhead light was weak and yellow, and she could see why the mercenary who'd been reading in here hadn't bothered with it. She turned so her body wasn't blocking the light from the door and yanked the lid off a random crate.

Bananas?

"What the hell?" She pulled the lid off another, the nails keeping it shut barely slowing her down. Ceramic ducks wrapped in plastic. She opened several more to find bolts of cloth, toys, more bananas, jars of pickled radishes.

Where were the guns? Or anything they could assault her island with? Were these simply smugglers, and there was more money in illicit fruit and ducks than she'd thought? She tried several boxes and crates on the bottom, but they seemed as full of nothing as the top. And Ligeia couldn't keep singing forever. She already sounded a little hoarse.

Helen hurried to the next building where she'd seen the TV, giving an apologetic look to Ligeia's wide eyes and snapping fingers encouraging her to hurry. Nothing in there but clothes, some personal items, a few hammocks. There was a two-way radio, but nothing as useful as cell phones or passports. Those might be in the mercenaries' pockets. She'd check after the final building.

Its door was locked, a good sign. She'd been hoping to disappear without a trace after putting the mercenaries back at their posts, leaving them wondering what, if anything, had happened. Ah well. With the aid of her godhood, she snapped the flimsy doorknob off. They'd just have to live with not knowing who had forced this door.

Nothing but shadows inside, more boxes perhaps, but the grimy windows didn't let in enough light. No window AC units hummed in here, no generator outside. All was hot and still and dark, no breath of air save what trickled in from the open door at Helen's back.

Goose bumps sprang up on her arms even under the sweat. She took a few steps, needed to hurry and open whatever she could find, just to guarantee that this operation wasn't a threat. And Ligeia's voice had begun to waver now, ratcheting up Helen's heart rate, but this room was setting off all her internal alarms.

It seemed almost an inevitable relief when the door slammed shut behind her, cutting off the sound of Ligeia's sudden scream.

❖

No matter how much bug spray one packed for traipsing around islands in the Caribbean, it wasn't enough. Every inch of Chloe itched, though how the mosquitoes had gotten through the heavy, camouflage flak jacket Jillian had insisted she wear, she didn't know. Maybe they had a magic all their own on top of their ability to make everyone they encountered scratch off a few layers of skin.

When someone screamed in the distance, it was almost a welcome distraction.

Fatma and Ali glanced at each other before hurrying toward the noise. David and Jillian had triumphant looks as they followed, and Damian grinned widely, his hunches proven correct.

Chloe's mom frowned, matching how she felt as they hurried to keep up. She should have been in the lead instead of running after everyone. She had the power, for fuck's sake. Clearly, no one had told them their gear might be useless in certain situations. They'd survived this long, so there had to be something in it.

When David pulled her down behind some bushes, she knew there was more to his survival than his gear, too. Just ahead, Fatma and Ali had taken cover behind some trees. Fatma had a pistol out, and Ali clutched something just bigger than a grenade. God, she hoped it wasn't a freaking grenade. She wasn't used to guns and explosives, but as she focused on the clearing beyond, she realized she'd have to get used to them real fucking quick.

Four thuggish people with handguns of various varieties stood around the siren Chloe had seen before. She lay on the ground, blood streaming from a wound on her temple. A crash sounded across the clearing from a large shed or portable building that rocked on its base.

"I'll go look," Ramses said, stepping through the plants between Jillian and Damian, who crouched on David's other side.

Chloe forced herself to wait, her mother's presence at her back a comfort as her mind raced. How had these people defeated a siren's song? She couldn't see anything in their ears, and earplugs small enough to go unnoticed wouldn't cut it. A shimmer near the collar of one caught her eye. It could have been the top of a sigil, and the way it glowed was a dead giveaway that it was magical in nature. It might even be invisible to those who weren't her.

The hair on Chloe's neck stood up. If these people were savvy enough to use magic in case of a siren attack, what else were they prepared for?

"Ramses," she thought as hard as she could, "get back here."

Her heart stuttered as something made a short *fzzt* like an overloaded socket. A trap?

"Ramses?"

The air left her lungs in a *whoosh*, like someone had clubbed her on the back. She had to fight to keep from doubling over as Ramses's presence faded from her mind, taking her back to when Helen had forced them to separate, a feeling she'd never wanted to revisit. "Ramses?" she croaked.

Everyone glanced her way, and she pushed up, her fear washed away in a tide of anger. How fucking dared they?

She slapped the magical helmet on her head, heard the gasps as she was surely lost from sight, and waded in where Ramses had vanished, determined to get him back or die trying.

Chapter Twenty-two

Helen gasped, breathing in old paper and stone. She darted for the door in the dark, intent on reaching Ligeia and Maurice, but a solid mass blocked her way: the softness of skin and the iron of muscle.

And the cold, slick feeling of scales.

A throaty laugh filled the stale air, and the muscled mass heaved into Helen's side, knocking her sideways and sending pain reverberating through her ribs. It didn't feel like an arm or a leg, more like the thick slab of a tail.

She'd know that laugh anywhere. "Lamia," she gasped as she caught herself on the heated metal of the wall.

"You really are a gullible fool."

Helen pressed against the wall and tried to follow the sibilance of the Lamia's scales in the shadows. She half wished the window was completely covered so her eyes could truly adjust. Gods, she had to think fast. The Lamia was strong, her bite was venomous, and if she transformed—

No, she couldn't do that, not with the cuff Helen had forced on her.

Well, if she'd gotten out of the sanctuary, she'd obviously removed that.

The air shifted. Helen ducked, and a clang over her head rewarded her effort. She rolled away, waving the kladenet to the side in case the Lamia was close enough to hit. In the darkness, it wouldn't be effective, needing light as much as most in order to fight.

She bumped into a wooden chair and clattered around it, putting it between her and where she remembered the door to be. The Lamia would be keeping her distance, too, lashing with that powerful tail until she could change shape.

Why hadn't she done it already?

"You've got me here, now what?" Helen said, skittering backward after she spoke, not wanting to give her position away. When she heard the chair splinter into bits and felt the sharp patter of pieces against her arm, she knew she'd made the right choice.

"Now you die."

"If you could kill me all this time—" She moved again, staying low, not wanting to be silhouetted against the meager light. She heard another thump where she'd been, but now she'd found a sofa or love seat and circled it quickly.

"Come and fight me, coward." The Lamia had to be close to the center of the room now.

Helen knelt behind the sofa and put her shoulder to it. She gathered her godhood in a rush, not wanting a glow to give her away before she had the chance to ram some furniture down the Lamia's throat.

When another small movement gave the Lamia away, Helen heaved, flinging the sofa across the room. The Lamia gave a strangled cry. Helen darted for the door, the path illuminated by her power. She braced herself, smacked into it, knocked it halfway off its hinges as she barreled through. With a grunt, she tumbled down the short steps and hit the ground in a roll.

Voices were shouting on top of one another, and she glimpsed a blue body on the clearing floor amid shuffling boots. Bastards.

But Ligeia would have to wait until Helen had dealt with the Lamia. She let go of the kladenet. "Guard." It would watch her as she rushed to put her back to one of the other buildings, keeping it between her and the mercenaries. No matter what else was going on, the Lamia was the biggest threat. She always was, always had been, it seemed.

But no one emerged.

When a cry came from the forest, Helen edged toward the other end of the building and peeked. A hazy white glow lit a patch of ground about ten-feet square. Inside, someone stood silhouetted against the trees. Well, not exactly. She could see the trees *through* him even as she could make out a few details of his clothing: a pleated kilt with a long belt, high sandals, and a tall, oblong crown upon his head, a figure straight out of a book about ancient Egypt.

Chloe's pharaoh.

Her *ghost* pharaoh.

How in the hell could Helen see him?

It had to be the hazy glow that surrounded him. He beat his hands against nothing like a mime trying to escape an invisible box, his face twisted in anger or pain. A trap of some sort? But if he was here…

Another shout drew her attention from where the mercenaries had been. She hurried back to the other side of her building, sparing a glance for the gaping door to the old one. The Lamia still hadn't come out. Before Helen could glance around the corner, one of the mercenaries flew past as if tossed by a giant.

Not even Maurice was that strong. "What in the world?"

Another mercenary went sailing into the trees on the right of the clearing as Helen glanced around. The others were struggling to rise, cradling various parts of their bodies. That looked more like Maurice's handiwork.

Then Chloe appeared out of nowhere and took a defensive stance near Ligeia's prone body. Helen smiled amid a surge of joy. Whatever else Chloe was, she clearly wasn't with these mercenaries.

That shouldn't have felt so good.

Chloe put the tarnkappe under her arm. No wonder she'd been able to throw the mercenaries around like toys. Next, she'd be wanting her pharaoh back.

Helen looked for him again, trying to spot the source of whatever imprisoned him. When she sensed movement behind her, she threw herself down just as a thick blue-black tail smashed into where she'd been standing, bouncing off the metal of the portable building with a *ting* that reverberated through the clearing. And leaving a huge dent in its wake.

The Lamia had finally decided to join them.

The kladenet slashed at the retreating tail but didn't advance, still in guard-mode. The Lamia seemed younger than the last time Helen had seen her. Perhaps that was an effect of seeing her in sunlight for the first time in years. She still wore nothing but a jeweled belt and an evil smile, the imprisoning cuff gone from her wrist.

And still no transformation?

When the Lamia's tail whipped around again, the kladenet blocked, and the contact made another too-metallic *ting*, along with a sound like cracking leather. And the blade didn't appear to cut her flesh. Something was wrong.

The Lamia's gaze flicked to the side. More shouts, maybe double the voices for the number of people Helen had seen. Reinforcements had arrived for someone. The Lamia cocked one shoulder back, her tail flicking as if she might strike again, but she hissed, recoiling as several somethings thwacked into her, each one preceded by a loud *thunk*.

Chloe marched past the edge of the building, a cordless nail gun in hand. "All window dressing, my ass," she said for some inexplicable reason. When her eyes met Helen's, she stutter-stepped a bit but didn't drop her formidable stance. "I guess cold iron works on a lamia, too."

"The," Helen corrected her automatically. She shifted so she and Chloe were nearly standing side by side. "And I guess it does." Though being shot by a bunch of nails was bound to make anyone cranky.

But it shouldn't have been enough to make the Lamia wheeze and fall back, one hand to her wounds, the other still cocked strangely behind her. Helen peered at where the nail heads protruded from the Lamia's flesh, certain they were oozing black blood.

"The Lamia doesn't bleed," she muttered.

Maurice's voice yelled something about a glamour. This wasn't the Lamia.

"It's a demon." Chloe dropped the tarnkappe and pulled a pentacle from her bag.

Helen could smell the anise from where she stood. "A demon?"

The faux-Lamia staggered back, its glamour slipping away to reveal pale red skin covered in barbs and a very muscular body. They had no eyes, the skin stretched tight over the upper half of their face like a mask, and the teeth were bare in a lipless grimace. A flaming circle stood upright just above the crown of their bald head, moving with them as they flicked a whip with a metal end, the Lamia's "tail."

"Gods," Helen mumbled just as Chloe said, "Oh shit." Helen wasn't well-versed in demons, and this one looked…challenging.

Thankfully, the demon spread black-veined bat wings and leapt into the air. Chloe fired the nail gun after them, and Helen commanded the kladenet to attack as the demon hovered in the air, but with several great pulls of their wings, they were off beyond the treetops.

The kladenet returned before it reached the limit of the magic that tethered them and settled in Helen's hand.

"Thank the fucking universe," Chloe said as she put the pentacle away, stripped off her gloves, and picked up the tarnkappe. "Ramses," she said to Helen, her eyes wide and worried. "Have you seen him?"

Helen pointed around the other side of the building. Chloe gave a strangled cry as she turned the corner. With a lunge, Helen caught her arm before she could run for where Ramses stood imprisoned. "Don't. The spell might catch you, too."

"Just what I was about to say," an older woman said as she joined them. She had Chloe's dark hair, her light brown skin, and the same pointed chin. A relative, maybe even her mother, judging by the protective, warning look she leveled at where Helen held Chloe's arm.

Helen dropped her hand but had to find something to say to Chloe's stricken expression. She still felt a pull between them, and they hadn't parted on *completely* antagonistic terms. Besides, Chloe had helped Ligeia, one of the creatures that most paranormal killers would be happy to see dead. "I'll help you figure it out, don't worry."

Chloe looked so grateful, Helen almost hugged her, no matter her mother's dagger eyes. But even her mother seemed distraught as she joined them and looked at Chloe's pharaoh.

"Ramses." Chloe's mother breathed the word as if she'd just discovered that a long-lost friend was still alive. "I never thought I'd see him again." She joined hands with Chloe, and the moment felt so weighty, Helen had to look away.

❖

Chloe dragged her fingers out of her mouth. She'd already bitten one nail to the quick, and if she let herself, she'd have ten bloody stumps instead of fingers. But Helen had been pacing around the prison that held Ramses for ten minutes instead of actually doing something, and Chloe was about to crawl out of her skin.

Fatma and Ali watched Helen from a distance, muttering to each other. A fairy flitted about Helen's shoulders, speaking in her ear. And the injured siren had recovered and begrudgingly stomped into the forest with a bandage supplied by David pressed to the side of her head.

The fact that Helen trusted Chloe enough to send one of her allies away did something to her insides.

"We shouldn't have let the siren leave," her mom said. Her insides were clearly the same as always. "She's probably bringing reinforcements."

"For what?" Chloe said. "The fight's over."

Her mom's sigh said she was still so naive. "Us, Chlo."

She shook her head, too nervous for real anger. "Helen wouldn't be helping Ramses just to turn on us."

"She could be faking, stalling for time. Maybe she plans to steal him for herself somehow."

Ludicrous. Paranoid. And maybe Chloe had the emotional space for some anger, after all. "She's not."

"How do you know?"

How? She...just fucking did. But she couldn't say that, didn't want to have this entire conversation. She wanted to get Ramses back, have a different conversation with Helen, then...make out with her for several days.

She pulled her finger from her mouth again.

"She is pretty impressive, I'll admit," her mom said.

The understatement of the year, but Chloe was glad someone else could see it. She was less glad when her mom stepped between her and the view with her lips pursed in a, *I know what you're thinking, and you should know better* look.

Chloe still said, "What?" in the faint hope that she was wrong.

"Chlo."

"Mom, if you lecture me right now, I swear to God, I will bite my nails down to my wrists."

Her mom gently removed her hand from her mouth. "Okay, I'll put the speeches away." But another look said they'd be back.

Yay, something to look forward to. At least for the moment, she got an unobstructed view of Helen. Pity it came with the sight of her best friend trapped in a hazy bubble, but even he would say beggars couldn't be choosers. After he'd reassure her and tell her to get him the hell out of there.

Gee, it was almost like she didn't need to hear him.

But she couldn't cheer herself up with bad jokes. She wanted him back like she needed a warm jacket on a cold morning. She'd forego making out with Helen forever in exchange.

Ramses would say, *let's not be too hasty. Forever is a long time.*

And she'd say—

She wiped a stray tear from her cheek, but there was another of the damn things right behind it, and her mother's hand on her shoulder was about to let more of them out, so she trudged away to see how David and Jillian and Damian were doing, knowing she probably looked like a grumpy toddler but lacking the mental energy to care.

David and Jillian had bound the thugs with zip ties taken from the thugs' own belts, but there didn't seem to be any need. They were docile as lambs under Damian's thrall. The sigils on their necks might have protected them from a siren's song, but that magic didn't do squat against a demon.

Of course, since they seemed to have a few demons on their team—or in charge—that could be by design.

David and Jillian both wore holy symbols around their necks. Damian stayed a good fifty feet away while they worked, but they still avoided looking at him. He didn't move back in until they'd shuffled away, and the thugs sighed at him as if he were a spring breeze.

"I know," Chloe said when Damian opened his mouth. "You're very useful."

He preened and gave a shallow bow. "I am, yes."

She rolled her eyes and nodded at the thugs. "They're not going to wither and die under your power, right? Or pine for you forever once you're gone?"

"We incubi do feed on sexual energy, but doing someone to death is just greedy." He waved. "Besides, just existing on this plane is like an all-day buffet. Humans think about sex *a lot*." He glanced between Chloe and Helen and smirked.

Her cheeks burned like the Sahara. "Ugh, stop."

He shrugged. "They'll be normal again after about twenty-four hours away from my presence."

Chloe sighed, relieved, even though she had no idea what they were going to do with these thugs anyway. It wasn't like monster hunters had a jail. And she wasn't about to murder anyone, even if they might not have the same qualms.

Just another question she had no answers to.

"What kind of demon was that one?" She pointed toward where the other had been. "Another incubus?"

He snorted. "Hardly. Many demons have the ability to take other guises, but her true form wasn't nearly stunning enough for one of us." He flipped his shoulder-length hair back.

She couldn't help thinking of the "popular" crowd in high school and feeling a jolt of not-so-long-ago loathing. "Are we all stuck-up in the incubus club?"

He pointed at his face as if that should have been answer enough. "She looked like a shock trooper, infantry used by greater demons."

"Fan-fucking-tastic. Seems like these people have hell on speed dial." She slapped at another mosquito bite. At least something stayed the same through all the worry and strife. "Probably immune to your power, huh?"

"I can feed off their energy but not enthrall them. And before you ask, I'm the quintessential lover-not-a-fighter type. I can't wrestle other demons to the ground."

Yeah, that sounded right, but... "Weren't you gonna rush me for insulting you back in my mom's bathroom?"

He had the grace to look sheepish. "Well, maybe, but I had no idea what I was going to do once I got you."

She shook her head. Even if she hadn't had the pentacle, Ramses would have possessed Chloe and kicked Damian's ass up one side of the apartment and down the other.

And now she was back to that pang in her chest, and her eyes were towed to where Ramses still stood in his glowing prison. He didn't seem to be in pain anymore—or was hiding it well—and was listening intently to something Helen said.

"No, I don't know anything about that kind of magic," Damian said quietly. "Also before you ask."

She had the strangest urge to take his hand and hoped his power wasn't now working on her. Or maybe she hoped it was. The alternatives were too bizarre to contemplate.

Chapter Twenty-three

Ramses seemed more angry than alarmed. His arms were crossed over his bare, muscled chest, and he glared at Helen from under a tall, imposing crown. If he looked worried at all, it was only when he glanced at Chloe waiting anxiously nearby. His sandal tapped a little faster, then.

Helen looked in that direction, too. In stark contrast to Ramses, Chloe seemed like she might dissolve into worry on the spot, either chewing her nails or twirling a stray piece of hair around one finger. It was touching and adorable and—

Not what she should be focusing on right now.

"Can you hear me?" Helen asked.

Ramses nodded. His mouth moved soundlessly.

She shook her head. "This spell doesn't allow me to hear you, it seems." But she wasn't sure how it all worked. Sigils glowed from a handful of trees around the clearing, different patterns than those on the mercenaries' necks. Maurice studied them now; Helen could hear him grumbling about power lines and focuses and other magical minutia.

She pointed to the trees in question. "We've tried defacing the sigils." With a sigh, she shrugged. "They resisted somehow. Maurice says it's like they twist out of the way. But he's not giving up." And while he worked, Helen had a few moments alone with a pharaoh. She wasn't going to waste them, even if speaking behind Chloe's back made her feel unreasonably guilty.

She switched to ancient Greek in case anyone was listening. "Can you understand me?"

Again, he nodded, and she remembered hearing somewhere that the dead knew every language. Even if he couldn't talk, he could still answer a few questions by mouthing the words or gesturing.

Finding out a little more about Chloe would only be a bonus.

"We may be able to help each other," she said.

He cocked his head and gestured around with his eyebrows up.

"Oh, I'm going to get you out whether you agree to any favors or not." Though she wouldn't elaborate on why at the moment, wasn't even really sure she understood that herself. It would put him in her debt, and as her quest for priests of Thoth had uncovered, she didn't have any connections to the Egyptian Underworld.

It was also the right thing to do, basic decency. Helen felt sorry for him, one demigod to another.

And Chloe wanted it. She looked so *sad*, and Helen could feel her pull from across the clearing. She couldn't just ignore it. "I realize you can't do much in there, but I would like some information when you emerge, however you can convey it."

Ramses waved, palm up as if gesturing for her to proceed.

Right. Good. First things first: "Do you know any priests of Thoth?" If the Lamia she'd fought here was a fake, having the real one on her team was still an option.

He seemed surprised, then looked skyward as if considering. He raised two fingers but jiggled the other hand side to side as if to say, sort of.

Well, if they were alive, they wouldn't be of the same caliber as when he'd reigned. Maybe he knew a few dead ones as well, but she'd concentrate on the living for the moment. "Can they write a contract with unbreakable clauses? Oath-sworn on the River Styx?"

His jaw dropped a little, and she could almost hear the, "Ah." After a long pause, he shrugged.

She smiled. "I appreciate your honesty. Could you provide the power behind such a contract?"

Another shrug, and she caught, "Never tried."

"I could reward you."

He actually fucking smirked. Maybe he didn't think she had anything to offer someone as grand as him, or as a ghost, he needed very little. Either way, she bristled.

He waited.

She let him.

But her time was running out faster than his. And something about being in his presence made her feel impossibly young. "I'm guessing you're still on this plane for a reason. Perhaps you chose to stay here.

Perhaps you couldn't pass the gatekeeper to your afterlife. Anubis, is it? Was your heart heavier than a feather?" She had done *some* reading.

She stepped closer to his prison. "Or were you offered, shall we say, less-than-perfect accommodation in a lower realm, and you chose here over going to hell?"

All guesses, but the smile gradually fell from his face.

"I have contacts in the Greek Underworld, and their current queen is good at finding ways through barriers. I'm sure I could discover a side door to where your family awaits you. You could finally rest."

He was still for so long, she worried that the prison had frozen him in place. When he moved again, he put one hand on the barrier that separated them, his fingers curled so that it was almost a fist. A myriad of expressions crossed his face too quickly for Helen to read, and the crown became a striped headdress and a short mess of red hair before settling on a crown again.

His power grew, prickling her skin even through the barrier, and blue light blazed around him. But was that anger? Hope? Frustration? A thousand shades of joy?

She had no idea, but it was beginning to get on her nerves. And she had a godhood, too. No matter how pissed off or excited he was, it was time he acknowledged that.

Helen summoned her power, gold lighting the edges of her vision. It flowed sluggishly, but she felt Ali and Fatma take a step back from where they watched the exchange, and she was certain everyone else would be looking this way.

Gods, she hoped she could make it last while Chloe was watching.

She clenched a fist, berating herself.

Ramses squinted, a calculating look, but his power receded a bit, and his hand fell to his side, though he didn't back up. He still seemed haughty, but that was fine. She could deal with arrogant men in her sleep.

"I think I've got it," Maurice called from the trees. He rattled off something about the magic existing on a slightly different plane or angle or something. She'd never bothered to learn all the terms since her magic came from within. But the fair folk she knew were as attracted to magic as they were to glitter.

Well, almost. "Can you break it?" she cut in.

His voice flew closer. "I'll need a few reagents." He started to name them.

"I have no idea what you're talking about." She waved toward where Chloe's friends sat with their bags. "They'll probably have it."

The soft flutter of his wings didn't move. "Don't wanna talk to humans," he mumbled.

She couldn't blame him. Especially self-confessed monster hunters. "What about Chloe? She's nice. You'll like her." Great, now she sounded like she was speaking to a small child, but she wanted him to like Chloe with a surge that surprised her. Ah, well, in for a penny. "And she can see the invisible, so she won't be surprised when you speak."

"Can't you get it?" His voice rose to a whine.

She rolled her eyes. "Sure, you asked for a golden what's-it, a rosebush, and a dusty silver something?"

His sigh could have filled a sail. "Fine." He fluttered away.

Ramses was staring at Helen with an amused smile now. She thought through what she'd said. Maybe it was her lack of magical knowledge that tickled him, or maybe it was what she'd said about Maurice surely liking Chloe. *Nice* Chloe.

Her cheeks grew hot. Oh, by all the fucking gods. She turned away before his damnable smile could grow any more.

Maurice and the others put their heads together after Chloe told them what he needed. Helen took the opportunity to speak with her while her mother was busy helping with the magical trap.

Cold and aloof, that was how she should play this. She should double her efforts to pretend she didn't feel a pull between them and that even though Chloe had come to her aid—inadvertently—there was no trust there yet.

If she'd been standing outside of herself, she would have rolled her eyes to the heavens. "It'll be all right," she said out loud, throwing all her plans for iciness out the window. As she knew she would. "Maurice can break the trap."

"Thanks." Chloe jerked her hand away from her mouth yet again.

Helen fought the urge to take it. It wasn't just the power linking them that prompted her. Chloe looked so open and vulnerable. How long had it been since Helen had seen someone wear their emotions like an uncomfortable coat? Not even herself. Out in the wider world, she had to wear a false face so often, she never got close to real emotions. And the denizens of the sanctuary either played verbal chess like the Lamia, or she already knew them inside and out, and the most common emotion they expressed was a sort of vague ennui or something a little more neutral.

Chloe was like a firework in comparison, no matter her emotions, though Helen would much rather see her smile. Or even be angry. She'd been very beautiful with color in her cheeks and her eyes flashing, nearly sparking.

"How long have you been together?" Helen asked, nodding toward Ramses.

Chloe took a deep breath, and Helen had to wonder if talking about him would only make this worse.

"I'm sorry. You don't have to answer."

"No, no, it's fine. A few years now. He was with my mom and was supposed to be with my sister, but…" She shook herself and tore her eyes from Ramses as if he'd been hypnotizing her. "She, um…" She bit her lip and shook her head as if chastising herself. "She—"

"I understand," Helen said quickly. She'd seen enough grief to recognize it in any form. "A family ghost, eh? And one who's older than I am."

"Don't meet many people who can say that?"

"Not any longer." She couldn't help sounding maudlin, and Chloe went wide-eyed, no doubt as embarrassed as Helen felt about bringing up a dead sister.

They both started speaking at the same time: "Oh, I'm sorry, you don't…"

"No, you didn't…"

They both laughed awkwardly, and Helen felt it to the tip of her toes, but it still felt…good? No, that wasn't the right word.

Alive.

But wasn't this emotional spark another reason she couldn't trust humans? Fireworks weren't the only things that exploded, and the closer one came…

"You okay?" Chloe asked softly. "I feel like everyone's worried about me, but your friend the siren got hurt, too, and I'm guessing these people were out to hurt the rest of y'all?"

The questions shouldn't have surprised her, but she let herself embrace the warmth they created in her chest. "Ligeia will be fine. And we figured they were out here to trap us, spying on our…on where we live." The copy of the Sphinx she carried around in her head worried about saying much of anything, but she'd already mentioned her sanctuary to Fatma and Ali. They had to have compared notes. "My sanctuary."

"Wow." Chloe brightened. "I can't imagine living out here in paradise." She looked thoughtful. "Well, except for the bugs. And the heat. And the humidity. And randos trying to kill you." She offered Helen a sheepish smile. "Still, living on a beachy island, that's lucky."

"No one's ever said that before," Helen said with a laugh. "They usually want to know about who lives there, especially if it's anyone dangerous or famous." Or both, but she didn't add that. "No one's just admired the fact that it's tropical." How long had it been since she'd meandered down to the beach and watched the waves or soaked in the sun?

"It's probably like owning a pool," Chloe said with a shrug. "It looks cool from the outside, and you might be obsessed for a month or two, but after that, you lose interest."

Another mature observation that seemed designed to pull Helen in even further.

Dangerous.

Before she could ask another question and become even more stuck in Chloe's gravity, Maurice yelled, "Victory!" The sigils on the trees around Ramses wavered and died, and he disappeared from Helen's sight.

Chloe ran to where he'd been, seemed close to bursting into tears as she spoke to empty air—no doubt the place Ramses was now standing— and leaned forward awkwardly, as if giving the breeze a hug.

Helen wanted to offer further words of comfort, but Chloe's mother got there first. She'd had her own teary speech to Ramses while he'd been trapped, but she was dry as a bone now, one arm curled protectively around Chloe's shoulders while she gave Helen a steady stay-back stare.

Fatma and Ali had gone through the portable buildings and said they held nothing of interest. Helen wouldn't have taken them at their word, but she could tell by their body language that nothing they'd found excited or alarmed them. Ligeia had kept the nereids apprised of the situation, and they'd taken a few cautionary jaunts to other parts of the island. Nothing to be found, even on the boats. It seemed like either an elaborate trap, some sort of staging area, or part of the smuggling arm of this operation. The people who'd been spying on the sanctuary would need capital from somewhere. And they had been prepared for sirens or ghosts. There could be more traps here that hadn't revealed themselves because the right creature hadn't shown up to set them off.

Helen was glad she hadn't completely given in to the Sphinx's demands and either brought more people from the sanctuary or failed to come herself.

Chloe's demon hadn't been affected by anything here, not surprising since the mercenaries had a demon working with them. Maybe now they'd stop trying to frame the Lamia, too. Unless this was some kind of double bluff that the Lamia would delight in.

Gods, she was tired. She stretched her neck and took another look at Chloe and her friends as they gathered their gear. Why were paranormal killers working with not only a ghost but a demon? Chloe claimed to only care about hunting if the creature in question was hurting people. Could the rest of them be the same? The looks her mother had given Helen, Ligeia, and the nereids weren't exactly friendly.

Helen approached Chloe again, her dull anger something of a shield. "Is Ramses all right?" she started, trying to ignore Chloe's mother's acid eyes.

Chloe nodded, red-cheeked and with a few tears still dribbling but happy. "Thank you. Really. I tried to thank Maurice, but he seemed really uncomfortable so..." She took a deep breath. "Thanks." The longer she looked at Helen, the more she seemed to light up, and the hum between them only grew.

Helen swallowed past a sudden lump in her throat. "Can we have another word in private?"

Chloe's mother stiffened, but Chloe gave her arm a reassuring pat. "It's okay," she mumbled in her mom's direction.

Her mother's mouth pursed, but she moved a few steps away. After a look at her and a sigh, Chloe gestured for Helen to come a few feet into the trees, out of earshot and away from prying eyes.

When Chloe stopped, she gestured to her other side. "I'm not really alone, remember, not now."

Right. Well, as long as Ramses couldn't butt in. But it annoyed her a bit that Chloe didn't send him away, too. Now that Chloe waited, staring with those big dark eyes, Helen found herself fumbling for what else to say. More getting-to-know-you questions? Now that Ramses was free, it didn't feel like they had the time.

She decided to stick with the business at hand, at least tangentially. "So you work with demons, too, huh?" She knew she sounded like an asshole even before Chloe frowned, but it was out there now. And maybe it was for the best. If she couldn't ignore the danger, she could still drive it away.

"Damian? Yeah, well, he was there when Ramses and I got through another trap, and he sort of stayed." She shrugged.

"Stayed with the people who hunt his kind?"

Chloe frowned harder, mouth twisted down. "Would you prefer that we killed him? Banished him back to hell to face being punished for failing? He begged us to help him, but I guess that wouldn't have worked on you. Would you have banished him or chained him up in the yard with your new wyvern?"

"The wyvern is resting comfortably in the sanctuary I run for the paranormal beings ruthlessly hunted by humans, thank you." Why on earth was she defending herself? "I'm sure Fatma and Ali told you something about it."

Chloe's cheeks flamed brighter, her tears all gone, her eyes flashing, one bit of dark hair stuck to her sweaty forehead. "Of course they did." But the way her eyes shifted didn't back her up. She straightened. "Look, all we want to do is keep humans safe like you want to keep mons— paranormal creatures safe. Shouldn't we be working together?" Her jaw seemed to tremble, and Helen sensed more from her than anger, more reasons to want to work together besides the logic behind it.

But Chloe had clearly been about to say *monsters*.

Yes, but she'd changed it at the last minute. Helen took a step forward, but her anger was quickly morphing into something else, something that reacted to seeing Chloe all hot and passionate again, something that wanted to see more.

"We…have to protect innocent people," Chloe said to Helen's lips as if she couldn't help staring. "Human or supernatural."

"And yet you allow human monsters to live. No room for rehabilitation for anyone else?" They had to stay on topic. Even as they stared each other down, nearly toe to toe, with Chloe a little shorter.

Chloe's eyes slid back up to hers. "If we had a paranormal prison, sure. But if the general public knew about these creatures, it would be far worse for them, believe me. I will grant you that there are lots more human monsters than supernatural ones, and they wouldn't stop at killing." She jerked a thumb at the clearing. "And as I've already proved, I don't destroy lives if I don't have to." She licked her lips.

By all the gods.

"And I…" Chloe stumbled as if she'd lost her place. "I won't let you kill those people we caught, either," she said in a rush, waving vaguely toward the clearing. "I mean, I'll try to stop you." Her voice was softer now, not hesitant, but as if there were other things she wanted to whisper but couldn't. "You should…you should work with Fatma and Ali to—"

"I don't want Fatma and Ali."

Chloe gasped, the sudden sound like a lure that Helen had to resist.

"I mean, I don't want to work with them. I want…" And she couldn't help looking at Chloe's parted lips because some things in the universe seemed inevitable, like Chloe's gravity. "Who are you?" This pull between them felt so damned genuine, like Chloe's emotions: hung on the outside for anyone to see. For all her anger, she cared. About Helen, about Ramses, her friends and family, Maurice and Ligeia, even the freaking mercenaries. Helen could feel it radiating from her like heat from an oven.

Helen could feel the desire too. That was practically a sun. The feeling pulled her in even more, magnifying her own feelings like a convex lens.

Chloe looked to the side, breaking the spell a little, talking to Ramses, no doubt.

Right, they weren't alone. Helen took a step back and breathed. "I'll leave the mercenaries in your hands."

Chloe seemed disappointed as she asked, "How do you know they're mercenaries?"

"I just assumed. I would like to know any information you glean from them. And I will give some thought to working with you. Let me give you my number." She patted for her pockets, then remembered she was wearing a wet suit. And now she looked like an idiot.

"Here." Chloe produced a pen from her bag, along with a slip of paper. "I'd write it on my hand, but it's so sweaty out here." Her cheeks turned pink again. "I mean, I'm sweaty. It's hot." She looked away as if having her own dumbass feelings.

Helen jotted one of her numbers down and handed it back, hearing the Sphinx calling her a fool.

"Do you want a ride home?" Chloe asked. When Helen looked at her curiously, she lifted her hands. "Oh, sorry, the sanctuary's location is probably secret, huh?"

How had they gone from angry to lustful to nervous so quickly? She chuckled, her memories catapulting her back in time. "This is like a very awkward first date."

Chloe went seven shades of purple, but she also laughed like some of the tension was leaving her. "Huh, well, I haven't had one of those in a while."

A surprise in itself. "I bet I've got you beat there, probably by several hundred years, maybe even a thousand."

"When you were in Egypt, right?"

Helen leaned back, nearly startled out of her shoes. "You know I was in Egypt?"

"I read that somewhere. I would have gone there too to get away from Menelaus. What kind of asshole was he? He married the most beautiful woman in the world, and now I find out you're intelligent and wise and obviously care a lot about people. And he still didn't treat you right?" Her lips curled in, and she cleared her throat, looking down sheepishly. "Um, I'm sorry. I get carried away. Like I said, I really shouldn't be here. My sister Jamie would be handling this a lot better than me." She glanced to the side as if hearing Ramses again.

Helen took her hand, her angry, lustful, embarrassed emotions tumbling once again to flattered and touched and awestruck and protective. "I didn't know your sister, but it's unfair of you to compare yourself to someone unproven. It's impressive that you're doing as well as you are if this is a job you were unprepared for." She ran her thumb along the back of Chloe's hand. "You should also take it as a compliment that everyone trusts you, likes you, humans and paranormal beings alike. Including me. I think you're doing very well indeed."

Chloe stared as if Helen was Aphrodite herself, and when she stepped forward, Helen waited, letting it happen, accepting the kiss with grace. Dignity.

Until Chloe's lips lingered on hers, and her body seemed to move on its own. She wrapped her arms around Chloe and nearly lifted her, bringing them flush against each other. When Chloe moaned, Helen leaned down and grabbed her ass, then her leg when she wrapped it around Helen's hips. Chloe's hands were in her hair, and their tongues had found each other, and even Helen's godhood was rising as if celebrating how fucking good it felt.

Until a shock to the ribs reminded her that Ramses was watching.

Helen nearly dropped Chloe's leg and had to steady her before they stepped away from each other. "Right," Helen said, breathing through the desire to keep kissing Chloe, to drop to the jungle floor and have earth-shattering sex no matter who was watching. "We can't…right." She rubbed her side.

"Did he shock you?" Chloe breathed like a bellows, and she was blushing as she looked to the side where Ramses was no doubt giving her an earful. "Yeah, I get it." She frowned darkly. "You mentioned a Lamia earlier, Helen."

She shook her head, still trying to gather her thoughts. "The."

"What?"

"*The* Lamia." She waved. "There's supposed to be one. I thought she was here, but that was the demon you saw in disguise."

"We've heard she's behind all these traps and such."

Helen shook her head. "She can't leave the sanctuary."

"So you do have her?"

Damn, damn, damn. And here she'd thought she'd never have to worry about verbal sparring with Chloe. That was it; no more kissing people she was supposed to be hiding stuff from. "Safely locked away."

Chloe looked doubtful.

"She is, I promise you. I've taken steps to make sure she can't even communicate with the outside world. And I'm taking even more steps to see if she'll actually help protect the sanctuary." She pointed back at the clearing. "Since some of those hunting us aren't nearly as altruistic as you are."

That seemed to mollify Chloe a little. "I don't suppose you'd let us talk to her."

Helen might let Chloe onto the sanctuary. Might. Someday. But the others? "Why?"

"Damian heard something about a, I mean, the Lamia when he was summoned. It might be another bluff, but could we ask her?"

Interesting. Helen would have to ponder that awhile. "I'm afraid not. But I will keep my eyes on her."

"And if you find out she's trying to kill you and everyone else?"

Helen took a moment to keep her anger at bay again, looking at where that had gotten her last time. "I won't let her be murdered."

"Even if she'll never stop trying?"

"Everyone can change. I should know. I've been around long enough to see it." Though she wouldn't acknowledge it about some people. Like Psamathe. But Chloe didn't need to hear about that.

To Helen's surprise, Chloe smiled. "Don't forget, I've also got someone with a few millennia's worth of experience to call on."

Of course. Helen couldn't forget about Ramses. She still had a tingle in her ribs to remind her.

CHAPTER TWENTY-FOUR

Every molecule in Chloe's body was on fire from that kiss. It had been a whole lifetime of things she didn't know she could feel packed into a few moments.

When she'd first seen Helen in her wet suit with her sword, braided hair, killer body, and kick-ass attitude, she'd stumbled. Even her anger about Ramses being imprisoned had given way to wow. How did anyone manage to look so beautiful with the sweat and dirt and bugs?

When Helen loosed her power, she glowed, her hair, eyes, and skin shifting through warm tones of brown, bronze, and gold. But when they'd spoken, her hazel eyes had held comfort, and her light-brown hair seemed silky, even pulled back as it was. Chloe was sure that, by comparison, she looked like she'd been dragged behind a bus.

But Helen had seemed as taken with her—for real this time—breasts heaving under that tight wet suit, and she'd stared at Chloe's lips, too. It was a wonder Chloe had been able to wait to kiss her until after she'd said that Chloe was doing a good job.

She'd untangle that psychological knot later on.

"I don't know whether to thank you or kick you," she said to Ramses as they hiked back to the Kareems' boat. "But I'm very glad you're with me again so I have the option."

He closed his mouth on whatever he'd been going to say and smiled. "It was neither the time nor place, and you know it."

"So if it happens in the right time and place, you'll discreetly withdraw?"

"We are still at somewhat cross-purposes with Helen if we want to stop violent paranormal beings, and she wants to shield them."

"Yeah, about that…"

He gave her a flat look.

She lifted her hands. "Not just because of Helen. I've been feeling sorry for these creatures ever since that poor wyvern."

"Chlo—"

"Ghosts are one thing. We only find out about the ones that hurt people, and summoned ones are too unpredictable to stay, but if Helen or Fatma and Ali have somewhere to put the creatures—"

"With those like the wyvern, you may have a point. It's really just an animal. But those who murder like this Lamia? The intelligent ones?" He sighed. "Helen was right in that people can change, but if someone who was murderous a thousand years ago still says, 'Gosh, I love to kill stuff,' it's time to believe them."

He was right. And Helen was kind of right. Everyone was a little right, and that just wasn't fair.

When they got back to the boat, Helen and Maurice—a for-real fairy Chloe had been incredibly tickled to see once Ramses had been freed—started down the beach. Chloe had hoped for a private good-bye, but Helen only offered a little wave to her and a slightly sarcastic bow to the others before she headed away.

"She looks as good going as she does coming," Chloe mumbled.

"Mmm," Ramses said. "And I appreciate the double entendre."

She wished she hadn't spoken aloud as her cheeks heated. "Would you mind not checking out my girlfriend? She's intelligent, thoughtful, and kind as well as being hot."

His eyes went wide. "Girlfriend? Does she know about her new title?"

"Excuse me while I do a little wishful thinking."

"Aha. Well, I'm happy to see you're acknowledging how much you're into her."

"Oh please, everyone knew before we kissed. I'm surprised the hired thugs didn't bring it up." The hired thugs they'd been forced to leave behind, though Fatma and Ali had taken their guns. No one knew what else to do with them.

And Chloe didn't want to think about them with the setting sun outlining Helen in oranges and pinks. "That kiss—"

"What kiss?" her mom said from behind her.

Yeah, she could have called that. Shit. "Run," she muttered to Ramses without turning around. "Save yourself."

"No way. Two Musketeers, baby."

When Chloe turned, she regretted her smile in the face of her mom's scowl. "Can we get on the ship before you tear me a new one?"

"Chloe—"

"I know." She gestured to the boat. "In relative comfort? Please?" Her mother stomped aboard.

After sailing out of sight of the island, Fatma and Ali dropped anchor, saying they wanted to stay in the area. They had intel on an artifact on a nearby island and wanted to poke around a bit in the morning, grudgingly admitting that they could use some backup.

Great, now her conversation with her mom wouldn't have any sort of time limit.

"Ramses already said everything you're going to say, I'm sure," Chloe said when she, her mom, and Ramses stood alone in the bow.

"Ramses is a pushover, and he knows it."

He seemed shocked, but the crown hadn't come out yet. His mouth worked as if he didn't know how to respond.

"It's only because he loves us, but there it is," her mom said.

Ramses might not know what to say, but Chloe did. "So you love me just enough to still order me around?"

"Don't be pedantic, Chloe."

"You're the one who said it."

Her mom folded her arms, and the Chloe of yesterday would have crumbled under that hard gaze, but today's Chloe had shot nails into a demon and kissed a goddess. She wasn't scared of shit.

"Mom, I know Helen and I are at cross-purposes," she said, borrowing Ramses's grown-up word. "But I truly believe we can find a way to work together."

"So you can give yourself permission to have sex with her?"

The bottom fell out of Chloe's stomach. "God, Mom, please don't say sex."

"I know about—"

"Please don't tell me what you know!" Chloe squeezed her eyes shut, not too old to put her fingers in her ears if that was what it took to make her mom stop.

"Chloe Annabelle, open your eyes this instant."

She opened one, compelled by that most ancient of spells. When her mom clearly wasn't going to pantomime sexual positions or anything, she opened the other.

"You don't know what you're getting into," her mom said. "Older women—"

Chloe closed one eye again in warning.

Her mom held up her hands. "I'm just saying that someone as old as her might know a great many ways to take advantage of someone like you…us."

Anger and a bit of shame burned in Chloe now. As well as a jot of fear because what her mom said was probably true. Hadn't Helen been trying to flirt information out of her when they'd first had a real conversation? No, no, she'd felt something between them during the kiss, something that couldn't be faked. She decided to let the anger run her mouth. "Because I'm so naive?"

"Compared to her, aren't we all?"

"Not Ramses."

He snorted. "Finally, someone remembers that I'm here."

"Oh my God," Chloe said loudly. "I cannot take attitude from two directions at once. Y'all take a number." She wished her mom could see the nearly identical irritated looks they gave her. "And Ramses is always with me, Mom. He'd let me know if she was playing me." Had already let her know, in fact, but she kept that quiet.

Her mom's eyes went wide. "Oh, he'll be with you whenever you're together? Every second?"

Chloe was grateful she didn't say sex when she obviously meant it. But how could Chloe say that she and Helen wouldn't need words when next they were alone, how she wouldn't care what game they were playing as long as they were playing together?

Her mom and Ramses were looking at her expectantly, and that was so not fair. She wanted to say, trust me, wanted to almost beg for it, and that made her angrier than ever. Say it, she told herself. *Trust me like you would have trusted Jamie.*

But the words wouldn't come out. She couldn't be the one to invoke Jamie's ghost, not when she was always afraid her mom was going to do it instead.

"If Ramses thinks I'm getting in over my head," she said, "he'll let me know, just like today when he shocked Helen during our…thing that we're not talking about."

Ramses nodded in satisfaction, and even Chloe's mom seemed a bit mollified that Ramses was dealing out punishment. Still, as relieved as Chloe was when her mom released her from the conversation, Chloe was still stewing over the fact that her mother didn't fully trust her, that her mom might still think she wouldn't have had these problems with Jamie.

"What did you and Mom talk about?" Chloe asked when she was alone with Ramses near the rear of the boat. "When you were trapped?"

"I couldn't talk, remember?"

She rolled her eyes. "Don't make me pull pedantic out on you like she did on me."

"That she was happy to see me. Missed me." He looked out over the water that was almost lost to night in the falling gloom. "But who wouldn't?"

The false conceit made her want to hug him. "I know I did, and it was only an hour or so."

He smiled sadly. "Before the accident, I'd never had the opportunity to share in the life of someone I was bonded to after that bond was broken."

Yeah, because they had to die for the bond to pass on. Or at least, their heart had to stop beating like her mother's had.

"I wish I could have spoken to her, but it was nice to hear her again as someone other than an observer. I wish I could be with both of you. You're so similar, if only you would see it."

She had to bite her lip not to argue. "Did she say anything about…" *Wishing I was Jamie, that the wrong daughter died?*

He seemed to read her mind without even possessing her. Her shoulders tingled as his spectral arm went around her. "She's so proud of you, Chlo. How can I make you believe it?"

He couldn't, and she was so tempted to invite him in at that moment. She never thought she'd ask for possession outside of a dangerous situation. It was uncomfortable, but it had been a helluva day, and it would have been nice to be enveloped by his comforting presence.

CHAPTER TWENTY-FIVE

"How are you feeling?" Helen asked Ligeia when they were alone.

"I'd be better if you'd have let me stay with you in the clearing the whole time," Ligeia mumbled. She slouched as she walked, making it look like her baggy clothing was still with her in spirit, even though she wasn't wearing a stitch.

Helen sighed. "You were safer—"

"I know, I know." She rolled her eyes epically, then groaned when Maera waved from down the beach. The rest of the nereids bobbed in the waves offshore. "But you didn't have to wait out here with them. Eudore is having this on-again, off-again thing with a selkie, and she will not, like, shut up about it. And the rest are all like, 'gimmie the hot goss,' and I'm like, there obviously isn't any because she told the same fucking story eight times. If I have to hear what this selkie's like in bed once more, I'm gonna puke."

Helen bit her lip to keep from smiling. That all sounded way worse than freeing a pharaoh and getting the kiss of the millennium. But since Ligeia hated talking about relationships—like, obviously—she wasn't about to share that last tidbit.

It was a nice thought to hold in her heart as she waded out to sea, and the nereids began transporting all of them through the waves, back to the sanctuary. All her fears and doubts concerning Chloe were still there, but someone had turned the volume down on each of them. She didn't have to focus on the danger since Chloe wasn't actually present; she could enjoy the tingles that ran all the way to her toes. How long had it been since she'd indulged her feelings like this?

How long since she'd actually felt them?

When the nereids brought her to the surface the third time, she realized how far they'd come without her paying attention. Even in the failing light, they'd never get lost. They knew all the currents by heart. Helen squinted into the darkness at a speck of light. Strange. The glamour should have hidden every light. The nereids pulled up sharply as if they'd detected something different, too.

"Ahead," Helen said, "slowly."

Maurice rested on her head as the nereids brought her closer. More lights shone through the trees. "Are we at the right island?"

The nereids glanced at one another. "We are," Maera said confidently.

Ligeia gasped. "Then..."

"The glamour is down." Cold fear seized Helen's heart.

"I'm going ahead," Maurice said.

Helen grabbed for him, but he was away like a shot. "No, Maurice, stay...shit." She grabbed Eudore's shoulders. "Let's go."

They swam quickly, and Helen caught a flicker of light from the east side of the island and a plume of smoke. *Fates protect us.*

They came ashore next to the smoldering ruin of the boathouse. The hut that housed the Sphinx's communication equipment had one door hanging off its hinges, and the inside was dark. Helen held her breath as she poked her head in and switched on the light, but thankfully, no one was inside.

A black pit sat in the middle of the beach like a hole in the world, the sand and trees beyond blackened as if the fire that had destroyed the boathouse had spread from that crater. She would have put money on some sort of missile. The yacht appeared to be missing, but Helen couldn't tell if that was a good or bad thing until she knew who had taken it.

"Stay near the beach," she said to the nereids. "Call the local dolphins and whales and try to find out what happened."

"Shouldn't we stay with you?" Maera asked.

Helen pointed back toward the sea, praying they obeyed. If whoever had attacked the sanctuary was still here, she wasn't risking anyone else. When Ligeia stayed on her heels, Helen almost shoved her. "You can't—"

"Fuck you if you think I'm letting you go alone."

Well, Helen didn't have time to force her. She jerked her head toward the path. They'd check her house first, the closest building to the beach. Her heart hammered like a drum, her imagination turning every dark mass into the Sphinx's body. The house was a wreck, and Helen winced at the sharp tang of blood in the air.

She cursed herself for feeling relieved when she discovered the corpses of one of the dryad sisters and a fire salamander but not the Sphinx.

"What the fuck happened?" Ligeia whispered.

Helen couldn't let herself begin to grieve, not yet. "Come on."

She found Pegasus just off the trail that led to the rest of the houses and enclosures. A sob came tearing out of her when she saw his white coat and wings nearly glowing in the grass. He was alive, thank the gods, but one of his wings was bloody, and his mane was matted to the side of his face by a sticky scarlet stain.

She and Ligeia felt over him, but the bleeding appeared to have stopped. "We can't leave him here alone," Ligeia said.

"You stay. I'll come back." How many of the others would be like this, barely alive? How many more would be like the poor dryad and the salamander?

"Helen?" Maurice's voice.

She ran toward it. "Here."

The sound of his wings zipped closer. "The survivors are gathered at the lagoon."

"Survivors," she whispered. "How many?"

"Dunno yet. The Sphinx said some humans with special weapons came to the island and tore through everyone like the Reaper."

The Sphinx was alive. Helen let out a shuddering breath. "Show me." She followed the sound of his voice into the trees. Rage began to take hold of her, filling her like coal in a furnace.

"Sphinx said a few of the others were kidnapped. One of the Pleiades, Dani the hippogriff, the wyvern, and the Lamia, maybe a few more they can't find."

The Lamia again. "Did she say how they were taken?"

"I only caught a few bits. That ain't the worst part."

"Right, the dead—"

"No." His voice sounded shallow, scared. "Come on."

With her heart clenching, she followed him into the copse around the lagoon. The wounded and scared looked at her from every angle, some weeping, others with hopeful faces, sure she would save them. She touched them as she passed, but her eyes kept going toward the large form of the Sphinx between two pale pillars.

"Can you collect a few people to bring Pegasus here?" she asked Maurice quietly. "Or get Maera if you need her."

"Right."

The Sphinx had bandages around both paws, each with blood seeping through. Another wad of bloody cloth dabbed at a long cut down the side of her face, an invisible fairy tending to her wounds. One of her eyes was swollen shut, and she had matted blood on the fur of her chest and haunches. Her head was down, eyes closed, but she opened them when Helen rested a hand on her nose.

"Sphinx," Helen said, her gaze wavering with tears. "Oh gods."

"Don't cry for me," the Sphinx said, her voice exhausted. She lifted her head slightly and offered a small smile. "My claws are bloody. I held my own."

"Of course." Helen tried to swallow her feelings, but her jaw was so tight, she had to speak through teeth and tears. "Who?"

"Humans. Beyond that, I don't know." She blinked tiredly. "Maurice told you who they took?"

"One of the Pleiades, Dani the hippogriff, the wyvern, and the Lamia." She'd never forget that list. Ever.

"That's not all." Her tone was like Maurice's, heralding worse to come.

But what could be worse than the Lamia out in the world? If she wasn't working with them, Helen hoped she'd get to sink her teeth into those who'd taken her.

"I couldn't stop them, Hel," the Sphinx said through a sob. "I'm so sorry."

"Shh, it's not your fault. We'll get them back."

"They found Charybdis's cell."

Time seemed to stop. Only the oldest inhabitants of the sanctuary knew Charybdis was even here. Her cell was carefully hidden, just as Charybdis herself was kept asleep. "How?"

"I don't know, but they were so prepared. Hel, what if they know how to wake her?"

Helen shook her head. Charybdis was so much more than the whirlpool-creating monster described in *The Odyssey*. She was a titan, a true force of nature, her hatred of humans so fierce, she would destroy the world to be rid of them.

And a group of humans had freed her? Gods help them.

Gods help us all.

Humans. Why had she ever gotten close to them again? This was what they did, what they always did. And she'd been off kissing one when she should have been here, protecting her people, keeping everyone safe, keeping the rest of the world safe if they did but know it.

Gods, what if Chloe had simply been keeping her busy while—

But everything in her rebelled at that idea. Unless the genuine parts of Chloe were an act, some subtle magic designed to beguile and confuse her. And Helen had mentioned the sanctuary, oh gods, gods!

She made herself breathe. If she'd been fooled once, she wouldn't be again. She calmed herself, but tremors still passed through her like the heralds of an earthquake. But it would be humanity who reaped that destruction this time instead of her own kind.

"Tell me from the beginning."

CHAPTER TWENTY-SIX

Chloe was startled awake by the howling of every dog in hell. She flailed in the dark, and it wasn't until she fell that she remembered she wasn't in her own bed or a hotel or in the back seat of her car. She was in a hammock. On a boat.

Or she had been.

Now, the floor had her full attention as she smacked into it.

She cradled her shoulder, moaned in pain, and rolled over. The dogs of hell became an alarm to her now-awake brain, and she joined everyone else in asking what was going on.

The alarm cut off abruptly with a sad *blart*. Ali yelled down the stairs, "There's something in the water."

Chloe pulled on pants and staggered up with the others. Ramses stood behind a sleepy-looking Fatma in the bow.

Ali held up a glowing silver decanter. "This set off the alarm. It detects the presence of oceanids."

"Like nereids?" Chloe's mom peered at the blackness of the water.

"How close?" Jillian asked just as David muttered, "I don't suppose it could be a coincidence."

After the day they'd had?

"All I can tell is that it's nearby," Ali said.

Fatma went inside the flybridge, and the underside of the ship lit up like Christmas, turning the water pea-green for about forty feet in all directions.

"There," Ramses said, but when Chloe looked, she saw nothing. He walked through the boat's side and started in that direction, hovering just above the water.

"Ramses is going to look," Chloe said. Her mother turned with worried eyes, but Chloe shook her head. "There's nothing to etch sigils into out here."

"You don't know that."

Chloe frowned, irritated and exhausted. "You try calling him back."

Her mother sighed. She knew damn well that he was always going to rush in no matter what anyone said.

"She's swimming under the boat," Ramses called. "She's carrying something that feels magical, but I can't tell what it is." And he really hated floating into the water, saying he could never see and quickly lost track of directions without gravity to guide him.

Chloe relayed this. Jillian bit her lip. "I've got a net that might—"

Ali rounded on them. "Let's try talking first, hmm?" Ironic coming from the master of angry silences. He blew across the top of the decanter, making a deep, hollow sound. Through the hum, he said, "Hello, we are Ali and Fatma Kareem. We mean you no harm." He gave the rest of them a dark look, daring them to argue. "We're ready to help if you need us."

All was still for a moment. Ramses rejoined them, peering over the side. He pointed as if to say the oceanid was still down there. Maybe she was just curious?

"Are you the humans from earlier?" a voice called from the water.

Chloe strained to see, but the slope of the ship hid them from view. Ramses floated closer. "She's here. She looks a bit like one of the creatures who were with Helen earlier. And she seems worried. The magical feeling is coming from a large conch shell."

"We met Helen earlier, yes," Chloe said. "On an island not far from here."

"And you helped her?"

"We did." Everyone clustered behind Chloe, and she tried to wave them back a bit. "Does she need us? Do you?"

"You have medical supplies?"

Chloe's heart seized. "What happened? Is Helen all right?"

"We have medicine," Fatma called. "And first aid kits."

"Will you follow me? Please?" Her voice grew thicker, the words slow with fatigue.

Chloe's mom and her friends looked doubtful. Damian just shrugged, but Fatma and Ali nodded. And it was their boat. "Yes, lead on."

With Ramses back onboard, they sailed into the night, the fleece letting them keep up with the oceanid's blip on the radar. She swam faster than anything Chloe had ever seen, and a good thing, too, because Chloe didn't think her heart could take the journey any slower.

They headed toward a brightly lit island that wasn't on the Kareems' sea charts, and the wind carried the heavy smell of smoke, too much for a bonfire or a friendly campout on the beach. Someone had attacked Helen's sanctuary.

Chloe went below and collected her bag and shoes. Fatma had already gathered all the medical supplies and loaded them into the Zodiac that nestled against the boat's side. Chloe tried to think of what else she could bring, but her mind was whirling too fast to focus. If someone had hurt Helen...

No, she wouldn't think about that.

But she would seriously fuck them up.

After just one kiss?

It was more than a kiss, always had been more than that. They'd been drawn to each other since they'd first met. She'd seen way too much magic to not believe such things were possible. And their future was still electric with possibilities, and she wasn't about to let anyone snuff those out.

She was going to be in so much trouble with her mom.

Chloe pushed that thought away too and climbed into the Zodiac once the yacht had stopped. When everyone tried to pile in with her, the oceanid called, "Only the human with the blood of Isis and her guardian spirit."

Ramses snorted and mumbled, "Guardian spirit," just as Chloe's mom yelled, "No way in hell."

"Mom," Chloe said sharply, "cut it out." She called to the oceanid, "It's okay," hoping her mom hadn't just messed everything up.

"It is not okay!"

"The demon may come also," the oceanid said.

With a smug smile, Damian hopped aboard.

Jillian crossed her arms. "Since when is a demon the most trustworthy one here?"

"Anyone else and we'll sink you."

"There are more of them now," Ramses said as he leaned over the Zodiac's side. The decanter in Ali's hands shone like the Fourth of July.

"Fine, then we'll leave," Chloe's mom shouted. "Good luck on your own."

Chloe glared at her, but the only thing to do was act before her mom could stop her. She waved to Fatma in the flybridge, and the Zodiac began to lower toward the water.

"No, Chloe." Her mom lunged, and David had to grab her to keep her from falling over the side. "Chloe Annabelle, you get back here this instant."

"I'll let you know what I find." She tried to tune her mother out as the Zodiac settled on the water but realized she had no idea how to drive it.

"Here." Fatma tossed something to her, and she hoped it was the driver's manual, but it was only a walkie-talkie. "Channel two. I can talk you through the controls."

"We will carry you in," the oceanid said over the side, and Chloe caught a glimpse of skin that shone like a pearl. "Hang on."

Chloe grabbed hold of the seat as a wave carried the Zodiac toward a fire-blasted beach.

❖

Helen felt a shift in the wind, then realized it was more of a hush descending on the lagoon. She turned and spied Psamathe at the edge of the trees. Her old betrayer. Helen felt required to throw a fit, but with a sigh, she sagged, lacking the energy to really care.

Psamathe wasn't even looking at her. She had a few boxes in her arms, one that looked like a first aid kit, and she began to pass those out to the wounded.

Good, Helen could ignore her if she was helping. But the hush persisted, and Helen turned again. She'd missed something. Or someone.

"You've got to be kidding me." The Sphinx grunted as if she might push to her feet.

"Lie back," Helen said, trying to be gentle but hoping the Sphinx read the threat in her words. If she had to, she'd—

Chloe stood at the edge of the copse, her demon beside her.

A human. In this place of sanctuary.

Another human. After they'd already committed such monstrous crimes here.

Chloe held a first aid box, the cross displayed like a shield. Her eyes were wide, horrified, and that was probably the only thing that saved her.

Grumbles now spread through the crowd like blowing embers soon to become a wildfire. Helen had a brief thought to let them catch. Everyone needed an outlet for their rage and pain. If the other humans had been standing with Chloe, she might have let it happen. Chloe alone? Trusting that Helen would protect her?

"Helen," Chloe said, her voice carrying above the murmurs, "I'm so sorry." Sympathy tinged her words rather than guilt.

The demon taking the first aid kit and kneeling next to an injured dryad seemed to help with the mumbling, and Helen moved toward Chloe, her feelings wound as tightly as tangled gold chains.

"The nereids told me a little. We came to help."

"Where are your friends?"

Chloe swallowed hard. "On the boat."

One sliver of good fortune. "Come with me." Helen led her into the trees, away from any mounting anger and leaving it to Psamathe to explain Chloe's presence to the Sphinx.

"They didn't tell me much. One of them woke us up, and we came as quickly as we could. Are you all right?" Her words were rushed, one hardly over before the next began, her southern accent mashing them all together.

"No, none of us is all right. Neither are you. Humans did this while I was on a wild-goose chase crafted by more humans, and still, you came here." She gritted her teeth and tried to keep her tears at bay, not knowing if she was grateful or appalled. She expected Chloe to deny, defend, cast aspersions in kind, and then she'd…she'd…

"I'm so sorry, Helen. How can I help? I'll do whatever you need." Her eyes seemed lit up, even in the dark. "We could get more supplies from another port. We could patrol around the island or try to trace the assholes responsible for this. We could…whatever you want." Her arms came forward as if to offer an embrace.

How did she know how to say all the right things? From anyone else, it might have seemed calculated, but the word genuine popped into Helen's mind again. What Chloe said was what there was.

Helen pulled her into a hug, delighting in the magical hum and resting her cheek against Chloe's soft curls. She let in a modicum of comfort, just a token, just for now.

Chloe's arms went around her waist and rubbed her back in soothing strokes. "It's gonna be okay. We're gonna figure this out," she said into Helen's shoulder.

Tempted to stay in those arms and let the tears come, Helen straightened, remembering that Chloe was never alone for long. Helen wouldn't be, either, not when the others had seen her go off with a human. "You can't stay here. It's not safe for anyone."

Chloe nodded softly. "I understand. Quick, though, tell me what happened."

Helen relayed what she knew, forcing herself to be distant from it, as if she was summarizing a novel. Chloe nodded, swiping at the tears Helen couldn't let herself shed, her determined expression saying she'd forget nothing.

Helen captured her hand when her tale ended. "I wish you could stay."

"Me too."

"Find out who did this. I don't think they were expecting you on that island, ghost-trap or not. They may not expect you now." It shamed her to ask for help, but she told herself not to be so precious. The sanctuary needed all the help it could get, and Helen couldn't lose herself in any feelings, tender or prideful. Rage was the only thing that would help her now.

Chloe nodded, fierceness showing through her sympathy. "Don't worry. We'll smoke these fuckers out if we have to." Her blush shone even in the dim light from the lagoon. "Sorry."

"Your vehemence is appreciated. Wait here."

When Helen returned to the lagoon, the demon, Damian—"my mom's a movie fanatic"—seemed content to stay and help. Though his power couldn't enthrall the sanctuary's residents, they seemed to find his aura comforting. Helen gave him a grateful nod, then turned to lead Chloe and Ramses back to the shore.

Eudore waited by the small craft that would carry Chloe to the larger boat bobbing on the water.

"The Kareems' yacht has all the bells and whistles," Chloe said. "I'm sure they'll be happy to keep watch for you through the night. And their alarms are loud enough for the devil to hear." She handed Helen a walkie-talkie. "Fatma said channel two would reach her, reach me."

Good. Helen didn't want to speak to anyone else. "If you find the whereabouts of those responsible—"

"*When* we find them."

Helen ducked her head and smiled, even though the lead weight of grief still hung around her shoulders, and she had to fight them both. "Don't go after them on your own. I need to be there. I will be there."

Chloe nodded. "I hear that. You didn't think I'd try to argue, did you?"

"Everyone else seems to object when I put myself in danger."

"Welcome to the club. So long as you let me come with you into the danger, you won't get a fight out of me." She shrugged. "Until we face the danger, of course."

Helen's first instinct was to object, but how could she after what Chloe had just said? "Thank you."

They stared at one another, a comfortable silence instead of an awkward one. So rare.

"Um," Eudore said from the water. "I think you'd better get back. That one woman keeps trying to jump in the water, and I don't know how much longer the others can hold her."

Chloe squeezed the bridge of her nose. "Mom," she mumbled. She snatched the walkie-talkie, thumbed it on, said, "I'm coming back now," and turned it off just as an angry squawk sounded from the other end. "I'll be in touch."

"Be careful." Helen didn't know what she'd do if something happened to anyone else she cared about.

"You too."

After another long look, Chloe stepped into the boat and was lost to the shadows among the waves.

CHAPTER TWENTY-SEVEN

When Chloe reached the boat again, she realized she didn't have much to go on. The intruders sounded similar to the thugs at the wild-goose chase island, but even Helen's info was secondhand. Chloe hadn't been able to talk to anyone actually present during the attack.

Not that she'd wanted to try. When she'd stood in that clearing, she'd felt the hatred seeping out of the ground. In her own encounters, she'd never fought an intelligent creature. That she knew of. How many of her ancestors or her mother and friends had left grief and anger like that in their wake?

Ramses was quiet, too, and when they reached the yacht again, Chloe could even tune out her mom, waiting to talk until everyone sat below except for Ali at the yacht's controls.

"I didn't see much of the sanctuary itself," Chloe said. "It was dark." She tried to marshal her thoughts and untangle them from her feelings. "The people who brought us here are called nereids, and Helen described returning to find the bodies of friends and family after a brutal attack. The survivors are pretty banged up." She sipped water and realized her hands were shaking. "Helen thinks someone lured her away on purpose, then attacked."

She looked at her mom but couldn't stop seeing bruised and bandaged faces half in moonlight, hatred or terror in their eyes while she choked on the stink of smoke and blood and fear.

Her mom squeezed her shoulder. "I never should have let you go alone."

Chloe surged to her feet. "This isn't about me, about any of us." Her voice kept rising, but she couldn't stop it. "We have to find out who did this and make sure they can never do it again." No matter what that took.

Her mom and Jillian talked over one another to disagree, but Fatma was staring with admiration or approval, and Chloe knew she had at least two allies in this.

Three counting Ramses. He gave her a proud smile, and she could take on the world.

"Where do we start looking?" Chloe asked over the protests. Funny how her childhood insecurities fell away when she knew she was right. Or maybe that was partly down to how tired she was.

"I'll make some calls," Fatma said before jogging upstairs.

"You can't be serious," Chloe's mom said.

Jillian touched her arm but aimed her words at Chloe. "Hon, I know what you saw scared you, but think this through."

Chloe wasn't even put off by the heap of condescension. "I have."

"Damian and I were looking at some of Ali's sea charts earlier," David said. He stared at the ceiling, his problem-loving wheels obviously turning. "If he can get some information about what kind of vehicles the attackers arrived in, I might be able to figure out where they came from." He seemed to notice Jillian's stare for the first time. "What?"

"Just how much time have you been spending in the company of that demon?"

He *tsked*. "Mind your own business, and come help me." He practically dragged her up the stairs.

Chloe's mom was looking at her as if they were strangers, a gut punch if there ever was one. Chloe wished she could lean into Ramses, so relieved he had her back.

"Ramses, please give us a minute alone," her mom said.

Well, so much for that.

Of course, she could always lie and say he'd left but wasn't sure he'd like that. "It's okay," she said when he hesitated. "Best get this over with."

Her mom tilted her head, and Chloe caught a glimpse of why her enemies feared her.

"Sorry," Chloe mumbled as Ramses walked through the wall into one of the cabins. "I'm tired."

"And not thinking clearly. That I understand."

"Mom—"

"This is not our fight, Chloe."

"Just listen—"

"After a good night's sleep and a hot meal, you'll see—"

"I'm not a goddamned child." No matter that she was yelling like one, but just like earlier, she had lost control of her volume.

Her mom crossed her arms, an immovable wall. "If we get in the fight over this island, we should get in on the other side."

Chloe went cold and felt the weight of generations in that stare. Who was she to say their ancestors had gone too far, to criticize them for not stopping their crusade at only those creatures who were still hurting people? She was nothing but an upstart, a novice in a long chain of knights forged in blood and sweat.

God, she wanted to call Ramses back so badly.

No, fuck that. She squeezed her hands into fists. "I know what I'm—"

"Jamie would have understood."

The world fell away. Chloe's stomach became a black pit full of every doubt, every mean thought she'd ever had about herself. It was all true. Tears bubbled inside her like a hot spring.

Her mom's steady stare waited for an apology.

Just like Helen and her people were waiting for help.

And she was the one with the power.

A new feeling rose in Chloe's chest, overtaking the tears and swamping them. It filled her limbs like the strength of the magic helmet, and a silvery glow tinted her vision.

Her mom took a step back, eyes wide. "Chloe...you're glowing."

That seemed only right. "I'm a fucking superhero, Mom, and it's time I acted like it. Screw what the world finds out. If humanity decides to come after supernatural people, well, I know where they can go for sanctuary, and I know who's gonna protect them." She stabbed herself in the chest with her thumb, just in case there was any doubt left in her mom's mind.

Still, the tears were coming. She had to get out of there.

But not before one more thing. "I'm not siding with anyone who hurts people like that." She pointed confidently in the direction of the sanctuary as if she could feel it through the wall. "I'm not Jamie, and I never will be, and you don't know that she wouldn't feel the same as me."

Her mom's face twisted in disbelief.

Chloe didn't stick around to hear any more. She barely made it into the cabin where Ramses waited before she collapsed, more tired than she'd ever been. Her mother's words still echoed in her ears despite her bravado. She opened her arms, and Ramses stepped into her without being asked, and she couldn't even feel guilty about needing someone else to take the wheel for a while.

He got them up off the floor. "Families of gods have to support one another."

Not always, it seemed. "Am I doing the right thing?"

"Your godhood rose, so you must be doing something right."

She couldn't even be that surprised. "Was that what that was? I'm hollow and nauseated, like I ran ten miles after eating a gallon of mashed potatoes."

"Now that it's manifested, you have to learn to save that power for when you really need it."

She had needed it. Saving it from now on was no problem; she had no idea how she'd called it in the first place. "You didn't answer my question."

"Chloe—"

"I know you'll always support me, but if you think I'm doing the wrong thing, you have to say."

"I—"

"Because godhood or not, I'll need your help and love, and…she said Jamie's name, Ramses, she actually fucking said it." If she'd been in charge of the body, she'd have been wheezing like a steam engine, all her feelings on the boil. "I feel like I'm coming apart at the seams."

He was quiet for a moment. "Finished? Because I never doubt that you'll do the right thing, especially when you take the time to think it through. Like you clearly have now."

"I know, right? Why can't Mom see—"

"No, it's my turn to talk." He sighed. "Helen made an offer to *free* me." The word had enough contempt to sink a freighter.

"What the hell?" Maybe it made sense on one hand; Helen helped paranormal people in trouble. But on the other hand was really annoyed. "How dare she—"

"It's still my turn."

Chloe hoped he could feel her look.

"She offered to get me around Anubis and into the underworld to see my family."

"Holy shit." His beloved Nefertari and the rest of his wives? His oodles of kids and grandkids and so on? The multitudes who'd worshiped him as a god king? "Maybe you—"

"It's still my turn."

The hordes who knew he could be kind of an ass?

"I heard that. Anyway, I didn't even consider it, Chlo, not really. I didn't outright reject it because I just wanted her to stop talking. All I could think about was your ancestors, your mom, you. You're alive. You have to grow, change, adapt, and I want to be here for you and tell everyone who comes after you how amazing you are. Eternity can wait."

If she'd been in charge of the body, the tears would have been choking, wet, and snotty. "Love you, too." She took a second to feel his love and share hers. "Can I talk now?"

"No. All that being said, I still have to answer your question. Yes, I think you're doing the right thing."

She sputtered a laugh. "You took forever to get there."

"Shut up and pull yourself together. The superhero does not burst into tears on the eve of teaming up with her lady love to save the day."

CHAPTER TWENTY-EIGHT

Helen forced herself to listen to each and every story about what had happened, even if most sounded the same. She was looking for clues the victims might not even realize they knew, but reliving the trauma also felt like her just desserts for not being there to suffer with them.

When the Sphinx finally forced her to get some sleep, laying one large paw across her legs so she couldn't move, she dreamed of unknown terrors in the dark and stirred at every cry from the wounded. No one else on the sanctuary had wanted to return home, so after feeding the more animal-like residents in their enclosures, everyone else bedded down near the lagoon.

She woke with a start to find dawn had already broken. The Sphinx's paw still lay across her, and she appeared to be asleep. Helen was loath to wake her, but now that the sun was up...

With a sigh, she felt around her for the walkie-talkie. She needed to think of something to tell Chloe. She needed to go home to change. Selfishly, she hoped someone else had cleared the bodies from her house. Where to keep the corpses: another thing she had to plan, as well as thinking up memorials for them. Some came from cultures that buried their dead; some would have wanted to be cremated or interred in stone. For others, she had no idea, and shame spiraled through her anew.

And where had the fucking walkie-talkie gone?

The Sphinx's paw shifted as she opened her tired eyes. "If you're looking for the walkie, Damian took it."

A thousand nefarious reasons came to mind. Helen hadn't known many demons, but their reputations—

She made herself breathe. She'd long ago ceased judging people by their pasts, shortly after "of Troy" had seemingly become part of her name.

Chloe had never mentioned that accursed city, another point in her favor. Helen shook her head, trying to arrange her tired mind. "Did he mention why?"

"He was asking about the ships that the bastards who attacked us landed in. He said Chloe was trying to find out where they might have come from."

Helen ran a hand down her face and pulled her knees to her chin. She'd thought every sound had awakened her last night, but apparently, she'd slept through a lot.

"And our yacht came back. A few residents managed to use it to flee from the attack."

"Thank the gods." She could happily cross those names off the list of the missing. The happy news gave her the energy to stand. "I need to get changed, then organize a…morgue."

"Already done. The Lamia's crypt."

Seemed fitting. "How much did I sleep through?"

"You might have been under the influence of Hypnos's Poppy."

A rather ugly potted plant blessed by the god of sleep. "You didn't." She clenched her fists.

"Just close enough to the lagoon that the wounded could get a good rest. The dryads just took it back to their grove."

"I'm not wounded," Helen said through her teeth. "You are."

"I had to take notes for you. And you needed sleep in order to be at your best, find those unholy children of Set, and rip them to pieces." She growled, her claws digging into the grass like plows.

Helen breathed through her anger again. The Sphinx had wronged her for the right reason; she could forgive that in the face of everything else. "Anyway, I'm glad you won't argue against me facing these monsters."

"I only wish I could go with you. You'll probably have lots of volunteers."

"Well, I won't argue for going alone."

The Sphinx flashed a fanged smile. "I like Chloe, by the way. She speaks like one of the Furies. Some of us have decided to just not think of her as human."

"You spoke to her?" The idea sent a swarm of bees loose inside her, though she couldn't say why.

"A little, over the walkie, after you were under the poppy's spell. And Damian has been a great comfort. I never really considered that a sex demon could give great massages, but I suppose it makes sense. Very good for pain and bruised muscles. Someone said that if he stays on this plane, he should consider a career in physical therapy. I bet he'd make a mint."

Helen barked a laugh, then another, and couldn't stop, struck by the absurdity. The Sphinx joined in, and they put their hands and paws over their mouths to keep the sound down. Like a crack in a dam, Helen's control threatened to give way to other emotions. She forced herself to stop before her laughter became sobs. The dead were seemingly piled in the Lamia's crypt. The injured still lay around the copse, and many of the sanctuary's buildings had been burned, the sense of safety stolen from them. "What are we going to do?"

"Rebuild. On another island if we have to. Or somewhere even harder to find."

"Like the center of the Earth."

"The fire salamanders would be happy."

With another shaky laugh, Helen rested her forehead against the Sphinx's fuzzy shoulder. "I'm so sorry I wasn't here."

"Don't you dare apologize. I have no qualms about biting a goddess. Now, go change into your best vengeance gear, and leave the island to me. When I see Damian again, I'll tell him to meet you back here with the walkie."

"I love you, Sphinx."

"Love you, too. Now run along."

Too much sentiment always made her edgy. Helen gave her a flick on the nose before setting off for the house. She forced down grief and fear and all worries about the future. She only had room for revenge now.

❖

Helen looked like every Lara Croft fantasy Chloe had ever had. Black boots, cargo pants, and T-shirt; the little sword she always carried at her hip. The only things missing were the shoulder holsters, but Helen never seemed to use real guns. Instead, she had an intriguing leather pouch strapped to one thigh. She seemed born to kick ass as she waited on the shore, her hair in a crown of braids and Maurice perching on one shoulder.

Someone else stood beside her, their much shorter form shrouded in a threadbare brown cloak with the hood up, but there was no missing the giant ax clutched in one gloved hand.

Chloe had never felt so normal in jeans and a blue T-shirt she'd borrowed from Fatma. Lil' Devil was written across the front in silver letters. Damian had been tickled pink by it when he'd returned to the boat and had called dibs on borrowing it next. David had opened his big mouth and suggested Damian just manifest the same shirt with his power, but Chloe had put her foot down.

"Don't you dare," she'd said. "We'll look like a friggin' dance team."

Looking at Helen now, she was so glad she'd shot that idea down. Chloe's side of this particular *Dungeons & Dragons* party already looked like amateur hour by comparison. They did not need to provide the comic relief, too.

After a tense night spent patrolling around the island and avoiding her mom, Chloe was more than ready to go to the beach with Ramses and Damian. When they arrived, Helen gestured to another yacht that had docked in the night, more survivors who'd been able to flee the violence. "We'll be taking that."

"Oh," Chloe said, hoping she didn't sound as clueless as she felt. "I see."

"Is there a problem?" Stone had replaced any earlier softness in Helen's features.

Chloe still didn't sense any menace toward her personally and tried to control her nerves at the thought of being in unknown territory again. "I just thought…"

"It will get us away from your mother and Jillian," Ramses said.

"That's a great idea." Chloe smiled.

"Do you have everything you need with you?" Helen asked.

Chloe patted her bag that now also contained the recharged nail gun. "And Ramses is ready, too."

Damian spread his arms as if to say he only needed himself. Chloe hoped for his sake that he wouldn't throw any random flirting Helen's way, and he seemed to have enough sense of self-preservation to hold back.

Helen handed over the walkie. "You'd better inform them of the change in plans."

Not ask. Chloe liked the sound of that but doubted her mom would. She nodded and hung back a few steps as they started walking down the beach before making the call. "Fatma, are you there?"

"Go ahead."

"We're going on Helen's boat. Can you tell my mom?"

"Coward," Fatma said, a smile in her voice. "Do you want us to follow?"

Helen looked over her shoulder. "No matter what they're using for speed, the magic of the nereids is faster."

"Sounds like you can't keep up," Chloe said, her mouth going dry in the face of Helen's badassedness.

Fatma was silent for a moment. "Do you have room for one more?"

Chloe looked to Helen, who paused, eyes on the sky. Chloe was about to point out that more allies could only be a good thing when Helen said, "One. And quickly."

After some shuffling of the Zodiac, Fatma arrived at Helen's boat bristling with so many weapons, she looked like a hedgehog with the NRA. Once Helen's boat was under way, Chloe asked, "What did the others say?"

"I sent most of them downstairs to work on an imaginary problem and only told Ali where I was going." She smiled sweetly. "I left it to him to explain later."

Chloe poked her in the arm. "Coward."

"Hush, Lil' Devil."

Her cheeks warming, Chloe frowned. "It's your damn shirt."

"A gift from my mother. She has an odd sense of humor."

"Lots of demons do," Damian said.

Fatma went stiff as a ruler.

Chloe's mind raced. "Wait, what?"

Damian blinked. "She and her brother are part demon, like half or something. Didn't you know?" He looked between them. "Is it supposed to be a secret?"

"A quarter demon," Fatma snapped in a low voice. "My father is half." She rolled her eyes as if the information was being dragged from her. "And for full disclosure, my mother's side is descended from one of el naddaha, a fresh-water sprite." She looked down. "Who may or may not have killed people occasionally," she mumbled.

"Why didn't you say?" Chloe asked. When Fatma gave her a look, she shrugged. "Okay, I see why you might have left out that last part, but what about the rest of it?"

"To a group like your mother and her friends?"

Fair point. "And it's probably not easy to slip that into the conversation."

"Like having the blood of Isis," Fatma said with another pointed look.

So she'd been talking to people, too. Or listening in. "Yeah, yeah, touché." She waved at the boat. "But you can probably admit it on this boat all you want."

A handful of nereids swarmed over everything, all exceptionally strong and exceptionally lovely in their swimwear; all the colors of the sea were in their hair, eyes, and skin. Helen stood talking to a large creature that seemed made of stone and muscle, a troll, if memory served, though Chloe had only seen one in pictures.

Ramses stood behind Helen, eavesdropping, though Chloe didn't see the need. The individual in the brown cloak had stayed covered, and Maurice perched on their head looking glum. Chloe gave him a wave that he hesitantly returned, but the person he sat on started a bit, then gave an enthusiastic wave in response. Cute.

They approached and took their hood down, and Chloe nearly screamed.

A friendly brown face, cheerfully marked by laugh lines, smiled through streaks of blood. It ran down their face in rivulets over dark, older stains. It matted the tufts of hair sticking out from beneath a sodden red hat and streamed over their shoulders, leaving patches that seemed to soak in and become part of their rust-colored clothing.

Before Chloe could ask if they were all right, the hat gave her a clue as to who this might be: a red cap, a goblin who was rumored to either kill everyone they met or act more like a cheery, helpful gnome, all depending on which folklore one consulted. The blood and ax seemed to point to the former, and the face belonged to the latter. And the hat might have been bloody, but it was also made of wool with a little bobble on top.

Fatma made a strangled noise, and Damian whispered, "Oh my gosh."

Chloe hurried over their words and noises with, "Hi, I'm Chloe," way too loudly and with a heap of fake cheer. "This is Fatma and Damian." She held out her hand before regretting it, but it was too late to draw it back.

"Robin," they said, red eyes shining as they blinked blood out of the way. They left a sticky red print on her palm that dissolved as she watched. "I'm so happy you waved. Not many people want to talk to me, put off by the mysterious cloak or…" They gestured up and down their face.

Maurice resettled on their shoulder. "Chloe," he said with a nod. "Welcome aboard."

"Thanks."

"You hang out with a lot of extraordinary beings for someone in your line of work," he said, a calculating look in his eye. Fatma and Damian were glancing around, no doubt seeking the source of his voice.

Chloe smiled, so not wanting to jump back into any debates. "As I'm finding out, we're all extraordinary here."

He smirked.

Robin *tsked.* "Leave her alone, Maurice. We don't get to meet many friendly new people. Or new people at all, and those from yesterday were most certainly unfriendly." They snorted with an incredulous expression, as if talking about someone who'd cut in line at the supermarket instead of trained killers. "I had to kill as many as I could and hope we never could have been friends. And they didn't even taste good." Their jaw dropped in exaggerated disbelief. "I fed lots of them to Cristos, he's a griffin, and the triplets of Wadjet, whom I can never tell apart."

Chloe didn't even know where to start. "Bummer?"

"I know!" They giggled. "Don't worry, even though you're mostly human, I won't try to eat you." They winked. "Or will I? Nom, nom, nom." They made as if to grab her arm while chewing air, then laughed. "Just kidding."

Chloe could barely stop herself from jumping overboard.

"Robin, can I see you for a moment?" Helen called.

"Sure thing." They turned back to Chloe. "So nice meeting you." With a cheery wave, they departed, Maurice chuckling on their shoulder as they went.

"I try not to judge," Fatma whispered, "but what the fuck?"

"We are so not in Kansas anymore," Damian said.

Chloe nodded. What in the hell had she gotten herself into? Her new pledge to spare intelligent paranormal beings shriveled a bit after meeting that particular one.

But something much more cheerful stuck in her brain, thank goodness. "Did you say, 'oh my gosh'?" she asked Damian.

He frowned defensively. "I can't really say the other G-word, now, can I?" He glanced around. "And I suggest you keep any holy symbols tucked away in the interim. Some of these people may not be as affected as I am, but I'm guessing many have a very problematic history with some symbology in particular."

Well, shit, she couldn't tease him after that.

Fatma grinned and said, "It's gonna be hard to remember to say gosh-damn," with seemingly no qualms at all.

"And gosh-awful," Chloe said, warming to it. "Thank gosh."

"OMG...OSH."

Damian stabbed a finger at each of them. "This is why no one likes you." He pointed at himself. "Beloved by everyone, MVP of every situation, voted most popular." He pointed at them again. "Back of the yearbook with no signatures."

Fatma burst out laughing, and Chloe had a brief thought that she could have fallen for that smile once upon a time.

If Helen hadn't gotten there first.

From her place near a set of stairs that led up to the bridge, Helen turned and caught Chloe staring. Her head tilted, and whatever she saw in Chloe's face seemed to bring out a smile. Just a small one, but it glowed with affection.

Helen said a few more words to her companions, then started toward Chloe.

"We should make ourselves scarce in case they want to make out," Damian mock-whispered.

"I dunno, that might be worth a look," Fatma said.

"Don't be creepy, Lil' Devil." He took her arm and led her away.

Chloe wished a steamy make-out session was on the agenda, both for its own sake and because it would have been nice to forget about their current troubles for a bit.

But Ramses's presence at Helen's side reminded her about appropriate times and places again, as much as she wanted to tell that whole concept to go to hell.

Chapter Twenty-nine

Part of Helen lamented having Chloe aboard. Yes, she was a comfort, and she looked positively edible in her tight jeans and devil T-shirt, and every time Helen looked at her, she wanted to forget the last several days in her arms.

Which was precisely the problem. Helen could not afford to stop being the spirit of vengeance. The sanctuary needed a sword, not a mourner wilting in her lover's arms.

She never should have entertained the idea of being with Chloe in the first place, should have turned on her heel the moment Chloe had arrived at Remora Island and left Ramses in his prison. She looked at Chloe now and told herself to feel nothing but regret. She would be steel.

Oh, bullshit.

She sighed. Being a demigod would have been so much easier without all the damned feelings. Some sword of vengeance she was.

Chloe's eyes shone with sympathy and kindness and not an ounce of guile. "I can guess at the answer," she said, "but the southerner in me would be appalled if I didn't ask how you are."

"Better now that I'm doing something." *And now that you're here.* But she was already smiling, damn her, when she should have been as cold as stone.

"We'll sort it all out." Chloe bit her lip adorably. "And I do mean we. I'll help from now on, Helen, leading creatures and paranormal folks to the sanctuary." She smiled hesitantly. "Though we might disagree on what to do with some of them, I hope we can work together."

Calm, cool, collected, Helen prepared herself to say something like, we'll be fine on our own, thank you. But her body disobeyed by taking Chloe's hand. "Thank you."

No, no, no. Too little, too late, she could have said. Or, generations of your kind led to the attack yesterday, and you can't make up for that. Or…

Helen told the sword of vengeance to shut the hell up already. She could not cease being herself, even for revenge. Chloe didn't deserve her vitriol, and they were stronger together.

Her inner voice grumbled but went silent.

Chloe was looking at her expectantly. "Do you have your own pet ghost you're talking to in your head that—" She looked to the side abruptly. "I didn't mean it like that, Ramses, I was just…okay, fine… Fine!" With an epic sigh, she looked back at Helen. "What I meant to say was, is there a guardian spirit accompanying you of their own free will that you were having a private conversation with?" She fluttered her lashes sweetly.

Helen grinned, wishing she could hear Ramses, too. A bolt of regret flashed through her. She never should have offered to help him separate from Chloe. Had he told her about that? Had he given it any thought at all? By the gods, what if he took her up on it?

She shook her head, telling herself those were all worries for another time. "No, just my inner monologue. It sounds like the Sphinx warning me about getting involved with humans."

Chloe's cheeks went pink. "Is that what we are? Involved?"

"You know we are." She stepped closer and hoped her expression showed her affection, her desire.

Straining on tiptoe, Chloe bit her lip again.

"If you keep doing that, I'm going to kiss you," Helen said. "Fair warning."

"Consider me warned." She slowly took her lip between her teeth again.

With another grin, Helen leaned forward.

"Oh my fucking gosh, Ramses," Chloe said, nearly leaping back. "I know, okay? We were just…" Her lips thinned into a white line, and she shook her head. "Unbelievable."

Helen could guess. "Not the right time?"

"Or the right place, apparently."

"Well, thanks for not shocking me again, Pharaoh."

"He says you're welcome," Chloe mumbled.

Helen cleared her throat. "Well, since the kissing portion of our trip is canceled, I think it's time for all of us to discuss exactly where we're going and what might happen when we get there." She turned toward the bridge and gestured to Fatma and Damian to go ahead.

And she was grown-up enough to admit that she waved for Chloe to climb the stairs first so she could admire the view.

Chloe paused. "I just thought of something. That was the Sphinx I saw at the sanctuary, wasn't it?" Her eyes went huge. "The actual Sphinx. Like, the Sphinx." She couldn't seem to say it enough.

Helen bit back a chuckle. "Not the statue that most people think of, but the actual entity, yes."

"Guardian of Thebes, riddle-telling Sphinx."

"Indeed." And the Sphinx would be tickled by the awe in her voice. "When you meet her again, ask for her autograph. She'll love you forever."

Chloe's smile was like a full moon emerging from the clouds before she turned and bounded up the stairs.

It wasn't lost on Helen that she'd said when, not if. Gods, the Sphinx would have something to say about that, too.

On the bridge, Eudore sat in the pilot's chair, steering the ship roughly toward the coordinates Ali and David had come up with. Helen led the others down a short flight of stairs inside the yacht to the large dining room with its highly polished, circular table.

Fatma whistled. "Swanky." She pulled out a chair that would let her see both exits. Smart.

Damian sat next to her but turned his back on the room to stare out the windows. Not so smart, but Helen supposed he had his uses.

Polyanthus the troll lifted one massive leg over the back of a chair and stepped over it to sit, the wood creaking under his weight. It wouldn't matter if he could see the exits or not. He would have been slow to turn if someone did come in, but most weapons would bounce off his cranium anyway.

Robin took the chair between Polyanthus and Fatma, laying their ax on the table with a clang. Helen assumed Maurice stayed with them. All the fair folk seemed to glean comfort from being near one another.

Chloe hesitated, seemingly looking around the room, clearly waiting for Helen to sit. Once she did, Chloe grabbed the seat next to her, forcing Maera to take the one between Chloe and Damian.

Helen fought the urge to sigh as they all looked at her. It had been a long time since she'd led a council of war, and each time, she'd hoped it would be the last.

Athena, please let it be so.

She paused. *And not because we've all died.* Though Ramses's presence signaled that death might not put a stop to such councils, either.

Maera cleared her throat. "Some of us can't be out of the water too long."

Helen laid her palms flat on the cool table and began to lay out what they knew so far. For two hours, they theorized, guessed, and suspected. Ideas ranged freely but kept butting into the concrete walls of the unknown. Number of enemies? Unknown. Full capabilities? They could only guess. Exact location? They had a few to choose from.

Even the information currently leading them could end in a fat lot of nothing, wild-goose chase number two. If it wasn't, their destination might be a mere stopover with nothing indicating where to go from there.

It had felt so good to finally be in motion, but with so many unknowns, this whole trip felt desperately premature.

But they had to do something.

From what the sanctuary residents remembered of the attacking boats, they were smaller than yachts or even large fishing boats, more like the Zodiac from the Kareems' boat or the small ship-to-shore craft on Helen's yacht. That spoke of a smaller range.

The Sphinx had thought they'd used a large helicopter to transport Charybdis's vault, but since there was no tracking that for now, their best bet was several small islands or a secluded port on Zile-de-Deyès, a larger, inhabited island to the southwest of the sanctuary.

Helen didn't want to waste time going to each island. If the nereids split up and asked the local dolphins for help, they could reconnoiter the smaller ones easily, but even with superspeed, it would still take time. No matter how meticulously she planned it, if they wanted to make sure the small islands were clear, they wouldn't arrive in Zile-de-Deyès until well after nightfall.

Stupid laws of physics.

"What's wrong with getting there after dark?" Chloe asked. "Wouldn't it help with the, you know, sneaking?" She still went adorably red when everyone stared at her.

Helen shook her head. "Most of the island is perfectly safe, but some of the ports, those infamous for turning a blind eye to smuggling, don't really come alive until dark. They'll be busier and more dangerous."

"Know a lot about smugglers, do we?" Fatma asked, her mouth twisting as if she couldn't decide on a smile or a frown. She seemed a lot friendlier than she'd been during the wyvern caper, but a hint of defensive anger still peppered nearly everything she said.

"Do we?" Helen said, giving her accusing stare right back to her. "I imagine such contacts have been useful to both of us."

Fatma managed to roll her eyes and look a little sheepish. Helen had the strangest urge to encourage her and Ligeia to spend some time together just to see if their collective scorn could create its own gravity. "Yeah, fine. It just sucks that the government is either taking bribes from the smugglers and turning a blind eye or 'cracking down' on crime just to shake the criminals down for more money."

Helen nodded. The circle went round and round. She had seen it all. "It can make the cost of doing business hard to anticipate."

"Even harder for the people who live there," Fatma said, no doubt building up to a good rant.

Damian clapped once, making everyone jump and neatly yanking Fatma's soapbox out from under her. "Okay, so we're relaxing tonight and heading into town tomorrow. Great." He smiled brightly and looked around the table. "Who's up for what? Cards? Dancing? Casual sex? What?"

Helen stood before they could start divvying up activities. She didn't care what they did, but she did not want to know. "I'll be on the flybridge." The look Chloe gave her said she'd be following soon.

Whew. What in the gods' names would she have said if Chloe had suggested a little demonic orgy? The fact that it was even a possibility in Helen's mind proved how little they still knew each other.

In the small flybridge, she leaned her elbows on the rail. She shouldn't be thinking of Chloe or smuggling or orgies. She needed to focus on the near future. The sanctuary had suffered attacks and setbacks before but never anything on this scale, never anything they couldn't handle alone. If she didn't have enough information about what they might find on Zile-de-Deyès tomorrow, she'd just have to plan for every contingency.

Sure, because that was possible.

When Chloe laid a warm hand on her back, Helen couldn't even be angry at herself for taking comfort from it. "On the deck of the Kareems' boat, it felt like my face was going to peel off from the speed," Chloe said. "How do the nereids avoid that?"

Helen snorted a laugh. "You can ask, but they might not tell you."

"You doing okay still?" Chloe asked. "If you need to talk…"

Even with the vast difference in their ages, that did sound helpful. But Chloe also had thousands of years of experience for the asking. Helen focused on the space around Chloe, trying to see exactly where the pharaoh was.

Chloe narrowed her eyes. "You looking for Ramses? I asked him to stay inside so we could talk. Should I get him?"

"No." Helen smiled. That tingly hum she always felt around Chloe was still there, only growing stronger the closer they stood, and it wasn't because of Ramses's presence. Not that she really believed that anymore. As recent events kept proving, perhaps she hadn't seen everything the world had to offer.

She kissed Chloe softly, not an explosion of passion like before—though that still waited below the surface—this was like a confirmation that what they shared was real. Even if it was still undefinable, a promise for later. If something dreadful happened, and they lost each other in this life, their souls would know each other still.

As they parted, Chloe's eyes shining with trust, Helen could almost hear the Sphinx labeling her thoughts romantic drivel, but she'd say it with a smile, and Helen resolved to carry that happy feeling with her.

"Spend the night with me?" Helen asked gently, but before Chloe's face could burst into flames, Helen placed a finger on her lips. "Talking, hoping, dreaming. I want to know everything about you."

Chloe went through so many expressions, it was like watching a film in a matter of seconds: setup, conflict, denouement. "I would love to." Her eyes shone, her proud smile saying it would be an honor, though Helen felt graced with her presence, not the other way around. She couldn't remember the last time she'd really looked forward to something like this. For the first time in centuries, there was more to live for than simple sanctuary.

CHAPTER THIRTY

Zile-de-Deyès, a tropical paradise Chloe had only ever read about, and she'd be there in a few hours. It was one of those places she'd always wanted to go, like Paris or Tokyo or London. Exciting? Well, yeah, but she was still too wrapped up in the memories of last night to really care.

She'd spent the night on one of the ship's many balconies, though she wasn't sure that was the right word. Porch didn't seem to fit. And it didn't matter because what it meant was being beside Helen in a lounge chair under a skyful of stars in the middle of the ocean. Romantic with a capital hell, yeah.

They'd talked, laughed, shared a bottle of wine, and eaten fresh seafood that the nereids had caught. A few cuddles here, a few kisses there—not easy with the chair arms between them—and Chloe had eventually fallen asleep with her head on Helen's shoulder.

Well worth the crick in her neck. And waking up damp with dew. At least her clothes wouldn't suffer. Helen had enough things onboard that she'd loaned Chloe some pj's and a robe so she could save her ass-kicking "Lil' Devil" shirt for today.

She drifted belowdecks to find Ramses waiting in the living room, though it was as weird to think of a boat having a living room as it was to think of one having a porch. Someone had set up an iPad for him at a table, and he paused his show as she came down.

"Good morning," he said, smirking just a tad.

She grabbed a mug of coffee from a carafe someone had left on a small table and dumped in copious amounts of sugar. "Morning," she said around a sip. "I should probably change." But the dampness hadn't penetrated the fluffy robe, so she sat next to Ramses instead. "In a minute."

"Did you go for a swim?" His tone was teasing.

"No. Slept outside."

"In someone else's clothes?"

"Helen loaned them to me."

"For your slumber party?"

She set her mug down with a thump and faced his grin at last. "We didn't have sex."

He lifted his hands, the picture of innocence. "I didn't ask."

"You didn't have to." But now her bubble had burst, and the reality of the day could come swarming in. She'd fought ghosts, the odd creature or two, but this felt different. She'd never felt the weight of other people depending on her before. Maybe Ramses, but they leaned on each other. At the heart of this fight were people like her mom's friends, who were still coming under attack, and the inhabitants of Helen's sanctuary, many of whom were helpless in the face of violence.

Who was she kidding? The person at the heart of her thoughts was Helen. If something happened to her, Chloe would feel the loss with a keenness she dreaded. Like the world had lost something, thousands of years of knowledge vanishing like a puff of smoke.

"I can practically hear you thinking," Ramses said.

She shrugged. "Now I'm nervous and weirded out, the usual when we're going looking for trouble."

His smile slipped. "I thought you'd be mooning over Helen for at least a few hours."

"I have never mooned and never will."

"Call it what you like."

"Falling in love?" came out before she even knew it was coming, but saying it felt both like a punch to the gut and a weight off her shoulders. She leaned her head back as a lovely floaty feeling wandered through her. "Holy shit, Ramses, I really could fall for her. Have fallen."

She expected at least an eye roll, but his smile was soft. "You're the only one of us who's even remotely surprised."

She glared. "After all the shit you've given me about getting close to her, you're not going to read me the riot act for saying that? Hell, for feeling it?"

He shook his head. "I'm resigned. I can no more stop you from falling in love than I can stop the sun from rising."

"I guess I feel a little like that." She picked at the cuff of the white robe. "Like my feelings are happening so quickly, I don't have any control over them. We got to know quite a bit about each other last night, but even before that, I felt like I've known her forever, and not just because of the history books." She sighed. "You don't think she has some kind of love power, do you?" Not that she bought that at all.

"Did you come across one in your studies?"

She shook her head. "But you know how vague myths can be."

He put his arms behind his head and stretched, his long legs hovering through another chair. "I feel so much magic from her that I can't tell. It might be your godhoods reaching out to each other. She might not be aware of why her own feelings run deep, either."

Deep, that was the word for it. Chloe's cheeks warmed. Their conversations last night had ranged from the shallow to the deep and back again. The real Helen, the one the history books didn't know, had so many facets, she would have flummoxed a master jeweler. They'd talked for hours but had only scratched the surface, and deeper was just what Chloe wanted.

She snorted at her own double entendre, but before Ramses could ask what was so funny, she stood. "I'm gonna change. We'll be at Zile-de-Deyès soon."

Ramses stood, too. "Time to get our heads in the game." His mouth twisted a bit, his nemes disappearing for a moment as he ran his hand through his hair. "I'm happy for you, Chlo."

"Are you?" God, why did it mean so much?

Yeah, you know why, she answered herself.

"Of course." He put a hand to his chest. "The father in me must add a pledge of bloody vengeance should she mistreat your heart."

"Duly noted. Thanks." She was going to bawl like a baby if she didn't get out of there and go change.

Afterward, she met up with the others on the deck as the ship approached Zile-de-Deyès. Helen's smuggling contacts used a harbor on the southern tip of the island, and if the people who'd attacked the sanctuary were moving weapons around, that was probably the harbor they used, too, but no one thought it was a good idea to just go sailing in there.

They docked at a marina a few miles away with other pleasure craft. Helen said a bribe might be in order to get them past customs, but Damian's power took care of that, and the swooning customs officer said they could do whatever they wished.

A couple of the nereids stayed with the boat while the others went swimming around to the destination harbor. If the mercenaries weren't there, maybe they could pick up a trail on land. Everyone else waited on the boat, anxious for news. Chloe fought the urge to bite her nails again and stared inland instead.

Mertrand, the town they'd come ashore at, was a colorful place, the buildings painted in the pastels so common in tropical isles. The sand was just darker than sugar, and the ocean was such a bright turquoise, it rivaled the dyed lakes of Disney World. Chloe wished she could take a stroll into town with Helen, pretending they were another couple on vacation buying souvenirs and silly hats and local delicacies.

If they had to go on land, Maurice planned to use glamour to hide Polyanthus and Robin, though Chloe would still be able to see all three. She considered giving the helmet to one, but Helen had told her that using it took some getting used to, and the last thing they needed was a red cap or a troll freaking out and using superstrength to destroy the town.

"Well, I should give it to you, anyway," Chloe said to Helen as they stood on the deck. She took a deep breath. The hot, crisp sea air still held no hints of the deepening autumn. "Seeing as how I stole it from you and all."

Helen smiled wryly. "You should hold on to it. Since you can see invisible things, you don't have to go through the mental gymnastics required when one can no longer see oneself."

Chloe didn't even know there were gymnastics required, mental or otherwise. Seeing the unseen was becoming handier than she'd ever thought it was.

It took a few hours for the nereids to return with a report, and morning was giving way to afternoon. "We saw two large warehouses right on the water," Maera said. "In a small cove between two long jetties."

Eudore nodded. "They have several piers, nothing for a big ship."

"No, shipping craft and cruise ships dock at the larger port down the coast," Helen said. "Did you see anyone?"

"A few people. Four fishing boats, a sailboat, and a few smaller craft tied up or hanging out of the water inside the buildings." Maera gestured at the other boats in this marina. "Nothing as busy as here."

"So what now?" Fatma asked, craning her neck as if she could see across the island by force of will.

"We get a look inside those warehouses," Helen said. "Do a little investigating."

Fatma rubbed her chin. "I can cover you from nearby." She had brought her arsenal onto the deck and gestured toward some kind of rifle with a scope. Chloe didn't miss the gleam in her eye as she looked them over. God.

"Or," Chloe said, "we can ask our invisible guardian spirit who is with us of his own free will if he wouldn't mind having a peek." She winked at Ramses.

He shook his head. "I simply objected to the word pet, as anyone might."

She didn't want to push him, so she hid her smile behind a cough. "Unless you think they might have a ghost trap."

"Depends on if they expected to be followed, doesn't it?" Damian asked.

"Did you see any signs of magic?" Helen asked Maera.

"No," she said, "but we're not always as sensitive to it as spirits or the fey." She nodded toward Robin.

They hefted their ax and grinned, rivulets of blood arcing around their lips. "I wouldn't mind having a peek. I'm good at getting through traps."

"I can walk them in with a glamour," Maurice said, "but that would take all my concentration."

Probably why he hadn't been able to spot any of the magic traps last time. "I should come with you," Chloe said.

"Why?" Helen and Ramses asked at the same time, and she both loved that they were worried about her and annoyed that they seemed worried about her the most.

"Because it seems like the only thing these people never plan for is humans." Since she'd discovered she had a godhood, she wasn't certain she actually qualified anymore, but nothing they'd seen would hold her like a ghost trap did Ramses or an iron cage would snare a fairy or demon.

"The plan to whip me to death via demon would have worked on you as well," Helen said, giving her a look.

"Let's go if we're gonna," Polyanthus said, his voice a low rumble. "Tired of talking. Hit stuff now."

Everyone tagging along seemed to make the most sense, and it would save them from any fights about who got to put themselves in danger and when. Of course, if their enemies sprung a trap, it might catch everyone, too. God, they seemed like the most unprepared assault team ever. It was the wyvern's barn all over again.

Chloe really should have brought her mom and the others, especially now that the team was looking at her and Helen as if they were co-authoring this particular *Choose Your Own Adventure.* "Right," she said. "Well, we don't know what we're facing or if any of us will even recognize the people responsible, but we've got god power, magic, glamour, troll fists, a sack of guns, and one very large ax. I don't see how we can lose."

That got wide grins from Polyanthus and Robin and even managed to coax a few smiles from the others, but Chloe still had a lead weight sitting in her gut.

They stuck close to shore as they worked their way around to the smuggler's cove, picking over the beach and through the dense jungle. The good news was that there weren't many people around, so Maurice didn't have to keep up a constant glamour. The bad news was that it felt like exploring the small islands all over again with the dense foliage, plenty of mosquitos, and enough walking on sand that Chloe's calves started to groan in protest. When the trees thinned, and she could see the sides of the warehouses, she was ready to head into any traps just so she wouldn't have to walk on the freaking beach anymore, burning quickly through their daylight.

She crouched with the others among the trees. With Polyanthus's help, Fatma climbed a palm tree that leaned into another, forming a perch she could lie along. She looked through her scope and spoke to Maurice so he could flutter down and pass it on.

Around six or seven people wandered in and out of the shadows of the large buildings. One or two more moved on the sailboat. No one seemed in a hurry or alarmed. She spotted two pistols on hips but no larger weapons like the one that could have burned the boathouse at the sanctuary. And she didn't report any large metal structures carved with runes like Charybdis's vault.

Fucking Charybdis. Chloe still couldn't believe it. When she'd asked what the infamous creature from *The Odyssey* looked like, Helen had paused and frowned in concentration. "Very hard to describe," she had said at last. "She can take many different forms."

Great, that would make finding her a piece of cake. "Maybe they've already let her out," Chloe said now. "They wouldn't need the vault, then."

Helen shook her head. "She's not loose."

"How do you know?"

"We'd know. This little cove would be decimated, maybe the entire island."

"She's that dangerous?" Damian asked.

Helen gave him another of those infuriating in-the-know looks.

Damian lifted an eyebrow. "I know we're trying this whole, save all the creatures, happy, sunny sort of thing, but maybe it would have been better to take her out of this world along with this Lamia who's becoming so infamous."

Helen glared. "A demon who advocates for murder, why am I not surprised?"

"Excuse me? Prejudiced much?" he asked.

Chloe stepped between them while Fatma hissed at them to be quiet from her perch. "Let it go for now," Chloe said softly. "What's done is done, and we'll have to deal with it."

Helen shifted that annoyed look to her, and she hated that it made her want to squirm. "Promise me that if we can recover her alive, we will. Same with the Lamia. I won't see them dead if it's avoidable."

"I know," Chloe said. "I know how important it is to you, and I promise to try."

Damian scoffed, and Chloe resisted the urge to kick him. "Hey," she said, "if I was the shoot-first type, you'd be banished as hell, son."

That made him shrink back a bit, and the smile she got from Helen made her day.

"Can we focus on the task at hand, children?" Ramses asked. "I think I should go ahead with Maurice. We're both invisible, and if he senses any traps, we'll pull back."

Chloe told Maurice, and Helen agreed to the plan, but before they could move, Fatma hissed again from above. "That woman," she said in a kind of whisper-yell.

Everyone on the ground shushed her, managing to be louder than she'd been in the first place. "What woman?" Helen asked.

"The one who was with you at the wyvern's barn," Fatma said. She kept looking away from the scope and then back again as if she couldn't believe her eyes. "The redhead. Is she one of your paranormal killers?"

She'd be answering for "killers" later, but Chloe's mind raced now, and she tried to remember the name of the pain in the ass who'd forced herself into the hunt for what Chloe and Ramses had been calling the Southern Mothman.

"Tabitha?" she and Ramses said together.

"Oh go…sh." Chloe said, her stomach twisting. "She couldn't keep her big nose out of it, and now she's gotten involved with murderers and smugglers. I knew we should have stuck around to talk to her at the hospital, Ramses, I knew it."

"Who is she?" Helen said. "I think I remember her, but—"

"A reporter," Chloe said. "Does she look like a prisoner? I hope to hell they haven't roughed her up." If they had, that was on Chloe. She wasn't sure how, but it was.

"I'm going in," Ramses said.

"Wait," Fatma called again. "She doesn't look hurt. In fact, it looks like she's giving orders."

What the hell? "Really?"

"She's pointing and shouting, and several people are hopping to obey."

Tabitha? Who ate jalapeño-flavored chips with sour candy chasers? Not that the people in charge of mercenary groups couldn't have quirky diets, but the two images wouldn't mesh in Chloe's head.

"Maybe she joined them after the wyvern," Ramses said. "For revenge?"

"And she's already bossing them around?"

"The only alternative is that she was part of their group the entire time."

Chloe shook her head. "What the actual fuck?"

"We need a closer look," Helen said. "Let's continue with the plan for Ramses and Maurice—"

"No," Chloe said, shaking her head, her confusion transmuting to anger. "She played us, lied to us. She could have known who I was the entire time, could have known about Ramses, could have suspected we'd follow her to that smaller island and set that trap. She could be planning the same thing now." She looked at Ramses and saw his stubborn face, but she had a helluva stubborn face of her own. "I'm going with you."

"Then we're all going," Helen said.

Chloe didn't argue. As long as she got to risk her life and liberty along with everyone else, she could be happy in the moment.

Until it was time to wring some information out of Tabitha.

Or kick her ass.

Chapter Thirty-one

Back straight, chin out, Chloe looked more like a sword of vengeance than Helen could ever hope to be. She seemed sick to death of these people being one step ahead. Or maybe she couldn't tolerate the thought of betrayal.

Helen could relate. Many a time, she'd thought of kicking Psamathe's ass. She felt a moment of pity for this Tabitha woman.

But only a moment.

Helen managed to slow Chloe with a hand on her arm. "I'm on your side," she said when Chloe leveled a hard stare in her direction. "But it's never a good idea to barge in on armed guards."

Chloe's mouth twisted reluctantly, but she slowed, and the seven of them approached from the side of the building where a lone door waited in the shadow of a tree. Fatma had stayed in her perch to cover them.

When they reached the door, Maurice whispered, "I'm not sensing any magic on the door."

Chloe pointed to a metal box set in the wall above. "Alarm."

Great, that ruled this door out. Helen was just about to lead the way around the front when Chloe grinned. "Let Ramses handle it."

A soft *bzzt* came from the door, and it clicked open, as if a magnetic lock had gone on the fritz along with the alarm. Helen's side tingled as she remembered the two shocks Ramses had given her. A ghost's electrical field was useful on more than one level.

"It's clear just inside," Chloe whispered. She held the door, waving everyone through. They walked into shadow, this side of the warehouse dimly lit in the face of the sun streaming in the other side.

Voices came from nearby, above the sound of the water slapping against the pier. Several boats hung from small cranes, and stacks of boxes and crates stood in piles about the floor, perfect for cover.

"I sense magic closer to the water," Maurice said softly.

Helen froze along with everyone else. She hardly breathed as she waited. When no explanation came, she said, "Well?" as softly as she could.

"Well what?"

She gritted her teeth. "What kind?"

"How the hell should I know? I'm not a bloody encyclopedia."

"Does it feel like a ghost trap?" Chloe asked with a hell of a lot more patience than Helen felt.

"Identifying magic by feel is a tricky business," he said peevishly. "I don't sense fairy glamour. I think."

Great. It looked like they wouldn't know until—

"I see the sigils," Robin said with a grin. "I'll set them off. Red caps and magic don't always get along."

"Wait, we're trying to sneak—"

But they were away before Helen could grab them. They struck out across the middle of the floor like they belonged there.

"Robin," Helen called as loudly as she dared. "Damn it." She drew the kladenet.

"Wait," Polyanthus said, their craggy face breaking into a smile that sent a scatter of shale falling to the floor.

A whistle like a teakettle on speed echoed through the room, the clear frontrunner in the competition for Most Annoying Sound Ever. Helen clapped her hands over her ears as two sigils carved into posts between her and the pier burst into flames, interrupted somehow by Robin's presence.

Didn't get along with magic indeed. But now everyone would know someone had broken in. At least the magic gave them confirmation that these had to be the killers who'd attacked the sanctuary.

Yes, that would be a great comfort when Robin was riddled with bullets.

Several mercenaries advanced with pistols drawn. A few more moved in from outside. No sign of the redhead who'd been with Chloe at the wyvern's barn.

"Drop the weapon," one of the mercenaries said.

Surprisingly, Robin let their ax fall to the floor. Helen started to move toward the back of the closest mercenary, but Polyanthus grunted again and shook his head.

"But—"

He nodded toward where Robin was now surrounded. One mercenary reached with his free hand and knocked back the hood of the cloak. He paused, looking at another mercenary, their expressions contorting as they got a look at the blood.

"The fuck are you?" one of them asked.

Robin burst into laughter. They lifted the ax on the end of their boot, the movement almost too fast for Helen to follow.

And one of the mercenaries was minus a head.

The others hesitated.

Thwack. Head number two.

The gunfire began before the heads stopped rolling. Robin hoisted one body aloft as a meat shield and took the legs out from under another.

Literally.

"Subdue," Helen said as she released the kladenet. They needed one mercenary for information, and she only hoped the kladenet could hit one before Robin killed them all.

Someone darted out from behind a stack of crates to the left, but Polyanthus punched a dent in their chest, and they collapsed. The fight had found the rest of them.

"To arms," Helen called, and the kladenet turned back toward her.

"There," Chloe said. She pointed at someone hurrying toward what looked like an office built into the side of the larger space. She didn't look to have a weapon, but Helen still reached out so Chloe couldn't go charging in.

And missed her by inches. She was outlined in a silver glow much like Helen's golden one. A spell? A trap going off?

A...godhood?

Helen darted after her, the kladenet trailing behind. There would be time to ask about the glow later. Shots echoed outside, and one of the mercenaries on the pier fell into the water. Fatma. She took another who looked to be heading for the office, clearing the way for Chloe to hurl herself into danger.

Damn. This was one more reason to only date in one's own age bracket. Young people had no patience.

❖

Chloe saw red and not just the color of Tabitha's hair. She'd been worried about the little shit, had walked on eggshells to keep her out of the know, then had put herself and Ramses in further danger to keep Tabitha from getting hurt.

Well, too hurt.

And now, here she was amidst a nest of guards in the Caribbean? Chloe was sure as shit going to find out why.

Ramses sprinted ahead, and a bit of sanity slapped into Chloe again. What if there was another trap? But if he wasn't going to give her a lecture about taking things slowly, she wasn't going to give him one, either, not when she knew Helen was following, those same words probably burning a hole in her brain.

The door was still slightly ajar, and Chloe barreled through after Ramses went through the side of the office.

Tabitha whirled from the other end, a phone at her ear. Ramses stood beyond a circle of glyphs that surrounded her. Nothing else waited in the rectangular room, but some writing that Chloe couldn't read had been carved into the wall at Tabitha's back.

She smiled, actually fucking smiled like they were old friends reunited. "Chloe, I guess you found what you were looking for out in the wilds of Texas? Thanks for the lift to the hospital, by the way. I had not planned for that evening to end in a concussion." As Helen stepped through the door, Tabitha grinned wider. "Oh, good, you're both here. I didn't really expect you to team up, either." She shook a finger in Chloe's direction. "You're not supposed to be fraternizing with the mythic entities you hunt. Except for the one, of course."

"What are you doing here, Tabitha?" Chloe asked, advancing until she stood at Ramses's side.

"Is he here?" Tabitha asked, face still annoyingly cheerful. "King Ramses?" She pointed to the glowing glyphs. "He should *not* step on these. Neither should you, really. No matter what, I never really wanted you dead." She glanced at Helen, and her smile slipped a little. "You might be a different matter."

Chloe just kept herself from stepping in front of Helen. She had her sword in hand again and looked ready to skin Tabitha alive. "Why did you do all this?" Chloe asked. "Killing people? Blowing up my fucking car?"

"Well, I had planned to do that in the boonies and strand you, but as I said, concussion." She touched the side of her head. "I wanted to strand you in Houston for a bit instead, but you're very resourceful. How in the hell did you persuade a demon to join your team? A has-been of a demigod is one thing, but a freaking demon? Naughty, Chloe."

Has-been demigod? Did she not know she was talking about the greatest woman in the fucking world? "All right, come out of there and tell me to my face what the hell it is that you want."

"Um, no, don't think I'll do that." She cocked her head. "But since you're all about making new friends, I'll let you come in." She batted her lashes. "It would be nice to have someone with the blood of Isis and a helpful pharaoh on my team."

"And what team is that?" Helen asked. She pointed to the writing on the wall with an elegant finger. "That's demonic script. And you're lecturing us about allying ourselves with hell?"

"Using, sweetie, not allying. There's a difference. Demons are hired guns just like any other. And mostly, they stick to their own shithole dimension. So I'm really curious what you had to offer your friendly demon." She narrowed her eyes as if studying them. "I mean, he's an incubus, so there's an obvious answer, but I'm sensing something else here." She moved a finger between them. "A little blood of the gods hanky-panky? Chloe, doll, you can do better."

Chloe had never really wanted to use guns, but one would have come in handy right about then. She drew the nail gun from her bag, needing to at least point something dangerous in Tabitha's direction. "I'm done listening to your lip. If you're not going to tell us anything useful, I will fill you full of iron."

Tabitha's mouth dropped in a delighted expression. "Oh my God, so badass." She fanned her face. "Pardon me while I swoon. Oh, but you really should have said, nail you to the wall."

Damn, that would have been good. "Just shut the fuck up and surrender."

Tabitha leaned forward. "No." She paused as if eagerly awaiting her fate.

"Shoot her, Chloe," Ramses said.

Yeah, she could do that, plant a nail right in her smug face, but she hadn't wanted to kill one sickly wyvern, how was she supposed to shoot a person?

"In the leg, Chloe," Ramses said as if reading her thoughts. "I know you're not a monster."

Oh, right. She tilted the nail gun down and pulled the trigger, grateful there was still enough of a charge for the nail to go sailing through the glyphs and bury itself in Tabitha's thigh.

She stepped back with a cry, hand to her leg. "You asshole, I didn't think you were actually going to do it."

And now that Chloe had, she could scarcely believe it, either. She hoped she looked confident as she shrugged, even though her brain was saying oh shit on repeat. "If you want to get shot again, just stay in there. Nails made from iron and soaked in anise will go through all this demon shit like a chainsaw."

Ramses smirked, and the look Helen gave Chloe said there would be some serious making out when all this was over.

It made her bold. "If you won't come out"—she drew the pentacle—"maybe we can muscle our way in."

And by the continuing sounds of fighting outside, they needed to hurry. If the goons out there hadn't already gotten reinforcements, they might soon, especially if the voices coming from Tabitha's phone meant she'd called this incident in.

"Try it," Tabitha said. "This circle will tear you all apart." But she backed up, limping, clearly not as confident as she felt. She bent lower, too, making herself a smaller target or shielding herself with her head as if knowing Chloe wasn't going to kill her.

Helen stepped to Chloe's side, but she was frowning at the script on the wall, muttering something like, "That chant."

"What?" Chloe asked out the side of her mouth.

"Let's go for it," Ramses said. "I'll possess you, and we use the pentacle to force a path through."

If they died, at least they'd be together, but Helen was still peering at the walls like someone with a particularly difficult crossword clue.

"Okay," Chloe said, taking a deep breath before Ramses's presence flowed through her. He raised the nail gun again, forcing Tabitha back another step, then moved the pentacle toward the invisible line that marked the edge of the circle. It glowed with a rainbow of light where the pentacle touched it, but the waves of color parted like the Red Sea before the pentacle's power.

"They're chanting," Helen said.

Chloe wanted to ask who, but she wasn't in charge of the mouth anymore. Ramses pushed into the path created by the pentacle, and it felt like trying to move through molasses. With a grunt, he shoved harder. Tabitha's back was against the wall when they finally got a leg through.

"Chloe," Helen said with a hand on her arm. "Something's wrong."

But they couldn't hesitate, and given a choice, Ramses would always rather go forward than back. "Almost there," he said. But it wasn't his body that felt like it was being squeezed in a steel press. They got their hips through the gap.

Tabitha breathed deeply, looking worried as hell. It should have been satisfying, but the moment felt off, like they'd all forgotten something.

Helen's grip on her arm tightened.

Tabitha's look of worry became a smile again as the voices from her phone grew louder. It sounded like someone singing.

Or chanting.

They'd forgotten how good of an actress Tabitha was.

Red and black lights burst to life behind her, and she sank into the wall as if it was made of cream. A wave of force yanked Chloe forward, shoes squealing on the floor as Ramses tried to keep their feet. The wall became a swirling vortex, hauling all three of them through the protective circle. Helen cried out as the edges no doubt clipped her, but Ramses didn't look, focusing on the whirlpool of magic. He crouched, but there was nothing to hang on to, and they skidded forward on their heels.

"Let go of the pentacle," Chloe shouted in their mind. If the magic was demonic, maybe the holy symbol would stop it.

He did; the vortex swallowed the pentacle and flared. The pull abated, thank God, and Ramses grabbed Helen, pulling her farther from the edge of the circle. She held her shoulder where the fabric of the shirt looked blackened, the skin beneath it burned.

Maybe it would be easier to get out of the circle than it was to get in.

A rumble came from the slowing vortex, its dying breath, perhaps. Something glinted in the very center like the sun reflecting off metal.

Chloe cried out in her mind as something snaked from that core, a thin line of fire that arced around them. Ramses only managed a step before it tightened like a noose and yanked them into the magical maelstrom.

CHAPTER THIRTY-TWO

Helen flailed against the whip that encircled them and against the panic seeping into her chest and the sharp ache of the burn on her arm. Against the feeling that she was being stretched thin by the portal she and Chloe were currently tumbling down.

Don't trip when you land, she told herself, don't hesitate, don't—

Darkness closed around her with a snap, the light from the portal disappearing like a snuffed candle. She swung the kladenet with her free arm, felt it bite into leather, but the whip tightened, pressing her into Chloe and dragging them both forward.

Don't fucking fall, Helen said again in her mind. She managed to keep her feet, but the demon wielding the whip was exceptionally strong. If Helen wanted to attack with the kladenet, she'd need—

Green light burst to life in Chloe's hand before it scattered over the floor. Long glow sticks like the kind cavers used brought to life a room about half the size of the one they'd left, also bare, though the pentacle gleamed where it lay on the floor.

Near the feet of the tall, angry demon currently pulling on the whip.

Helen released the kladenet. "Attack." It shot toward the demon. The whip slackened as the demon brought the handle up to block with the metal-capped end.

Chloe darted forward, drawing a knife from her bag. Helen sensed Ramses possessing her before she even rolled to grab the pentacle and sprang upright again. She held it in front of her like a shield as she advanced.

"Assault," Helen cried, the command word for a concerted attack, but the kladenet often had trouble with that one, sometimes unable to tell friend from foe when weapons were pointing in every direction. She glanced around for Chloe's nail gun, but it was a pile of broken pieces on the ground.

Helen dug in the pouch on her hip and took out a small golden pin in the shape of a spear, a holy symbol of Athena that should work against a demon, but she wasn't going to depend on that alone.

She pricked her finger with the sharp point of the spear and the clasp at the same time. With a small pop, a full-length spear replaced the pin, the head shining gold. She wasn't a fair hand with a spear but sensed that an ancient pharaoh just might be.

"Ramses, catch." She tossed it to them, and the head flared as it neared the demon.

Chloe-Ramses dropped the knife and pentacle and grabbed the spear with both hands. The demon leapt away, wings snapping open. With one flap, it pushed almost to the wall and turned its eyeless head toward the door, no doubt calculating if it could escape before Ramses was on top of it.

No, they couldn't let it go. Helen grabbed Chloe's knife and pentacle before running for the door to guard it.

The demon brought the whip back and around. Chloe-Ramses dodged, and the metal tip struck sparks against the floor. The kladenet hovered as if unsure where to go. Chloe-Ramses leaned far to the side and threw the spear with a grunt, sinking it in the demon's chest.

"Gotcha," Helen said, elation filling her.

The demon roared, and black blood spurted from the wound. The spiny skin smoked, the holy weapon burning it and filling the small space with the stench of sulfur. It grasped the shaft, but Chloe-Ramses was already on the move, along with the kladenet.

"Assault," Helen yelled again, desperate to remind the weapon as Chloe-Ramses kicked the butt of the spear, driving it farther into the demon's chest. It shrieked, flailing, and the kladenet buried itself right where an eye would have been. The whip fell, and the flaming circle above the demon's head dimmed as its screams rattled the walls.

"Yes," Helen yelled.

Chloe-Ramses yanked on the shaft. The demon lurched forward, sagging, but the blade didn't come free. The kladenet wiggled, no doubt trying to drive in deeper. With a groan, the demon grabbed it with one hand.

And wrapped the other around Chloe's throat.

They released the spear and pounded at the demon's elbow. Its grip didn't slacken.

"No!" Helen leapt, sinking the knife into the demon's arm while she pressed the pentacle against its hand, her godhood rising, giving her strength.

With a roar, the demon elbowed her in the head, sending stars across her eyes as she flew to the side, ears ringing. The pentacle bounced away when she hit the concrete floor, and pain ricocheted up her arm. The demon howled above her, its cries weakening.

But Chloe had nearly stopped kicking, too, going limp in the sickly green light.

No, no, no. Helen pushed to her feet. She had to get the tarnkappe from Chloe's satchel. Her godhood rose again as she darted for it, her glow lighting Chloe's desperate face.

No, the silver glow had returned, pouring from Chloe's skin, mingling with Helen's. A godhood. Chloe's godhood.

So beautiful, even as it flared, blinding Helen and pushing her back again.

❖

Ramses's voice became a dull roar. Chloe felt him flow out of her, forced to leave as darkness threatened. Huh. She'd always wondered how close to fucked a person had to be to boot a ghost from their body.

She was dying.

And what would her obituary be? Killed by some faceless demon in a nondescript room in the back of beyond? Here lies Chloe, she knew a lot of exceptional people but proved quite ordinary in the end. Fell at the first real danger.

Fuck that.

Something inside her shuddered, something deep and primal and beyond sick of this fucking demon. Grace filled her, the only word for something so beautiful, fluid, as delicate as a flower unfolding and as powerful as the sun that drove it.

Compared to that, what was a demon?

Nothing but ash.

It crumbled and blew away like dandelion fluff, the knife and spear *tinging* against the floor as Helen's sword returned to her. Power filled the pain in Chloe's neck, dispelling the ache in her cheeks, her eyes, returning her to wholeness, another state of grace.

In the silver light, Helen's and Ramses's faces were beyond beautiful.

And pretty damned shocked.

Chloe's power dropped like a stone, taking her with it, her legs no more able to hold her than she could lift a mountain.

"Chloe," Helen and Ramses called at the same time, solid and spectral arms going around her.

"Don't…fight over me." She paused to wheeze. "Plenty to go… around."

Helen had tears in her eyes. "That was your godhood, your connection to Isis. Oh, Chloe, it's been so long since I felt…" She ducked her head as if forcing herself back in control. "It was so lovely."

Chloe stroked her cheek. "I only discovered it since I met you. You bring out my inner superhero."

Helen kissed her hand.

But how would Isis feel about her blood being half a world away, her Egyptian heritage a mere percentage on a DNA test? If the pride shining in Ramses's eyes was any indication, maybe she would have smiled.

"Now, if you can only figure out how to do it at will," he said.

"One thing at a time." Some of the feeling was returning to her legs. "Help me up?"

Helen frowned in concern. "Are you sure?"

"Not even a little, but I want to get after Tabitha before she pulls any more demons out of her hat." She stood with help, her legs like Jell-O left in a warm car. They held, though, and that was the only thing that mattered in the moment.

Helen grabbed the spear that had become tiny once more and led the way out, gripping her sword and looking every inch the warrior of old.

Chloe dug out the magic helmet. "Just in case there are more demons." When she donned it, strength flowed through her, and she went from pudding legs to feeling like she could leap a building. But a short one. In a couple of bounds.

Helen threw open the door, and blinding sunlight flooded in. When nothing came from the glare to attack them, Chloe stumbled after Helen into a hot mugginess just a bit less miserable than the last place they'd been. She didn't need the sky and trees and weeds to come into focus to know this place like she knew herself.

Central Texas.

And by the look of things, she was again in the middle of a pasture, standing outside the remains of what looked like a Cold War bunker. A herd of cows watched Helen warily from off to the left, and some muddy car tracks to the right spoke of someone hauling ass out of there not too long ago. Fucking Tabitha had stranded them, probably not far from where they'd met.

Great.

Chloe pulled off the helmet. Helen turned in a slow circle, her hair shining in the sun. "It's Texas," Chloe said. "Central somewhere."

"How can you be certain?"

Chloe snorted. "Ever had someplace where you just know the air?" Saying that it was dry grass and manure didn't sound nearly as poetic.

"A few times." She smiled wistfully, and Chloe was reminded of the gulf of time between them and some of the stories Helen had told her about last night, places she'd known as well as she knew herself before the world had changed around her.

Chloe hugged her from behind. "I'm sorry."

"For what?"

"All the bad shit that's happened to you lately. Or ever. Because you've had to suffer douchebags throughout history."

Helen's chuckle vibrated through her, and the hand resting on Chloe's was comforting, warm. "I'm lucky. I've had more good than bad." She turned in Chloe's arms. "Like you. And none of the bad shit is your fault."

"Except, it kinda is." She rested her cheek against Helen's collarbone and breathed in her scent, delighting in the way their bodies felt together. "I should have changed the way my family does things earlier, smartened up sooner."

"Chloe, look at me."

Gladly. She tilted her chin up to stare into those gorgeous eyes, noticing a slender ring of gold around the pupil like in a bird of prey's.

"We are none of us responsible for the sins of our ancestors." She tucked a strand of hair behind Chloe's ear. "And your guilt serves no one. The important thing is that you've recognized the mistakes of the past and are determined to fix them."

A bit of a departure from the things she'd said before, but they felt right when spoken in each other's arms.

Helen ducked her head as if coming in for a kiss, then paused. "Ramses isn't watching, is he?"

Chloe snickered. "You shy or trying to avoid another shock?"

"Both."

And he had been conspicuously silent. He stood a few paces away, discreetly watching the cows.

"He's giving us some privacy. Or maybe scanning the horizon for Tabitha."

"Good," Helen said through a smile Chloe felt against her lips. The kiss started sweet like the one on the boat, but Chloe added a little spice with her tongue, missing that fire of their first one.

Helen pulled her closer, one hand strong and sure between her shoulder blades. The other cupped her cheek, fingers playing along her jaw and skimming her lower lip. Helen had to have spent at least a hundred years practicing kissing on some very lucky volunteers.

Chloe gripped her hips and pulled them together harder, but Helen lifted her head before Chloe could really embarrass herself. "It's almost evening," Helen said, a little breathless. "And we need to keep on Tabitha's trail."

Chloe grinned, so proud to have the most famous face in history looking at her like that. "You're right. We'd better start walking." But her hands did not want to let go.

With a grin, Helen kissed her nose. "Once we find out where we are, we can make a few calls, arrange some transport, check on the others, find some way to track Tabitha." Her eyes went half-lidded, her voice dropping into a deep, pre-orgasm range. "Find somewhere to bed down for the night." She quirked an eyebrow. "Spend the night with me again?"

Chloe's insides nearly boiled. That look said this would not be an innocent night full of talking and cuddles. She was beyond tempted to put the helmet on, throw Helen over her shoulders, and run for civilization faster than Speed Racer on meth. But she settled for taking Helen's hand and starting down the dirt track. "It's okay, Ramses," she called over her shoulder. "You can look now. We're going."

She wanted to fall completely into the welcoming arms of anticipation, but she couldn't help wondering about the rest of their gang, too, praying they were okay even if she didn't quite know who to pray to anymore.

Chapter Thirty-three

Helen was grateful that Tabitha proved easy to track. There was only one winding dirt road through the acres of rolling pasture. A very pretty walk through the country, but evening was fast approaching, Texas was proving muggier than Helen expected, and both she and Chloe were exhausted from the fight and the loss of adrenaline. By the time they reached the two-lane blacktop with more nothing in either direction, they were both, as Chloe put it, dragging ass.

"I'm tempted to ask Ramses to possess me so I can just ride in the body for a bit," Chloe said.

"Can he possess both of us?" It would feel really good not to have to walk anymore.

She chuckled. "He says he's never tried."

That reminded Helen of the conversation they'd had about Thoth and helping Ramses find his way to the Egyptian Underworld. Her cheeks burned with shame, and she ducked her head. She should have admitted that before now, had been tempted to admit it last night, but she hadn't wanted to spoil things. "I have to confess something," she said as they turned south, the direction they ultimately wanted to go. "Back at the first island, I offered to help Ramses reach the underworld if he helped me locate a priest of Thoth."

Chloe was silent for a moment. Or maybe she was too tired to yell. "I was wondering when you were gonna say something about that."

"You knew?" Her heart stuttered. "Since when?"

"The day after. Pretty much the first opportunity Ramses had to tell me. Did you think he wouldn't?"

Helen stumbled over her thoughts, over all their interactions since. "How are you not, well…"

"Going for your throat?" She smiled crookedly. "I was a little pissed at first. But helping people is what you do, especially if you think they're trapped." She held up a hand. "Which Ramses is not, thank you very much. He chooses to stay with my family. Our bond is more so he can appear wherever I am rather than be tied to a statue like any old ghost. And so he can possess me, but no other ghost is able to."

She said it so calmly, and Helen wanted to hang her head even more. "I apologize to both of you. I should never have made such an offer without more information, or I should have at least made it to both of you at the same time, rather than trying to hide it."

Chloe gave her a fuller smile, then shrugged. "Like I said, it's what you do. We forgive you." She sputtered a laugh. "And like Ramses just said, it's a mark in your favor that you said it now before—" Her ears went very red. "Anything else happens between us. Especially since you didn't know if I'd be pissed enough to sleep alone tonight."

Helen felt her body warm, too, though she was in no way embarrassed by her desire for such a wonderful woman. "I didn't even consider that, at least not consciously."

"Good to know your subconscious will never let you down," Chloe said with a wink.

Helen wanted to kiss her but was afraid that if they stopped walking, they'd never get started again. "How are we going to find Tabitha?" she asked, hoping an angrier topic might keep them moving.

Chloe sighed and put her hands on top of her head as she went. "I don't even know. I think that last island was probably the one where Damian was summoned, but if he went to Houston, they clearly have other locations they can teleport to. Maybe the others will find some clues."

"Do you know her last name?"

"It's probably on the original article I tracked her down from. If that was her real name." She dug her phone out of her bag. "We might need a bit more civilization to get a signal."

Night had fallen by the time they reached a larger road and were able to get cell service reliable enough to order a ride. Helen felt tired from summoning her godhood. She imagined Chloe must feel the same, even more because she was unused to it on top of everything else. But figuring out just how tired they were would have to wait until they were behind closed doors.

They opted for the closest motel that seemed the cleanest and safest from the reviews and wound up at a Super 10 Motor Court near the closest freeway outside of Waxahachie, Texas.

The fact that Chloe had known their approximate location by feel struck a chord in Helen. It was true that she could also recognize a few places in the same way, but there was something about the mix of love and resignation in Chloe's voice that felt endearing.

It was one of many things that prompted her to put her arms around Chloe and kiss her when they were finally as alone as they could be. "I'm going to have a shower," she said softly when they parted, loving the dumbstruck look on Chloe's face. "Will you see if you can reach Fatma's sat phone?" She ran a finger along Chloe's jaw. "I'd invite you to join me, but I don't want your first glimpse of me naked to include the amount of sweat, grime, and demon ichor I'm currently carrying on my body."

Chloe sputtered a laugh even as her eyes darkened. "Agreed. And ditto, by the way."

Helen kissed her nose. "I'll save you some hot water."

❖

Holy shit, holy shit, holy shit. Helen of freaking Troy was in the shower cleaning up in preparation for a night of wild passion. With *Chloe.*

"Fucking holy fucking shit, Ramses."

He'd already vanished to wherever he usually went, but she heard his voice in her mind. "I just left, and now you want me to come back? For the nudity?"

"Ew, no. I mean, yes, but just help me. I'm freaking out."

He appeared at the end of the bed, eyebrows up. "You've already spent one night in each other's company. I know you don't need me to talk you through this one."

"No, but that was…and she's just so…and I'm…sex!"

He squinted. "Am I supposed to know what that means?"

"It means…it means…holy shit." Her stomach was in knots. She was so far out of her league, she was playing a different sport.

"Chlo." The slight tingle of his spectral hands on her shoulders forced her to focus on his kind expression. "Neither of you is better than the other. She obviously likes you, and I know you like her. Relax. Enjoy yourself. Don't be afraid to ask for what you want, even if what you want is to stop." He ducked a little to meet her eyes. "Okay?"

"Okay."

"For the gods' sake, don't cry, Chloe. This is supposed to be a joyous expression of affection."

She wiped her cheeks, but any tears were more for her tumbling emotions than impending sex.

With Helen. Holy shit.

"Make the call," Ramses said. "Use the time to calm down. I'll be a thought away if you need me." With a cheeky wink, he was gone again.

Chloe took a couple of deep breaths before she plugged in her phone with the charger from her bag and tried Fatma's number.

She picked up on the second ring. "Chloe? Fuck, girl, are you okay?"

Chloe had to laugh, touched by the concern. Fatma seemed like one of those people who took a while to get to know, but once she called someone a friend, she was all in. Chloe told her what had happened, and Fatma relayed that everyone else had come through the fight okay, though Robin had sustained a few injuries—"but who can tell?"—and Damian had a bullet graze to one leg that had almost healed, but "he will not shut up about it."

Fatma sighed. "And Polyanthus seems to be missing a rock from one shoulder but also doesn't seem to care, and one of the nereids got a bit of dry-land sickness." She lowered her voice. "I can't remember which one she is, and that feels a bit racist, but I don't know what I can do about it."

Chloe snickered. "That's one of the reasons I love the word y'all. You don't have to remember everyone's names to ask how they're all doing."

"I'll remember that. In the meantime, we'll tear this place apart for clues if you can get your mom to stop blowing up my phone."

"Shit." Yeah, she'd noticed the oodles of missed calls, too. "Maybe after Helen and I get a good night's sleep and head toward the coast to rendezvous with y'all, I'll call her back."

Fatma had an audible smirk when she said, "Good night's sleep, huh? Alone at last?"

Chloe's face warmed even as pleasant tingles started in her middle. "Shut up."

Fatma actually giggled and made kissy sounds, and Chloe heard Damian in the background saying, "What is it, what's she saying?"

"Hanging up now," Chloe said loudly. "Don't call unless it's dire."

Fatma said something, but the words were drowned out by the sight of Helen emerging from the bathroom in a towel.

"Yeah, thanks, you too," Chloe said vaguely before she hung up on autopilot. She forced her eyes away from the acres of glistening bronze skin barely covered by the thin hotel towel and said, "Good, um, shower? Nice...water?" She could almost hear Ramses giving her a slow clap and a ten on the suave scale.

But Helen's throaty chuckle made her forget anyone else even existed and dragged her gaze to eyes that reflected a desire as heady as her own. "Shower. Quickly."

Chloe didn't need to be told twice.

❖

Helen drew on her vast wealth of life and forced herself to be patient. Her time with Chloe felt limited, perhaps because they'd spent so much of their acquaintance running from or toward danger, even after the quiet night they'd spent together.

And now, she'd almost lost Chloe earlier, and she wasn't prepared to waste any more time.

When Chloe emerged from the bathroom, Helen reached for her quickly and caused both their towels to fall to the floor. She forced her passion to cool a degree or two, savoring instead of consuming, though with every kiss or caress, she wanted more.

The same humming tingles passed through her as whenever they were near each other, but now Helen knew what they were, one godhood recognizing another. When she briefly opened her eyes while kissing a path down Chloe's neck, she saw their glows mingling like their bodies, embracing like old friends.

Memories hurtled through her: mainly Menelaus and Psamathe. Something like this had happened between her and them, too, a god's blood recognizing itself, one of the things that had attracted her to them.

But this felt like more, a half-remembered dream, a call she'd felt when passing through ancient Egypt or Babylon, that she'd never been able to forget. The call of one soul to another.

Her blood and the blood of Isis? Could souls fall in love?

At the moment, who cared?

Before she could break herself from Aphrodite's spell, she buried her face in Chloe's neck, sucking lightly when Chloe moaned her name at a certain spot. Who cared about reasons when she had this gorgeous soul in her arms right now?

Helen stepped back, guiding them toward the bed so they could lie down and explore each other fully. The hum in her ears grew, perhaps the herald of the first climax between them. Quick, but that was fine. They had time for more than a few.

But now the hum was getting very loud.

"What's wrong?" Chloe asked, her voice love drunk.

"Can you hear that?" Helen leaned up, glancing at the door.

With a bang, it flew off its hinges as if summoned, clattering to the floor at the foot of the bed.

Dust filled the room as Helen launched to her feet, coughing, her ears ringing. She grabbed Chloe's legs and yanked her off the bed, away from the window. She cried out, but Helen's eyes were on the door. Was it another demon? She couldn't see anything through the dust except the yellow glow of halogen lights in the dim parking lot.

"To arms," she called, summoning the kladenet from her pile of clothes in the bathroom. After a brief clatter, it flew into her hands, shaking off a bra as it came.

Chloe scrambled for the bathroom, too. "Ramses, it's a ghost!"

Ah, that explained why Helen couldn't see anything. The energy that filled the room crackled like two storm fronts meeting, and Helen guessed Ramses had engaged the intruder.

Chloe was dressing quickly. Helen followed suit, not bothering to do up the laces on her boots, just wanting to have everything covered.

"What can I do?" Helen asked. "Ghosts are your area of expertise."

"Here." Chloe threw her bag over her shoulder and handed Helen a few long iron nails and a hammer. She looped a ring made of branches and red thread over her own arm and held a baggie of red and white powder in her hand. "Ramses will wrestle him into a position where I can hit him with salt and cayenne." She lifted the baggie. "Drive in those nails where I tell you, even if it's in midair."

Helen nodded. "I trust you."

Chloe's glow surged for a moment. With her smile confident and her shirt on backward, she stepped into the room, eyes darting as if searching for an opening. Helen waited, hammer and nails ready, and watched the door for whoever had surely summoned the ghost to attack.

❖

And now Chloe could add, interrupted fantastic sex with the woman of her dreams, to the reasons she hated ghosts.

And not just any ghost. It was a gigantic man wearing fur and leather who looked like he had stepped from a book called, *Huge Viking Anglo-Saxon Fuckers*.

He roared and swung an ax at Ramses's head. Though ghostly weapons were no longer sharp, Ramses ducked; the weapons could still connect, and the ghostly energy roiling off this one was nearly as great as Ramses's. That combined with the wild look in the ghost's eyes and how massively pissed off he seemed pointed squarely to him being summoned. It had to be Tabitha.

Goddamn it, what were the odds of her picking this same motel?

Given its proximity to the bunker and the low rating of the other motels nearby? Pretty damn good.

She had to be nearby to be boosting this ghost. And since the Super 10 Motor Court probably didn't have any statues of ancient Vikings in the parking lot, she had to have brought a figurine or totem of a real person with her. Hell, Ramses might have been fighting Erik the Red or some famous Celt, though in this confused and angry state, he might not even remember his name.

That wasn't right, not by a long shot. Rage burned in Chloe's belly. She couldn't hate this ghost now—just like she hadn't been able to hate the Ada Lovelace lookalike—no matter what he'd interrupted. He'd been at rest, and Tabitha had yanked him back to this mortal coil. She was going to pay for that.

If Chloe could get around where Ramses and the Viking currently had their arms locked, both trying to force the other back, teeth gritted, sparking with blue-white energy.

"I see something outside," Helen said.

Chloe barely heard her above the roaring of the giant man, but Helen wouldn't be able to hear it much, if at all.

"Should I go?"

Chloe grabbed her arm. "I don't know what will happen if you run through all that energy."

Helen nodded, still trusting her as the expert, and it was such a turn-on.

Goddamned Tabitha.

"I can almost see the ghost," Helen whispered.

Chloe nodded. "That's their spectral field. It takes a ton of energy for a ghost to show themselves to most people, even briefly, but they're using a lot to fight each other. And Ramses is between me and the other guy. I can't get a clear shot."

Ramses and the Viking were stumbling through the bed and desk, but the Viking seemed determined not to leave, probably sent after Helen and Chloe rather than Ramses, but he was holding his own, his strength more than a match for a ghost who seemed to be relying mostly on strength of body instead of will.

"Can I get past?" Helen asked.

Chloe bit her lip, wanting to give her a hundred reasons to stay, but they'd already agreed to let each other put themselves in danger if necessary. And as soon as Chloe could nail this Nordic bastard to the floor, she would be hot on Helen's trail.

"Not yet," she said. Ramses and the Viking were still pushing at each other like Sumo wrestlers. The ax had long since faded away. "Outside, look for someone doing a summoning. They'll need a circle and a focus, a statuette or figurine."

"Right." Helen gave her a look so full of confidence, it made Chloe weak in the knees. "And if I see Tabitha, I'm clear to kick her ass, right?"

"So right." Chloe wanted to give her a kiss good luck, but Ramses wrenched the Viking sideways through the bed, clearing a path to the gaping door. "Go."

Helen leapt into a run as gracefully as a deer, bolting through the doorway.

The Viking bellowed a war cry as she left and took a half step back. Ramses shoved, his energy crackling like a popping ember, knocking the Viking to one knee.

Chloe pulled a handful of salt and cayenne and darted forward, but when she threw, the Viking fell sideways away from her, pulling Ramses with him.

Right into the spray.

He froze on the spot, crying out as the salt and cayenne held him in a crouch near the floor.

"Shit, I'm sorry." Chloe stuffed her hand back into the baggie, but the Viking slapped at her, and a jolt of energy shot up her arm like an electric shock. Her fingers went numb, the baggie falling to the floor. She gripped her arm in agony, then groped for her hammer and nails.

That had just gone outside with Helen.

The Viking stood between her and the door as if reading her intentions, chest working like a bellows, his eyes wild.

"I can put you to rest," Chloe said. She held the ring of rowan and red thread up like a shield, but it wouldn't do much good on its own.

The Viking's head tilted like a cat facing down an interesting bug, deciding whether to eat or torment it. Either way, it'd be dead. He stepped forward, reaching for her with one meaty hand.

Chloe threw herself past him onto the bed and bounced across it. As she hoped, the Viking ran around the bed rather than through it.

And left the foot of the bed clear.

Chloe bounced onto it again, using it to land right on Ramses as the Viking's hands *whooshed* over her head.

Ramses collapsed into her as if falling into her arms, but as soon as he possessed her, being frozen in place no longer mattered. He flipped their shared body, somersaulting toward the bathroom before pushing to his feet.

Chloe had managed to keep hold of the rowan ring, and Ramses waved it like a bullfighter. The Viking paused, clearly very confused and probably getting angrier by the second.

"I'm so sorry I salted you," Chloe said in their mind. "And cayenne-d you."

"It's okay."

"So amateur."

"It's all right."

"If we die, I'm so damned sorry."

"You're not going to die, and I'm already dead."

Chloe forced herself to focus. The Viking stepped around the bed, blocking the way out again, but Chloe doubted Ramses would have escaped even if they could. He was always loath to leave an enemy once the fight was on, but without the baggie or the nails—

"Wait. We have a vial of iron filings," she said. "It's for fey, but they might work against a ghost, especially one as newly summoned as this guy, and it's sure as shit not just window dressing." She directed Ramses to the right pocket, and he pulled the plastic vial and popped the cork off with his thumb.

When the Viking hesitated again, eyeing the vial, Ramses gestured him forward. "Come on, you son of a pig. Or will you be a coward and shame your family?"

Confusion or not, that seemed to get through. With another battle roar, the Viking charged, hands out for Chloe's neck.

Ramses ducked and managed to turn while bending sideways, bringing his arm up to throw the iron filings in the Viking's face. The roars cut off mid-bellow, and the Viking fell, clawing at his eyes as if blinded, too interested in protecting his face, even though it wasn't nearly as vulnerable to a ghost.

Pity and the Viking's strangled coughs turned Chloe's stomach. "Hurry, Ramses."

He grabbed the baggie and tossed a handful of salt and cayenne onto the Viking, freezing him in place before stepping out of Chloe's body. She didn't know what might happen if he was actually possessing her while she did a banishing, and she didn't want to find out.

"I don't have the nails," she said, shrugging off twinges from muscles that weren't used to moving the way Ramses forced them to.

"*Mostly* window dressing, remember?"

Right. She went through the motions with the rowan ring anyway, saying the words and feeling the power building in herself where she'd thought it was the tools before. The power stuttered a few times, and she made herself fall back into the ritual, using that to prop up her self-confidence.

When the Viking finally faded, his eyes seemed grateful. It made her life that much more worthwhile.

"You okay?" she and Ramses asked at the same time before they both chuckled.

"Let's go see if Helen's kicked Tabitha's ass yet," Chloe said. She paused on the walkway outside. A haze stretched in front of her before bending through half the rooms on either side of theirs and arcing overhead. It glistened iridescently, as if she stood inside a giant soap bubble.

"It's magical," Ramses said.

"No shit."

He grumbled, no doubt something about trying to be helpful, but a gleam from the parking lot caught Chloe's eye, and her insides froze solid.

Helen's kladenet lay on the ground, winking at her in the glow of the halogen lights.

CHAPTER THIRTY-FOUR

It had all gone swimmingly in Helen's imagination. She'd run out of the room and seen Tabitha kneeling in the back of a pickup amidst several glowing kerosene lamps. Her head had jerked up, red curls framing her pale, wide-eyed face. It should have been simplicity itself to close the distance, leap onto the open tailgate, and either stab Tabitha or punch her into unconsciousness.

Should have been.

After a step, Helen had passed through some force field that felt like a mass of cobwebs, but it had yielded easily, and all the chirps and croaks and trills of an evening in the country had surrounded her. That should have been a clue that more magic than a simple summoning was in play.

But it took another few steps to realize there was a second force field, this one as solid as stone.

Pain, shock, stumbling back, her head ringing and on fire: those were easy to remember now as her vision went in and out. Air rushed past her as if she was flying, taking a jaunt on Pegasus yet again, perhaps, until something else squeezed her, a vise-like feeling she'd experienced recently, but she was having such a hard time focusing.

How could she have been so stupid? The rough tautness of rope bit into her wrists behind her back. She strained to snap them but couldn't. Was she falling? Darkness surrounded her, but another jolt to her body turned her mind off again.

Awake, she was lying down now. With Chloe? No, the surface beneath her face was hard, rough, and filled her nose with the scent of mustiness and earth, the smell of time itself. When she lifted her head, it throbbed, and something sticky trailed from her cheek to the floor. She tasted more metal. A bloody nose, maybe worse.

Voices.

Tabitha was one. But where were they?

She had to get loose. Chloe was counting on her. Helen had to at least slow Tabitha down, both to save Chloe the worry and to get her revenge.

But more fucking carefully this time, or the Sphinx would never forgive her.

Her wits came back in fits and starts. She rolled onto her shoulder. Dim light came from behind her, turning the wall from a mass of shadows to a row of shelves, all filled to the brim with stone or pottery or boxes with bundles of straw and packing materials cascading down the front. Her feet were free, and she managed to roll over slowly. Shutting her eyes, she forced herself to breathe through the pain and dizziness and called for her godhood.

Nothing.

She nodded weakly. More magic at work. It must have been why she couldn't just snap the ropes, why her injuries weren't already healing the way they should have been. When she opened her eyes again, a beautiful face was smiling down at her.

The Lamia. At last. But was it the real one this time?

And why was her hair a startling shade of red rather than her usual dark blue?

"Awake, are we? That was quick, especially without your god powers." The voice was a little different but still throaty, seductive.

Helen breathed a laugh. "You don't even have the voice or the hair right. Pathetic, demon."

The faux-Lamia laughed where a demon might have bristled at the insult. What kind of creature was this?

Helen cried out as she was lifted upright, her head throbbing and the world spinning. The faux-Lamia placed her in a wooden folding chair as if she weighed nothing. When she managed to open her eyes again, the faux-Lamia had backed off a few steps, letting Helen take in the red-and-black striped tail of her lower half and the ochre skin of her upper. She wore as little as the real Lamia, and their faces and figures were nearly identical, but this one's necklace and belt and bangles were all silver, and she didn't wear the magical imprisoning cuff Helen had put on the real Lamia all those years ago.

"Who are you?" Helen asked, breathing through the pain.

"I'm the Lamia, of course." She held up a hand with long scarlet nails. "Not the one you're used to. That's my sister."

"Mmm-hmm, sure." Helen tried to feign nonchalance while looking around the room. Tabitha bent over a table behind the faux-Lamia, busily sorting through a box on a table lit by an electric lamp. Beyond her stood more shelves and double doors. The walls and floor were concrete. No one had bothered to turn on the overhead lights. Would the motel have a storeroom like this? "You can pretend all you want if it amuses you."

The faux-Lamia laughed again and leaned back on the table, biting her lip playfully with one fang. "You don't have to take my word for it." She put a hand to the side of her mouth. "Sis? You busy?"

A creature who looked much more like the real Lamia slithered through the double doors, the colors right with her blue hair, green skin, and black, iridescent tail. But her mocking, eternal-teenager energy had been replaced by a scowl. And her left arm ended in a bandage instead of a hand. "It'll take forever for this to grow back," she said petulantly, seeming to aim the comment at both her "sister" and Helen.

Helen frowned. If the Lamia had to chop off her hand to remove the cuff, then was this the real Lamia? She fought to stay quiet, to let them reveal whatever they wanted to, but she couldn't help saying, "But you're *the* Lamia."

"Yes." The blue one gestured back and forth between herself and her sister. "The Lamia."

"Twins," her sister said, linking their arms.

"That's not how *the* works," Helen snapped, beyond tired of whatever nonsense was going on here.

The Lamias gave the same elegant shrug.

No, it couldn't possibly be true.

Could it?

"I didn't know you were going to take her," the blue Lamia said. She didn't look happy as she tilted her chin at Helen.

"I wasn't, but she'll work marvelously as long as her magic lasts." The red Lamia gave Helen an appraising glance. "Mind you, that might not be too long. She's fairly used up."

"And sitting right here, thank you," Helen said. *Rude.*

The Lamias ignored her. "It would have been better if she'd been asleep for centuries like Charybdis, but..." The red Lamia shrugged again. "She'll last longer than the wyvern, at least."

"What are you talking about?" Helen said, getting angrier by the moment. "That wyvern is old and tired and deserves a rest. And the others don't deserve whatever it is you're going to do to them, either." She glared. "And if you're the real Lamia," she said to the blue one, "you should know that releasing Charybdis will do nothing but put the entire world in jeopardy, you included."

The blue Lamia narrowed her eyes. "Still thinking you know everything, same as always."

"We're not going to let her go, hon," the red Lamia said to Helen. "You don't have to worry your pretty little head. In fact." She slithered closer and walked her fingers up Helen's chest as she spoke. "You don't have to worry about anything until it's your turn." She ended with a light touch on her nose.

It was almost worth the energy to try to bite her, but Helen needed to save it all for escaping.

"All you have to do is sit there and be bait," the red Lamia said as she backed away.

"Don't talk about your plans." The blue Lamia crossed her arms, and Helen got the sense that she found her sister as irritating as everyone else found her. Served her right. "You're not a Bond villain."

The red Lamia laughed delightedly and slithered for the doors. "All right, I'll leave her to you. Make sure you keep enough of her left for our…" She shut her lips with a snap and winked. "Mysterious plans." She snorted as she went through the doors. "Come, Tabitha."

With only a slight glare, no doubt at the summons, Tabitha scurried after her.

Helen stared the Lamia down, something in her saying this was the real one, something she hadn't felt in the presence of the imposter: centuries of animosity. "Well, are you going to get your revenge or what?"

The Lamia sighed and sagged on the table far more resignedly than her sister had. "I don't feel like having revenge."

"Did she give you a personality transplant when she cut off your hand?"

That earned her a smile. "Her lackeys did this." She lifted her arm and scowled at it. "I put the bandage on. It didn't seem right to leave it bare even if I don't bleed."

"I didn't know you could regrow limbs."

"There's a lot you don't know."

Ah, the attitude Helen was far more familiar with. Maybe she could use it to get more information.

Like the Lamia had ever given up any info for free.

"If you can regrow your hand, why didn't you chop the cuff off a long time ago?"

The Lamia rolled her eyes. "Just because one can do a thing doesn't mean that thing is pleasant."

"But for your freedom?"

Another elegant shrug, but this one seemed half-hearted.

"You didn't really want to escape, did you? You just liked to bitch." Helen expected some bristling, but the Lamia smiled, her gaze faraway. "You liked living in your crypt and playing your video games and being near Melusine's sleeping body."

"They left her behind." It was so soft, Helen nearly missed it.

And her heart went out to the Lamia for once. Well, probably more than once. "The Sphinx won't let anything happen to her."

The Lamia's gaze snapped to hers. "Trying to butter me up?"

"Do I need to?"

Another smile, brighter this time. "You know, I'm actually going to miss sparring with you."

"Why should we stop?"

The Lamia's mouth opened before she shut it and smiled slyly. "Just like I'm not a Bond villain, you're not Bond. I'm not revealing my sister's dastardly plans."

"So she does have a dastardly plan?"

"So you do acknowledge that she's my sister?"

And the tap dance continued. But not for much longer, it seemed, with whatever the red Lamia had planned for Helen and Charybdis and the others. "Used up," she said, trying to think. "Power-wise?"

"It's certainly not your looks," the Lamia said, winking lasciviously. "Your charm, maybe."

"Screw you."

The Lamia burst out laughing before a shadow passed over her face. She didn't like her sister's plans. Helen had been on the right track there.

"She needs our power for something. Mine, Charybdis, those I understand. Even the hippogriff and the Pleiades and the dryad. But the sick old wyvern?"

As usual, the Lamia's face gave little away.

"What could it do for you? What could the others really do? Was that all her lackeys could get their hands on? I'm assuming she didn't free you just to use your power in some way."

"No, she'd never turn on me."

So whatever the red Lamia was going to do to Helen and the others, it wasn't good. But she hadn't really expected it to be. And the few who had been kidnapped from the sanctuary might have been all that the mercenaries could get at the time, but they hadn't been the only supernatural creatures targeted for capture.

There was Ramses.

They wanted a powerful ghost, too.

And Helen was the bait.

She tried to force herself to remain calm, but something of her thoughts must have shown in her eyes because the Lamia studied her, head on one side.

"You never should have gotten involved with another human," the Lamia said softly.

Helen fought to speak through her clenched jaw. "Would that have stopped this?"

"No, but it might have hurt less." She slithered out the door without a backward look.

CHAPTER THIRTY-FIVE

No way in hell was Chloe losing Helen after everything they'd been through.

And before the actual nudity.

She shook her head. No, after everything they'd been through sounded way more ethical, not to mention classier.

"They can't have gone far." Ramses stepped through the bubble before they even had a chance to find out what it was.

Chloe bit her tongue, relaxing only a fraction when nothing happened to him. *In for a penny...*

The sounds of the outside world came rushing back as she passed through, startling her into wondering why she hadn't missed them in the first place. It was some kind of silence bubble, maybe so no one in the motel would hear what had gone on. The door lying on the floor of the room would be a dead giveaway later.

Ramses stood near the back of a pickup. "Over here."

Chloe hurried over, one hand on her bag. When she glanced at the lanterns and the figurine in the middle, she knew what this was: a summoning circle. She took the figurine of some Anglo-Saxon warrior and smashed it on the ground, just in case Tabitha came looking for it.

There was more around it, a circle of beeswax, flecks of metal, and flower petals. In the light of her flashlight app, they looked like a mix of gladiolas and bluebells, flowers said to represent strength and resilience. Bluebells could also stand for hope, but Chloe doubted Tabitha meant that. They were clearly part of some strength spell for the ghost, maybe for Tabitha, too, maybe even for some kind of trap that Helen had run into.

Chloe gnawed on her thumbnail. That sounded like some ancient spell. She'd never met anyone who could actually make such old magic work. "You don't think Tabitha has a godhood, too, do you?"

"Absolutely not."

But could he be sure? "This is old magic, Ramses. And she's summoned at least three spirits that we know of, one that seemed pretty powerful. She's pulling power from somewhere, and if she doesn't have god blood, where's it coming from?"

He rubbed his chin and frowned, no doubt casting his mind back through the millennia. "Some kind of godly token? Or even a smaller god that she's pulling power from?" He twisted his hands as if wringing a washcloth, and Chloe winced. *Ouch.* "A river god, something like that."

"Who's still around after all this time and has the mojo to serve as her battery? Any god like that would put her on her ass, wouldn't they?"

"Unless she's formed some pact with them."

Great. So Tabitha might have a god in her pocket, but what in the world could she have promised them in order to use them like that?

And what the hell did she want?

That would have to wait until Chloe had more room to think. "If Tabitha took Helen somewhere, she had to leave a trail."

She and Ramses spread out, looking through the parking lot, but it wasn't like following tracks through the mud, and Tabitha hadn't left any helpful breadcrumbs. They went down the row of rooms, but like most hotels, the Super 10 Motor Court had doors that shut automatically, so no open rooms beckoned to them.

"A drop of blood," Ramses called from close to the office.

Chloe ran that way with her heart turning over, happy for a trail to follow but scared as hell by the blood. Luckily, it was only a few drops that led along a covered walkway and through a gate to the pool.

"She can't be that hurt," Ramses said as they paused. The pool light was on, turning the water a sickly blue-green. Several insects paddled ineffectually near where the light glowed just under the surface. "From the look of things, Tabitha was carrying rather than dragging her." He pointed to another spot of blood, and Chloe followed. "If Helen's hurt, she'd be leaving more marks if she was dragged."

That spoke to strength again. Tabitha was fairly petite, shorter than Chloe, and Helen would have been head and shoulders above her. Maybe Tabitha had a monstrous ancestor instead of anything godly? Using her own blood or something to grant herself power?

The trail led to a small pool house, little more than a shed, with a red-and-white striped safety ring hanging on the side that looked as if it had never been used.

Ramses started toward the wall, but Chloe said, "Wait. They've already laid one trap for you where they were sure we would follow."

He frowned but nodded and stood behind her, ready to possess her at a moment's notice.

She threw open the door.

And nearly screamed when a long-handled pool brush fell out at her.

Ramses let out a breath as if he too had nearly spun into action and killed the hell out of some cleaning equipment.

Chloe brought up the flashlight app and scanned the inside of the shed, though she was certain Helen wasn't there. When she saw the marks on the wall, she froze. They were the same as from the office in Zile-de-Deyès, the ones that had been part of the portal.

"On the ground," Ramses said.

A folded piece of paper lay neatly beside a bucket of chlorine tabs close to the wall. Chloe nudged it with her foot, and when it didn't explode, she chided herself and snatched it up.

"Tag," it said. "You're it."

What followed read like instructions for opening the portal, an invitation if ever there was one. At the bottom, just to drive the point home, was an obvious smear of blood.

"It's a trap," she and Ramses said together.

"A big, obvious trap," Chloe said.

"Huge."

"But we're going anyway, right?"

"Of course we are."

But not without some serious preparations. Chloe quickly called Fatma's number. "I need to know how to make things go boom in a hurry."

❖

Helen had no doubt it would be her turn in the funhouse sooner than expected, though she doubted it would be much fun at all. Once the blue Lamia had gone, she stood, but she'd never get far with her hands bound behind her back, so she leaned on the table and wriggled and squirmed until she managed to pull her legs through her arms.

She rubbed her wrists raw in the process and almost got stuck halfway. That would have been embarrassing as hell if they'd found her, but thanks to the gods and yoga, she managed to succeed.

Unluckily, her captors hadn't left her with anything like a knife to free herself with. The shards of pottery felt too fragile to get the job done. Tabitha or one of the Lamias had also taken the hammer and nails Chloe had given her.

Then what was that heavy feeling at the top of her boot?

After a quick peek at the door, she sat again and dug around, finding a lone nail that seemed to have fallen through a hole in her pocket. A small victory, but she'd take it. She did up her boots more tightly while she was at it, then went to work picking at the rope with the nail. It felt as if it might take forever, but when she managed to gouge one thread until it snapped, she felt a smidge of power, and her face hurt a little less.

She smiled so widely, it hurt. All she had to do was break enough threads, and her power would return enough to snap the rope, heal her, and let justice run down like waters.

When she heard footsteps, she hurried to the side of the doors and put her back to the shelves, not going to let the opportunity for a sneak attack pass her by. When Tabitha paused just inside the room, Helen reached for her neck, but Tabitha grabbed her with hands like steel and turned with a smile on her face.

"So predictable. That's the trouble with you immortals."

Helen tried to twist away. She kicked Tabitha's thigh where the nail wound had been, but it was like smashing her sole against concrete.

"It's a strength spell. You're never gonna break it," Tabitha said. "But hey, good job on getting your hands around your front. Now you'll be able to put them up when you say, 'Oh gods, please stop.'" She laughed obnoxiously, yanked Helen forward, and hoisted her over one shoulder like a sack of grain.

"Get your fucking hands off me." Helen squirmed with no effect. She considered trying to stab Tabitha with the nail but doubted it would do any good. And would give away the fact that she had it in the first place. She hid it in her palm instead.

Tabitha carried her down several hallways, talking over her cries of protest. "Yeah, yeah, get it all out of your system. You're only making what comes next better for me."

The world went topsy-turvy as Tabitha slung her down onto another hard floor. The air rushed from Helen's lungs as she stared up at a dome made from stone and rusting metal. Shop lights dotted the large space, their powerful glow highlighting dozens of strings crisscrossing overhead. Prisms had been woven into the strands as if a very fancy spider was nesting there.

Helen didn't have much time to gawk before Tabitha hauled her upright and forced her into a large metal ring that clasped around her waist. She strained forward, and the ring felt as if it could give, like it might be pieces joined by some kind of stretchy cable. She couldn't stretch it with her current strength. Another metal bar in the back held her in place like a doll's stand.

She breathed hard, rage building in her throat. "When I get out of here—"

"I've heard it all before." Tabitha looked almost sorry for her but spoiled it with a smirk. She crossed to where the red and blue Lamia fiddled with some kind of altar. The entire room was strewn with magical whatnots, glyphs, and reagents. Helen was starting to wish she'd spent more time listening to Maurice when a shadowy lump from a corner of the room caught her eye.

The wyvern, unmoving, finally at peace, but she doubted he'd gone easily. Oh, these bastards were going to pay for that.

The blue Lamia came over and followed her gaze. To Helen's surprise, she sighed. "Sacrificed to power a human's strength spell. A waste."

Right, it would be the waste of power and not the actual loss of life that saddened her. "Just to get me here?" She managed to keep her voice level.

The Lamia looked at her curiously. "When either I or my sister could have done it as easily? Yes. She likes to pretend she's stronger than she is, that one."

Helen ground her teeth. "That's what you're doing with all the creatures you kidnap? Using their lives to power your magic? Her magic?"

The Lamia had no expression as she leaned forward. "Until she's no longer useful, of course."

"I imagine sacrificing me and Charybdis will give you all the power you need."

"Well, Charybdis might." The Lamia leaned back, her smile returned. "Look at you putting all the pieces together and even getting some information out of me. Though, it did take you quite a while to figure it out. I'm both embarrassed for you and proud at the same time."

Oh, no, their sparring days were done. Helen forced herself to remain expressionless, hoping the Lamia would see they were nothing to each other now, not even hated enemies. She would still have her revenge, but she would feel nothing when she did. "Everyone always said I should kill you. I had lots of reasons not to, but they all seem silly now. You really are a monster. The only true one I ever met."

The Lamia's eyes turned a bit stricken before she shook her head. How could any being have a conscience when their soul was dead? "You're going to regret saying that."

"Is the portal ready?" the red Lamia asked without looking up.

"Yeah." Tabitha gestured to another side of the room. Helen recognized those symbols from the office on Zile-de-Deyès, the same kind of portal spell. "I left Chloe instructions on how to open it. We should have enough juice to power it with her." She gestured at Helen with her thumb before giving her a sneer. "Though who knows for how long?"

"Shut your mouth, you grubby little shit," Helen said, her control slipping.

Tabitha's face darkened, turning nearly purple.

The red Lamia laughed. "I'm going to miss you," she said to Helen over her shoulder.

"You're never going to be a true archvillain like that, sis," the blue Lamia said. "You keep the lovers alive so that they can watch each other die. It's practically a rule."

"And I have missed you." The red Lamia looked at her sister fondly. "So effortlessly cruel. Well, I suppose I can indulge you since she tortured you by boredom for so long. Okay, bring one of the others. We'll drain them dry instead."

"No," Helen yelled. "Use me if you have to. Leave them alone."

The red Lamia shivered as if beyond delighted. "Even better. We get to hurt you before your love even arrives."

Tabitha burst out laughing, as comfortable with evil as any demon in hell. She tinkered with a few more bits and bobs as she neared the door.

Helen raged against her bonds, stabbing at the inside of the rope with the nail, a red mist covering her sight. The gods could not be this unfair.

The blue Lamia sidled to a similar contraption as the one that held Helen. "Where did you learn all this stuff, sis?"

"Here and there. Tabitha researched quite a bit for me. She's so efficient."

"And now you've got it all figured out?"

The red Lamia nodded and glanced around as if surveying a job well done. "All we have to do is snap another soul into this crucible"—she patted the metal ring—"and we can take every ounce of energy they have."

"Good." The blue Lamia darted forward, nearly a blur, and snatched Tabitha off her feet and slammed her into the metal ring, shutting it before Tabitha could even cry out.

Until the metal ring glowed and sparked. Then she shrieked as if her very molecules were tearing themselves apart.

Helen's jaw dropped as the prisms glowed, and the glyphs seemed to twist in place. Those in the portal corner hummed as if charged. It was over in seconds, leaving Tabitha's body to sag like a broken puppet, her eyes wide, terrified, and her skin as pale as dust.

"Well, that was uncalled for," the red Lamia said with a scowl.

"I was sick of her mouth. Besides." The blue one stuck her lip out in a pout. "I didn't like how close you seemed to be getting."

"Oh, my dear sister." The red one smiled and opened her arms. "All is forgiven." When they embraced though, the red one seemed to be holding her tighter than necessary. "But don't forget whose plan this was. Next time, ask permission."

The blue one broke away with a snort. "Permission. As if."

They shared a laugh in front of Tabitha's corpse. It was just one more thing Helen would remember when getting her revenge.

Right now, she had other things to worry about. Their portal was powered, and if she'd heard right, Chloe knew how to open it. She and Ramses would know it was a trap; Helen would stake her life on that. They wouldn't actually fall for it, wouldn't charge through hoping to outsmart the perpetrators of such an obvious snare.

Oh, who was she kidding. She'd be doing the same thing, could almost see them coming up with a plan. The idea was marginally better than just charging through. Fractionally. A minuscule amount.

She fought the urge to sigh and kept stabbing at the rope. The enemy team was down a member, a point for their side. But they still had two magic-wielding Lamias who weren't even in their fiercest forms. Not to mention any hench-demons wandering about the place.

Maybe when the portal inevitably opened, Helen could shout, "Don't bother, save yourselves."

Not that they would listen.

She glanced at the magical apparatus again. There was no doubt something in there that could hold a ghost, too, and she shuddered to think what they could do with a power like Ramses as well as Charybdis.

She might as well ask. What could it hurt? "What are you going to do with all this power? Destroy the world?"

The red Lamia gave her a flat look. "Don't be an idiot. We'd set Charybdis loose if we wanted that." She slithered closer. "It's more power, darling. It's always about power, the threat of a world-ending weapon. The magic will just allow our strikes to be a little more...tactical."

Helen thought fast. "World domination?" Like the blue Lamia had said, true supervillainy. "If you can destroy anyone or anywhere in the world, humanity will have to do what you say?"

"You should rejoice," the blue one said. "Quite a few of our extraordinary brethren will be on our side."

"And the world will become their sanctuary." The red one tipped her head back and forth. "For some of them, anyway."

Those whose power the Lamias didn't need for their murder machine.

Helen's belly went cold. She couldn't fight a picture of what the world would look like. It wasn't a vision for the future she'd ever considered, not one she really wanted, but she was curious to see how it would go.

In the end, she'd never know because she'd either thwart the plan or be dead.

Or maybe she would see it even then. With the veil between the worlds weakened, the Lamias might be able to punch a hole into the underworlds and have the dead at their disposal like never-ending batteries. At least until the spirits dissolved, forced into actual oblivion.

She shivered, terrified by the very idea, but when she looked up and met the blue Lamia's expressionless gaze, she knew it would be useless to reason with them. There was only one way forward.

She stabbed harder with the nail, feeling a few more strands snap. She jabbed herself in the hands and wrists but kept going, didn't dare look to see how far she had yet to go.

The wall in the portal corner began to swirl, the vortex opening, and she stabbed even harder. "Chloe, don't," she cried, needing to try. "Stay away, it's a trap."

But the Lamias darted for the portal faster than Chloe could ever be, even with Ramses in charge of the body. The vortex pulsed, and they held their arms out to catch whoever came through.

Something sailed low between them, far too small for a person. The sound of breaking glass was quickly drowned out by a *whomp* of displaced air.

Helen just had time to suck in a lungful before a cloud of pale green gas exploded outward. Enough of her godhood had returned to give her a burst of speed, and she pulled her shirt over her face. Her skin still stung, her eyes burning. She squeezed them closed.

Gods, the Lamias had to be lamenting their lack of fashion choices at the moment.

And Helen fell more in love with Chloe by the second.

CHAPTER THIRTY-SIX

All Chloe could do was hope Helen wasn't in the room when the chlorine bomb went off. Or that she had a little time to prepare. The gas shouldn't kill her—especially with her godly powers—and it probably wouldn't kill any supernatural creatures, but it should give everyone a helluva headache.

As Fatma had said, "We don't always have to rely on iron and salt. Sometimes, good old chemistry and ammunition does the trick."

Though Chloe wouldn't be messing around with guns anytime soon.

She and Ramses went in together, him steering the body. If these fools had a ghost trap, it'd just have to grab him out of her. Until then, they were stronger together.

They stayed low, appearing between two half-snake women who were coughing and gagging and grasping at their faces and throats. Chloe had donned her gloves and wrapped hotel towels around her head, figuring she and Helen had screwed themselves out of any deposit already. She wore sunglasses, hoping that would keep out the worst of the gas already settling toward the floor, heavier than normal air, and seeping toward a large grate in the center of the room.

Two people were imprisoned in wide metal rings, one slumped, one with its shirt pulled over its head. Gods, what if the slumped one was Helen?

"Use that anger," Ramses said in their shared mind as he stabbed at one of the snake women with the golden spear they'd retrieved from the pouch Helen had left in the bathroom.

Chloe felt that same spark inside her as when her mom had pissed her off. She yanked on it, hoping to raise her godhood, but when she looked hard at the power, it fled like a scared rabbit.

Ramses scored a gouge to the snake woman with the red-and-black tail. This had to be the Lamia. Or one of a pair because except for coloring, they looked almost identical. The striped one cried out as the spear pierced her snake half, but she didn't bleed, the wound gaping like dead flesh.

The Lamia doesn't bleed, Helen had once said.

Still, it seemed to pain her.

Good.

That same spark reappeared inside her. Chloe kept her metaphorical eyes off it, letting it come, surrendering to it. Ramses grabbed it once she let it rise and used it to power his swings as he stabbed at the Lamia with the green skin, blue hair, and iridescent tail. Her eyes were red-rimmed and streaming, but she slapped the strike away, and the one with the striped tail pulled her behind a tangle of string and crystals.

"Get to Helen," Chloe said.

Ramses turned, and Chloe caught a glimpse of red curls from the slumped figure. Tabitha fallen into her own trap? It didn't matter right now. Ramses darted for the other, though how they were going to break the metal ring was—

Chloe screamed in her mind as pain shot through her, and the world turned white around the edges. She was falling toward the thin layer of light green gas that crept across the ground, but Ramses could catch them in time.

She smacked into concrete, her head ringing, and her limbs under her control.

"Chloe!"

She pushed out of the gas, staggering to her feet, her limbs jerking in mid-spasm. Helen peeked out the top of her shirt and pointed. Chloe turned to find Ramses stuck in one spot, his arms outstretched like a scarecrow, face contorted. He opened his mouth as if screaming, but no sound came out.

"Shit." She couldn't feel him, just like before. They really should have watched where they were stepping, but the ground was still obscured. Hoisted by their own petard.

Chloe banged the sigils on the ground with her spear, trying to gouge them, but that hadn't worked before. Maurice had needed a whole list of ingredients to shift them. She tried to remember what they were and whether she had them.

The Lamias were advancing, snarling, tears streaming down their beautiful, snotty faces. Even if Chloe remembered the exact combination, she wouldn't have time to use it.

She grabbed for her godhood, but like before, it was slippery, and she couldn't relax in the face of the Lamias enough to let it flow. And though she had felt Ramses use the spear, she couldn't replicate his moves.

Time to buy some time.

She ran for what looked like an altar, hoping the Lamias wouldn't be quick to barrel into their magical setup. Chloe recognized prisms and flowers and all kinds of metals and herbs. More old magic, but there was no little god standing around waiting.

When the Lamias came for her, one on either side of the altar, she rolled under it, the remaining gas burning her exposed skin where the towels or clothes had slipped, and her eyes and nose and lungs were aching, too, the gas finding little ways in. Maybe the spear would be tough enough to break the metal ring that held Helen in place.

She sprinted for her, Wait, no, she couldn't risk stabbing the ring. If she jammed the shaft between Helen and the metal, maybe she could pry it open? She crammed the butt of the spear down across Helen's back.

Helen said something through her shirt, but Chloe couldn't hear. She leaned on the spear, trying to pop the metal ring, but it only stretched, solid pieces joined by some kind of cable. She yanked hard. If she could stretch it enough, Helen could slip out.

Come on, godhood, you useless piece of shit.

It ignored her.

Well, she couldn't blame it if she was going to talk to it like that.

Helen yelled something right as Chloe's foot was yanked out from under her. She smacked onto her tailbone, losing her grip on the spear still stuck behind Helen.

The blue-haired Lamia held her foot. She'd used Chloe's trick, coming in low. She opened her mouth, and her fangs caught the light. Chloe kicked, aiming for her face.

The blue-haired Lamia pulled back just as her striped twin shot forward. With a smile, she grabbed Chloe's leg out of the air and sank her fangs into it.

❖

When Chloe shrieked, Helen cried out, too. Her eyes were beginning to clear, her godhood healing her now that she'd broken several of the rope's strands. She'd tried to get Chloe to cut the rest of them with the spear but obviously hadn't gotten her point across.

And now the fucking spear was stuck along her back.

She turned to see Chloe reeling from the red Lamia's venomous bite. Gods, how much time did she have? Seconds? Could her godhood save her if she couldn't control when she brought it forth?

Helen couldn't wait to find out. She summoned as much of her own godhood as she could, pulling harder than she had in a long time, making her ears pop, and a fresh trickle of warm blood cascaded over her lips.

Never mind. It halted abruptly as power filled her, cleansing her eyes and lungs with a golden glow. She snapped the rope around her wrists and wrenched the spear out from behind her. With a cry, she buried it in the red Lamia's tail, driving all the way through to pin her to the floor.

Her shriek rattled Helen's teeth far more than Chloe's had, but it only filled her with satisfaction. She pushed on the metal ring, expanding it enough to slip out. The blue Lamia was reaching for her sister, but Helen kicked her in the shoulder, sending her falling to the side.

Helen grabbed Chloe under the arms and pulled her away from the red Lamia and closer to Ramses. She knelt and put a hand on the bite as the last of the gas streamed down the grate in the floor.

"Chloe?" Helen yanked the towels and sunglasses off her head. Her eyes had rolled back, her complexion ashy.

Helen ripped the leg of her jeans open. Two half-moon punctures marred her calf, the fang holes seeping blood and the veins outlined in black, the venom coursing through her. "Chloe, summon your godhood." Helen pushed her own power toward the wound, but she'd never healed anyone but herself. "Chloe?" She smoothed the sweaty hair from her forehead and tried to push all her loving feelings through their connection just as she'd tried to lend her power. "Remember the demon, how your godhood came when you needed it. Do it now, Chloe. We need you, Ramses and I."

The blue Lamia yanked the spear from her sister's tail. The hole didn't bleed, but a little plume of dark smoke swirled out, the Lamia's essence. If too much escaped, she'd die like anything else.

Right now, she was very much alive and pissed off, and Helen couldn't fight the two of them on her own.

Especially as the red Lamia's form shimmered and blurred, heralding her transformation.

"No, no, no." Helen stood over Chloe, but she really didn't know what she would do against a dragon.

CHAPTER THIRTY-SEVEN

Chloe felt like she'd been here before: breathing shallowly, people depending on her, life in the balance, Helen at her side. The dragon was new.

More remarkably, she couldn't even care as the world went round and round, and her veins were full of fire. She couldn't see Ramses, wasn't sure he still existed. Wasn't even sure she existed. Everything felt fuzzy and faraway and none of her concern.

The white light shining from her left was more interesting. If she looked straight at it, it was a long, glowing tunnel. From the side of her eye, it seemed more like a door. When she didn't look at all, it smelled like a garden in bloom, the spring sunshine lying gently on her shoulders. It felt as much like grace as her godhood had felt before.

And Jamie was standing inside it, waiting for her.

Chloe couldn't see her clearly, but she knew her sister in that moment as she knew the back of her hand. She wanted to cry out, reach for her, but that felt like so much effort. There was something going on at her other side, too, with Helen and a dragon, but she didn't know what to do about that, either.

She only knew she had to choose.

"I can't help you decide," Jamie said, seemingly able to read Chloe's mind, just like when they were children. It had driven her nuts, then.

"Just the wisdom that comes with experience." Jamie didn't sound as smug as she used to, as if she'd grown in death the way she never would in life. "You have to make the choice, Chlo."

Why? Couldn't she stay in this in-between place where she had Helen and her sister? Ramses had to be nearby. The dragon could even stay, too.

Jamie chuckled, but the sound carried a hint of exasperation. "You know the answer. If you don't decide soon, someone's gonna choose for you, and I know how much you hate that."

The curse of the younger sibling. What if they could switch places? Jamie would have been better at this job, anyway, would have never made the same mistakes. Even their mother thought so.

"She knows that's not true," Jamie said. "She was speaking from a place of worry and pain, and she's realized that by now. The shame haunted her after you left. Part of her thinks she drove you to it."

Jamie felt closer now. All Chloe had to do was reach out a hand.

"I won't stop you. Whatever way you want to go." Jamie's breath seemed to tickle the hair near Chloe's ear, she was so close. "The truth is, there were times when I never wanted the legacy, either, when I wanted to trade places with you. I had fears and doubts. You've done so good, though. I'm so damned proud."

Chloe felt like crying, but again, the effort was too great. All she had to do was turn and throw her arms around Jamie, and there would be time. They'd have eternity together.

Leaving their mother alone. Leaving Ramses alone. Leaving Helen alone.

With a dragon.

And maybe her mother and Ramses and Helen wouldn't be alone for long because they'd all be dead, too. If the Lamias and the dragon even stopped there. This place between realms brought clarity as well as grace, and she knew how the Lamias and Tabitha were getting their power, draining it from their victims, and if they wanted Ramses, they had a way to drain ghosts, too, creating a separate death for the dead.

Oblivion.

For her mother.

For Ramses.

For Helen.

Everyone.

Well, that was simply unacceptable.

Something bubbled inside her, something that bridged the span between worlds sort of like she was doing now, but it wasn't connecting her to the realm of the dead. It connected her to some other place, another power—ancient, undeniable—thousands upon thousands of years leading behind her in a chain to a being she could barely comprehend. Someone who transcended physics and nature and space-time itself.

Humans had called her Isis and many other names, but that only touched a fraction of what she was. She lifted a hand, stretching through the dimensions that separated them.

All Chloe had to do was take it.

"I'm sorry," she said to Jamie, her consciousness gathering steam.

"We'll meet again someday. Everything'll keep until then." Her voice faded as if Chloe was on a train speeding away from her. "Love you, Chlo. Trust yourself."

"I love you, too," Chloe said, opening her eyes.

Helen stood in front of her, facing a fucking dragon.

Huh, Chloe had almost been convinced she'd imagined that bit. She took Isis's hand and used it to pull herself up. It was time to get to work.

❖

Helen's godhood rose in her like a wave, power filling her limbs like she hadn't experienced in hundreds of years. Her glow was so bright, she could barely look at herself, and she had a moment to wonder what had happened.

Then she felt Chloe's power at her back.

"I love you, too," Chloe said.

Had Helen said that aloud? It didn't matter. She fell back a step. The blue Lamia and her dragon sister had backed off, too, no doubt driven by Helen's golden light and the cascade of silver flowing from Chloe's every pore. "And I love you." Their godhoods mingled around the edges in a sparkling fountain of color to rival the most beautiful jewel.

Helen expected Chloe to turn the Lamia sisters to ash as she had the demon, but she seemed hesitant, as if she had the power but was unsure what to do with it.

"Allow me." Helen stretched their mingled power over Ramses first, freeing him from his trap.

He came loose with an angry roar, and Helen marveled at the fact that she could still see him, hear him, even. He stepped to Chloe's other side, his blue power lending its glow to theirs. If they wanted, they could reshape the world.

Chloe was staring at her hands as if thinking the same thing. Helen knew because she'd been here before, but those same thoughts had led the Lamia to where they were now. And history had taught her that a hero would always rise to combat that sort of ambition.

She put a hand over Chloe's. "It's enough right now to stop them."

"We can always sort out the world later," Ramses added.

Chloe grinned. "Everything'll keep until then."

The dragon roared, no doubt angry with them for acting as if she wasn't in the room. She bared her sharp teeth, her reptilian face pulled into a snarl, her unfurled wings nearly filling the whole space, sending the strings and their trinkets bouncing and jangling together. Her crimson skin shone as red as blood, and her claws were as long as scythes. Everything about her screamed, fear me.

They should start there.

Helen could almost see the magic that made her, the patterns it created, the lines and flow and planes that Maurice was always talking about. It seemed simplicity itself to give them a yank and watch them crumble in on themselves. The dragon squawked and shuddered, form rippling and shrinking until she was the redheaded Lamia again.

Her eyes were wide, terrified, one hand on her heaving chest as she leaned against the wall. "What have you done?"

"It's like I can see how she's tied to the world," Chloe said.

"Mmm." Ramses tilted his head. "And it would be so easy to cut her out of it."

To cut them both out. "But it would leave a hole," Helen added. "The loss of every species takes a piece of existence away." It was something she'd always known but had never been able to articulate, one of the reasons she'd started the sanctuary in the first place.

"She can't be trusted," Ramses said.

Helen nodded, seeing the faces of those who'd been killed in the sanctuary, of the wyvern, of who knew how many others. "And vengeance demands a price."

Chloe said nothing. Helen hesitated. She couldn't use this power unless they were all in agreement. Anything else felt exploitative, wrong on a very deep level.

Helen looked to Chloe and waited.

❖

Well, shit, this was a pickle.

It should have been simple. Even Helen was saying that they ought to get rid of the Lamias, but Chloe couldn't help recalling her earlier words about the sanctuary and how everyone could be redeemed. And she also heard Ramses saying that unrepentant murderers should be put down and her mom saying that humans had learned the hard way that beings like the Lamia could never be trusted.

Everyone was still a little right, and that still wasn't fair.

A choice had to be made, but who had the right to make it?

The blue-haired Lamia was on the move. Chloe hadn't even noticed her go to the altar with all the magical whatnots. She was slithering back toward her sister now. Funny, all their attention and power had been focused on the dragon, the red-haired Lamia, and how she fit into existence. They'd ignored the blue one, but why? She was just as dangerous.

Trust yourself.

If she was coming to give her sister some relic loaded with power, if the Lamias filled themselves with some godhood they'd found, this could turn into a fair fight real fucking quick.

Trust yourself.

"Chloe?" Helen asked.

Something glinted gold in the blue-haired Lamia's hand.

"Chloe." Ramses's voice held a warning note, but he hadn't moved yet, leaving it to her to decide.

Something inside her said, "Wait," and she trusted it.

She put a hand on Helen's arm and touched Ramses's spectral elbow with the other, feeling a tingle pass through all three of them. "Look."

The red-haired Lamia reached for the blue one as if asking for help, and the blue one surged forward as if desperate to put something in her hands. At the last minute, the blue one swerved slightly and clapped the golden object around the red Lamia's wrist.

"Oh shit," Helen said.

The red Lamia shrieked and grasped her arm as if burned. Light swirled around her in a multicolored vortex, bouncing around every prism in the room until she was engulfed in a tornado of rainbows. With a howl, she winked from view, the tornado shrinking around her until it was no more than a tiny swirl of dust settling on the floor.

"What the hell?" As if the shock pulled a cork from a bottle, Chloe's godhood fled, and she dropped like an empty sack, her legs folding. Her stomach felt like a hollow pit, and her legs were strands of wet spaghetti.

Helen and Ramses knelt at her sides, but she waved for them to pay attention to the Lamia that was left. "Just winded," she managed. She couldn't get enough of looking at both of them and was so happy she'd chosen this life over the afterlife.

And that her heart had never stopped, or she'd have lost Ramses all the same.

"So," the blue-haired Lamia said, drawing everyone's attention. She stood calmly, as if willing to wait for them to get themselves together, her hand folded over the stump of her wrist. "Here we all are."

"You put the imprisoning cuff on her," Helen said as if she couldn't believe what she was saying. "You banished her to the sanctuary."

The Lamia sighed. "I know. I'm the one who did it. I'd decided a while ago not to go along with her plan. I tried to help you several times, but you wouldn't let me."

"Wouldn't let you?" Helen seemed ready to kick her ass.

Chloe tried to get her legs under her to help, but they'd decided they weren't speaking to her anymore.

"Several times." The Lamia glanced away as if she couldn't be bothered to actually care. "And now she's somewhere she can't hurt anyone, and no one can hurt her, so…"

"So? She has to pay for what she's done."

"Agreed," Ramses said, but without Chloe serving as a conduit, it seemed like Helen couldn't hear him.

"Yeah, a few hundred years in your boring-ass sanctuary should do it." The Lamia put her hand on her hip. "It did it for me. Notice how I'm not killing all of you, even though I had the chance." She examined her nails as if the three of them were no more of a threat than a breeze through her hair. "I just want to get back to waiting on Melusine and playing *Call of Duty*."

The terrifying, blood-sucking Lamia, eater of human flesh, who had a dragon as her final form, sounded tired as hell, for all her show of bravado. Maybe time was the great redeemer Helen had always been searching for.

When Helen looked at her incredulously, Chloe shook her head. "I'm the ghost expert. This one's on you." She took her hand. "And I trust you like you trusted me."

Helen gave her a look so full of love and appreciation, Chloe had to give her a quick kiss.

"Time and place," Ramses muttered. "When will the two of you learn?"

Chloe sighed and turned to him. "Do you have an opinion on this?" She nodded toward the Lamia.

He raised his hands as if in surrender. "I'm leaving this one up to the living. I'll just help deal with the consequences."

His way of saying he trusted her, too, maybe even trusted Helen a little by proxy.

Helen stared at the Lamia for a good minute, and Chloe had to fight the urge to squirm, especially when the Lamia stared back, neither of them giving an inch.

When the Lamia finally raised an eyebrow, Helen took as deep a breath as if she'd been underwater all that time. "You'll take the oath on the River Styx?"

The Lamia rolled her eyes so hard, Chloe was surprised she couldn't hear it. "Fine."

Helen smiled. "Let's go home."

Epilogue

The sanctuary's first inter-species barbecue was a tense affair, humans on one side and everyone else on the other. Chloe did her best moving between the two groups, along with Fatma, Damian, and Ali, but she couldn't keep tap dancing for long, and her forced grin was starting to hurt her face.

Ah well, the beer was nice and cool, and the smell from the grills was enticing, and she decided to enjoy herself in spite of her mom's scowl.

"She'll come around," Ramses had kept saying, flying in the face of impossibility. It was much harder to trust him in situations like this than when they were imperiled. Well, their lives might be safe right now, but her mom's expression was blistering her spirit a bit.

Then Helen, the best thing in the world, appeared at her side in a yellow sundress, looking magical as could be, and Chloe didn't give a shit if everyone started killing one another.

Well, much of a shit.

Helen squeezed her hand as they stood between the two groups, and even though the lines around her eyes spoke of a tense morning, she looked relieved and happy. "The Lamias aren't coming."

"Some good luck at last."

Helen gave her a wry smile. "We're supposed to be fostering goodwill."

"You'd pick those two to be your ambassadors, huh? The one who tried to take over the world or the empress of disdain?"

"Good point." The longer Helen looked at Chloe, the more tension seemed to melt from her expression, just like it was falling from Chloe's shoulders. "I love you, you know."

"I know." She waited before Helen's face began to twist into amused disbelief before she added, "I love you, too." It was a new feeling—at least to say it out loud—and they both giggled like schoolgirls. Their souls, their godhoods, felt like they had been in love much longer, as if the magic that infused them was either the same or bound in ways they couldn't begin to imagine.

Maybe anyone who carried a piece of that magic always found their soulmate in life.

Her mom had groaned so loudly when Chloe had told her that, it was a wonder she hadn't thrown up. She'd read Chloe the riot act up and down the harbor when they'd reconnected, then for the entire ride home, then at her apartment, then Chloe's apartment, and countless times over the phone for the first couple of weeks Chloe had been home.

It hadn't made any difference. Chloe had read it right back to her, certainty and Ramses on her side. She had told herself time and again that she wouldn't say anything about her conversation with Jamie's ghost, but she'd finally laid it out there in person one day after her mom wouldn't stop calling.

Her mom had gone still for a good minute and a half, just breathing, staring at nothing, her eyes swimming with tears that had finally dribbled down her cheeks.

Chloe had expected Ramses to hop in with some advice, but he'd fled, and she'd supposed that was only right even as she'd longed for him to return. But she'd still known he'd always have her back.

"She…it can't…you…" Her mom's words had seemed unable to connect themselves, but her shaking head had conveyed that she didn't want to believe it.

Chloe had crossed her arms and waited. She wouldn't lie about such a thing; her mom would figure that out.

She'd had Chloe go through the whole thing three more times. For the last, they'd sat on the couch, her mom watching her eagerly as if solely wanting to hear news of the daughter she'd lost years ago.

They'd cried in each other's arms, her mom blubbering things like, "I'm so proud of you, too, baby," and Chloe had bawled and hiccupped and managed, "I'm proud of you, Mom." They'd said they loved each other and loved working together, and even though that last part wasn't exactly true, it felt good to say it amidst all the snot and tears.

After that was sorted out, Chloe had spent most of the three months since at Helen's sanctuary. For the first week, she hadn't left Helen's house at all, spending the days helping fix the place up when she wasn't in Helen's bed. At night, she didn't even try to pretend that being in Helen's arms *wasn't* the primary reason she'd come to the sanctuary in the first place.

Little by little, Helen had introduced her to the residents, and she'd helped repair other parts of the island, and at some point, she and Helen had hit upon the idea of this get-together to introduce the two spheres of their lives. Fatma and Ali had been happy to help, both in giving Chloe a lift to the sanctuary, and by granting the residents a chance to know outsiders who were only partly human.

David helped now, letting Damian lead him among the residents. Many of them chuckled over the Lil' Devil T-shirt Damian had finally managed to borrow off Fatma. According to Jillian, David and Damian had been spending a lot of time together out in the world, and Chloe finally knew for sure who had taken advantage of Damian's offer that day in her mom's apartment.

And she still wasn't thinking too hard about it.

Jillian finally took her mom firmly by the arm and forced her to stand closer to Chloe and Helen, just close enough for the sanctuary residents to do the same on the other side. Eventually, they all scooted forward enough to speak, exchanging pleasantries while Helen and Chloe served as a buffer. When one of the fey started talking about magic and reagents, Jillian and Chloe's mom perked up a bit, always happy to talk shop.

But keeping back the reasons they'd become involved in said shop in the first place.

Helen knocked her beer bottle against Chloe's. "Mission accomplished," she said in Chloe's ear. "Ish."

Chloe shivered. "Stop tickling my ear unless you want to vanish for at least an hour."

Helen grinned. "At least? I'm intrigued." She bit her lip like Chloe was always doing, and it was just as much of a turn-on as Helen said.

"Knock that off. My mom is watching."

"So? She'll see that we're in love."

"And that's all I want her to see, thanks very much."

Helen laughed delightedly.

It melted Chloe on the spot. She would have used her godly power to give Helen anything in that moment. Lucky for her, Helen had her own power and could get whatever she wanted for herself.

With a smile and his hands clasped behind his back, Ramses appeared at Chloe's side.

She startled, dribbling beer on her shirt. "Shit." She wiped it off as much as she could and flicked it from her hands.

"Ramses?" Helen asked with a smile.

"Ah," he said with a smile of his own, his head bare in the mild sunshine of a Caribbean winter. "I like how she always senses when I'm here."

"Me dumping drinks on myself is a dead giveaway," Chloe said.

He shrugged. "I prefer to think of her as a natural leader, always aware of her surroundings."

"Always wary of getting something spilled on her."

He gave her a flat look. "Why are you trying to spoil my good time?"

"I thought you were spying on conversations over there. Why didn't you just walk over?"

He waved as if to say he couldn't be bothered, but she knew part of him liked scaring the hell out of her.

"You're gonna make me old before my time." To Helen, she mouthed, "Sorry."

Helen was still watching with that amused, loving look. "I'm just sorry I can't see or hear you unless our powers are joined, Ramses."

They'd been practicing, though Chloe still found raising her godhood an exhausting exercise, and it was damned hard to do unprovoked. Still, they were getting better.

"Tell her it is a shame," Ramses said. "I've enjoyed our conversations."

"He says he likes talking to you, too."

He gave Chloe's shoulder a warning tingle, and the striped nemes covered his head again. "Not like that. Friendlier. And you forgot the first part."

"The meaning is the same."

"But my words were better."

Chloe put on her most maniacal grin. "'Tis a shame, m'lady fair. He doth adore speaking to you forthwith as well. Verily."

"I'm going to shock the shit out of you."

"Bring it on, chum."

Helen burst out laughing, and they both stared at her. "It's so fun filling in his side of the conversation. I could watch you two all evening. You're like a sitcom."

Chloe glanced at Ramses, and his frown echoed how she felt. "Is she making fun of us?" she asked.

"I think she might be," he said.

"You shock her a bit, and I'll tickle her?"

"Verily."

Helen backed up, her hand and the beer held out in front of her while her eyes were filled with mock alarm. "Mercy, my lords!"

They had a short, laughing chase through the crowd, and everyone smiled as they watched, seemingly caught up in the good mood that spread far more easily than godly power.

Such a small gathering didn't speak of peace forever, but it was peace for now, a grace they could all take sanctuary in.

About the Author

Barbara Ann Wright writes fantasy and science fiction novels when not hoarding glitter. She has been a finalist in the *Foreword Review* Book of the Year Awards and the Lambda Literary Awards. She's won two Golden Crown Literary Awards and five Rainbow Awards. Her first novel, *The Pyramid Waltz*, was one of Tor.com's Reviewer's Choice books of 2012 and made *BookRiot*'s 100 Must-Read Sci-Fi Fantasy Novels by Female Authors. *Lady of Stone*, the prequel to *The Pyramid Waltz*, was recommended on Syfy.com.

Books Available from Bold Strokes Books

Coasting and Crashing by Ana Hartnett. Life comes easy to Emma Wilson until Lake Palmer shows up at Alder University and derails her every plan. (978-1-63679-511-9)

Every Beat of Her Heart by KC Richardson. Piper and Gillian have their own fears about falling in love, but will they be able to overcome those feelings once they learn each other's secrets? (978-1-63679-515-7)

Grave Consequences by Sandra Barret. A decade after necromancy became licensed and legalized, can Tamar and Maddy overcome the lingering prejudice against their kind and their growing attraction to each other to uncover a plot that threatens both their lives? (978-1-63679-467-9)

Haunted by Myth by Barbara Ann Wright. When ghost-hunter Chloe seeks an answer to the current spectral epidemic, all clues point to one very famous face: Helen of Troy, whose motives are more complicated than history suggests and whose charms few can resist. (978-1-63679-461-7)

Invisible by Anna Larner. When medical school dropout Phoebe Frink falls for the shy costume shop assistant Violet Unwin, everything about their love feels certain, but can the same be said about their future? (978-1-63679-469-3)

Like They Do in the Movies by Nan Campbell. Celebrity gossip writer Fran Underhill becomes Chelsea Cartwright's personal assistant with the aim of taking the popular actress down, but neither of them anticipates the clash of their attraction. (978-1-63679-525-6)

Limelight by Gun Brooke. Liberty Bell and Palmer Elliston loathe each other. They clash every week on the hottest new TV show, until Liberty starts to sing and the impossible happens. (978-1-63679-192-0)

Playing with Matches by Georgia Beers. To help save Cori's store and help Liz survive her ex's wedding they strike a deal: a fake relationship, but just for one week. There's no way this will turn into the real deal. (978-1-63679-507-2)

The Memories of Marlie Rose by Morgan Lee Miller. Broadway legend Marlie Rose undergoes a procedure to erase all of her unwanted memories, but as she starts regretting her decision, she discovers that the only person who could help is the love she's trying to forget. (978-1-63679-347-4)

The Murders at Sugar Mill Farm by Ronica Black. A serial killer is on the loose in southern Louisiana, and it's up to three women to solve the case while carefully dancing around feelings for each other. (978-1-63679-455-6)

Fire in the Sky by Radclyffe and Julie Cannon. Two women from different worlds have nothing in common and every reason to wish they'd never met—except for the attraction neither can deny. (978-1-63679-573-7)

A Talent Ignited by Suzanne Lenoir. When Evelyne is abducted and Annika believes she has been abandoned, they must risk everything to find each other again. (978-1-63679-483-9)

All Things Beautiful by Alaina Erdell. Casey Norford only planned to learn to paint like her mentor, Leighton Vaughn, not sleep with her. (978-1-63679-479-2)

An Atlas to Forever by Krystina Rivers. Can Atlas, a difficult dog Ellie inherits after the death of her best friend, help the busy hopeless romantic find forever love with commitment-phobic animal behaviorist Hayden Brandt? (978-1-63679-451-8)

Bait and Witch by Clifford Mae Henderson. When Zeddi gets an unexpected inheritance from her client Mags, she discovers that Mags served as high priestess to a dwindling coven of old witches—who are positive that Mags was murdered. Zeddi owes it to her to uncover the truth. (978-1-63679-535-5)

Buried Secrets by Sheri Lewis Wohl. Tuesday and Addie, along with Tuesday's dog, Tripper, struggle to solve a twenty-five-year-old mystery while searching for love and redemption along the way. (978-1-63679-396-2)

Come Find Me in the Midnight Sun by Bailey Bridgewater. In Alaska, disappearing is the easy part. When two men go missing, state trooper Louisa Linebach must solve the case, and when she thinks she's coming close, she's wrong. (978-1-63679-566-9)

Death on the Water by CJ Birch. The Ocean Summit's authorities have ruled a death on board its inaugural cruise as a suicide, but Claire suspects murder and with the help of Assistant Cruise Director Moira, Claire conducts her own investigation. (978-1-63679-497-6)

Living For You by Jenny Frame. Can Sera Debrek face real and personal demons to help save the world from darkness and open her heart to love? (978-1-63679-491-4)

Mississippi River Mischief by Greg Herren. When a politician turns up dead and Scotty's client is the most obvious suspect, Scotty and his friends set out to prove his client's innocence. (978-1-63679-353-5)

Ride with Me by Jenna Jarvis. When Lucy's vacation to find herself becomes Emma's chance to remember herself, they realize that everything they're looking for might already be sitting right next to them—if they're willing to reach for it. (978-1-63679-499-0)

Whiskey and Wine by Kelly and Tana Fireside. Winemaker Tessa Williams and sex toy shop owner Lace Reynolds are both used to taking risks, but will they be willing to put their friendship on the line if it gives them a shot at finding forever love? (978-1-63679-531-7)

Hands of the Morri by Heather K O'Malley. Discovering she is a Lost Sister and growing acquainted with her new body, Asche learns how to be a warrior and commune with the Goddess the Hands serve, the Morri. (978-1-63679-465-5)

I Know About You by Erin Kaste. With her stalker inching closer to the truth, Cary Smith is forced to face the past she's tried desperately to forget. (978-1-63679-513-3)

Mate of Her Own by Elena Abbott. When Heather McKenna finally confronts the family who cursed her, her werewolf is shocked to discover her one true mate, and that's only the beginning. (978-1-63679-481-5)

Pumpkin Spice by Tagan Shepard. For Nicki, new love is making this pumpkin spice season sweeter than expected. (978-1-63679-388-7)

Rivals for Love by Ali Vali. Brooks Boseman's brother Curtis is getting married, and Brooks needs to be at the engagement party. Only she can't possibly go, not with Curtis set to marry the secret love of her youth, Fallon Goodwin. (978-1-63679-384-9)

Sweat Equity by Aurora Rey. When cheesemaker Sy Travino takes a job in rural Vermont and hires contractor Maddie Barrow to rehab a house she buys sight unseen, they both wind up with a lot more than they bargained for. (978-1-63679-487-7)

Taking the Plunge by Amanda Radley. When Regina Avery meets model Grace Holland—the most beautiful woman she's ever seen—she doesn't have a clue how to flirt, date, or hold on to a relationship. But Regina must take the plunge with Grace and hope she manages to swim. (978-1-63679-400-6)

We Met in a Bar by Claire Forsythe. Wealthy nightclub owner Erica turns undercover bartender on a mission to catch a thief where she meets no-strings, no-commitments Charlie, who couldn't be further from Erica's type. Right? (978-1-63679-521-8)

Western Blue by Suzie Clarke. Step back in time to this historic western filled with heroism, loyalty, friendship, and love. The odds are against this unlikely group—but never underestimate women who have nothing to lose. (978-1-63679-095-4)

Windswept by Patricia Evans. The windswept shores of the Scottish Highlands weave magic for two people convinced they'd never fall in love again. (978-1-63679-382-5)

An Independent Woman by Kit Meredith. Alex and Rebecca's attraction won't stop smoldering, despite their reluctance to act on it and incompatible poly relationship styles. (978-1-63679-553-9)

Cherish by Kris Bryant. Josie and Olivia cherish the time spent together, but when the summer ends and their temporary romance melts into the real deal, reality gets complicated. (978-1-63679-567-6)

Cold Case Heat by Mary P. Burns. Sydney Hansen receives a threat in a very cold murder case that sends her to the police for help where she finds more than justice with Detective Gale Sterling. (978-1-63679-374-0)

Proximity by Jordan Meadows. Joan really likes Ellie, but being alone with her could turn deadly unless she can keep her dangerous powers under control. (978-1-63679-476-1)

Sweet Spot by Kimberly Cooper Griffin. Pro surfer Shia Turning will have to take a chance if she wants to find the sweet spot. (978-1-63679-418-1)

The Haunting of Oak Springs by Crin Claxton. Ghosts and the past haunt the supernatural detective in a race to save the lesbians of Oak Springs farm. (978-1-63679-432-7)

Transitory by J.M. Redmann. The cops blow it off as a customer surprised by what was under the dress, but PI Micky Knight knows they're wrong—she either makes it her case or lets a murderer go free to kill again. (978-1-63679-251-4)

Unexpectedly Yours by Toni Logan. A private resort on a tropical island, a feisty old chief, and a kleptomaniac pet pig bring Suzanne and Allie together for unexpected love. (978-1-63679-160-9)